HIGHEST ORDER

A NOAH WOLF THRILLER

HIGHEST ORDER

In the course of protecting the security of a nation, governments must often make choices that are best kept away from public notice. Society being what it is, people are wont to believe that everyone has some innate good within them, and that when necessary, they will do the "right thing."

Those who choose public service, however, whether it be through law enforcement or political office, soon learn the truth: that even the finest examples of men and women are capable of horrific acts under the right circumstances, while the worst examples view those acts as nothing more than taking care of business. Such people are often beyond redemption, and in many cases they are far enough ahead of the rest of society that they avoid being detected, exposed, and caught. While it may be obvious to some that they are evil, the vast majority of society never sees it, and so would never sanction the kind of action that is necessary to eliminate such evil.

For this reason, such actions are carried out by shadows, people who do not exist as far as society is concerned. Every nation has had such people, including the supposedly civilized western nations. Over the years, the United States of America has publicly denied the existence of assassins within the ranks of the CIA and FBI, which it can do because the Alphabet Soup Groups that are known to the American people honestly do not engage in such things, or at least, only when there is absolutely no other alternative at the moment when such action must be taken.

Instead, there is a special organization that is so secret that even most of the government knows nothing more about it than that it does exist, including some of those Alphabet Soup Groups. Whenever one of those organizations comes upon an individual whose departure from the world would leave it a notably better place, a request must be filed through a highly secure computer network. The request must include as much information about the person or persons to be eliminated as possible, an explanation in great detail as to why the requesting organization believes it necessary to resort to elimination, and a projection of the benefits to society if the request is granted.

That request will be delivered to a single person who has demonstrated a capacity for common sense and a willingness to accept responsibility. She alone will determine whether the request will be granted or denied, and if it is granted, she will assign the mission to eliminate the target or targets to one of several teams that work for her. These teams specialize in doing just that—eliminating those persons whose presence in the world can no longer be tolerated.

Her name is Allison Peterson, and she runs a nearly invisible department known as E & E, which stands for *Elimination and Eradication*. This department was established under a secret order from the President of the United States, and given absolute autonomy. Allison alone can grant or deny requests for elimination, and no one, not even the president, can order her to approve one.

The missions she assigns are carried out by teams that normally consist of only four people. One, the team leader, is the assassin. He or she is aided in missions by three support specialists: transportation, intelligence, and muscle. Each team is named after something from mythology, which has led to her department getting the nickname of Neverland.

Noah Wolf is Allison's star pupil, recruited because of something that most people would consider a character flaw, but which she saw as potentially the greatest strength any assassin could have.

When he was only a child, Noah Foster was present when his father murdered his mother, and then committed suicide. Something inside the seven-year-old boy broke, and from that day on, he has been completely without emotion—or conscience—of any kind. He would probably have found himself in an institution not long after that tragedy, but for the help of a genius friend that he met in foster care. Her name was Molly, and she was one of those rare children with an IQ so high that it was almost impossible to measure. While she lived at the foster home with Noah and other children, she was taking high school and even some college classes in a special education program, and one of those classes was psychology. It didn't take her long to figure Noah out, and to realize that if he continued to act so differently from everyone else, he would soon find himself locked away.

Molly convinced him to use his own surprisingly intelligent mind to study the actions and mannerisms of people around him, and mimic them in order to conceal his emotional state. She compared him to Mister Spock from *Star Trek*, the famous Vulcan, because Noah had instinctively turned to logic. He naturally examined all sides of any given situation before attempting to react to it, and by the time he was ten years old, he could arrive at a conclusion so quickly that his reactions seemed natural and brilliant.

As he grew older, he continued to mimic others, keeping his logical nature as secret as he could. He was considered an asset to any task he undertook, because he would simply examine the problem, decide what needed to be done, and then do it. He was never selfish, never lazy, and always willing to do whatever it took to ensure the success of any project he was involved in, for himself as well as for others who worked with him.

A combination of circumstances led him to join the Army when he was only seventeen, and he found it to be exactly the kind of environment he needed. The rules, structure, and discipline fit perfectly into his concept of how the world should be, and he excelled as a soldier. He rose to the rank of Staff Sergeant, served three tours of duty in Afghanistan and Iraq, and had more than a dozen different commendations in his file.

None of that did him any good, however, when his platoon leader, Lieutenant Daniel Gibson, one day decided to engage in sport with some Iraqi civilian girls that the platoon had stumbled across on a patrol. Unfortunately, the girls, of course, objected to being raped, and so he ordered them killed. Noah had been assigned to sniper cover that day, and was unaware of what was going on until he was called down from his position. Only one of the girls was still alive, and Gibson offered Noah the chance to take advantage of her before she met her own fate.

Noah assessed the situation, and concluded that his commanding officer had committed and condoned the rape and murder of Iraqi civilians, which could be considered an act of war against Iraq by forces of the United States. He refused to participate, and demanded the situation stop, but Lieutenant Gibson told him to shut up and then shot the one surviving girl through the head.

Noah's computer-like brain saw that the situation was completely out of control, and took what he considered to be logical action. He shot and killed his platoon leader, and then attempted to place the rest of the platoon under arrest. The other men fought, and he was forced to kill several of them before the remainder surrendered.

Unfortunately, when they returned to their base, it was his word against theirs. When it turned out that Lieutenant Gibson was the son of Congressman Gibson, the up-and-coming presidential hopeful, the political pressure came down from Washington and Noah was arrested for multiple counts of murder. He was railroaded through court-martial and sentenced to die.

That's where Allison found him, sitting on death row at Leavenworth. She visited him there in disguise, explaining that if he was willing to put his talents and abilities to work for her, she could arrange for him to have a second chance. Of course, it would mean never having any contact with anyone from his past, since the official story would include that he committed suicide in his prison cell.

Noah made the logical choice, and agreed. Days later, he was taken out of his cell in the middle of the night and transported to the department's training compound in Colorado. The morning news carried the story that the renegade soldier who had murdered the son of Congressman Gibson had killed himself in his cell. His unclaimed body was interred in the prison cemetery only two days later.

His codename was Camelot, and he was the most effective assassin the world had ever known.

Prologue

Chidi Abimbola wiped the sweat off his brow and looked up at the sun. It was high and it was hot, but that was normal in this part of western Algeria. He and Oni were walking along the path through the Sahrawi refugee sector, occasionally returning the smile of someone they passed by, or nodding to an acquaintance on their way. They were barely twenty miles from the border with Western Sahara, and only a few miles southwest of Tindouf. Chidi, the *Wali*, or territorial governor, had his office there.

"General Zaki says we are ready," he said to his aide, Oni. "The only thing standing between us and independence, now, is Algiers. We have secured the support of Mauritania, Western Sahara, and Morocco, all of whom will recognize us as a separate nation. The announcements will go out at four o'clock today throughout the world, and we are prepared for any military action Algiers may decide to take."

Oni inclined his head. "Our people have waited long for this day," he said. "Freedom is their dream, and whatever the cost, we will pay it."

"I suspect it will be high, Oni. Zaki has only forty thousand troops, less than a dozen warplanes and a single artillery division. President Belkacem can hit us with three times our numbers within a matter of days. If our allies fail us, we will all be hanged for treason."

Oni maintained his reverent posture. "Morocco and Mauritania will stand with us," he said. "We will control enough natural gas reserves to be worth defending, and our iron mines are the most productive in this part of Africa. Western Sahara may waver, but I believe they will follow Mauritania. Individually, none of them have the mili-

7

tary strength to stand up to Algiers, but together we can throw off the oppression we have labored under for so many years. Mauritania enjoys strong relations with the United States, so the Americans might recognize us. Europe receives most of our natural gas, so we could see support from them, as well."

"All of that is only speculative," Chidi said. "We must plan as best we can for our own defense, but I agree that Mauritania and Morocco will at least rattle their swords on our behalf. That should be enough to make President Belkacem think twice before launching an all-out offensive."

Oni finally looked up at him. "Zaki has been playing at training exercises for the past few weeks, to cover up the fact that he has been placing troops into defensive positions along our border. His officers are loyal, he says, and he expects loyalty from almost all of his troops. Arranging housing for the families of the soldiers who were stationed here was a stroke of brilliance. It gives them all more than enough reason to want to stay in West Algeria, once we split from the rest of the nation."

Chidi smiled. "Seems to me I remember someone suggesting that to me. It was brilliant, yes, but it was your idea, my friend. So many of the things that have brought us to this point were from that powerful mind of yours, but you always let the world think they were mine. Don't you ever get tired of being in the shadow of your own puppet?"

Oni glared at him, but there was friendly affection hidden in it. "Chidi, you are anything but a puppet. I have served you for more than fifteen years, and I've seen how hard you have worked to protect the people of Tindouf. When Belkacem apportioned our resources to benefit Algiers, you fought against him and almost faced prison, but you prevailed. There is no one better to serve as our first president than you."

"But you still refuse to take a post in the new government?" Chidi asked. "You could be vice president, the people would not object."

"I prefer, my good friend, to remain in your service. I do not believe I could bear the stress of political life, but I have learned that you are not so much a politician as a man who loves his people. Together, I think we have found ways to do things that neither of us might have accomplished alone. Do you disagree?"

"Not at all, Oni. I know full well that I would not be where I am today without your wisdom and advice, and I am incredibly grateful for both. We are about to enter a new age for all of us, and I do not know how I could go further without you, but I also do not wish to keep you from the rewards you have earned. Our new country owes you a great debt, and I will make certain that the people know this."

Once more, Oni bowed his head modestly. "I need no accolades, and no reward. The freedom of our people is the reward we have both sought for so long, and now you are making it come to fruition. Only let me continue to serve, and I am happy."

They entered one of the many huts in the area and were greeted by a woman who led them through a curtain, to where her elderly husband was waiting. He was sitting on a bench at a table, and invited them to sit and join him as he ate *shakshouka*, a dish of eggs poached in a tomato sauce and covered with diced vegetables.

"A pleasure," Chidi said, as the old woman spooned eggs and sauce onto plates for both of them. "We thank you, Doctor Benyamina. I trust you have been well, and your wife and family?"

Benyamina smiled. "We are as we are. And you, old friend?"

"I have been well," Chidi said. "I have been busy, as you can imagine, but all will be finished as of today. Are your people ready for the events to come?"

"We have been ready for many years, Chidi. Algiers has ignored our province for decades, either letting us wallow in poverty or raping our resources to enrich the rest of the country. It is time for us to stand up for ourselves, and I only give thanks to Allah that I have lived to see this day come."

"It could not have come without you, old friend. You, and those who worked with you in secret are the true heroes of our cause. One day soon, I shall be able to throw back the veil that has kept you hidden for so long."

Benyamina grinned, his toothless mouth stretching across his wizened face. "I was among the first to speak out for independence more than twenty years ago, as you know very well. Syphax Rezgui and I were the ones who devised the cell system that kept us all out of prisons, though I suspect that is no secret any longer. Only the government's fear of the younger ones in our movement keeps me from being arrested these days."

"As long as it works," Oni said, his own smile showing his reverence for the old rebel. "But I think there have been enough rumors of your death to confuse the issue. I heard four different stories in the past month alone, how you fought off eighteen soldiers before they got you, or how you outran an assassin for more than an hour before your heart gave out. And, of course, we have taken pains to keep your location a great secret, as well."

"Indeed," the old man replied. "Without your help, I think someone would have collected a bounty on me by now. Perhaps I should just be grateful in general, and not worry about how I have managed such a long life?"

The three of them shared a chuckle at the joke, and fell to eating and small talk. They spoke of mutual friends, Benyamina told stories of his great-grandchildren, and Chidi boasted of his own year-old grandson. Oni had no children, and so he only spoke admiringly of the little ones.

When they were finished eating, and Benyamina's wife had left them alone, Chidi looked into the old man's eyes. "We are only hours from our declaration of secession," he said. "All of the arrangements have been made, and it will be broadcast from my office. Will you come and be beside me for this moment of history?"

"Allah be praised, Chidi, I would love to be there, but this is a time for the political minds to be wary. You don't need an old revolutionary, even a quiet one like me, to cast the hint of treachery over this day. Make your announcement, and let the world see men of words acting to make this a peaceful transition, rather than a violent one. We have accomplished this marvel without resorting to the tactics of the jihadists, without resorting to any kind of violence. Bask in the glory, old friend."

Chidi bowed his head respectfully. "As you wish, then," he said. "We must be going. It is a long walk back to the car, and then another hour to my office." He got to his feet and clasped his hands around one of the old man's. "Thank you, Mourad, for all that you have done to help us bring this to be."

He turned and walked out, as Oni made his own respects to the old man. Once Chidi was out of the room and far enough away, Benyamina looked him in the eye. "Does he suspect anything?"

"No, Sahib. I have taken great care to be sure, and always show him only how concerned I am for his safety. He will take us to independence, and then our new nation will mourn his loss. As a martyr, he will live forever in the hearts and minds of our people and keep them from ever bowing the knee to Algiers again."

"Yes, but without his sacrifice, they may not last through the troubles to come. Men will fight for freedom until their children begin to cry from hunger, and then they will begin to wonder whether they were better off under the old regime." He smiled, but there was a sadness in it. "Everything is arranged?"

"Yes. It will happen on the eighth day from today. Belkacem will make his strongest move against us at that time, and we will need a martyr. Chidi is so beloved by the people that his death will rally them when we will need the momentum the most."

"Go, then," Benyamina said. "Don't let him wonder what we are talking about. And remember, Oni, you must take your place to lead us once he is gone. Do not shirk the duty that has fallen to you."

"I will do as I must, Sahib," Oni said, and then he left the room quickly to catch up with his oldest friend.

"Was Mourad berating you again over his daughter?" Chidi asked with a smile, as Oni took his place beside him. "You know, she isn't all that ugly. Perhaps a wife would be good for you."

Oni made a face. "She looks like a camel," he said, "and she spits like one. Besides, I have never considered marriage for political gain to be worth the sacrifices it entails. If I ever marry, it will be to a woman who only wants a man to keep her comfortable, and doesn't expect romance. So much simpler that way."

Chidi laughed. They talked of simpler things through the rest of the long walk back to where they had left the car, and then Oni drove them back into Tindouf.

The office of the provincial governor was nothing special. It was housed in the only government building in the entire city, on the third floor overlooking the market area. Chidi spoke with his secretary when they arrived, taking the slips of paper that told him who had called while he was gone. None of them were relevant to the events that were about to unfold, so he set them aside when he got back to his desk.

Oni went to the cabinet near the side wall and began setting up the video camera. Arrangements had been made for the broadcast of the announcement of secession, and all they had to do was connect the camera to the computer that would transmit the video signal to all the major news organizations in the world. BBC, CNN, Pravda, EuroNews, Al Jazeera and more would receive it live, and it was expected that most of them would turn it into a major story. After all, it wasn't every day that a large nation split.

It took him only a few moments to get everything set up, and then he called to confirm that the connection was working. The local TV station would be the intermediary, and would broadcast a short warning to all of the agencies that a major announcement was coming. It was possible that many of them would simply stream it live to all of their affiliates.

At ten minutes to four, the warning went out. At exactly four o'clock, Oni activated the camera, which was focused on Chidi Abimbola.

"Greetings to the world," Chidi said. "I am Chidi Abimbola, governor of Tindouf province in Algeria. I come before the world today to announce the secession of West Algeria from its mother country."

On the video screen Oni was monitoring, a map appeared that showed the newly proposed border between Algeria and West Algeria.

"The map you are seeing shows the border between our two countries. The people of West Algeria have been forced to take this unprecedented action because of the excesses and neglect of the government of Algeria. Our resources have been plundered to enrich the rest of the country while we struggle in poverty, and our pleas for aid and assistance to help us care for our people have fallen on deaf ears in the capital of Algiers. This is why, after careful consideration that has gone on for many years, we have approached some of our neighbor countries for recognition and alliance, and we hereby declare our independence from Algeria. We expect the next few weeks to be full of challenge and surprise, but we are prepared to stand firm in this decision. We welcome opportunities for cooperation with all nations, and will pledge ourselves to successfully integrating our new nation into the councils of the world. Thank you."

Oni cut off the camera and smiled. "The press releases are already going out," he said. "They include the minutes of the meeting of the

West Algeria Formation Council, naming you as interim president. I would imagine that your phone is about to..."

He was cut off, as the phone on Chidi's desk rang suddenly, with all of its lines lit up.

Chapter ONE

"**I** thought we might get the boat out," Noah said. "Looks like it's going to be a beautiful day, we could invite Neil and Jenny, and Marco and Renée. Just spend the day out on the lake. What would you think?"

Sarah sat down at the table across from him and smiled. "After this last winter? I am ready for some sun, trust me. Will it be warm enough for sunbathing?"

"It's supposed to get up to eighty by eleven," Noah replied. "You girls could soak up the rays while us guys do some fishing. Sound all right?"

"It sounds wonderful. Give me a few minutes to finish my coffee and I'll call them all. We can pack up some sandwiches and stuff, for lunch out on the lake."

"That's exactly what I had in mind," Noah said. He took a sip of his own coffee and was about to add something else when his phone rang. He glanced at it and saw that it was Allison calling, then answered.

"Hello," he said.

"Briefing," she said, "conference room, ten a.m. I'll notify everyone else."

"Yes, ma'am," Noah said. The line was dead before he finished, and he looked up at Sarah. "Looks like we have to postpone," he said. "Mission briefing at ten."

Sarah made a face that expressed her opinion of mission briefings that interfere with sunbathing. "And it was gonna be such a good day," she said. "That sucks."

"I agree," Noah said, "but work has to come first. Besides, the weather might be even better by the time we get back. I want to get a shower before we go." He got up and headed toward the bedroom, and Sarah followed a moment later.

Sarah had showered as soon as she got up, so she got dressed and put on her makeup while Noah finished up. They had actually slept in a bit, and it was already past nine. They left the house at nine thirty, which would give them plenty of time to make it to the briefing.

Neil hadn't come home to his trailer the night before, but his Hummer was parked in the garage under the headquarters building, along with Marco's latest hot rod, a 1970 Chevelle he had found a few weeks before on eBay. The car was covered in primer, a sure sign that it was on its way to being completely restored.

They rode the elevator up and stepped out to go to the conference room, and ran into Donald Jefferson, who served as second in command of the organization, helping to coordinate all of the intelligence and data necessary for each mission. He was just coming out of his own office and smiled when he saw them.

"Noah," he said. "Good to see you. Everything going okay?"

Noah nodded. "It's been nice to have a few weeks off," he said. "I gather that's coming to an end, today."

"Yes, I'm afraid so. I'll let Allison brief you, of course, but you're going to be headed for Africa in a couple of days. Hope you're ready for the desert."

"Can't be worse than Afghanistan," Noah said. The three of them walked together into the conference room, and Noah and Sarah helped themselves to the ever present donuts and coffee before they took their seats.

Marco and Neil were already there, but they were surprised to see Jenny. After a moment of passing greetings back and forth, they all turned their attention to Allison.

"I don't know if you've seen the news this morning," she began, "but there has been a major rift in Algeria. The entire province of Tindouf, along with portions of several other provinces, two hours ago declared themselves in secession from the rest of the country. They have formed a new country called West Algeria, and that they've already garnered some pretty powerful support from a number of other nations. Mauritania, Morocco, Egypt, Saudi Arabia, Israel, and the EU have all recognized them as a sovereign nation, and Algeria and its own allies are in an uproar. President Belkacem is threatening military action, with Libya and Niger both offering support. The potential for war in that region is staggering at the moment, and with Algeria's ties to Russia, this could become a major conflict within a matter of days."

"I'd heard about it," Noah said. "Their secession, I mean. I take it the U.S. wants to avoid the war?"

"Actually, the war is probably inevitable but we don't think it will last that long. The problem for us is that West Algeria has some powerful strategic potential, and we need to establish diplomatic relations with the new interim government as quickly as possible. Our intelligence sources in the area, however, have uncovered a potential problem." She pressed a button on the remote in her hand and a photograph appeared on the big, wall-mounted display screen. "This is Chidi Abimbola, the interim president of West Algeria. He was appointed by the West Algerian Formation Council to serve as president until they can hold public elections. He's probably the best possible man for the job, because he was the provincial governor for the last fifteen years, and the people absolutely love him. He stood up to the Algerian government on numerous occasions, and managed to prevent a lot of problems. He even accomplished a lot for the Sahrawi refugees that have been living in their own communities around his province since the nineteen seventies, getting them medical care and making it possible for them to work more freely in the country. Those refugees now make up a large part of his population, and may well decide to become citizens. It's the perfect time, from their perspective. They would come in as equals with everyone else, something they haven't known in a long time."

"Okay," Noah said. "So far, this doesn't sound all that bad. Where do we fit in?"

"American intelligence agents working in Algeria have uncovered a plot by the Formation Council to turn President Abimbola into a martyr. They're planning to assassinate him, quite publicly, and blame it on the Algerian government. Their reasoning is actually fairly sound, since they believe the people will cave in to pressure and reunite with Algeria if the conflict actually breaks out. The Algerian military would do everything it could to cut off supply lines to the region, and the Council fears that the potential for famine would undermine everything they have accomplished. This could be true, and in fact, almost certainly will be. Right now, we are predicting a ninety-seven percent chance that West Algeria will fold within ninety days. They will return to provincial status within Algeria, but will get some very important concessions from the government there in exchange. By establishing diplomatic relations with them while they are temporarily separate, we can make inroads that will last after the reunification and give us the ability to counter a lot of Russian influence within the country."

"So," Marco said, "we don't want the temporary president to get assassinated, right?"

Allison looked at Donald Jefferson. "That's correct," Jefferson said. "His martyrdom would make it almost impossible for the people to accept reunification on peaceful terms, no matter what concessions the Algerian government might offer. The conflict would last much longer than it needs to, and would lead to the possibility of involvement by major world powers, such as Russia, China, and the United States. What we need to do is stop the assassination from taking place, but that means that we have to remove some of the people involved in setting it up. That's your mission."

Allison leaned forward. "This mission is of major importance, because it will lead to the possibility of an even more significant alliance for the United States in northwestern Africa. Algeria is one of our allies in the war against terror, and was the first country to stand up for us after the attacks of 9/11. We maintain an air base in southern Algeria for drone flights, mostly surveillance flights to keep track of what Al Qaeda and ISIS operatives are doing. This opportunity to expand our relationship with Algeria could be critical as we work to bring an end to international terrorism that tends to originate from that region."

She pressed another button on the remote and another face appeared on the screen. "This is Oni Zidane, Abimbola's personal aide and best friend. Unfortunately, he is also a member of a very secret organization known as West Algeria Defense Initiative Revolution, or WADIR. This organization is the one behind the plot to assassinate Abimbola, and intelligence indicates that Oni is the prime actor. He has reportedly abducted an Algerian soldier who is loyal to the current government, and will allow him to be captured immediately after the assassination. That will make it appear that the Algerian president ordered the assassination, and will without doubt inflame the people against any possibility of reunification. It will also propel Oni Zidane into the interim presidency, a calculated move that WADIR considers the most emotional appeal they can make to the people. Chidi Abimbola and Oni Zidane have been close for so many years that many people believe there is a clandestine romantic relationship between the two of them. Because this would be considered an abomination from an Islamic point of view, the vast majority of the population considers it to be something of a joke and pretends not to have such thoughts about them."

"What does our intelligence say?" Noah asked. "Are they actually lovers?"

"Not as far as we could tell," Jefferson said. "Our intelligence sources have found no indication that the rumors have any substance, but it's essentially immaterial to our purposes. Regardless of Chidi's relationship with Oni, allowing him to be assassinated would be a disaster from an American political point of view. Your mission, therefore, is to eliminate Oni Zidane and other members of WADIR who might be able to complete his plans. To do so, you will go into West Algeria posing as part of a delegation the president is sending in to discuss the possibility of American diplomatic and military support for their independence. It is absolutely critical that there be no connection between your cover identities and the mission, however. If you are discovered or captured, the Secretary of State will have no choice but to disavow all knowledge and declare you impostors. There will be absolutely no possibility of rescue if that were to happen, not even from within our organization."

"Noah?" Allison asked. "Are we clear on that?"

"Yes, ma'am," he said. "If any of us are captured, it's up to us to do whatever we can to affect a rescue, but without any support from the government or from E & E."

The corners of Allison's mouth twisted upward slightly. "That's not exactly what we said," she said.

"No, ma'am," Noah said. "It's the way I interpret it, however. I wouldn't do anything to jeopardize American interests, but I do not leave anyone behind."

Both Allison and Donald Jefferson laughed. "As if we don't know that about you," Allison said. "This is what brings up Jenny's presence. She will be accompanying you on this mission, because there may simply be more than you can handle alone, or even with Marco. Jenny's own specialties in securing and eliminating her targets are likely to come in handy with some of these men, anyway." She turned and looked at Jenny. "Cinderella, you are temporarily assigned to Team Camelot. You will be under Noah's orders for the duration of this mission, and you are expected to obey them instantly and implicitly."

Jenny was grinning from ear to ear as she clung to Neil's hand. "Yes, ma'am," she said. "You won't have any problems out of me."

Jefferson turned to Noah. "Unfortunately, you don't have a lot of time. The assassination is scheduled for just over a week from today, but we do not have any specific details as to where and how it will take place. That means you have to get in and eliminate your targets in plenty of time to keep that from happening at all."

Noah nodded his head. "I understand. Will we have any kind of support in country?"

"We don't have a station of our own there," Allison said, "but there is a CIA station, and they'll be ready to lend what support they can. Weapons, logistics, vehicles—you know the drill. What they do not have is any kind of support staff, unfortunately. There is no embassy there at this time, so the station is a clandestine one. You'll have their contact information before you leave."

"What about targets?" Noel asked. "Other than Oni, do we have other names?"

Jefferson nodded. "There are several," he said. "Unfortunately, it's very difficult to confirm which of them might be on the committee behind the assassination. We don't have time to turn this into an investigatory mission, so you will have to eliminate all of them to be certain of getting the key players. Most of them are part of the Sahrawi Polisario Front, an organization of refugees from Western Sahara who opposed the occupation of part of its lands by Moroccan forces. The United States recognizes them as a legitimate rebel faction, so we don't want to alienate them. The problem is that it's highly doubtful that the leadership of the Polisario is even aware of the actions of the Formation Council and the secret committee planning the assassination of Abimbola. That makes it doubly imperative that you not be caught or discovered, because we could lose allies on many sides of the equation."

"Noah, you'll be given the file listing all of the targets," Allison said. "As I mentioned a moment ago, it's probably going to be more than you can handle alone, and will require at least three of you to be active. You, Marco, and Jenny will be the strike team, with Sarah and Neil as your support. Sarah, traffic laws there are very similar to those in the States, so you shouldn't have any problems."

"Any special equipment we should take with us?" Noah asked.

"Feel free to visit Wally and get whatever you think you might need. Remember that a lot of the equipment he provides is still highly classified, so be certain it doesn't get left behind." She turned and looked at Jefferson. "Donald, anything else?"

"Not at this moment," he said. "I need you all to come back this afternoon for ID kits. I just haven't had time to put them together yet. While we sort of knew this was coming, it's come to a head about a week earlier than we actually expected. Our intelligence people were never able to get the actual date of the secession, so it caught us a bit off guard this morning."

"I'm just curious," Neil said, "but what's the global political climate on this? Who's happy and who's upset?"

"To be honest," Jefferson replied, "I don't think any country is happy about this. Seeing Algeria split this way could actually trigger similar divisions in a few other countries. Chad, Nigeria, and Libya are actually possibilities, and the Sudan is pretty much on the verge of civil war all the time. If West Algeria were to get away with this, I'm afraid we might see a lot of new countries on the African continent. Hell, we might see a few on North America. There are parts of California that are trying to secede and become a separate state, and Texas is constantly threatening to break off from the U.S.A."

"Then, where does Russia stand on it? Do they have a lot to lose if this happens?"

"Not strategically, but it could hurt them economically. They've long been a major customer of the iron ore that comes out of Algeria, and most of that would be controlled by West Algeria. It would actually be a perfect time to look for better prices from other buyers, which could even include the U.S.A. or the U.K. If they do, the Kremlin isn't going to be happy."

"Okay," Neil said. "I was just curious. I know they aren't real fond of us, and I sure would hate to end up on their radar."

"Then, unless you have any questions," Allison said, "I think you should start making your preparations. Remember to come by this afternoon—three o'clock, Donald? Okay, around three, to pick up your ID kits. We'll have the details on your flight by then, as well. It'll be a diplomatic flight, so you can take along whatever equipment you decide you need."

The newly mingled team rose from their seats and left the conference room, riding the elevator down together to the garage level.

"Imagine," Neil said, "how surprised I was when Allison called me this morning and told me to report for briefing and to bring Jenny with me. I'm trying to figure out how she knew we were together."

"Because we're almost always together," Jenny said with a giggle. "It's not like it's a big secret, and we couldn't keep it secret if we wanted to. I'm pretty sure everybody notices that we hold hands a lot, don't you think?"

"Do you think I pay attention? I could care less what anybody thinks. I'm happy and you're happy, and that's all that matters to me."

"Personally," Marco said, "I think the Dragon Lady has cameras hidden in all of our houses. She always knows when Renée spends the night. Doesn't bother me all that much, but Renée gets a little spooked by it now and then."

Neil shook his head. "Nope, no cameras. I check periodically, at my place, at Noah's and now I check at Jenny's. Believe me, if they were there, I'd find them. I just think she's that good at predicting what we might do, that's the only way I can explain it."

They got into their cars and left the garage, heading out to R&D. Wally, the mad genius who ran the research and development department, was delighted when they came through the door. He had left standing orders with the front desk to notify him the moment Camelot came in, and he had a comical habit of running down the hall as soon as he got the call.

This day was no exception. His running footsteps could be heard almost half a minute before he came sliding around the corner into the lobby. He hurried up to Noah and shook his hand.

"Noah!" Wally said. "I was beginning to think you forgot where we were. I haven't seen you in weeks."

"That's because he's been spending time with me," Sarah said. "You know, his wife? How have you been, Wally?"

"Doing good, doing good," he said. "Got some fantastic new toys to show you. Allison told me you're headed out for a mission, but she didn't have the details. What are you up to?"

"We're going to Algeria," Noah said. "Somebody wants to turn the new president of West Algeria into a martyr, and I guess our president doesn't want that to happen. Allison said they were expecting to have a little more time to plan for this, but the sudden announcement this morning of West Algeria's secession from its mother country caught them off guard."

"Algeria," Wally said, almost with awe. "Lots of desert there, isn't there? It's going to be hot and miserable. Boy, oh boy, have I got some things to show you. Come on, follow me."

With Wally almost skipping along in front of them, they followed him down one hallway and turned into another. He led them to a particular door and then through it, and they saw a couple of people working over what looked like sewing machines.

"This is something that Dennis, here, came up with," Wally said, pointing at a young man. "Dennis, I'm going to let you explain it. These folks are Team Camelot, and they're about to be headed into the desert, so this is perfect timing."

Dennis grinned and got off the stool he was sitting on, walking over to extend a hand to Noah, and then to each of the others. "I'm delighted to meet you," he said. "I've heard an awful lot about you." They all shook hands with him and then followed him to the bench he had been working at.

There was a t-shirt laying on the bench. "This is a new fabric we developed here," Dennis said. "It's thin, but has some amazing absorption and evaporation properties that mean it will keep the wearer cool even in the hottest weather. It's based on work done at Stanford University, but we take that a few steps up the ladder from what they came up with. Basically, what the fabric does is block visible light so that your body won't absorb heat from the sun, but it also is transparent to infrared light. Now, infrared radiation, or infrared light, is how we lose heat from our bodies. It's dissipated out into the air as infrared radiation. By being transparent to infrared but opaque to visible light, we managed to release the built-up body heat you've already got, while preventing you from gaining more through sunlight. Added to this is a capillary action that actually wicks the moisture when you sweat away from your body, so that it can be released into the air. Drawing that moisture off dissipates even more heat, so that even when the sun is beating down on you and it's a hundred and fifteen degrees in the desert, just wearing this fabric will make you feel like you're sitting in air conditioning."

Noah's eyebrows actually rose a half-inch. "Is there any kind of limitation on how it can be used? What types of clothing, that sort of thing?"

"Not really a limit," Dennis said. "As long as it's dyed in light colors, it should remain pretty effective."

"I'm thinking of desert clothing. Our mission is going to be into the deserts of Algeria, and we'll need to fit into the local culture. I'm thinking khakis, long-sleeve shirts, short-sleeved shirts, underclothing. Could several pieces be put together for each of us quickly?"

Wally stepped up. "That would be our costuming department," he said. "They've already got an ample supply of the fabric, Dennis just likes to keep trying to improve it. We'll talk to Martha down there in costuming in just a bit, I know she's got all your sizes on file."

"Excellent," Noah said. He turned to Dennis and shook his hand again. "Great work, thank you."

The young man beamed as Noah and the rest of them followed Wally out the door. He turned to the other man in the room, who simply grinned and shook his head.

"He puts his pants on the same way we do, Junior," the older man said.

Out in the hallway, Wally turned to Noah again. "So, what other kind of things do you think you might need? What about weapons, for instance?"

"I want eight of your smart guns," Noah said, referring to the little computerized, tripod-mounted, brick-shaped guns that used facial recognition technology to watch for specific targets and then fired with deadly precision. "I want a pair of M107s in fifty caliber, two Miktor MGL grenade launchers with two dozen HE rounds, and five MAC 11s. Give me four loaded magazines for each of the MACs."

Wally's eyes were wide. "Holy cow," he said. "No problem, I just wasn't expecting you to have a list all ready to go. I'm kind of impressed."

"Seriously?" Neil asked. "You're surprised? This is Noah you're talking to, remember?"

Wally chuckled. "Good point, good point," he said. "Okay, we've got all of that. And, by the way, we've made some improvements to the smart guns. They now have built-in sound and flash suppressors, so they're about as quiet as they can possibly be. Put them in the right locations, and no one will know where the shots came from. What else?"

"A couple of aerial surveillance drones. High-resolution, long-range cameras, drones that can stay up high and out of earshot while still giving me a good look at what's going on on the ground."

"Got just the things. Small, quiet, a two hour flight time. Facial recognition follow-me system that can track a person through a crowd. That sort of thing you're looking for?"

Noah glanced at Neil, who was nodding and smiling. "That'll work," he said. "How soon can you have it all ready?"

Wally shrugged. "Let's go see Martha, first, then work on the rest of it."

Letting Martha take measurements to make sure they were up-to-date took only a few minutes, and they were assured the clothes would be ready by the following afternoon. When they finished there, Wally took them to the armory and asked one of the technicians to show them the improvements to the smart guns.

"They're basically the same as they were the last time you used them," the technician said. "We only added a few little features. You see the sound suppressor, it looks like somebody stuck a big beer can on the end of the gun? It uses a combination of wakes and baffles to muffle the sound." He picked up one of the guns and aimed it at a target down the range, then pressed the manual fire button. There was a slight *phhzt* sound, but nothing that any of them would normally associate with the firing of a gun. "One of the things that makes it so quiet is that the ammunition is subsonic. It doesn't travel quite as fast as the speed of sound, but that also limits its range. While the targeting computer is very precise, the maximum effective range of this gun is only about two hundred yards. Any further than that, and bullet drop is going to start interfering."

"Okay, I can work with that," Noah said. "What else is new?"

"Two other little things. We added the ability for the guns to communicate with each other, so they all know which targets are still at large. And they can notify you, via a smartphone app, each time they fire. Each one will tell you when it fired, at which target, and the results of the shot, such as whether the target was hit, or if the target managed to run away. The second feature is an automatic self-destruct. These new models are built on a frame made of magnesium, and we built in an electronic igniter. If it gets the self-destruct signal, which can be through the same app or by setting it to activate at a specific time or after all targets have been taken out, there won't be anything left of that gun but slag five minutes later. The circuitry will be melted beyond any possible recognition, the camera will look like a melted decoration of some sort, and any remaining ammunition will have exploded. No one is going to figure out anything other than that it was some kind of a gun at one time or another. Wally wanted that, just because we don't really want any of our allies or enemies getting their hands on this toy."

Noah looked at the technician and took out the gun. "Perfect," he said.

Chapter TWO

"Noah," Jefferson said when they returned for their ID kits, "you'll be going as James McConnell, and your credentials identify you as having formerly been the commercial attaché at our embassy in Venezuela. Officially, you are there to meet with President Abimbola to discuss the possibility of placing an embassy in Tindouf. Sarah will be Elizabeth Roth, your assistant. Neil, your identity is Garrett Stevens, and you are the IT technician. Jenny, you'll be going as Neil's assistant, Connie Marchand. Marco, you are the only one among you who speaks French, which is a common language throughout Algeria, so you will serve as interpreter. You will be Pierre Lafontaine, child of French immigrants to America who grew up in Baton Rouge. That should account for the slightly Cajun accent in your French."

"*Mais, oui*," Marco said. "Y'all do know my French is pretty rusty, right?"

"You'll get some practice for the next couple of days," Allison said. "You're going out to Character Development to work with Lisette Charpentier. She's our expert on French and French accents. Report to her tomorrow morning at eight a.m."

"Okay, question," Jenny said. "While my boyfriend may be a computer genius, I have trouble checking my Facebook on anything but my phone. How am I supposed to pass myself off as his assistant?"

Jefferson chuckled. "Just look at him the way you always do," he said. "Nobody will expect you to know much about computers, they'll figure he pulled strings to get you the job."

Jenny pretended to look shocked, but Allison smiled. "Sadly, he's right," she said. "It's amazing how often a secretary or assistant to

29

someone in foreign service turns out to be nothing more than a secret lover. Just about everyone involved in politics will naturally think that's what you're doing there, anyway, so we might as well play on it."

Jenny closed her mouth and shrugged. "Works for me."

"Here are your ID kits," Jefferson said, passing out large envelopes, "along with back stories and target files. Be sure to look over your back stories, so that you can answer questions if you need to. All of the information in the back stories is already included in the files that their intelligence service will receive as part of their due diligence in checking you out, so you might need to prove yourselves a bit. Just don't let them trip you up; if they ask about a place you wouldn't know, don't try to fake it. The Algerians learned a lot from the French, whose idea of espionage is to always try to force the other fellow into a mistake."

Noah was looking through the wallet and papers he had been handed. "All right," he said. "When do we leave?"

"Six p.m.," Allison said, "the day after tomorrow. That gives Marco two days to work on his French with Lisette. He'll be your interpreter when you need one, because just about everyone over there speaks French, even though Arabic and Berber are the official languages. Anyone you'll need to speak to in the government will understand and speak fluent French."

"Our clothes will be ready tomorrow evening," Noah said. "Since we're traveling on a diplomatic flight, Wally is sending our weapons along with us. Do we anticipate any problems at Tindouf?"

"No," Jefferson replied. "Abimbola knows and respects our Algerian ambassador, Daniel Ford. Daniel spoke with him by telephone a few hours after the broadcast this morning, and received assurance that you will be treated as a diplomatic envoy of the United States. That was last night, to them, but our State Department will also be speaking with Abimbola this evening, during his morning. They'll make certain of your diplomatic status."

"Then I guess we're all set," Noah said. "Is there anything you want the rest of us to do while Marco is taking French lessons?"

"Just study your back stories," Allison said, "and the list of diplomatic concessions you're going to ask for. You probably will only have a couple of hours with Abimbola, so it shouldn't interfere greatly with your actual mission. Pay close attention to the list, because there are a few concessions we actually want in the event this secession doesn't fail. Mostly just access to a few hundred acres of desert, a strategic place for a drone base. We've already got one in southern Algeria, but another in Tindouf province would be beneficial. The State Department said to make sure we get that locked in before you make any other agreements."

Noah nodded. "I'll do my best," he said. "Anything else?"

"Yes, before I forget," Jefferson said. "The cell phones in your kits are satellite phones. They won't look out of place, because almost every diplomat in that region carries one. That's because they don't have nearly as many cell towers as they need, so a direct connection to satellite is necessary. The reason I'm pointing it out to you is because you will need them if you need to communicate while you're in the desert. You'll also find in each of them a contact identified as Prudence Mays. Prudence is the CIA station chief in Tindouf. Her cover is manager of a charitable organization that works with the Sahrawi refugees; that will come in handy, because she can move through the refugee camps without anyone paying much attention to her, or anyone with her. CIA simply asks that we try not to out her, because she's invaluable over there."

"We'll remember that," Noah said. "For now, I think we're all going to go and get some dinner. Would you care to join us?"

Both Allison and Donald Jefferson seemed surprised at the invitation. "Where have you got in mind?" Allison asked.

"We're going out to the Sagebrush Saloon," Sarah said. "Kind of our favorite watering hole, and they know us well enough to always give us a table off to ourselves."

"Sure, I'll go," Allison said. "Donald?"

"I hate to do it," Jefferson said, "but I'll need to take a rain check. I've got a little bit of paperwork I want to finish in my office, and then I promised my wife and daughter I'd come home at a reasonable hour tonight. It's my wife's birthday, and we're celebrating at home. I'd love to come another time, though."

"We understand," Sarah said. "Tell her I said happy birthday, okay? And tell Elaine that we miss her."

Jefferson smiled softly. "I sure will," he said.

"Can you kids give me ten minutes before we go?" Allison asked. "I need to finish up a couple things myself, just so I can pretend to earn my paycheck."

"Sure," Sarah said, and Jenny echoed her. "We'll wait in your lobby. By the way, who's the new secretary?"

"Hell, I can't remember her name," Allison said. "We rotate them through a pool, now, because we found out that blasted Monique actually had my secretary spying on me. As it stands now, not even I know who will be on duty from day-to-day. In fact, I don't think I've seen the same girl twice in the last month."

"That's one way to keep everybody confused," Marco said.

"Sure does keep me confused," Allison said. "On the other hand, none of the girls in the pool are ever likely to overhear anything critical, and probably wouldn't recognize it if they did. it's really not that bad an idea, and I'm grateful to Donald for thinking of it."

Noah, Sarah, Neil, Jenny, and Marco all walked out of the office and settled into the chairs around the lobby. The current secretary, a middle-aged brunette, just smiled at them and said nothing.

Marco couldn't leave it at that. "Excuse me, ma'am," he said. "Allison was just telling us that you secretaries are all on some kind of rotation, now?"

The woman smiled at him again. "Yes," she said. "It's a security precaution."

"Okay, yeah," Marco said. "Only I'm just wondering, is it confusing when you come up here for the first time? I mean, how do you know what to do?"

She reached into the upper right drawer of her desk and picked up a small ring binder. "Orders of the day," he said. "We are told to check this book before doing anything else. It tells us where the appointment calendars are, what the computer password of the day is, who sits in what office on this floor and what their telephone extensions are. Pretty much everything we need to know is in this book." She dropped it back into the drawer and shut it.

"Well, now, ain't that a thing," Marco said. "Makes sense to me, I guess."

"Even better than that," the secretary said, "it makes sense to us. Imagine what a nightmare this would be if it didn't."

"That's a good point. Has anyone ever gotten it confused up here?"

She looked at him askance. "Do you think they would admit it if they had? I know I wouldn't. Far as anybody downstairs needs to know, I aced it up here today. And since it will be at least two months before I ever sit in this chair again, who's going to argue the point?"

"Marco, you might want to stop," Neil said. "I'm pretty sure she's smarter than you are, and it's starting to show."

Marco gave him a dirty look, but sat back in his chair and was quiet.

Allison came out a few minutes later, and they all went down the elevator together. Neil offered to let her ride with him and Jenny, but she insisted on taking her own car. They made their usual little convoy, with Noah's Corvette out front, Neil's Hummer behind him, Marco's Chevelle on his tail, and Allison's Cadillac bringing up the rear. Marco called Renée, who promised to meet them there.

There was a bit of construction on the road to the Sagebrush Saloon, so the drive took almost an hour. By the time they got there, it was nearly six o'clock. Renée had already arrived, so they waited until everyone was parked and all walked in together.

The hostess, whose name was Carla, knew Noah, Sarah, Marco, Neil, and Jenny as regular customers, but it turned out this was Allison's first time out to the place. Sarah introduced her to Carla as "the Boss Lady," and they were led to a large, round table in a corner of the dining room that was partially isolated from the rest of it by the layout of the building.

Carla, they had learned, was the wife of Jack Zigler. Jack was the security chief at R&D, and so Carla had enough of the security clearance to know that her husband worked for a secret government organization. She also knew that Noah and the rest worked for that organization, so meeting "the Boss Lady" seemed a bit exciting to her. In the circles that she and her husband ran in, there were rumors about the infamous Dragon Lady who ran the whole operation. Carla privately thought that Allison didn't look nearly as vicious as rumor would have one believe.

"This place is pretty nice," Allison said. "I've heard of it, of course, but I've never been here before."

"It's a good place to relax and have a good meal," Noah said. "They do serve alcohol, and they even have a band on weekends, but we never do any actual drinking out here."

Allison looked him in the eye. "Glad to hear it," she said. "That's what the Assassin's Club is for. I put it in because I know that everybody, even people in our business, have to be able to let their guards down once in a while."

"Oh, we love the place," Sarah said. "Especially when it has a good band, so we can get up and dance."

"Yeah," Renée said. "You should see Marco dance, he's really very good."

"I don't dance," Neil said, "but Jenny likes to drag me out there and dance around me. I just kinda keep my feet planted and sway to the music, but everybody ends up watching her, so nobody really notices me at all."

"God, I haven't been dancing in—a really, really, really long time," Allison said.

"Well, you should come with us, sometime," Jenny said. "There's probably a hundred guys out there that would love to dance with you."

Allison gave her a mock scowl. "Somehow I doubt it," she said. "I don't think too many guys go for middle-aged blondes, especially when she's also the boss."

"Okay, but that's where you're wrong," Renée said. "There's a lot of guys out there that don't work for you. We've got military officers, people from other sections of the government, even a few from the CIA. From what they say, the Assassin's Club is about the only bar of its kind in the entire world. My roommate met her boyfriend there, and he's with the DEA."

"DEA?" Allison asked. "What was he doing here?"

"I don't know," Renée said. "Oh, he was here to talk to that kid Noah brought back a few months ago. I guess that boy has turned out to be a treasure trove of information on drug trafficking in the south. That's what I heard, anyway."

"Hrmph," Allison said. "Any other agency that sends people in to Neverland is supposed to check with my office first. Maybe I need to look over some of our security and see who might be sleeping on the job, because I don't remember any DEA requests coming through in the past few months."

"Is it something only you can approve?" Noah asked. "Couldn't Mr. Jefferson handle it?"

"He can, and he would," Allison said, "but he's always let me know about it when a request comes in. He knows that I sometimes come up with ideas on the spur of the moment, and it could be necessary for me to know about an outside officer being on site. I suppose it's possible he did tell me, and it really slipped my mind. I mean, it's not like I don't have other things to think about, right?"

"Oh, no," Neil said, "not you. I couldn't believe you might forget something."

Allison stuck her tongue out at him. "Go ahead, poke your fun," she said. "I'll have you know there isn't a lot that I ever forget. For example, your high school locker number was 451. You lived at fifteen forty-nine Baker Street, and you had a cat named—don't tell me, I know this—its name was Charlie, because you said it reminded you of Charlie Brown."

Neil was grinning and nodding. "Yeah, I found him when other kids were kicking him around in the street. Seemed like Charlie Brown was always getting picked on, so it was the first name that came to mind."

"See? I don't forget very many things. Once I know something, I pretty much know it for life."

"That's interesting," Noah said. "I didn't know you had a photographic memory."

"Oh, I don't," Allison said. "I just took some courses on memory management several years ago, and they stuck with me. I learned how to build a mental mansion, and put every little thing I learned into its own place in the mansion. You'd be shocked at how easy it is to remember things using that little trick."

"You got any tidbits on me?" Jenny asked.

"You," Allison said with a grin, "are an entire collection of tidbits, as you put it. Your first car was a Toyota Prius, and your license plate number was 465-WXR. You were a cheerleader your freshman and sophomore year in high school, but you dropped it in your junior year because you wanted more time for your drama club. You played the Ghost of Christmas Present in your senior class play, which was, of course, A Christmas Carol. Oh, and you can't stand red M&Ms. You pick out the red ones and throw them away."

"Holy moly," Jenny said, her eyes wide and mouth hanging open. "How do you even know all that stuff?"

"Honey, did you think we only grab you because you're a killer? It takes more than that to become one of ours. We went through a complete background investigation on you, even down to interviewing some of your friends. Of course, they thought it was a pre-sentence interview. They kept hoping that something they said would make the court go easy on you. Pretty much everyone you knew felt like you should have been given a medal, rather than being arrested for murder. I guess they all knew your sister and liked her, so they figured those boys got what was coming to them."

"They all would have," Jenny said, "if I hadn't been interrupted. But, hey, I'm not complaining. If it hadn't been for you getting me out of that prison, I never would have met Neil." She looked up at him adoringly.

"You know, I've been meaning to ask you kids," Allison said. "How is it all working out for you? I mean, Neil works for Noah on Team Camelot, but you, Jenny, you are the leader of Team Cinderella. And yet, when I see the two of you together, you look like a perfectly normal couple. How do you do that?"

"It's not always easy," Jenny said. "I've had a few rough moments, when Neil and I would get into a fight and I would start to think violently. I found a way to stop that, though, by just leaving Cinderella outside the door. When I'm with Neil, I'm not Cinderella anymore, I'm just plain old Jenny. Scared, insecure, submissive little Jenny." She smiled, and her nose crinkled. "It makes it all work, because I have to be all tough and in charge when I'm Cinderella. Jenny can just be—she can just be me."

Allison looked at her for a moment, nodding slightly. "And are the two of you thinking about making a permanent relationship, like Noah and Sarah did?"

Neil and Jenny looked at each other, then turned back to Allison. "We talk about it," Neil said. "I think it might be something we want to do, but neither of us is sure that we want to do it very soon."

"Yeah," Jenny said, "and besides, it's not like we can really be normal. I mean, I always thought I'd have a couple of babies someday, but I don't see that happening now."

Allison looked at her for a moment longer, then turned to Sarah. "What about you? Do you think about babies?"

Sarah looked up like she was a deer caught in headlights. "Um—I don't know," he said. "I mean, yes, I think about it, of course I do. I think it would be abnormal if I didn't think about it, don't you?"

"Of course it would," Allison said. "Do you want to be a mother?"

Sarah's eyes got even wider. "I, well, I—I guess I always thought I would be, sometime. I mean, is it something I'd want? Sure, if it was possible. I just don't see it working out too well when Noah and I don't even know if we're both going to come home alive. In this business, you just never know, right? I don't think it would be fair to bring a child into our marriage, our family."

Allison looked at her for another moment without saying anything. They were interrupted a few seconds later by the arrival of the waitress, who took their orders and was gone again.

"I think you're actually right," Allison said. "It wouldn't be fair to the child, when it could lose one or both parents at any time. Of course, now that I think of it, that could happen even if you work at a factory, or at a fast food joint. With the way the world is nowadays, everyone is a target, everyone is at risk. You simply have the benefit of knowing that the work you do carries certain extreme inherent risks. On the other hand, you are basically just intelligence agents. There are an awful lot of intelligence agents who have children."

Sarah, Jenny, and Renée were all staring at her, while Neil and Marco were doing their best to look anywhere else. Noah seemed to be studying the three girls.

"Allison," Jenny said softly, "are you implying that it might be possible for us to have children?"

"Well, that would be for your doctor to decide," Allison said. "All I'm saying is that if it were to happen, I don't think it would necessarily be the end of the world. Sarah, you could probably stay home; I'm sure I could find Noah another transportation specialist. Jenny, I'd probably move you into training, or use you for some of the simpler assignments that come in, if you had a baby waiting at home. I would certainly increase your team. However, before either of you starts decorating a nursery, let me make something perfectly clear. I would want advance notification, as far in advance as you can possibly give it to me. Do you understand?"

Sarah managed to close her mouth after a couple of tries, then opened it again. "I understand," she said. "But, I'll be perfectly honest and tell you that I don't think I'm ready for that just yet. Maybe I need to see how Noah and I do for a while, first. I don't mean how we do as a couple, I mean how we do on coming home alive. Does that make sense?"

"It makes perfect sense," Jenny said, "because it's exactly the same thing I was thinking. Noah may be the assassin, but Neil is at risk every time he goes out, too. And, while the thought of a little blessing has its appeals, I'm not ready for diapers and three a.m. feedings right at the moment."

"And you'll give me warning, if you change your minds?"

"Oh, yeah," Sarah said. "We definitely would."

Allison grinned. "Well, that's one worry off my mind, then. Now if I could get rid of a few hundred others, I could really relax and have fun."

"Is something causing you a problem?" Noah asked.

"When is it not? I've got eighteen sanction requests sitting on my desk, and only four working teams—well, five, if you count the new one that we just approved for the field. We've reactivated Team Unicorn with a new group. The assassin came to us from the U.K., a former member of Group 13, Britain's version of E & E. They apparently downsized a couple of years ago, and this fellow decided to go independent. We caught him through a sting operation that was tracking hit men in New York. Once we realized who we had caught, I went to pay him a visit."

"Well, he ought to be good at what he does," Noah said. "Are there any others coming online anytime soon?"

"Well, yes," Allison said. "That kid you brought in a few months back, Ralph Morgan? He's actually done well in training. He'll be heading Team Pegasus in about three more months. The problem is that I'm getting more requests than we can handle. Andropov really did a number on us last year. It's almost like we're starting over."

"That would bring you up to six," Noah said. "Has Ralph been out in the field at all?"

"Actually, yes," Allison said. "I sent him out with Hercules last week, just as additional muscle. Hercules said he did exceptionally well, though there was no wet work involved. I just thought he ought to get a taste of it, and he came back rather enthusiastic."

"That doesn't surprise me," Noah said. "Like I said when I brought him in, the kid seems to be a natural."

Chapter THREE

The team, loaded down with luggage and equipment, boarded a 747 at the Kirtland airfield on Saturday evening. The flight lasted almost 20 hours, and they arrived at the Tindouf airport at just after eight p.m. on Sunday. While they slept through a good part of the flight, each of them spent time studying the files they had been given. It was important for each of them to be able to recognize the targets, so that none would be missed. They had seven targets with photographs, though it was possible they would learn of even more potential targets once they were on site.

Four rooms, including one that would be used as an office, were already reserved for them at the Hotel Bijou de Tindouf. They made up an entire floor in the hotel, which was not far from Abimbola's offices. That floor had been officially designated as short-term diplomatic headquarters of the U.S. A large parcel van that had obviously been hastily painted with the emblem of West Algeria was waiting to transport them and their luggage and equipment to the temporary embassy.

Nine U.S. Army soldiers accompanied them on the journey, to serve as security for the diplomatic mission. Each of them, while they were on the plane, had quietly identified himself as an Army intelligence officer, even though most of them were posing as NCO's. Officially, there were three lieutenants, three sergeants, and three corporals. They would stand guard in three-man teams at the temporary embassy, adding to the cover Noah and the team would have for carrying out their real mission.

Unfortunately, because it was so late in the evening, there wasn't much they could do. With the first shift of Army guards in place, they sat down in Noah's room to continue going over the target files.

"This guy Oni is the primary," Noah said. "He's also President Abimbola's closest friend, so I'm planning to use discretion and deception in his case. The others are primarily Polisario Front, so we don't need to be quite as circumspect in dealing with them. There are regular hit squads moving in and around the Polisario all the time, and any of them could be targeted for a number of reasons."

He pointed at several photos laying on the bed. "These four," he said, "are likely to be targets of opportunity. I think we'll program them into the smart guns and look for concealable vantage points."

"Good thing they're quiet, then," Marco said.

"Yes," Noah said, "but we still can't take the chance of letting them be found intact. The refugee camps are divided into five sections, so we need to program them all and spread them out among those sections. The problem we are going to have is that the camps are mostly in fairly flat desert. Finding a place to conceal the smart guns is not going to be easy. The buildings are low, mostly made of sand brick or concrete, but a large percentage of the populations live in tents."

"Then what we need to do," Neil said, "is go out there and let me scan it with the drones. I should be able to spot the best vantage point, somewhere to place them with some cover."

Noah nodded. "Okay, we'll plan on that after I meet with the president in the morning. Neil, you won't be going to this meeting, so you can make contact with Prudence Mays and arrange a tour of the refugee camps for us. Let her know that we'll be needing at least two vehicles, and another interpreter if we have to split up."

"You got it," Neil said.

"I think that covers it," Noah said. "We might as well relax for what's left of the evening and get some sleep. The next few days might be pretty intense, so get whatever rest you can while we have the opportunity."

Neil and Jenny went to their room, and Marco went to his own. Noah and Sarah decided to share a shower, then got into bed. An hour later, they drifted off to sleep.

They rose early the next morning, as soon as the sun began to peek over the horizon. There was a small restaurant attached to the hotel, and they all, except for the guards on duty, went down to breakfast together. It was a simple affair, with rich coffee and French pastries.

As soon as they were finished, a limousine arrived to take Noah and his team to visit President Abimbola. Marco had to interpret, but his French was definitely up to the job.

"The driver says we will be taken directly to his office," he said. "The president is waiting for us, and I guess we were supposed to be there earlier."

"Really?" Noah asked. "It's only seven thirty, now. According to the itinerary they gave me, we weren't supposed to meet with him until nine."

"I'm just telling you what the man said," Marco said. "It sounds like there might be something going on that makes them want to hurry up and take whatever deals with the U.S. they can get."

The ride took only about fifteen minutes, and the driver then escorted them directly to the president's office. A secretary sat in the foyer, but kept her eyes down as they passed. A moment later, they stepped into the office of the President of West Algeria.

Chidi Abimbola was seated behind the desk, while Oni Zidane was standing beside it. Oni smiled and addressed them in perfect English.

"We welcome you, Mr. Ambassador," he said. "May I present President Chidi Abimbola, temporary executive of West Algeria."

"I'm James McConnell, and I'm delighted to meet you, Mr. President," Noah said, "but I must correct Mr. Zidane. I am not an ambassador, simply a career foreign service officer who's been sent to pave the way for future diplomatic relations. If we come to a successful agreement, a new ambassador will definitely be appointed right away. He would certainly have more authority and flexibility than they've given me." He withdrew an envelope from his pocket and held it out with both hands to President Abimbola. "I present my credentials, Mr. President."

Chidi smiled as he glanced at the papers inside, then kept the smile as he looked at Sarah and Marco. "And these are?"

"Mr. President, this lovely lady is my assistant, Elizabeth Roth," Noah said. Abimbola smiled at her and bent over her hand in a bow, gently brushing her fingers with his lips. "And this gentleman," Noah went on, "is Pierre Lafontaine. He was sent along because I didn't score very well when I studied French back in high school."

Abimbola held out a hand, and Marco shook hands with him. "Mr. President," he said, "it is an honor to meet you."

Abimbola smiled and turned back to Noah. "Mr. McConnell, it is not necessary for us to concern ourselves with titles or positions today. It is my understanding that you are here to open negotiations on diplomatic relations between your country and mine, and that is all I could ask."

Noah smiled back. "That's exactly my purpose," he said. "And may I first congratulate you on your independence. My home country went through something similar when it was formed, and I can only hope you have fewer problems than we did."

The president chuckled. "Don't we both," he said. "Please, seat yourselves." He pointed at a conference table on one side of the room, and rose from his chair to move toward it. He took the chair at one end, while Oni held the chair to his right for Noah. Sarah and Marco took a couple of the other chairs, and then Oni sat down at the president's left.

"Mr. McConnell," Oni said, "can you tell us what level of support and recognition your country is prepared to offer?"

Noah had carefully studied the paperwork he'd been given regarding this meeting. "The United States of America is prepared to recognize President Abimbola's government as the legitimate interim government of West Algeria. If we can come to certain agreements regarding mutual defense and the establishment of a U.S. military presence within your country, then we are prepared to offer both political and military support, as well as sponsorship for your application to the United Nations."

Chidi's smile grew slightly wider. "Then let us discuss that military presence. I presume you have an outline of what your country would want, as far as location and the size of your base?"

Noah opened the briefcase he was carrying and took out a file. He opened it and withdrew several papers, passing one each to Chidi and Oni. "If you'll take a look at this," he said, "the area we would like to acquire is roughly eight hundred hectares about a hundred kilometers southeast of Tindouf. This would primarily be a drone base, but we would maintain a couple of fighter squadrons and a battalion of ground troops there, mostly just for rapid response to our allies throughout north and northwest Africa. These allies include Mauritania, Morocco, Tunisia, Egypt, and Mali, and this particular base would be designed for air support and rapid deployment of troops in support of those allies when needed. For that reason, we would need to build a couple of air strips, maintenance hangars, storage hangars, administrative buildings, as well as housing and barracks for all of the personnel."

Oni lowered his eyebrows. "Eight hundred hectares? That would be quite a large drone base, would it not?"

"Which is why we specify that we would maintain troops and air squadrons there, as well. As part of the agreement, West Algeria would become another ally of the United States, so those troops and aircraft would be available for the defense of your country, as much as any other ally."

"So what you are saying," Chidi said, "is that if we agree, you will commit your forces within our country to aid and assist our own defenses? Does this include any actions that take place during what may amount to a civil war?"

"It does," Noah said. "While we regret the reality, the fact is that Algiers is unlikely to let such a large portion of the country split off without a fight. The troops we would station here will be a full battalion from the 101st Airborne Division of the United States Army. They are some of the finest troops we have, and could offer a great deal of training to your own soldiers. Our experience in Afghanistan, Iraq, and Iran has given us a clear insight into desert warfare. These soldiers know what they're doing, and would be of terrific benefit to your country."

Chidi looked closely at the map on the paper Noah had given him. "The place you have marked is in a very rugged area. There are currently no actual roads in that region. I presume your military would be responsible for all of the construction, including roadways?"

"That's correct. Our goal is to acquire the base with the minimum impact on your country, both economically and ecologically. Since that area does not have any sources of fresh water, we would need to establish roads quickly so that water can be tanked in until a pipeline can be run. We anticipate that the establishment of the base in that location might create as many as a thousand peripheral employment opportunities for some of your citizens."

"The most direct route," Oni said, "would be straight through Boujdour and Smara refugee camps. I would expect that the Sahrawis would welcome the opportunity for work, and your road would probably be lined with market stalls and restaurants."

"American soldiers have always welcomed native entrepreneurship," Noah said. "You'd be very surprised how much money a couple of thousand American military personnel can spend on local food and merchandise. You could be talking about as much as a few million dollars a year finding its way into the Sahrawi economy in those camps."

"Two thousand soldiers?" Chidi asked. "I thought we were talking about a single battalion."

"The Airborne Infantry Battalion I'm referring to amounts to about eight hundred soldiers, but we are also talking about forty-eight jet fighters in two squadrons, several transport aircraft, maintenance facilities and personnel for the aircraft, a motor pool for trucks and vehicles plus their own maintenance personnel and facilities, a medical facility and personnel for the troops, not to mention administrative personnel—yes, I think we're talking about a couple thousand people, and possibly more. There would also be several hundred jobs on the base for native employment, so that would probably add a few million more dollars to the local economy."

Oni smiled, and turned to his president. "I believe, Mr. President," he said, "that Mr. McConnell has come bearing gifts. Between the military support such a base would offer and the economic opportunities that it presents, I believe we have little to lose and very much to gain in such an agreement."

Chidi nodded. "I tend to agree," he said. "Mr. McConnell, you mentioned political support. Can you explain what you mean by that?"

"Yes, sir," Noah said. "Political support for your country means that our State Department and diplomatic corps will work to negotiate peaceful resolutions to protests that some of your neighboring countries might make regarding your secession. For example, we anticipate that Morocco is likely to expect West Algeria to take a strong position supporting the Sahrawis and the Polisario. That could lead to border conflicts that could potentially devastate your country. We would send diplomats to Morocco and to West Algeria to try to negotiate a peaceful agreement or settlement that would avoid such conflicts. Based on recent intelligence we picked up in Morocco and Western Sahara, it is even possible that we could get them to sit down at the table and discuss repatriation of some of the refugees. Our State Department believes this is far more likely with West Algeria than with your former mother country."

Chidi nodded. "I believe you may be correct about that. I have spoken with many Moroccan officials who believe that the time for repatriation and cessation of hostilities over Western Sahara is long overdue. Algiers has managed to keep the matter out of reasonable negotiations for quite some time, however."

"That's the position our State Department has taken, as well. We think that it's very possible that a crisis that began in the nineteen seventies could finally be nearing its end, and that West Algeria might play a pivotal role in the talks that could bring it about."

Chidi looked into Noah's eyes for a moment, then slowly nodded his head. "Let me ask you, Mr. McConnell," he said, "what other conditions of alliance with the United States might there be?"

Noah smiled. "We'd like to buy a lot of your iron ore," he said. "We understand that Russia has been your biggest customer, but the trade agreements between Algiers and Moscow have left your mines getting what we consider inferior prices for your ore. If we can establish a trade agreement that will give us first right of refusal on your iron ore, we will pay you the same prices we pay to Europe and South America. That will be about a threefold increase over the prices you've been getting from Russia."

"And our natural gas?" Oni asked. "Would you want first right of refusal over that, as well?"

"Actually, no," Noah said. "Transporting natural gas across the oceans is expensive, and we couldn't pay you the kind of prices you're already getting from Europe. We prefer to stay out of the gas market over here, other than what we would purchase through your local distribution outlets for the purposes of our military base."

The conversation continued for another hour, with very little argument from the West Algerians. It seemed that Noah had done a very good job of presenting the American position, and he and Sarah and Marco finally left with a promise that the agreement would be drawn up and ready for the president's signature by the following morning.

The driver was waiting outside the office for them, and bowed as they came out. He spoke quickly in French to Marco, who broke into a smile.

"He says we are invited to a dinner this evening," he said to Noah. "The president and his advisers will be hosting it. I get the impression that turning it down might be the same as slapping the president's face."

"Have you ever heard of a diplomat turn down free food?" Noah asked. "Tell him we'll be delighted, and find out about time and place and transportation."

Marco spoke with the driver for a moment, then turned back to Noah as they were led to the elevator and back to the limousine. "He'll pick us up at seven thirty," he said. "The dinner is here in this building, apparently there's a big dining room downstairs."

"Sounds good," Noah said. The driver held the back door open as they all climbed inside, and then they were on the way back to the hotel.

When they arrived, they were surprised to find not just Neil and Jenny in the room set aside as an office, but another lady. She smiled and held out her hand to Noah, who took it and shook with her.

"Prudence Mays," she said. "I'm supposed to let you know that any support I can give is yours."

"Thank you," Noah said. "We were hoping to get out and take a look at some of the refugee camps today, but it turns out we have an appointment this evening. Are any of them close enough that we can be back here by six thirty? We've been invited to dinner with the president, and I don't think we can afford to miss it. It's even possible that I'll be able to identify some of my targets there."

"Oh, I agree," Prudence said. "Boujdour is nearest. We could probably get there and back in plenty of time. The others might be a bit tricky."

"Then let's go to that one today, and save the rest for tomorrow. Do you have vehicles for us?"

"Yes," she said. "I've got you two G-Class Mercedes SUVs. They're sitting outside right now. It's almost ten thirty, are you ready to go now? The sooner we get started, the better."

Noah nodded. "Let us gather up a few things," he said, "and we'll be ready to go. Marco, let's get two of the smart guns, and Neil, you grab one of the drones. If anyone asks, we're doing a survey of the camps to help us make recommendations for additional aid."

Prudence nodded. "That's a good cover," she said. "My cover story here is that I run the U.S. Refugee Child Welfare Program. Since we provide a lot of food and medical care to the refugees, and not just the children, nobody is going to think much of me bringing diplomats to look it over. If anyone asks you, tell them that I'm making demands for more food and medicine. They know me, they'll believe it."

They took one of the soldiers with them, a reputed PSC named Jorgensen. He drove one of the cars with Neil and Jenny, while Prudence drove the other with Noah, Sarah, and Marco. Prudence took the lead and surprised them all when she followed a faint dusty track across the desert.

"Not a lot of roads out here," she said. "We have to make our own most of the time. Of course, that means paying close attention to the weather, the sky, and the horizon. I don't know if you've spent much time in the desert, but a Sahara sandstorm can just about strip your skin. These cars have to have the oil changed weekly, along with air filters and a thorough washing. The sand can get into places where it can literally grind away at important metal components. You'll notice there aren't a lot of old vehicles running around, because the sand has weakened them to the point that they aren't worth fixing."

"I was in Afghanistan for a while," Noah said. "I've seen what the sand can do. It didn't take long to figure out why the natives wear the kind of clothing they do."

Prudence nodded. "Yeah, you need something that can protect your skin but still let air move around." She glanced at the khaki pants and shirt Noah was wearing. "Light colors, that's good, but you might find that's a little heavy for out here in the desert."

"Or not," Noah said. "This is a special fabric, designed to keep us cool even in the hottest desert. It draws the moisture away from the skin and evaporates it in a hurry."

Her eyebrows went up. "Really? Wonder when they'll get around to letting us have some of that." She caught Sarah's eye in the rearview mirror. "You and I are about the same size," she said. "If you accidentally left some behind..."

"I see what I can do," Sarah said with a grin.

It took almost an hour to get to the camp, which was a large area with scattered buildings and tents everywhere. There seemed to be thousands of people wandering around, and Noah tried to figure out where the main thoroughfare might be.

"About thirty-two thousand people in Boujdour camp alone," Prudence said. "There's not a lot of industry in this one, unless you count the shepherds. A lot of Berbers here, and an awful lot of the mutton that we eat back in Tindouf comes out of this camp."

"Any idea who out here might be involved in the plot to assassinate Abimbola?" Noah asked.

Prudence shrugged. "I can think of two or three possibles," she said. "Zacharia and Chabane Leberteaux, they're brothers, they'd be in the thick of it. Also Amed Wassim, he's part of the Formation Council. Those three, they're the only ones I could point to as likely. Would you like to meet them? They'll be at the administrative building, probably just throwing their weight around. They aren't actually part of the administration here, but they've been deep in the secessionist movement for many years, so a lot of people are afraid of them."

Noah cocked his head. "Zacharia is on my target list, and so is Amed. Do you think Zacharia's brother is actually involved?"

"If Zacharia is in it, then so is Chabane. Those two are into anything that might build their power base or enrich them financially. If they can turn Abimbola into a martyr, it could have both effects. His death will incite a monstrous wave of national pride and indignation, which will mean the government will be able to institute some form of protectionism. They'll undoubtedly stop accepting any kind of imports from Algeria, and the Leberteaux family controls an awful lot of the sheep and chicken farming in all of the camps. As for Amed, he only wants one thing: power, and all of it he can get. He's been claiming that he will soon be named to the advisory council for the government. If that happens, there is no doubt in anyone's mind that he will run for president in the first open election."

"A refugee?" Marco asked. "Running for president?"

Prudence nodded emphatically. "You betcha," she said. "One of the premises West Algeria is being founded on is that the Sahrawi refugees will be granted full citizenship, while still being able to return to Western Sahara whenever repatriation actually can happen. Going home won't remove their West Algerian citizenship, which will allow them to move freely between the countries. It's a prime position for people who have been feeling like they were completely unwanted and without a home of their own for decades."

She pulled the car up to a building and parked, and they all got out, following her inside. The roof blocked the sun from beating down on them, but did little to cool the air inside. Noah saw a small fan powered by a car battery and was suddenly grateful for the special clothing, because Prudence began pouring sweat instantly.

"Prudence," said a man seated at a desk just inside the door. "You have brought guests?"

"I have," she said. "Meshac, this is Mr. James McConnell. He came from the United States government to discuss diplomatic arrangements with the president, and he wanted to come out and see what it is we do. I told him that the RCWP provides food and medicine for your people, but that we never have enough of either. He's going to try to get my allowances increased, so don't let them know I was lying." She winked.

Meshac rolled his eyes and looked at Noah. "I will never come to understand what this woman considers humorous," he said. "Welcome, Sahib. May you live long and have many wives and sons."

Prudence slapped his shoulder playfully. "You complain about my humor? Your people haven't used blessings like that in centuries. Don't let him fool you, Jim, he's just trying to pretend he's a stupid Berber, when he's anything but. Meshac is the man in charge, here. President of the *wali*. Back home, we'd probably just refer to him as the mayor."

Meshac chuckled. "Forgive me, Mr. McConnell. So many Americans come here expecting us to be like something out of *The Arabian Nights*. I've learned to play the part, especially if I'm going to be begging."

"You don't need to be begging with me," Noah said. "All I get to do is report back to the State Department. They'll make any decisions on whether to increase the aid funding Ms. Mays receives."

"Okay, is the pissing contest over yet?" Prudence asked. "You both established that you're smart and tough, so now let's get down to the real thing. Meshac, I need to take Mr. McConnell and his party and show them around. They need to get a really good look at the conditions here, because I'm trying to get some better construction materials sent in. Some of the buildings around here are starting to fall apart, and I want to show them just how bad it's getting. I want McConnell to go back and tell State that they need to send concrete this way."

Meshac grinned. "As always, my dear Prudence, you are welcome anywhere in the camp. If anyone troubles you or tries to interfere, simply send them to me."

She smiled. "Meshac, you old desert dog. If you keep being so nice to me, I'm going to start thinking you like me."

"Well," the old Berber said, "I always have room for another wife."

Chapter FOUR

They left the administration building a few minutes later and got back into the cars. Prudence drove slowly, often having to wait for people, sheep, or chickens to get out of the way, but a few minutes later, they emerged onto a wide roadway. There were a few cars driving on it, but it was mostly foot traffic.

"You wanted to see the main road," she said, "this is it. Just about everyone in the camp passes down this section of track at least once a day. See the buildings on either side? That's where we distribute commodities, and the smaller building on the left is my outfit's wellness clinic. Pretty much everybody needs something from one of these buildings at any given moment, so this area is always pretty crowded."

Noah looked around at the concrete and sand brick structures that lined the roadway for three hundred yards in each direction. "I need a high spot that can look down over this area."

She pointed. "See that?" 'That' turned out to be a water tower, basically a large wooden tub at the top of a steel scaffold. "Tanker trucks bring fifty thousand gallons of water down here a few times a month, and pump it into that tower. It's barely fit for human consumption, although you have a hard time telling that to the children. It's mostly used for cleaning, sanitation, that sort of thing. Some of it gets smuggled out for watering small gardens, even though it's not supposed to be used for that purpose. Nobody ever climbs up there, so if you can put your toys up there somewhere, they probably won't be noticed."

"Yeah?" Marco said. "What about when one of them takes off somebody's head?"

"You want to know the sad truth? Most of the people would just walk around the poor guy, until one of his friends finds him. There's a lot of rivalry inside these camps, and it's not uncommon for someone to get shot. It's usually a simple matter of one-shot taking out somebody's personal enemy, and then it's over. Most of the refugees simply give thanks that they weren't the target and go on about their business."

"Well, that's pretty sad," Sarah said. "But how would we get it up there? That tower is up about what, a hundred feet? Anybody climbing up it would be noticed from just about anywhere in the settlement."

"It would have to be at night," Prudence said. "I can drive you back out here after dark, after your dinner."

"That sounds like the best plan," Noah said. "Let's do it."

"Okay," Prudence said. "If we're done here, we actually have time to visit Smara camp. It's only about a half hour south of here, and we can make it back to Tindouf in time from there."

"All right, let's go." Noah climbed out of the car and walked back to let Neil, Sarah, and the soldier know what was going on, then came back and buckled in again.

Prudence took her foot off the brake and drove slowly through the throng of foot traffic for a moment, then found a clear path out of the camp. As they left, she followed another faint track across the desert.

"What might surprise you," Prudence said after a minute, "is that we are actually less than twenty miles from Tindouf. I don't know if you've noticed, but this sand is so soft and fine that it's often like driving on snow. That's what slows us down out here, not the distance."

"Yes, I noticed," Noah said. "Do these vehicles get stuck out here very often?"

"Nah," she said. "One of the benefits of the fine sand is that, as long as you don't stop, one of your wheels is going to grab something at some point. That's the trick, just like when you're driving in slushy snow, you just don't stop."

They reached the camp known as Al Smara and Noah was surprised to see that it was even less modernized than Boujdour. The previous camp had a few amenities, and he had even seen the occasional solar panel on top of one of the roofs.

Here, on the other hand, there was no water tower and he saw no solar panels. The roads, if the pathways between structures could be called such a thing, meandered like wild rivulets. There was no order to the layout of the community, and he couldn't spot any kind of central business district.

"No electricity here?" he asked.

"Car batteries," Prudence replied. "These people get pretty inventive. You'll see an old car sitting on blocks, but the engine is purring like a new one. If you look closely, you'll see that cables are hooked up to dozens of batteries at once. A bunch of people pool their money to buy a few gallons of gasoline, then pour it into that old car so they can charge up the batteries. If you went inside any of the homes, you'd see old taillights used as lamps, and old heater fans hooked up to draw a little cool air into the house. Not that there's much cool air around to draw, but they try. Oh, they try. Oh, and then, of course, you'll hear the radios. It's cheaper to have an old car radio that runs off a half-dead car battery than it is to buy new double-As every few days."

"And these people have lived like this for decades?" Sarah asked.

"Yep. More than two thirds of them have never known anything else, but if you asked them how they felt about it, they'd tell you it's just temporary. As soon as the UN or somebody else can work out the details of a peace treaty with Morocco, they all plan to go home. Home, of course, being the Western Sahara."

"I feel sorry for them," Sarah replied. "To live your whole life in exile, that's horrible."

"Don't tell them that," Prudence warned. "These people are the most stubborn you'll ever meet, because they simply don't know how to give up. It's not in their DNA, I guess. If you or I had to live under these conditions, it would probably drive us to depression. These folks, they still laugh and joke and expect it all to come to an end some day. And when that end comes, they say that's when they'll go home."

"That's amazing," Sarah said. "Hey, listen, I don't suppose there's a restroom around here somewhere? I kinda need to go."

Prudence burst out laughing. "Honey, the closest thing they have to a restroom here is a little square mud hut with a hole in the floor that's about the size of a small pizza. You squat, do your business, and then dip some water out of the bowl beside you to clean yourself up. I've learned to hold it, but if you really need to go..."

"Never mind," Sarah said. "It's not that urgent."

"Smara is, in some ways," Prudence said, "kind of a seat of government for the Sahrawis. All of these camps are actually made up of small villages, and this one," she pointed at a group of buildings and tents that seemed set off by itself a bit, "is 27th February village. February twenty-seventh is the day the Sahrawi Democratic Republic was founded. The SDR is a nation without its own land, which is probably why, even though these people are Islamic, they get a surprising amount of support out of Israel. And just to put your mind at ease, these aren't the jihadist types. In fact, you'll hear the *muezzin* call at various times during the day, but most of these folks are too busy to stop for prayers. I'm not saying they aren't faithful to their religion in their own ways, but sometimes survival takes precedence over tradition and custom."

"I'll ask you the same question I asked in the other camp," Noah said. "Who would you expect to find here that might be involved in the assassination plot?"

"Tariq Doumaz," Prudence said. "He is part of the Formation Council, and one of the most devious men I have ever known. If there is any kind of plot going on to turn Abimbola into a martyr, he will be in the thick of it."

"Doumaz," Noah said speculatively. "That's not a name on my list. Think we can find the guy?"

"It's possible. His wife pretty much runs this camp, along with a few other women."

"Women run it?" Sarah asked. "I thought women didn't hold positions of power in this part of the world."

"That's true in a lot of Islamic countries," Prudence said, "but not in the camps. If you want my personal opinion, it's because the men figured out that letting the women run things means they have more time to sit around and relax. Okay, I guess that's an oversimplification. Let's just say that the women run things, but they also answer to their husbands. If Tariq doesn't like something his wife does, there's a good chance she'll reverse herself on it. That make any sense?"

Sarah rolled her eyes. "Makes perfect sense," she said. "Sounds like the Baptist Church my family went to when I was little. Seemed like the women ran everything in the church, as long as the men were okay with whatever they decided to do."

Prudence chuckled and nodded. "That's a very good analogy," she said. "And I know just the kind of church you're talking about."

"How about Farouk Harachi?" Noah asked. "He's on my list, and is supposed to live in this camp. Do you know him?"

Prudence looked at him, her eyes wide. "Harachi?" she asked. "I know him, but I can't believe he would be part of the assassination plot. He's a loyalist, a lot of the Sahrawis are. By that, I mean that they have pledged loyalty to Tindouf province, and it's understood that loyalty is now to the current government in West Algeria. If the secession succeeds, these people would be a lot more likely to defend

Abimbola than be any part of the plot to martyr him. Any idea where that intel came from?"

Noah met her eyes with his own. "I had actually assumed it came from you," he said. "According to what we were told, this is all CIA intelligence."

She nodded. "Okay, I'm catching on. I'm the station chief for Tindouf town, but there is another small CIA station in Dakhla camp. The station chief there is a Sahrawi, himself, Rashid Aruj. He was recruited not long after the refugees started coming into Algeria, back in the nineteen seventies. Of course, he was a young man, back then."

"Any reason to believe his intelligence might be tainted?" Noah asked. "Would he have a grudge against Harachi that might make him single the guy out?"

Prudence sucked on her cheek for a moment. "I wouldn't think so," she said at last. "Rashid's intelligence has always been damn reliable, so I'd have to say it would be better to take his opinion than mine, at least on this. Harachi could be involved, if they managed to convince him that is the best thing for the secession movement. I'm just surprised, that's all."

"Okay. Where would we look for Doumaz?"

Prudence pulled the car up in front of a mudbrick building. "This is where we'll find Dalia, his wife. She'd be surprised and suspicious if American diplomats asked for him, so let me do the talking."

They all got out of both cars and followed her inside the building. The structure had only one room, and the entire back wall was missing. They walked through it and into a tent that was attached and extended another fifty feet.

Several women were sitting together near the center of the tent, and the rest of the space was taken up with what appeared to be bags of grain and boxes of canned goods. One of the women looked up and smiled when she saw Prudence.

"Welcome," she said. She glanced at Noah and the others, then turned her attention back to Prudence.

"Thank you, Dalia," Prudence replied. "This is Mr. McConnell, who was sent to open diplomatic negotiations with the new government. He wanted to learn more about the humanitarian aid we provide the camps, so I'm taking him on a tour. He's hoping to get some increases to our funding when he goes home."

Dalia smiled at Noah. "May you be successful," she said. "We are all grateful for the assistance that your country and others provide. This is inhospitable country, and it is difficult for us to survive on our own."

Noah inclined his head in a respectful bow. "I hope that we can do more to help in the future," he said. "Seeing the conditions your people live under has given me a great appreciation for your strength and stamina."

Dalia burst out laughing. "You mean our stubbornness? We are a very hardheaded people, but it serves us well under the circumstances. Forgive my humor, sometimes it strikes me at precisely the wrong moment."

Noah gave her a smile. "There's nothing to forgive," he said. "I'm not sure I would be able to maintain a sense of humor under these conditions, but I'm certainly glad that you can."

"Dahlia," Prudence said, "would you know where I might find your husband? Why we're here, I wanted to talk to him about an idea that I had."

Dalia rolled her eyes. "Of course," she said. "He and Shakir are in his market stall. He got another load of camel skins yesterday, and they are selling well. The Norwegians are buying all the camel skin bags and clothing we can make, and it is helping some of our people, letting them learn to be more self-sufficient."

"Oh, that's wonderful," Prudence said. "Is he still in the same place?"

"Yes, right where he's been for the last fifteen years. If you go to see him, please tell him to remember to bring meat home with him."

Prudence smiled. "No problem, I'll be glad to." She collected Noah and his team by eye, and they filed out of the building and into the cars.

The market was not far away, and it took only a couple of minutes to get there. Most of the delay was caused by foot traffic, but that seemed to be a common factor in the refugee camps. When they arrived, Prudence climbed out once again, followed by everyone from both cars.

The market was similar to an old world bazaar, with stalls set up in a haphazard grid work. It took her only a moment to find the one she was looking for, where two men were surrounded by a dozen women speaking rapidly in French.

"Looks like we'll have to wait a minute," she said softly to Noah. "Sales are definitely brisk, aren't they?"

"Very much so," Noah said. "Incidentally, I noticed that most of the people we've spoken to in the camps seem to speak English quite well. Why is that?"

"Schools," Prudence said. "Most of the schools in the camps teach both Spanish and English. French and Arabic are so common that everyone learns them, but with Spain so close, it seemed logical for the people here to learn Spanish. As for English, a lot of their teachers have actually been to school in the U.K. As far as they're concerned, English is pretty much the universal language outside of Africa. As you can see, they had quite an effect on the refugees."

Slowly, the haggling women walked away, some of them burdened with several obviously heavy camel hides. One of the men turned and noticed Prudence standing there, and gave her a smile. As soon as he finished with the customer he was talking to, he immediately turned and beckoned her closer.

"Hello, Prudence," he said. "Are you looking for a camel hide?"

Prudence laughed. "No, not today," she said. "I wanted to ask you about the tractors. Are they holding up for you?"

The man smiled. "As long as we have fuel," he said. "I plan to buy more tomorrow."

"Good. Tariq Doumaz, I'd like you to meet James McConnell. Jim is here to talk with the president about diplomatic relations, and he wanted to see the camps. What would you think about using the tractors for moving water containers? I think I can get a few old trailers and hook them together, so that we can put water tanks on them. If the tractors could pull several of them at a time, it would make it a lot easier to distribute water around the camp."

Doumaz seemed to think about her question for a moment. "It would depend on how large the tanks are," he said, "but I'm sure each of them could pull three or four. If we could bring them to the tankers when they come, then set them back out in the villages—that would certainly be better than having to walk so far with jugs of water."

"I thought so, too. Okay, let me see what I can do. Oh, I saw Dalia a few minutes ago, and she wanted me to remind you to bring home meat. Are you having a special dinner tonight?"

"Hah! Every dinner with my beautiful wife is special. But thank you for reminding me, I probably would have forgotten." He shook his head. "And then I would never hear the end of it."

"You're welcome, and I'll see you again soon," Prudence said. Noah bowed briefly to the man, and then they all went back to the cars.

"It's almost 4," she said. "By the time we get across the desert again, it'll be getting close to six. We probably should start back towards Tindouf."

"I agree," Noah said. "The only problem I see, here, is that there's no place to put a smart gun. If Doumaz is a legitimate target, I may have to come back and hunt him down."

"Too bad," Prudence said. "He's actually a likable old cuss. That doesn't mean he wouldn't cut your throat for a dollar, if he got the chance, though. I can show you where he sleeps, if necessary. A gunshot would probably bring his neighbors running, I'm afraid. Things are different here than in Boujdour; there aren't as many shootings, here."

"I don't have to use a gun," Noah said. Prudence looked at him, but said nothing.

They made it back to the hotel before six, which gave Noah and the team a chance to shower and get the desert dust off of themselves. They didn't rush, but they were all dressed and ready for quite some time before the driver arrived to pick them up again.

This time, Noah chose to bring Neil and Jenny along. The limousine had two fold-down jump seats in front of the big back seat, so Neil and Marco took those, leaving the comfort of the back seat for Noah and the girls.

They pulled up at the same building they had visited that morning, and the driver held the door open as they all climbed out. Oni appeared as they prepared to enter the building, and greeted them with a smile.

"Mr. McConnell," he said. "The President is so glad you could make it. Please, follow me."

He turned instantly and led them into the building and through the hallway on the main floor to a large room toward the rear that had been set up as a dining hall. There were two long tables with a dozen chairs or more on each side, and Oni escorted them directly to the far end of the right-hand table. President Abimbola was sitting at the head of the table, and rose to his feet when he saw Noah.

"Mr. McConnell," he said. "It is good to see you again, and your lovely assistant. I see that you have gained a couple of people?"

"Yes, Mr. President," Noah said. "May I present Garrett Stevens, my computer expert, and his assistant, Connie Marchand. They do their best to make sure I know how to check my emails."

"It is my pleasure to meet you both," Abimbola said. "Please, please, be seated. There is tea, and I believe we have coffee, if you would prefer it."

"Tea will be fine," Noah said, and the others agreed. They took their seats, with Noah in the place of honor at the president's right, and the rest of them taking chairs along the same side. They were just getting seated when a courier came rushing in and whispered into Oni's ear.

Oni suddenly stared at the courier wide-eyed, then bent down to whisper into the president's ear. Abimbola seemed startled by what was said, and looked suddenly at Noah. He stared into Noah's eyes for a moment, then suddenly burst out laughing.

"Mr. McConnell," he said through his laughter, "someone has just sent me an amusing message. Apparently, there is someone within our country who believes that you are an assassin, sent to kill me."

Chapter FIVE

Noah's eyes went wide as he stared at the president.
"Mr. President," he began, "I can assure you..."

"Please, Mr. McConnell," Abimbola said, "I don't believe this for a moment. This is only the latest in a long line of ridiculous rumors that have been coming my way since we announced our secession. If it comforts you, I have also been told that the Russian emissary, who will arrive tomorrow, plans to poison me. Despite these stories, I think I probably have several years left in these old bones. I told you about it to share the laugh, not to worry you."

Noah allowed himself an expression of amused wonder. "Well, I'm not sure I can find it in myself to laugh about it," he said. "I promise you this: you would be the last person on any target list I might have."

He turned and glanced at Sarah and the others, who were all staring at him and the president. Sarah's eyes told him that she was wondering if they had somehow been exposed, so he turned quickly back to Abimbola.

"I'd be curious to know where this rumor came from," he said, "if that might be possible. To be honest, I can't believe anyone would think such a thing. I mean, do I look like some kind of assassin?"

"Of course not," Abimbola said. "As I said, I have lately been warned that almost everyone I know wants me dead. Why, even Oni, who has been my friend and adviser and aide for many years, is reported to be planning to have me assassinated. I know that cannot be true, because I have repeatedly asked him to serve as my vice president, but he has declined. I do not believe he would stand to gain anything from my death, so the entire idea is ludicrous."

Noah smiled. "If you can't trust your oldest friend," he said, "who could you trust? Personally, I would think people might want to see how you do as interim president before they start thinking about getting rid of you."

Abimbola beamed at him. "Exactly," he said. "They should at least wait to see whether I get us through this fantastic endeavor. Then, if I were to fail, they will have to bother trying to kill me themselves. President Belkacem will be more than happy to do that for them, if he gets the chance." He waved a hand in dismissal of the entire conversation. "Forget all that," he said. "Let us enjoy ourselves for this evening. Our dinner tonight is traditional fare for our region, *couscous* with lamb. If you have never had it, you are in for a treat."

"I'm certainly looking forward to it," Noah said with a smile. "It'll be a new experience for me."

"I've had it," Jenny said. "Personally, I love it."

"Oh, I know," Sarah said. "I had it a couple of years ago, I thought it was wonderful."

Noah shrugged. "Seems like the ladies know more than I do about it," he said.

Abimbola chuckled again. "Isn't that always true?"

Noah's phone vibrated at that moment, and he slipped it out of his pocket, holding it below the table as he glanced at it.

All E & E operatives are trained in certain signals, and one of them involves a call from a contact named Horatio. Any call from Horatio was an order to immediately cease all operations and disappear, then wait for further contact.

The caller ID said Horatio.

Noah looked up at the president and gave him a shy grin. "Mr. President, I hate to do this, but I need to take this call. It's a friend of mine, and he's been looking after my mother for me."

Abimbola was on his feet instantly. "Of course, of course," he said. "Please, you can have privacy if you step through that door. It goes into a smaller dining room, but no one is in there right now."

"Thank you," Noah said. He rose and started toward the door, putting the phone to his ear. "Hello? Horatio?"

"Hey, Jim," said a voice that Noah recognized as Donald Jefferson. "I hate to bother you, old buddy, but there is a problem. Are you by yourself?"

Noah stepped into the room and shut the door behind him, touching a button on the side of his phone. "Yes," he said, "and the phone is scrambled."

"Good. God help us, Noah, Allison's been arrested. Apparently, there was a secret Senate committee investigating some of our operations, and it's been decided that the Morgan Mafia case violated the civil rights of Morgan and his crew. We don't know what's going on for sure, but it seems like some kind of witchhunt. We've got FBI on the way down here to go through our records, but they'll play hell trying to break through our encryption. And, Noah—they've got warrants for you and your entire team. The only one with you at the moment who is safe is Jenny, because they don't have anything on her. You need to abort your mission and get out of Algeria as quickly as possible."

"Will anybody else be coming in to take over? I think this is an important mission..."

"Team Unicorn is already on the way. Make whatever excuses you have to, but get out of that country. Cut all ties with any of our intel assets over there and make whatever exit you can. If CIA gets dragged into this, and they almost certainly will, you could have crosshairs painted on all of your foreheads before morning."

"Right at the moment, we're at a dinner with the new president. It'll take a couple of hours, I'm sure, before I can even get out of this building. What about our cover identities, are they compromised?"

"Not yet, but I don't know how long they'll be clean. Noah, this almost feels like some kind of coup. There is already talk of replacing the entire senior staff here, including me and Parker."

"All right, let's look at it from another angle. Who would be out to get Allison?"

"I've no idea," Jefferson said. "I'm sure she has a few political enemies, but I am frankly shocked that even the Senate could pull this off. We've got a call in to the president, now, but haven't gotten any answers yet. This all went down about twenty minutes ago, and I've been swamped until just now. Get the rest of your team, let them know what's happening, and get out of that country. If you can make it to Barcelona, we have our own station chief there who will give you whatever support you need. I'll text you the number."

"All right," Noah said. "We'll get there as soon as we can."

"Good," Jefferson said. "Get to Barcelona, any way you can."

Noah ended the call and put the phone back into his pocket, then turned and went back to the main dining room. As he took his seat at the table again, President Abimbola looked at him with concern in his eyes.

"I hope everything is all right," Abimbola said, making it sound like a question.

"Mom seems to be having a rough time," Noah said. "I'm afraid the State Department has been notified. They've decided to recall me and send a new team in to take over. The agreements we made this morning will still stand, but there will be a new emissary here by tomorrow sometime."

"Oh, I'm so sorry. Do you need to leave now?"

"Mr. President, I would not want to in any way dishonor or insult you or your country," Noah said. "We can make arrangements after the dinner."

Abimbola smiled and inclined his head. "Then let us dispense with all of the formalities," he said. He turned to Oni. "Oni, if you would be so kind as to tell the servers that we are ready to eat?"

Oni Zidane bowed to the president and hurried away. A moment later, the servers appeared and began setting bowls of *couscous* before each of them. Following Noah's lead, the others ate slowly and made small talk with the people across the table from them, although Jenny and Neil were forced to rely on Marco to interpret. Their opposites spoke no English, so they resorted to French.

"Your mother," Abimbola said, "is she ill?"

"Apparently," Noah said. "I was informed that she was suddenly taken to the hospital today, quite unexpectedly."

"I will pray that it is nothing serious. Has she had health problems like this before?"

"No, actually. Until now, she's always seemed to be the picture of health. Everyone always relies on her, but sometimes it seems that she takes too much on herself. This may be one of those times, but I won't know the details until I'm back home."

"I see. Is there anything I can do to expedite your return? I presume you have an airplane waiting for you?"

"No, our plane was only passing through when we arrived," Noah said. "We'll have to get to Barcelona, and then the arrangements will be made from there to get us on home."

Abimbola's eyes went wide. "Barcelona? My goodness, that is a difficult journey by automobile, and to fly would mean going through Algiers. That may not be a good idea for you, considering the purpose of your visit here at this time." He closed his eyes in thought for a moment, then opened them and turned to Oni, who was standing beside him. "Oni, does General Zaki have an aircraft that could fly our guests to Barcelona tonight?"

"I'm certain he does, Sahib," Oni said formally. He always spoke formally when there were others present. "Shall I call him?"

"Please do. Explain that our friend Mr. McConnell and his party is in need of immediate transportation to Barcelona, so that he can get home to be with his ailing mother, and to make the arrangements as soon as possible."

Oni bowed and stepped out of the room. He was back in less than ten minutes and leaned down to whisper to Abimbola, who broke out into a smile and turned to Noah.

"It seems that, as the president, I have some influence with the chief of our military forces. We have an airplane that can leave in two hours and take you directly to Barcelona. It is being fueled as we speak. Perhaps it will help you to reach your mother more swiftly."

Noah tried to look humble. "Mr. President, I don't know what to say. That would be most helpful."

"It is nothing," Abimbola said. "If my mother were living, she would want me to do this for you. Consider it an act of good faith on our part, to show your government that we understand honor and family."

Noah glanced at Sarah and the others, who were watching him closely.

"I guess you overheard," he said. "Mom is very sick, and she's been taken to the hospital. Mr. Donaldson is arranging for someone else to take over our mission here so that I can go home to be with her. President Abimbola has graciously offered us a flight to Barcelona, where we can pick up a diplomatic flight back home."

Sarah leaned slightly, so that she could look directly into Abimbola's eyes. "Thank you, Mr. President," she said. "Jim's mother is very special, and he should be there in case this is serious."

Marco, Neil, and Jenny all echoed her, and Abimbola smiled broadly. "This is true of all of us," he said. "Mothers deserve their children being with them when they are suffering. I am only pleased that I am able to offer this minor bit of assistance."

Noah finished eating while he and Abimbola continued to talk. He mentioned that he had a tour of a couple of the refugee camps, and suggested that the president request further humanitarian aid from the United States as part of the deal for the new military base. Abimbola seemed very pleased with the suggestion, and went on to tell him a great deal about the Sahrawis and their situation.

Noah, who didn't anticipate ever having to come back to the region, still filed the information away in his mind. The Sahrawi strength of spirit and resilience was something he wanted to remember as part of his constant study of human nature.

An hour later, Noah and the others made their excuses, thanked the president individually, and were driven back to the hotel to pack. On the way, Noah called Prudence Mays one more time.

"Mr. McConnell?" Prudence asked as she answered the call. "I'm just about ready..."

"I'm afraid there's been a change in plans," Noah said. "I'm being recalled, and President Abimbola has arranged an immediate flight out of the country. Unfortunately, I won't be able to take some of my special equipment. I need you to meet us at the hotel and take charge of it right away."

"Oh, okay," she said, confused. "That seems unusual. Is something wrong?"

"I don't know the details," Noah said." You know how it is, they don't tell us what's going on while we're out in the field. Another team is coming in to take over for me, so I'm sure they'll be in touch with you as soon as they arrive. You can turn this equipment over to them. I just need it out of the hotel before we leave."

"All right," she said. "I can be there in about fifteen minutes. I'll see you then."

"Boss," Neil said, "what's going on?"

"I'll fill you in when we get to the hotel," Noah replied. "I need to check on Mom once more before we talk about it."

All of them, including Sarah, appeared nervous. Being recalled from a mission had never happened before, and they were quite sure there was considerably more to the story. Still, they knew not to ask questions when they might be overheard, so they waited as patiently as their worries would allow.

They arrived at the hotel ten minutes later, and Noah stopped them before they entered the building. He waited until they were away from the limousine and there was no one in earshot, then lowered his voice.

"I got a Horatio call," he said. "Allison has been arrested, but we don't know all of the details, yet. There's something about a Senate committee investigating some of the missions she has sanctioned, and the mission we handled in Arkansas has apparently sent up some red flags. The committee has apparently issued warrants for Team Camelot, so Donald wants us to get out of the country immediately. If we can get to Barcelona, the E & E station there can give us some assistance. Abimbola may have saved our asses by arranging this flight, but we don't dare try to take our weapons with us. Donald told me to cut all ties with other intelligence assets, but I had to call Prudence to come get our equipment."

"She's here now," Sarah said. "Her car just pulled into the parking lot."

"Good. Let's get everything ready, and then Marco and I will haul it down to her car."

They waited until Prudence caught up with them, then entered the building and took the elevator up to their floor.

"So, what's going on?" Prudence asked in the elevator.

"I'm not really certain," Noah said. "I got an emergency call telling me that we are being recalled and another team is coming in to take over. Because of the urgency, and the fact that we don't have a plane waiting for us, the president offered us a special flight from their military and I accepted. We have to be at the airport in just under an hour, so we'll help you load all the stuff up."

Prudence rolled her eyes. "Something about this is bothering me," she said. "I've never seen any of your people be recalled in the middle of a mission before. Should I check in? Maybe I can find out something for you."

Noah shrugged. "That's your call," he said. "On the other hand, if this means any kind of problems, it's always possible that being too close to us could be unhealthy for you. I wasn't specifically told not to tell you, but I was told to leave the country with as little impact as possible."

Prudence looked at him, and the apparent innocence in his face must have been convincing. "Okay, fine," she said. "Last thing I need is to get tangled up in anything that could expose our mission here. Just do me a favor, and let me know if you hear of anything that might affect me or my people. Can you do that?"

Noah smiled. "I'll be glad to," he said.

The elevator opened on their floor and they went to their rooms. Marco and Noah quickly repacked all of the weapons and equipment, then carried the four cases down to Prudence's car. Only two of them would fit in the back, so the others went into the rear seat.

"You want to get those secured as quickly as possible," Noah said. "There's some high tech in there, and we don't want it exposed to the locals if at all possible. It would be best if you could leave the cases sealed until our replacements get here."

"Yeah, trust me," Prudence replied. "I don't want to mess around with any of your stuff. I can just imagine what getting caught with it could do to me, you know?"

"Good thinking," Noah said. "Just get it stashed somewhere no one will bother it, and hopefully our replacements will get here within the next twenty-four hours."

She shook her head ruefully. "I damn sure hope so," she said, and then she got into her car and drove away. Noah and Marco went straight back upstairs, where Sarah, Neil, and Jenny had their luggage packed and ready.

"I ran a quick sweep for bugs," Neil said. "We can talk, if we need to."

Noah sat down on the bed. "Here's the thing," he said. "The only one of us that doesn't have a warrant out right now is Jenny. I think we should put her on a commercial flight back home as soon as we get to Barcelona. That way..."

"What are you smoking?" Jenny asked. "I'm not leaving you guys, not in the middle of this."

Neil scowled at her. "Jenny, you don't need to get mixed up in whatever's going on. Noah's right, we need to get you away from us before you end up in trouble, too."

Jenny looked at Sarah. "You want to explain it to them?"

Sarah sighed, but there was humor in it. "She's saying that she won't leave Neil," she said, "for the same reason I won't leave Noah. If you guys can't understand that, then I don't know what to tell you."

"Yeah, that pretty much sums it up," Jenny said. "Besides, if things get nasty, you might need me. I'm not letting anything happen to Neil, or to any of you. You've all become part of my family, and that's just how it is. Besides, you know what lengths I'll go to for family."

Noah nodded. "I expected as much," he said, "but I felt it was necessary to try. All right, let's go. It's ten o'clock and the flight is scheduled to leave at ten thirty."

They gathered their luggage and carried it down the elevator, then loaded it into the trunk of the limousine. The driver held the back door open as they climbed inside, then got behind the wheel and started toward the airport.

Despite the fact that the airport was only two miles away, the ride took almost 20 minutes. Most of that time was spent maneuvering through city traffic, which was surprisingly heavy for that time of night. They arrived without incident, however, and the driver was waved through a gate and pulled up beside the airplane. Noah recognized it as a Beechcraft Super King Air, a large twin turboprop.

The flight crew, as it turned out, spoke no English. Marco stepped up to interpret, because they did speak fluent French like most Algerians, and then turned to Noah.

"We must rate," he said. "Turns out this is the West Algerian version of Air Force One. This plane was assigned to the president, himself, but he's never even seen it. This will actually be its very first flight as a diplomatic aircraft."

Noah nodded. "Thank the flight crew for us," he said. "Let's get aboard. The sooner we're in the air, the better."

They climbed on board and took their seats while the flight crew stowed their luggage in the cargo compartment. Five minutes later, the engines started up and the plane slowly began to move, taxiing to the beginning of the runway. Noah, who was sitting just behind the cockpit, could vaguely hear the tower approve the airplane for takeoff.

Noah's phone rang at that moment, and he glanced at it to see that it was Prudence Mays calling. He answered the call and put the phone to his ear as the engines revved up to full power and the plane began its takeoff roll.

"Hello," he said.

"Mr. Wolf," Prudence said. "Are you out of the country?"

Noah hesitated for a second, until the wheels left the ground. "We are."

"Damn good thing," she replied. "I just received orders to arrest you, using any force necessary. Not sure I want to get into any kind of a gun battle with you, so I'm glad to hear you're out of my jurisdiction."

"So am I," Noah said. "I'd hate to be the reason you were compromised."

"You and me both, buddy. Look, the message I got said that your agency went rogue and has been performing missions that were off the books. Your director and some of her staff have been arrested, and there are warrants out for you and the people with you. I'm not sure going home is a real good idea for you, right now."

"I think it's going to be necessary," Noah said. "There is some kind of screwup back home, and I want to know what it is. Can't really do much about it if I'm sitting in Africa, now can I?"

"You ever read Rudyard Kipling?"

"Yes," Noah said. "Why?"

"Because you're a better man than me, Gunga Din. If I was facing the kind of things they're saying about you, I'd be heading for the outback of Australia."

"Care to give me a heads-up? What kind of things are they saying?"

"Murder for hire, basically. Word is that your team took out a number of Americans on American soil. The story is that it violates the prohibition on intelligence activity within U.S. borders. According to the relevant Executive Orders, such activities can only be pursued against foreign nationals, not against American citizens."

"I'm familiar with that executive order," Noah said, "but it only applies to the CIA. Our organization is not part of the CIA, nor under its purview. Sounds to me like somebody is twisting some facts around to try to achieve a specific end."

"Hey, I'm just relaying the message. You and I both know there are some bad actors in the government, and it's times like these when they stand up and shout for attention. I don't know who your people pitstop, but they seem to have some clout. Anyway, I'm just glad you're out of my hair. Do me a favor and stay that way, will you?"

"I think you can count on it," Noah said. "Try to stay safe. Things might get ugly before this is over, and I'd hate for it to splash onto you."

"Goodbye, Mr. Wolf."

Chapter SIX

Four Hours Earlier

Allison looked up when she heard the commotion in the hallway, and slipped a hand under her center desk drawer. The Mac 10 she kept in the holster mounted to its bottom slid easily into her hand, as she watched her office door closely.

A knock came on it a moment later, and then it opened slowly to reveal her secretary of the day. She hadn't even bothered to learn the woman's name, but the look on her face made Allison wonder if she shouldn't have made the effort. The gal seemed positively terrified, even though she had seemed fine only moments earlier, when Allison had come back from lunch.

"You okay?" Allison asked. "What's going on?"

"Ma'am," the secretary began, "there are some men..."

The door burst open and the woman was shoved out of the way. Six men entered, and one of them had a pistol in his hand. Allison started to reach quickly for the Mac, but the gun was aimed at her face and she knew she'd never get it out in time.

"What the hell? What is this?" Allison demanded.

"Allison Michelle Peterson," one of the men said, "I am United States Marshal Glenn Howard, and pursuant to the warrant I present to you now, you are hereby placed under arrest on the charge of disenfranchisement of citizens of the United States of America, and on the charge of conducting clandestine operations relevant to foreign security on U.S. soil. I'm instructed to take you into custody and transport you to a federal holding facility."

Allison stared at him for a moment, then shook her head in confusion. "What on Earth are you talking about?" she asked. "What you mean, disenfranchisement of American citizens?"

"Ma'am, I am not at liberty to discuss these charges with you. I need you to get up out of your chair and turn around, right now."

Don Jefferson came through the door at that moment, his face white. "What on Earth is going on here?"

One of the men pushed him against the wall and put a hand on the gun in the holster strapped to his belt. "Sir, please step back," he said.

"I'm being arrested, Donald," Allison said. "Some bull crap about disenfranchising American citizens."

She got up from her chair and calmly turned her back, and the marshal put her in handcuffs. When he turned her around, she saw Jefferson clenching his teeth in rage.

"Chill out, Donald," she said. "Just get yourself busy finding out what's going on. Somebody is playing games, and I want to know who it is."

Jefferson shoved down his anger and got himself under control. "I will," he said. "May I see a copy of that warrant, please?"

"Are you an attorney?" The man who was holding Allison asked the question.

"Yes, as a matter of fact, I am," Jefferson said. He held out a hand in expectation, and the copy of the warrant was placed into it. He snatched it open and began to read, but the marshals began leading Allison out of the room.

"This is ridiculous," Jefferson said. "This is referring to Executive Order 13470. That doesn't even apply to this agency. We were created under an entirely different order, and we are not part of the elements of national intelligence, nor under the oversight of the NSA. And I see nothing about disenfranchisement of anyone. Where did that come from?"

The marshal glared at him. "Sir, we are acting under the direct orders of the Senate select committee on intelligence. I read the charges to the accused exactly as they were given to me, and any questions should be directed to them. Senator Diana McCaskill is the chair of the committee, and you can direct any questions to her office. Now please, step out of my way."

"Donald," Allison said, "under our articles of organization, you are now the acting director. Get busy and find out what's going on."

The marshal looked at Jefferson and seemed to smirk. "For now, anyway," he said. "I've heard there might be a shakeup in the top levels of your outfit."

Jefferson was still staring at the warrant, and his eyes were wide. "Marshal, what is this? There are vague references to other people to be arrested, but no names."

"That, sir, is an open warrant for any and all of your personnel who were involved in a recent mission to Arkansas. According to the committee, those personnel caused the deaths of a number of American citizens in clear violation of their civil rights. Since their names are not known to the committee, you will be contacted by the FBI with orders to reveal their names and assist in bringing them into custody."

"This is some kind of madness," Jefferson shouted. "This agency is directly answerable to the President of the United States, not to the Senate or the House or the joint Chiefs or any other arm of the government but the executive. Allison, I'll get Parker and we'll get started on this."

Allison nodded to him. "You do that," he said. "And Donald? You take care of my kids."

Jefferson looked her in the eye. "You know damn well I will."

The marshals escorted her out of the office and to the elevator, and then she was gone. Jefferson went to her desk and picked up the phone. He pressed a single button and waited for an answer.

Doctor Nathan Parker was a psychiatrist who evaluated potential agents and employees for the organization. He had spent more than thirty years working with the CIA, where he had actually developed testing regimens that could help predict which human assets were at risk for psychological issues. Allison had recruited him to help her evaluate specific individuals and determine their capacity for killing without suffering adverse psychological effects.

"Parker," came a gruff voice.

"Don Jefferson. Doc, we got a problem. Federal marshals just came in here and arrested Allison."

"They what? What are you talking about?"

"Just do me a favor and get over here," Jefferson said. "I'm calling in the attorneys to try to figure out just what's happening. Doc, the warrant doesn't make any sense, but it's not just for Allison. They're also trying to identify and arrest all of Team Camelot."

"I'll be there in fifteen," Parker said. "Camelot is in country on a mission; get somebody else on the way to take over, and call them out. Tell them to get out of Algeria immediately, and go to ground. Hell, give them a Horatio."

"I'll do that as soon as I know more," Jefferson said. "The mission is critical and time sensitive, I don't want to abort unless we absolutely have to."

"Trust me, Donald, you have to. There are too many out there who know who Noah is. By the time you get any more information, word could be on its way to the CIA in Algeria to try to arrest them, and that might not go very well."

Jefferson sighed. "All right, I see your point. Let me get another team started on it, and then I'll call them."

"Do that," Parker said. "I'm on the way."

Jefferson hung up the phone, then picked it up again. He called Molly Hansen and told her to get all of the information together on the Algerian mission and meet him in the conference room in five minutes. As soon as he finished that call, he consulted his cell phone and then dialed another number.

"Unicorn," answered Jeremy Schaefer.

"This is Donald Jefferson. Briefing in the conference room in thirty minutes. Bring your team."

"Yes, sir," Schaefer said. Jefferson hung up the phone and leaned back in the chair, rubbing his hands over his face.

Donald Jefferson had begun his career in the intelligence field as a case officer for the CIA in Brussels, recruiting foreign students who were attending the many universities there. Several of his recruits had gone on to be highly valued assets when they returned home to their own countries. Donald's success had led to promotion, and he was eventually running a lot of the HUMINT operations throughout Europe.

Once again, he had excelled in his position. A few years down the road had seen him move through a number of posts until he was finally named as a deputy director, only a couple of steps down from the director, himself. That's where Allison had found him five years earlier, when E & E had been created and dropped in her lap.

Donald had never been the squeamish type; on a few occasions back in Brussels, he had been forced to eliminate some of his potential recruits who were attempting to subvert his operation. Allison had come across references to him in some of the reports she had analyzed, and remembered him when POTUS had tapped her to build and operate an assassination division.

It was actually Donald who had suggested an expansion, adding "Eradication" to "Elimination." Eradication, in his view, meant making it appear that someone had been killed in order to achieve a greater purpose than his death would bring about. Allison had liked the idea, and immediately named Donald as her second-in-command.

He had been there ever since, almost since day one of E & E's existence. He and Allison had become close friends and confidants, sharing not only the day-to-day burdens of operating the organization, but also learning that they could lean on one another even during personal tough times.

Donald, who had been married for more than twenty years, had even toyed with the idea of a romantic involvement, but Allison had carefully failed to recognize the one time he had actually flirted with her. He knew from the look on her face that she caught it, but her words seemed to assume he was only joking. He got the message, and the thought was never allowed a moment in his mind again.

All of this went through his thoughts in a matter of minutes, and then he got up from behind Allison's desk and went to the conference room. Molly was already there and waiting for him, and he explained quickly what had happened.

"Team Unicorn is coming in to be briefed," he said. "Under the circumstances, I'm going to let you handle it. Get hold of idea development and get them started, and let Wally know they might be coming out. Call Georgette down in the travel office and get the necessary arrangements made. Remember, they are going in as a diplomatic mission. We got an email packet earlier today from Noah, telling about the arrangements he made with President Abimbola regarding the new military base. We want that, even if the secession fails."

Molly was staring at him. "They want to arrest Noah and his team? But why?"

"It's got something to do with the Morgan Mafia mission in Arkansas," Jefferson said. "At the moment, it looks like they're trying to say we aren't authorized to operate within the U.S., but the charter specifically refers to 'within and without the United States.' I'm meeting with Doctor Parker and our attorneys in just a few minutes to try to figure out what we can do about this."

Molly shook her head. "Okay," she said. "Please keep me posted, will you? And find out if I can go visit Allison. That might help her while she's going through this."

Jefferson chuckled. "I suspect she's going to be pretty busy, just reaming the asses of whoever was stupid enough to try to question her."

"Yeah, but find out anyway."

Jefferson went back to Allison's office and arrived just as Parker got there.

"What did POTUS say?" Parker demanded instantly.

"I haven't called yet," Jefferson replied. "To be honest, I think he'll respond better to you than to me. Since he's been in office, I've found that I don't have nearly as many friends on the Hill as I used to."

"Fine," Parker growled. "Gimme the damn phone and hit the button."

Allison, like many of the senior directors of organizations dealing with national security, had a direct line to the President of the United States. Jefferson handed over the receiver as Parker took the chair in front of the desk, then pressed the green button that would dial straight to the president's body man.

"Dog robber," said Keenan Davis. He served as body man to the president, making sure that the Chief Executive of the United States always looked perfect and had everything he needed.

"Keenan," Parker said, "it's Parker. What's he doing?"

"At the moment, he's talking to the British ambassador. It's not official, they were just both passing through the rotunda. Is it something important?"

"Would I bother calling if it wasn't? Get him on the damn phone."

In Washington, D.C., Davis' eyes went suddenly wide. "Yes, sir, just a moment." He muted the phone and approached the president, holding it out and waggling it to get attention. "Mr. President? It's Doctor Nathan Parker."

The President of the United States smiled at the British ambassador and promised to invite him to lunch at the White House very soon. The two men shook hands and the president turned to Davis, taking the phone and putting it to his ear, then taking it down again to unmute it. He put it back to his ear and said, "Parker? Why are you calling me?"

"To find out what kind of idiots are running loose in the Senate," Parker said. "The damn Senate permanent select committee on intelligence has had Allison arrested."

"They did what? Why would they do something like that?"

"Well, I would suggest, Mr. President, that you get somebody to ask them that question, because I sure as hell don't know. They are claiming that the agency has been operating illegally in the United States, probably back to that Arkansas situation."

"I'm headed back to the Oval Office," the president said. "I'll get on this the minute I get there, and I'll call you back. I don't know what they think they're doing, she doesn't answer to them."

"Hell, she doesn't answer to anybody. She has presidential autonomy authority, remember? As far as operating illegally in the United States, our charter specifically authorizes actions within the borders of the U.S.A., as well as outside the borders. Somebody is playing games, and that's a dangerous occupation when it goes to messing with the Dragon Lady."

"I'll call you back," the president said, and the line went dead. Parker passed the receiver back to Jefferson and leaned back.

"He says he'll find out what's going on and call me," he said. "Have you called Noah out yet?"

"Not yet, no," Jefferson replied. "He's got a mission phone, and I've got to get the number." He picked up the phone on the desk again and called out to the ID development department. It took a few minutes to get the right person on the line, but then he got the number of the special satellite phone Noah was carrying.

Parker had gotten up and walked out of the room while he was on the line, but Jefferson didn't feel he needed to wait. He punched the button on the desk phone for the number designated as Horatio, then dialed the number he had written down.

It rang several times before coming to life. "Hello? Horatio?" Noah said as he answered.

"Hey, Jim," Jefferson said. "I hate to bother you, old buddy, but there is a problem. Are you by yourself?"

There was the sound of footsteps and a beep. "Yes," Noah said, "and the phone is scrambled."

"Good," Jefferson said. "God help us, Noah, Allison's been arrested. Apparently, there was a secret Senate committee investigating some of our operations, and it's been decided that the Morgan Mafia case violated the civil rights of Morgan and his crew. We don't know what's going on for sure, but it seems like some kind of witchhunt. We've got FBI on the way down here to go through our records, but they'll play hell trying to break through our encryption. And, Noah—they've got warrants for you and your entire team. The only one with you at the moment who is safe is Jenny, because they don't have anything on her. You need to abort your mission and get out of Algeria as quickly as possible."

"Will anybody else be coming in to take over? I think this is an important mission..."

"Team Unicorn is already being briefed. Make whatever excuses you have to, but get out of that country. Cut all ties with any of our intel assets over there and make whatever exit you can. If CIA gets dragged into this, and they almost certainly will, you could have crosshairs painted on all of your foreheads before morning."

"Right at the moment, we're at a dinner with the new president. It'll take a couple of hours, I'm sure, before I can even get out of this building. What about our cover identities, are they compromised?"

"Not yet, but I don't know how long they'll be clean. Noah, this almost feels like some kind of coup. According to some of the rumbles from the feds, there is already talk of replacing the entire senior staff here, including me and Parker."

"All right, let's look at it from another angle. Who would be out to get Allison?"

"I've no idea," Jefferson said. "I'm sure she has a lot of political enemies, but I am frankly shocked that even the Senate could pull this off. We've got a call in to the president, now, but we haven't gotten a response yet. This all went down about twenty minutes ago, and I've been swamped until just now. Get the rest of your team, let them know what's happening, and get out of that country. If you can make it to Barcelona, we have our own station chief there who will give you whatever support you need. I'll text you the number."

"All right," Noah said. "We'll get there as soon as we can."

"Good," Jefferson said. "Get to Barcelona, any way you can."

He hung up the phone and leaned back, once again running his hands over his face. He was still sitting like that when Parker came back in.

"The damn lawyers are here," Parker said. "They'll be in here in just a moment. Do you have the copy of the warrant?" Jefferson passed it over, and Parker read through it quickly. "This is bogus, Donald. Somebody is playing games with us."

"Yes, but what's the goal? I can't see this actually standing up, can you?"

"We are living in a crazy time," Parker said. "I'm not sure of anything, right at the moment."

The phone rang suddenly, and Jefferson snatched it up. "Donald Jefferson," he said.

"Mr. Jefferson, this is Kathy, out front. I have the president on line two."

"Thank you," Jefferson said. He passed the receiver to Parker and punched the button for line two.

"Hello," Parker said.

"It's me," said the president. "I don't know what's going on, but we've got a situation. E & E is a creature of my predecessor, but I'll be damned if the Democrats aren't trying to find some way to use their existence to impeach me. What the hell is going on over there? I'm hearing about Allison selling assassinations on the black market, for crying out loud."

"That's bull," Parker said. "Not only has no such thing ever happened, Allison would kill anybody who tried it, and that's with no pun intended. She agonizes over every single sanction request, and believe me on that, because I know. I'm the one who gets the phone calls at three o'clock in the morning when she can't sleep because she isn't sure she made the right decision. On top of that, the particular mission this is based on was requested by the DOJ, and she damn near turned it down. If it hadn't been for the fact that the people involved were so dangerous, she probably would have."

"Who is Lee Ringgold?" POTUS asked. "Apparently, he testified that he was present when the request was made, and that it only included six people. The way the committee got it, your people went to Arkansas and had a killing spree. Were there really forty-five dead in that mission?"

"I don't have the file in front of me, but I know it wasn't that many. We also managed to expose dozens of corrupt law enforcement officials and prosecutors. All in all, I'd have to say the mission was a rousing success. It sure as hell isn't something to use to shut us down."

"They are not trying to shut it down," the president said. "What they're trying to do is take it away from me. They want to put it under senatorial oversight, maybe even make it report to the intelligence committees in both houses, and use it to undermine my entire administration. Now, I'll be honest, I've read through everything my predecessor wrote about needing such an agency, and I agree with every bit of it. On the other hand, Allison Peterson is the only director of any agency who has real autonomy. I think that's what has them scared."

"As you know, Mr. President," Parker said, "the reason your predecessor gave her autonomy is because he trusted her judgment. He didn't want anyone to be able to order her to approve a sanction, and that reasoning is still valid and still stands. If E & E goes under the supervision of any of the committees, you'll end up with politicians demanding sanctions on their rivals. Mr. President, you don't dare let this happen."

"I may not have the power to stop it," the president replied. "I'm going to keep digging, but you need to see what you can learn on your end. There is somebody behind this, and I don't have any way to find out who it is."

"Trust me, Mr. President," Parker said coldly. "I intend to get to the bottom of it."

PARKER STORMED OUT of the office as soon as he got off the phone with the president, and ran into Molly Hansen as she was coming out of the conference room. She gave him a weak smile, and he waggled a finger to call her closer.

"You got the relief team on the way?" Parker asked her.

"They'll be leaving within the next three hours," she replied. "Doctor Parker, do you have any idea what's happening? How is Allison, do you know?"

"We don't have any contact with her right now. As for what's going on, it's some kind of convoluted nightmare. Officially, the Senate permanent select committee is trying to say that we've violated some rules that keep the CIA from running their own clandestine operations within the United States, but they don't apply to us. There's a lot more going on in the background, but I can't say what it is at the moment. Trust me, as soon as I'm able to let you in on details, I will. We're going to need that brain of yours, I guarantee it."

"Just let me know," Molly said. "I'll do anything you need me to do."

Chapter SEVEN

Allison was taken to the parking garage level and pushed into the back seat of a black SUV. Marshal Howard slid into the back seat beside her while two others got into the front seat and the rest climbed into another vehicle.

"So where are you taking me?" Allison asked. "Somehow I doubt you're going to haul me to the county jail."

"Our orders are to take you to Denver," Howard said. "The committee feels you might be an escape risk, considering the kind of people who work for you. There is a special facility in Denver that they believe is secure enough to keep you."

Allison laughed. "You think I'm going to try to escape and run away? That's ridiculous, especially since this entire case is nothing but a whitewash of some kind. I don't have a clue who is behind this, but somebody is trying to make fools out of all of you people. If you took a look at the charter of my organization, which came from the President of the United States during the last administration and was ratified by the current one, you'd find that I am immune from prosecution for any actions taken in the performance of my duties. I can be removed from my job, but I cannot be prosecuted. Trust me when I tell you that you, and a lot of other folks, are going to feel really stupid when this is over."

"Yes, ma'am," Howard said. "I feel pretty stupid already, if you want to know the truth."

Allison narrowed her eyes and looked at him. "You do? Why is that?"

"Because I work for the government, if you must know. I've been a U.S. marshal for more than twenty years, and I'll tell you that I haven't seen nearly as much ridiculousness in all that time as I've seen in the last six months. It's like there's some kind of mental illness spreading in D.C. You've got Democrats blaming the Republicans for everything, Republicans are blaming the Democrats and nobody seems to want to take responsibility for anything. It doesn't take a rocket scientist to see just how crazy they're all acting, does it?"

Allison nodded and let a grin appear on her face. "Well, well," she said. "An honest man. Don't see many like you anymore. Of course, I understand you're just following orders and doing your job, so I'm not blaming you for this at all, but there surely has to be some kind of madness going on."

"Ma'am," Howard said, "I couldn't agree more."

THE PLANE LANDED AT just after two o'clock in the morning, and Noah and the others thanked the flight crew profusely as they took their luggage and walked into the terminal. Their diplomatic passports got them through customs without anyone bothering to check them out, and they got into a cab as soon as they got outside again.

"Americans, yes?" The cab driver was a local, and spoke very good English. "Tourists? I can show you around, if you like."

Noah smiled at him. "Well, it's a little late for sightseeing," he said. "How about showing us a cheap hotel?"

"Ha. You're in Barcelona, my friend. The words cheap and hotel don't go together very well, here."

"Oh, come on," Noah said. "There's got to be something. We had a mishap on our flight, and my credit cards were lost. I won't be able to get them replaced until tomorrow, and I'm running low on cash."

The driver shook his head. "Not in hotels," he said. "There is a hostel, though, run by my cousin. You can get rooms there for only ten dollars American."

Noah grinned. "Sounds like just the place," he said. "Let's go."

The driver smiled and cranked his meter, then put the minivan in gear and drove off. The cab was in rough condition, and the transmission didn't seem to want to shift into high gear until the engine was revving so fast Noah expected it to blow up. Somehow, however, it got them where they were going. The driver hopped out and helped carry luggage for the two women, then kicked the front door of the building until a sleepy woman came to open it.

"Carita," the driver said. "I have brought you guests. American guests. Open up for them."

Carita suddenly seemed more awake, and held the door open to allow Noah and the team to enter.

"Welcome, welcome," she said in decent English. "We are happy to have you. You need rooms?"

"Yes," Noah said. "Three rooms, please. I'm afraid I don't have any euros, will American dollars be okay?"

Carita's eyes narrowed. "American dollars? Okay, okay, will be sixty American dollars."

Noah only nodded. He pulled three twenty dollar bills out of his pocket and handed them to Carita, who smiled brightly. She handed Noah three keys, and never even bothered to ask for their names. "Okay, three rooms on second floor. Second floor, okay?"

"Second floor will be fine," Noah said. He handed a key to Neil, and another to Marco, then led the way up the stairs.

The building was old, and had definitely seen better days. When they got to the rooms, Noah quietly beckoned all of them into the room he would share with Sarah. He waited until they were all inside and the door was locked, then looked at Marco.

"I get the feeling this might not be the safest place," he said. "You and I got sleep on the plane, so we'll keep watch for the rest of the night. I'm going to call Jefferson in a moment, just to let him know we got here, so by tomorrow we should be able to look for better accommodations."

"No problem," Marco said. "How about I take first watch? I'll go to five, and you can take over after that."

"Sounds good. Everybody try to get some rest, and we'll see what tomorrow brings."

"Hey, Noah," Neil said. "Do you want me to see what I can find out about what's going on back home?"

Noah shook his head. "No, I want you to get some rest. We'll find out soon enough, and I'll let you all know in the morning if Jefferson has any news. I want us all as alert as possible when we leave here in the morning."

"Okay." Neil took Jenny's hand and started out the door, but she stopped and turned back to Noah.

"Don't worry, Noah," she said. "Yeah, yeah, I know you never really worry, but this is all going to work out, somehow. Don't let it drag you down. We'll get through it, together. All of us."

She turned and followed Neil out the door and to the next room, which would be theirs. Marco went to his own, and Noah took out his phone. He dialed the number for headquarters, and was not surprised when a gruff voice answered.

"Camelot?" Parker said. "Where the hell are you?"

"We made it to Barcelona, sir," Noah said. "We're in a hostel for the rest of the night, but I'm going to need money and assets. Any word on what's going on?"

"It's some kind of damn foolery," Parker shot back. "I've got the president himself hopping on this, but it seems some of the Democrats think they can use this against him. There is even talk of trying to impeach him, just because we exist. I don't think it's going to go anywhere, but we definitely have a nightmare on our hands."

"It sounds like it. Is there anything we can do?"

"You can stay the hell out of the U.S., for now," the old man said. "The stupid warrant is open-ended, it just says they want to arrest all parties who were involved in the Arkansas mission. It doesn't actually name any names, but I'm quite sure the CIA knows who you are."

"Yes, the station chief in Tindouf actually called me as we were leaving the country. She said she had just received orders to arrest us, and wanted to be sure we got out of her jurisdiction. I'm half surprised they weren't waiting for us when we got here."

"I've been rattling cages. Both Donald and I spent a lot of years with the CIA, and we've each got contacts. We been spreading the word that this is pure bullshit, and that nobody wants to be on our bad side once we get it straightened out. I think most of the CIA would just assume we should handle this as an internal matter, and do their best to stay out of it."

"How is Allison?" Noah asked. "Any updates on her?"

"The only thing I've managed to find out is that she's being held in a secret lockdown in Denver. Word has it that some of the senators are coming to talk with her tomorrow, but I don't know if that's true or not. We aren't allowed to talk to her at the moment, and the FBI showed up here a few hours ago demanding access to everything. There was almost a gun battle when they tried to get into the restricted area; it took the chairman of the Joint Chiefs calling the Attorney General to get them to stand down before our Marine guards took them out."

"Sir, I get the feeling there's more to this than just an end run around the president. It's almost like somebody is planning to use Allison and the agency as some sort of shock propaganda. If they get her to admit anything..."

"I'm way ahead of you, kid," Parker said. "But don't you worry about Allie. The interrogator hasn't been born that could crack her. She'll have them telling her what she wants to know long before they find out anything. I've seen her work, you can trust me on this."

"All right, sir. Mr. Jefferson told me to check in when we got here, and that he would put me in touch with our station chief."

"Yep. I don't want you giving up your location, not to anybody, not even me. I'm going to give you his number, and I want you to call him tonight. He's already been warned, so you don't have to worry about waking his ass up." He rattled off a number, and Noah committed it to memory. "Give him a call and make arrangements for whatever you need. I don't know how long you're going to have to be off the grid, but try to enjoy it while you can."

The line went dead. Noah dialed the number he was given and put the phone back to his ear.

"Yeah, hello?" a sleepy voice answered, and Noah wondered if the chief had gone back to sleep anyway.

"Camelot," he said. "We've arrived in Barcelona."

"Good job," the voice said, suddenly sounding wide awake. "I'm Jorge Rivas. I've been expecting your call. Are you safe for the night?"

"Yes. We got in about an hour ago, and found some rooms. Low-end, low profile."

"Good thinking. I spent half an hour on the phone with Parker as he filled me in. I've got new IDs in the works for you. Since none of you speak Catalonian, however, I've decided it might not be best to keep you here. How would you feel about becoming rich ex-pats in England?"

"We could live with it. What about money, resources?"

"I'll have new credit cards for all of you, with pretty much unlimited funds. You won't have to worry about running out of money anytime soon. If you're okay with England, I'll call my opposite number

in London and start the process of getting you established. Do you
want all of you to stay together?"

"Yes."

"Okay, that will actually make it a little easier. One house, a couple of cars. You're supposed to be rich, so we'll probably put you on
some country estate, one of the smaller communities. The kind of
place nobody would think to look for you."

"That sounds good," Noah said. "When should I contact you
again?"

"Call me about lunchtime," Jorge said. "I should have things pretty well set up by then, and we can start working on getting you on the
way to your new home."

Noah thanked him and ended the call, then turned and pulled
Sarah into an embrace.

"Noah," she asked, "what do we do if it all blows up?"

"We retire," he said. "We're going to England for now, but I don't
know if it would be a good idea to stay there if we had to go AWOL.
I'm sure we could manage to make it to somewhere safe, and then
we learn how to go native. I'm thinking Brazil, Australia, somewhere
English is commonly spoken and there are lots of expatriates."

Sarah smiled up at him. "You almost make me wish for it," she
said. "That would be nice, if we could just retire and settle down,
somewhere. But do you really think we could? Don't you think we'd
be hunted?"

Noah released her and started taking off his clothes, and she did
the same.

"I don't think anyone would get very serious about it, depending
on just how things go back home," he said. "I'm pretty sure we could
manage to disappear, if we wanted to. And, to be honest, I don't
think there'd be much chance that anyone would come after us, not if
E & E is either shut down or stripped of power. CIA would be more

likely to just be glad we were gone, as long as we didn't stay in the intelligence game."

"Maybe for you and me," Sarah said. "But what about Jenny? Do you think she could give up killing? She'll tell you herself, she actually gets off on it."

"She'll have to, if she wanted any kind of normal life. If she stayed in the assassination business, they'd catch on to her sooner or later. If she couldn't shake it off, I'm afraid she'd either end up dead or in prison."

They crawled into bed and Sarah cuddled up to her husband. Noah held her for a few moments, and then felt her breathing slow as she drifted off to sleep.

ALLISON WAS DRIVEN to Denver, and arrived at the facility she would be held in at just about the same time Noah got back to his hotel in Tindouf. It looked like an old factory building, except for the armed guards standing around the perimeter and manning the gate. The car was waved through when it arrived, and then was driven through a large overhead door into a sally port.

"Just sit still for a few minutes," Howard said. "This is an extremely secure facility where we house terrorists and such when it's necessary to have them in Denver. They go through a lot of procedural crap here." He climbed out of the car and walked up to a window, passing some paperwork through a slot like you might see at a bank drive up. Armed guards inside the building could be seen through the window, and two of them looked the paperwork over carefully.

When they seemed satisfied, a door beside the window opened and three men came out holding submachine guns. Howard walked around to Allison's side of the car and opened her door, then took hold of her arm as she climbed out.

"No quick moves, just walk slowly with me. These guys have the itchiest trigger fingers I've ever seen."

"Yeah? You should hang out with some of my kids." Allison smiled at him, and he barely contained a chuckle.

The guards let them proceed through the doorway, and they ended up in a hall that led straight into the building. Another guard was waiting for them beside a door, and opened it when they approached.

"Inside," the guard said.

Allison stepped inside as she was told, and the guard removed her cuffs before closing the door. She saw that she was in a room that held nothing but a shower and a bench. A panel in the wall slid open and a woman's face appeared.

"Take off your clothes and pass them through the window," she said, "then take a shower and put these on." A stack of clothing was passed to her, and she took it and set it on the bench.

Irritated, Allison stepped out of her clothes and tossed them through the window. The shower was simple, with a single knob that controlled temperature and pressure. She turned it on and waited for it to warm up, which took only a matter of seconds, then stepped in and let it run over her. There was a bottle of soap that was labeled for both hair and body, so she lathered up quickly and then rinsed off.

There was a towel with the clothes, so she dried herself as quickly as she could and then got dressed. The clothing, though it was nowhere near the quality she was used to, fit her perfectly.

As soon as she was dressed, the panel slid shut and the door opened. The same guards were waiting for her, along with Marshal Howard, and her cuffs were reapplied. She stepped out and let them lead her farther down the hall. They stopped in front of a door and opened it, and one of the guards motioned for her to enter.

Allison glanced into the room and was surprised at what she saw. Instead of a sparse and stern jail cell, it looked like a room in a moderately priced motel. There was a nice-looking double bed, a TV on the wall, and a table with three chairs. If she had seen a mini fridge, she wouldn't have been surprised.

She stepped inside and the guard shut the door. A slot in the door opened, and the guard told her to squat down and put her hands through the slot. A moment later, her handcuffs were removed and she was able to stand up again, rubbing her wrists.

Marshal Howard appeared at the window in the door. "My understanding is that some of the committee will be coming to see you tomorrow," he said. "I know you may not believe this, but I really hope you get this all straightened out pretty quickly."

Allison turned and smiled at him again. "If I do," she said, "and if you want a better job, you make sure to come see me. Okay?"

Howard glanced to his left, then faced her again. He winked, and then was gone.

"Curiouser and curiouser, said Allison," she said to herself. "Well, if I have to be locked up, this is the place to do it." She looked around and saw a basic bathroom with toilet, sink, and shower. She looked inside and decided it would do, then stepped back into the main room. She sat down on the bed and found it comfortable, then picked up the remote and turned on the television.

She scanned for news, but there was no mention of anything going on that might be connected to her situation. She finally settled on a movie and was about to make herself comfortable when the slot opened the door again. She glanced over at it and saw a youthful female face smiling at her.

"Hi," the girl said. "I'm Jeannie, I'm on the night staff. Do you want anything to drink? A snack? Anything like that?"

Allison looked at her, a bemused grin on her face. "I'll tell you what," she said. "This has got to be the most unusual jail I've ever seen."

"Yeah, no kidding," Jeannie said. "I think it's really for when important people get in serious trouble, because they want to be treated better, know what I mean?"

Allison got up and walked over toward the door, then squatted down so she could look Jeannie in the eye.

"That's probably true," she said. "So, you really pass out drinks and snacks?"

Jeannie pointed behind herself, where Allison could see a cart with cans of soft drinks and many different kinds of snacks, such as you might find in a vending machine.

"That's my job," she said. "Want anything?"

"Hmm, sure. Do you have orange soda? And maybe some potato chips?"

"Yep," Jeannie said. She produced a can of ice cold soda and a decent size bag of rippled chips and passed them through the slot. "Anything else? Oh, I've also got things like toothbrushes and toothpaste, shampoo, that kind of stuff. You can have any of it you want, but only one of each at a time."

"Oh, great," Allison said with a smile. "How about a toothbrush, and do you have Colgate?"

Jeannie handed her a small bag that contained a toothbrush, a small tube of Colgate toothpaste, a comb, and a small hairbrush. "There you go," the girl said. "I gotta make the rest of my rounds, but if you need anything else, just bang on the door. My little cubicle is right down at the end of the hall, so I'll hear you."

"Okay, thanks," Allison said. Jeannie shut the slot and waved at her through the window as she pushed her cart down to the next door.

Allison took the soda and chips back to the bed and sat down on it, dropping the bag with the toothbrush and such on the blanket beside her. She opened the chips first, then popped the top on the soda and leaned back against the wall as she watched her movie.

Now, she thought, *if only I had a phone.*

Chapter EIGHT

When morning came, Noah and the team went looking for breakfast. They found it in a small, open-air eatery a short distance from the hostel and enjoyed strong, flavorful coffee with *bikinis*, which turned out to be toasted ham and cheese sandwiches. They were quite delicious, though the waitress explained that most people ate them for second breakfast, rather than first. Second breakfast usually happened around ten a.m., but Sarah told the girl that they were American tourists and just didn't know any better.

"I'm pretty sure she figured that out for herself," Jenny said when the waitress and walked away. "I think it kinda shows."

"Well, we've never been here before," Neil said. "It's hard to know the customs at a place you've never been, right?"

"Actually, I was here once before," Marco said. "It was a couple years ago, I was on loan to Team Aladdin for a mission. We were only here for a couple of days, and spent most of that cooped up in a hotel room. I actually wanted to get out and see the place, but it just didn't pan out."

"It's not going to this time, either," Noah said. "Jorge said to call him around lunch time. I'm guessing that would probably be around one." He looked around at the neighborhood they were in. "I suppose we could walk around here for a little while. There are some interesting buildings."

"Yeah, you and architecture," Neil said. "Noah loves looking at buildings, especially older ones."

"We might as well," Sarah said. "We may never get another chance."

They finished eating and began to stroll around, just admiring the city around them. They were all a bit surprised at the amount of foot traffic, and Sarah and Jenny made a point of holding onto Noah and Neil. It seemed that people just walked wherever they wanted in Barcelona, and moving down the street was a lot like fighting your way through a river. No matter which direction you were going, it seemed to be against the flow of traffic.

Unfortunately, this put a limit on the amount of actual sight-seeing they could do. There weren't very many exciting buildings, though they did see a couple that looked like they would be more suitable as sculptures than as buildings. A plaque near one of them, with legends inscribed in both Catalonian and English, explained that it was known as La Pedrera, and had been built in the early nineteen hundreds. It was the work of architect Antoni Gaudi, revered in all of Barcelona for his Art Nouveau styling.

"It's interesting," Noah said, "but not really to my tastes. I prefer Anglo Gothic or Russian styles, especially in older buildings. The curves in this one, the odd little patterns of ceramic items that cover the outside, that just doesn't strike me as functional."

"I can agree it doesn't seem very functional," Marco said. "Me, I like more primitive constructions, like log cabins and old American buildings. Those are the kind that appeal to me."

"That's because your brain is primitive," Neil said. "Neanderthal, almost."

Marco grinned. "I resemble that remark," he said.

They continued looking around a while longer, and then Noah decided it was time to check in with Jorge. He took out his phone and dialed the number again, and Jorge answered on the second ring.

"Camelot," Noah said.

"Good timing. Okay, I've got everything set up for you. Can you get to the airport?"

"Yes, we can take a taxi."

"All right, perfect. There's a store in the duty-free area called Tascon. Meet me there in forty minutes. You'll know me when you see me, I'll be wearing a purple hat."

"We'll be there," Noah said. He put the phone in his pocket and pointed at a taxi across the street. The driver agreed to take them back to the hostel to get their bags, and then on to the airport.

Finding the store proved to be the most time-consuming part of the trip. The duty-free section was rather large, and the store was close to one of the ends. When they finally found it, they had no trouble spotting Jorge. His purple hat was the center of attention for a group of children, who were pointing at it and laughing.

Noah looked around carefully before approaching him, just to be sure no one was paying attention. When he didn't see any apparent surveillance, he told the others to wait while he walked up to the man who was E & E's local operative.

"Jorge?" Noah asked.

The man turned and smiled at him. "Jimbo," he said. "Man, I thought I'd missed you. You guys ready for some lunch?"

"Sure," Noah said, returning the smile. He waved at the rest of the team, and they came walking toward him.

"Okay, come on," Jorge said. "I found a quiet spot close to one of the pizza places. You guys all like pizza, right?"

"Love it," Neil said. "In fact, I've been craving it all day."

"Then I've got you covered," Jorge said. He led the way to the food court area, and bought several large slices of pizza in different varieties, then took the group to one of the picnic style tables that was away from other diners. They all sat down and began eating, while Jorge lowered his voice.

"Okay, this isn't the best way to do this," he said. "I've got ID for each of you, including American drivers licenses, passports, and a couple of credit cards each. The cards draw on special accounts we keep back for this type of situation, something nobody else in the government would even know about. If you don't go crazy, you could live on them for a couple of years." He carefully slipped a hand up under his shirt and began passing out envelopes under the table. "Take them into the bathrooms to look at them, don't open them out here. You'll also find a few hundred euros and around two hundred pounds sterling, British money, your plane tickets, and a set of codes to reset your cell phones with new numbers. You are on British Airways flight 1429, which leaves in about an hour and a half. You'll need to be past security at least twenty minutes before departure time, so eat up and get going."

"Okay, I just got to ask," Jenny said. "You're American, right? With that accent, I mean?"

Jorge grinned. "Born and raised in Columbus, Ohio, but I've been over here for almost 4 years now. I get the same question from locals all the time, who think I must've been raised right here in Barcelona."

"I'm just glad you speak English," Marco said. "I can handle French, but Spanish was the worst subject I ever had at school."

"Well, around here, we speak Catalan, although most people can speak Castilian as well. That's what you call Spanish. I actually like it when some of you come over, because I get to practice my English."

"Well, you haven't lost it," Neil said. "Thanks for everything, Jorge."

"No problem, that's my job. You guys better get moving, if you're going to make the flight. You'll meet up with the London chief when you arrive at Heathrow. He'll be there waiting for you, so look for the sign with your name on it." He aimed that last at Noah. "Listen, guys, have a good trip and stay safe. I've got to get going, I have a local job I have to take care of, as well."

Jorge walked away, and Noah told Sarah and Jenny to hit the ladies room, while Neil and Marco went to the men's. Noah would stand guard over their luggage until they came back, and then he would make his own trip to the restroom.

Marco was back within minutes, and Noah slipped into the men's room and went straight to a stall. He closed the door behind him and opened the envelope.

The ID documents told him his name was Travis Lightner, originally from Memphis, Tennessee. He rid himself of the ID he had been using for the mission, tucking it into the now empty envelope. He took the precaution of breaking the credit cards and ripping up the passport, since they were now replaced with new ones.

Reprogramming his cell phone was a simple matter. A slip of paper held four strings of numbers. When he entered the first string, it opened a special settings menu. He chose "Reset Number," and then entered the second string. The phone then asked for a confirmation code, which was the third string, after which it went back to normal. The fourth string of numbers was his new cell phone number, which was on a British exchange.

As he left the stall, Neil was also coming out of one. They nodded at one another but said nothing until they were back at the table with Marco and the girls.

"I'm Travis Lightner," Noah said.

"Somebody was watching over us," Sarah said with a grin. "My name is Penny Lightner."

"John Davis," Marco said.

Neil shrugged. "Gary Jamison. At least they won't be hard to remember."

"I'm Stacy Jamison," Jenny said, looking at Neil with a grin. She held up her hand and showed him the simple wedding band that had been in her envelope. "Maybe we can consider this a trial run?"

That got her a smile from Neil.

Noah nodded. "All right," he said. "Let's exchange phone numbers." It turned out that all of the numbers were assigned to the same exchange, and it took them only a minute to add in the new contacts. "Good. Marco, I'm sending you through security first. Once you make it to the gate, send Neil a text message. Sarah and I will come next, with Neil and Jenny coming last. Once past security, we don't acknowledge each other until we land at Heathrow."

"You got it, boss," Marco said. He picked up his bags and walked away, passing through the duty-free once again. He stopped and bought a book at one of the stalls, then proceeded to the security checkpoint.

Fifteen minutes later, Neil's phone chirped to indicate a text message. *Weather's nice over here,* it said. *Come on over and visit.*

Noah and Sarah went directly to security and checked in, while Neil and Jenny hung back for a few minutes. When a few other people had gotten between them, they also stepped up to the line, and fifteen minutes later, the five of them were sitting on benches at their departure gate. They all sat quietly, pretending to be tired, and only occasionally speaking when another tourist addressed them.

"Any idea when we'll know something?" Sarah asked softly.

Noah shrugged. "I'm going to check in after we get settled in London," he said. "Maybe Uncle Don will know something by then."

Sarah sat beside him, leaning against his side while he kept an arm around her. "You know, as much as I wouldn't mind getting out of this life, I don't want anything bad to happen to Aunt Alice. She's never been anything but good to us."

"Yeah. I feel the same way. You know, it's possible I'll have to take care of some business to help her out. I might need to go back home for a while."

She looked up at him. "I know," she said. "Because I know you. You couldn't leave her stuck with a problem like this, any more than you could leave me in a bad situation. That's just how you are, but you're not going without me. I'm pretty sure everybody else would feel the same."

Nodding, Noah said, "I figured that out. We'll just have to wait and see. For now, we're going to do exactly what we're supposed to and stay low."

A dozen feet away, Neil and Jenny were having a similar conversation.

"What will you bet," Neil asked her, "that Noah decides to go back and try to rescue Allison?"

"Um, how about we don't bet? There's no way he'd leave her in this situation, and neither would the rest of us. If he goes, you know we're all going to go."

Neil grinned and pulled her closer. "That's where I was going," he said. "If this goes bad for her, I think we'll end up breaking her out of wherever they put her. She can go off the grid with us."

"Well, I'm hoping it doesn't go bad," Jenny said. "I—I need this job, you know? It takes care of that certain part of me. If it comes to an end, I'm not sure how long I'd last."

"We'll figure something out," he said, and then he chuckled. "This has got to be the weirdest romantic conversation ever," he said. "I'm trying to reassure my girlfriend that I'll help her cope with it if she has to give up her hobby, which happens to be something terribly frowned on in polite society."

Jenny looked up at him, and her face reflected sadness. "Are you starting to regret being with me? Because of my—hobby?"

"No, and don't even think that," Neil said. "Baby, while I might not always do the things you do, we are in the same line of work. I've had to do those things before, and I can even tell you that I understand how it can become—I'm looking for the right word, maybe addictive? The first few times were hard, but after that, I started to realize that I could do it when I need to."

Jenny looked at him for a long moment, but didn't say anything more. They sat quietly together until the flight was finally called, and then they were the first ones to board the plane because they were closer to the door.

Their seats, it turned out, were directly behind Noah and Sarah. Since Noah had suggested they not board together, they pretended not to notice. Neil had allowed Jenny to take the window seat, and Noah did likewise with Sarah.

Marco boarded last, and found that his seat was all the way at the back of the plane. He ignored the two couples as he made his way down the aisle, then buckled his seatbelt and opened the book he had bought.

Twenty minutes later, after some last-minute minor delay, the plane was in the air. The flight wasn't a long one, a little less than two and half hours. Noah, Sarah, Neil, and Jenny watched a movie on the seatback screens and tried to relax, but it was difficult with so much unknown.

The flight landed at Heathrow at just past two thirty in the afternoon. It took a few minutes for all of them to get off the plane, and then they met up at the baggage claim area.

"Don't look now," Sarah said, "but we've been spotted."

"What do you mean?" Noah asked.

"Well, if I remember correctly," Sarah said, "we are actually supposed to be staying out of England, right? Which is probably why an old friend of ours is standing over there grinning at us right now. The only question is whether she's here to say hello or to drag us off to jail."

Noah turned and looked, and saw Catherine Potts, E & E's liaison with MI6, coming toward him.

"Mr. and Mrs. Lightner?" Catherine asked. "I trust you enjoyed your flight?"

Noah gave her a smile. "We did," he said. "We weren't expecting to see you this trip, though."

She winked and leaned close, lowering her voice to a whisper. "The station chief was supposed to meet you," she said softly, "but he was unavoidably detained by a friend of mine. I thought I'd rather come and see you settled in safely, myself. I hope you don't mind."

"Then I take it," Noah said, "you're here in your capacity as our resident liaison? Rather than as an official of the British government?"

"I'm here as your friend," she replied. "I picked up a memo that was intended for Mr. Kendall, the station chief, and managed to decipher it. It made reference to 'Arthur's abode' coming here to drop off the radar for a while. Doesn't take a bleeding rocket scientist to figure out what that means, so I wanted to come and see to you myself. Kendall is dealing with one of my superiors, trying to explain his way out of a little mess I might've created for him; he's the tourism officer at the American embassy, and a couple of tourists got into some minor trouble yesterday. He'll be fine, but he was glad to let me take care of this for him. Have you got everything?"

They had all picked up their luggage, and followed Catherine out through the terminal. She had a diplomatic transit van with her, and invited them all to climb inside. It was roomy and spacious, with large, comfortable custom seats. Noah and Sarah sat just behind the driver's compartment so that Noah and Catherine could talk.

"All right, we can speak freely in here. I think you know that, besides my dual capacity between E & E and MI6, I'm also a special ambassador to Her Majesty. Because of that, I felt it absolutely necessary to brief her on your situation, and she instructed me to ask you not to cause any kind of trouble while you are guests in our country. She also told me to wish you luck in whatever the situation is that brings you here, and that she regrets she will not be able to meet with you. Officially, you are not here at all, and no one but myself, Mr. Kendall, and Her Majesty are aware of your presence."

"Please extend to her our thanks," Noah said, "and our pledge to stay as low and quiet as we possibly can. That's the whole point of coming here, to be off the radar for a while."

"Right, I know. Now, can you tell me what the hell is going on stateside? All we've been told over here is that Lady Allison has been removed from her position as director, and that there is an investigation going on."

"At the moment, that's about all we know. If you're certain this vehicle is clean of wiretaps, I'll try to find out something now."

"I had it swept thoroughly an hour before I left to pick you up," Catherine said. "I'd love to know what's actually going on."

Noah took out his phone and dialed the office number. It was answered right away.

"Brigadoon Investments, how may I direct your call?"

"Would Mr. Donaldson happen to be in? It's Mr. Arthur calling."

"One moment, please." Hold music began, but it vanished only a few seconds later.

"Camelot, report," said Donald Jefferson.

"We are in the fog," Noah said. "All secure and comfortable. Any news on your end?"

"Nothing worth talking about," Jefferson said. "Some members of the committee are supposed to go and see Allison today, but we don't know what's going on. So far, we can't even find out who started this witchhunt, and we've been allowed no contact with Allison at all. Your orders are to stay off the grid and out of sight until further notice. Unfortunately, I have no idea how long this might last."

"Understood, sir," Noah said. "Is there anything we might be able to do to help?"

"Lord, no," Jefferson said emphatically. "I don't want you anywhere near the U.S.A. until this is over, you got that? Right now, these people don't know for sure who you are, but there's very little chance we're going to be able to keep it that way for very long. Best you get accustomed to your new identities, because they may be the last ones you ever use. And by that, I mean that I expect you to live a long time under those names."

"Yes, sir. I can assure you, we will do our best. You know how to reach us if you need to?"

"Absolutely. Our text message system can find your phones no matter where they are, or what numbers are assigned to them. I can promise you that we'll let you know as soon as we have any information that can help you."

"Thank you, sir. Camelot out." Noah ended the call and dropped the phone into his pocket. "No new developments," he said. "There's a Senate committee that seems to think we've been violating some rule about not operating within the United States, even though it doesn't apply to us, and only the DOJ can request actions within our borders. They decided to go after Allison, but they're also trying to identify my team and arrest us, as well. Jefferson says we are not to return to the United States at all until this is settled, and to get comfortable in our new identities."

Catherine shook her head. "What a bloody mess," she said. "Well, as for getting comfortable, I'm going to help you with that. Kendall had already made arrangements for your accommodations, which is where I'm taking you. You'll be living just outside the city, near Guildford. It's actually an old manor house, called Feeney Manor." She grinned at Noah in the mirror on her sun visor. "It's not quite a kingdom, but you get to be the lord of the manor."

"We're actually supposed to be keeping a low profile," Noah said. "Is this going to work?"

"Of course," Catherine replied. "Kendall said he was told to give you means, so you are now the owners and stockholders of a company that sells books through the internet. As far as anyone can tell, it's making you quite the tidy fortune."

Chapter NINE

The drive to Feeney Manor took just over half an hour, and Sarah, Jenny, Neil, and Marco were all excited when they got a good look at it. The house was huge and built of stone, with a dozen chimneys protruding from its tiled roof.

"Limestone," Noah said. "I wouldn't think there would be a good limestone quarry around here."

"And you'd be correct," Catherine said. "The stone for this mansion was transported from Brighton, nearly a hundred kilometers away. That was back in the time of William the Conqueror, around 1070. It was once owned by William Sutherford Feeney, who was Attorney General during the early 1900s. That's where it got its name, of course."

The front door opened suddenly and a man stepped out, followed by three other men who hurried down and took their bags. Noah glanced at Catherine, who was smiling.

"I meant to warn you," she said. "The house comes with a staff. That's the butler, Thomas, and the other men are his sons. They take care of the grounds and do the general labor. His wife is the housekeeper, and there are three maids and three cooks. They are all paid by your company's bookkeepers, so you don't need to bother about them. They don't, of course, know anything about who you actually are, but since you won't be involved in any actions, it shouldn't be a problem."

She turned and smiled at Thomas. "You'd be Thomas? I'm Catherine Beasley, the estate agent."

"Good afternoon, Miss," Thomas said. "Your office rang that you were on the way with the new owners."

"Yes," she said. "Thomas, I would like to introduce Mr. and Mrs. Lightner, and their friends, Mr. and Mrs. Jamieson and Mr. Davis. They own the corporation that has purchased the manor. Mr. Lightner, Mr. Thomas, your new butler."

Noah extended a hand, and Thomas looked at it for just a second before reaching out to grasp it firmly.

"Thomas, it's a pleasure," Noah said. "I hope you can put up with a bunch of Yanks running around the place."

Thomas smiled, and Noah could tell that it was genuine. "To be frank, sir, I've found most of our American guests have been considerably more polite than my own countrymen who have stayed here. I was quite pleased when I learned that the old place had been sold, and that we would be permitted to stay on."

"Well, after one look at this place," Noah said, "I sincerely doubt we'd be able to handle it without you. Are those chimneys from fireplaces?"

"Indeed they are, sir," Thomas said. "However, there was added six years ago a new heat and air con system. The hearths are now used mostly for delight, rather than for warmth. May we show you in, sir?"

Noah glanced at Catherine, who nodded. "By all means," he said. "Lead on."

The three younger men lined up behind them as they followed the butler into the house. They were shown a pair of sitting rooms that flanked the hallway just inside the front door, and then led through the passage to the Great Hall, a large room that looked like it could almost be used as a theater. One end seemed to have a raised dais.

"The lord of the manor would hold manorial court in this chamber," Thomas said. "In modern times, it is used primarily for social gatherings, holiday parties and such things."

Sarah and Jenny were staring around themselves in delight, while Noah, Neil, and Marco were looking closely at the suits of armor and numerous swords and battle axes and other weapons that decorated the walls. Some of them were polished and shining, but others showed signs of having actually been used.

"This is incredible," Noah said, doing his best to look like the amazed American.

Thomas smiled and led them further into the house. They were shown the private dining room, the kitchens—there were two of them—and a number of rooms dedicated to the staff. The butler explained that the staff all lived on the ground floor, so that "the Family," which meant anyone who was a permanent resident of the house without being an employee, could have the upper floors to themselves.

After this tour was completed, they went up to the second floor. This was where they would be staying, and it took only moments for Thomas to show them the six available suites. Noah and Sarah were instantly placed into the master's chamber, Neil and Jenny took the one across the hall from theirs, and Marco was given one at the other end of the hallway. Thomas' sons put their bags into the appropriate rooms, and then seemed to vanish.

Catherine had followed along, smiling as she watched the young people. This was obviously far beyond anything they had anticipated, and she actually found herself hoping they would be able to stay for quite some time.

"Mr. Lightner," she said. "Will you be needing me for anything else today?"

Noah turned and looked at her. "I think you were supposed to arrange some vehicles?"

Her eyes went wide, and her smile got even bigger. "Oh, yes," she said. "The estate comes with several, and I thought they might meet with your approval. Thomas?"

"Yes, miss," the butler said, and he led the way down the stairs and directly out the back door. A large barn sat a dozen yards behind the house, and had obviously been converted to a garage. He opened one of the swing-up doors, and Noah saw a beautiful Bentley sedan that he guessed was from the late seventies. A second opened door revealed a nearly new Land Rover, and a third housed a 1963 Jaguar XKE roadster.

"There is also," Thomas said, "a small utility truck, which we commonly use for fetching supplies."

Noah smiled at him. "I think these will do nicely," he said. "The Bentley; what year is it?"

"Nineteen seventy-nine, sir."

Noah turned to Catherine. "I suppose we're all set, then," he said. "You'll let us know if you come across anything else we need to deal with, right?"

"I certainly will," she said. "I'm going to be on my way back, then. Do let me know if you learn anything more about that other matter."

Noah agreed, and Catherine got into the van and drove away. Thomas showed all of them where the keys to the vehicles were kept, in a small cabinet just inside the back door, and pointed out that there was also another barn off in the distance that held the tractors and other equipment necessary to maintain an estate with more than three hundred hectares.

"Will you be wanting something particular for dinner, sir?" Thomas asked.

Noah glanced at the others, then shook his head. "I'm certain that whatever the kitchen provides will be perfect," he said. "Should we dress for dinner?"

"It is not necessary, sir," Thomas said. "It is only customary on Sundays, but this is your home. The choice is entirely up to you."

They had begun walking back toward the house, and Noah glanced at his phone to check the time. It was growing close to four o'clock. "What time is dinner served?"

"Customarily at six thirty, sir. If you would prefer a different timetable, you need only let me know."

Noah grinned and shook his head. "I think it might be best if we try to learn how to be on your schedule," he said. "I've got a feeling you folks know what you're doing, and we're all new at this. I don't know if anyone told you, but we actually just sort of fell into money. Our website just sort of took off, and the next thing we knew, we were rich. If you happen to think of any advice you can give on how we can avoid looking like total fools, we are more than happy to listen."

Thomas smiled. "In my humble opinion, sir," he said, "you have just managed to prove beyond the shadow of a doubt that you are anything but fools."

They went back into the house and Thomas went his own way. The five of them went upstairs and gathered in Noah and Sarah's room.

"Dude," Marco said, "if this is what happens when everything falls apart, I'm ready for a whole lot more bad luck."

"I know, right?" Jenny asked with a smile. "Do you have any idea how glad I am that I got sent out with you on this last job? I could live like this for the rest of my life."

"Yeah, me, too," Sarah said. She and Noah were sitting on the bed, and she was snuggled up against him. "This is the kind of thing I used to dream about when I was a kid. Almost like hitting the jackpot in a fairy tale, right?"

"Okay, I like it too," Neil said. "But am I the only one that's worried? What happens if they really start looking for us? Do you honestly think we could stay here?"

"As long as we keep a low profile," Noah said, "and continue to use the identities we've been given, we'd probably be okay. These identities are pretty solid. If you remember from training, any time we get a Horatio call, the idea is to lay low and blend in. However they have us set up, we don't need to be drawing any attention to ourselves to make money, or do anything else. We could probably last a long time, here."

"Okay, maybe. Do you mind if I set up my computer and try to find out more about what's happening?"

"Of course not," Noah said. "I was going to ask you to. And that brings up another point; for now, you can all stop thinking of me as the boss. Unless something changes, I think we need to think of ourselves as equals in this situation. We're apparently business partners, and we know that we can get along well, even when we're not on the job. I think we need to lean on our friendship and dedication to each other, rather than any chain of command concept."

Neil and Marco looked at each other, then turned to Noah. "Oh, no," Neil said. "Noah, we need you in charge. You're the only one who can really think things through clearly, so don't even think about trying to ditch your responsibility."

"I agree with them," Jenny said. "I learned in China and Russia that your instincts are better than any of ours. We might be friends, but that's partly because we have learned to trust you completely. We need that leadership now, more than ever."

Sarah smiled up at him. "They got you, babe," she said. "You're Camelot, no matter what."

Noah locked eyes with each of the for a second before moving to the next, then nodded his head. "All right," he said. "Logically, you are correct. I just didn't want to assume leadership if it wasn't necessary."

"It's necessary, boss," Marco said. "Trust me on that. If the shit hits the fan, you're more likely to see it coming than anyone else. We need you to tell us when to duck."

"All right, we've agreed. It's been a rough couple of days, I think I'm going to grab a shower before dinner."

"That sounds like a good idea," Neil said. "Honey?"

"I'm in, pumpkin." The two of them left the room, holding hands.

Marco watched them go. "Shower, my ass," he said. He turned and looked back at Noah, then blushed and turned to leave the room. "Yeah, my ass needs a shower, too."

Sarah chuckled as he went out the door, closing it behind himself. "I can't help but feel sorry for him," she said. "If this goes on too long, he's going to be a wreck without Renée. I think they were getting pretty serious."

"I agree," Noah said. "On the other hand, this brings up one of the risks of our position. Suppose Neil and Jenny were to be married, and then one of them gets a Horatio call while out on a mission. How could they cope with it?"

"Yeah, right," Sarah said. "If I were back home when this happened, I'd go crazy. He can't even call her, can he?"

"Protocol says absolutely no contact except through secure channels," Noah said. "I doubt they would consider Renée secure. If she were to slip and mentioned that she talked to him, it could blow up in all of our faces."

Noah got up and opened the suitcase, taking out clean clothes. Sarah stayed on the bed and looked up at him.

"So, if you were sent out without me and this happened, I'd just be out of luck? That would be it, I'd never see you again?"

Noah stopped what he was doing and looked into her eyes. "Eventually, the situation should come to an end and I would be able to come home to you. You know me, though. I don't want to be without you. If I came to believe that the situation would never be resolved, I would use whatever resources were necessary to come and get you."

Sarah smiled. "You would, wouldn't you? Babe, you walked into almost certain death for me, I should have known you wouldn't let something like this keep us apart." The smile faded into a frown. "So, if this goes on, what are we going to do about Marco?"

"I suppose we would have to mount a mission to go and get Renée," he said. "The only question would be whether she wanted to come."

Sarah narrowed her eyes and gave him a seductive grin. "Have you seen the way she looks at him? Trust me, she'd come."

The shower was a nozzle that was attached to a large, claw-foot tub, and a metal oval overhead held a curtain that went all the way around. Noah got the water set to the temperature he liked, then climbed in. He wasn't surprised when the curtain opened a moment later, and Sarah stepped in with him.

Downstairs, Thomas walked into the kitchen, where his wife Caroline was watching over the cooks.

"Well, they're here," he said. "The new owners. Seem like some lovely young folk."

"That's good, then," Caroline said. "You can introduce me at dinner. I peeked out, and they look very nice."

"They seem so. There's something about that Mr. Lightner, though. He's polite enough, but there's a hard core underneath. Strikes me he might've been a soldier."

"Nothing wrong with that," his wife said. She leaned over one of the cooks, who was using a rolling pin to flatten a piecrust. "Susan, you needn't beat it to death."

"Yes, mum," the girl replied. She laid the rolling pin aside and carefully folded the crust over before picking it up and pressing it into the pie pan. Caroline continued to watch as she spooned in the banana cream filling, then turned back to her husband.

"Three men, and only two women. What's the other lad like?"

"Mr. Davis? Seemed bright enough, and a bit to the quiet side. Definitely the manly sort."

Caroline's lips pressed into a thin line. "We'll be watching the girls, then," she said.

"Well, and that's a bit of wisdom in any case, innit? Let's get everyone together, so we can make all the introductions at dinner."

"They're all here. What are the boys up to?"

Thomas smiled. "I sent them out to check the fields," he said. "Thought Brendan's eyes were going to pop out at the young ladies. I'll be having a word with him later on, as both of them are wed. Little Tom and Chauncey were well behaved, but they could stand to hear it as well."

"You needn't worry about Chauncey," Caroline said. "He fancies Diana, which is why I keep her on the upstairs staff. When they get in the same room, neither of them can manage to think."

That got her a chuckle from Thomas. "I suspect they can think just fine," he said. "I'd wager it's that they don't want you to know what they're thinking about that keep them so quiet."

"You're probably right," his wife said with a grin. "He's your son, after all."

NOAH AND THE REST CAME down shortly before six thirty, and Thomas met them in the dining room.

"As master of the house," Thomas said to Noah, "you should traditionally take the head of the table. Your lovely wife will be seated at your right hand, and the rest should be seated according to your own preferences."

The table was one that could be expanded, and Thomas had taken out sections to make it only six feet long. Noah took the chair he had indicated, with Sarah directly at his right, but rather than taking the other end of the table, Neil and Jenny sat down at one side together, with Neil directly across from Sarah and Jenny on his left. Marco grinned and took the chair directly opposite Noah.

"I thought this might be a good time for you to meet the rest of the staff," Thomas said. "Would that be all right?"

Noah smiled. "Certainly, that would be fine," he said.

Thomas bowed stiffly and walked out of the room, returning only a moment later with a small crowd following him.

"Mr. and Mrs. Lightner, Mr. and Mrs. Jamieson, Mr. Davis," he began, "I should like to introduce you to my wife, Caroline. She is the housekeeper for the estate, and supervises the maids and cooks in the performance of their duties."

"Caroline, we are delighted to meet you," Noah said. "Let's be a little less formal, though, can we do that? I'm Travis, and this is my wife, Penny. That's John down at the other end of the table, and this is Gary and Stacy. If you go talking about Mr. Lightner, I'm probably going to look around and see if my father has found me."

Thomas and Caroline both smiled. "That would be fine, sir," Thomas said. He held out a hand and indicated the rest of the staff. "These young men are my three boys, who take care of the grounds and the house. First is the eldest, Thomas Junior, but we all call him Little Tom. After him is Brendan, and that's Chauncey."

Each of the young men bowed briefly as he was introduced, and then Thomas moved on to the ladies who were lined up behind them.

"These are the maids," he said. "First is Julianna, who happens to be our daughter. She sees to the downstairs, and makes fine work of it. Next is Constance, and then Diana. They are sisters, and actually grew up just up the road in Guildford. They are the upstairs maids, so they will be seeing to your rooms. Feel free to let them know about anything you need, and when you want them to do your rooms. They will take care of your washing, so tell them about any special requirements for your laundry."

The young ladies each offered a curtsy, which made Sarah and Jenny smile. Noah thanked them for the work they did and told them to let them all know if they did anything to make the work harder, but the girls only smiled nervously.

"And these are the cooking staff," Thomas said. "We have Beatrice, who is the chef, and her helper, Lynn, and that leaves us with Susan, the pastry cook. She bakes cakes, pies, and biscuits, and you'll always find some ready and waiting."

Beatrice seemed to be the oldest of the ladies, and the least intimidated. "Now, don't any of ye be shy about lettin' me know what ye like," she said, her accent thick and Welsh. "I know the ways of American cookin', and many others, so tell me what ye'd like and it'll be me pleasure to make it fer ye!"

Noah smiled. "We appreciate that," he said, "but I think we're all looking forward to trying new things, so we'll be happy to let you make those choices."

She smiled. "Well, then, and I hope ye like beef. Tonight I've prepared a roast, with potatoes and peas, and a gravy such as ye never had." She clapped her hands together and her helpers followed her to the kitchen. A moment later, they returned and set large bowls on the table.

Chapter TEN

Allison was awakened when the slot in the door was opened. With no windows, it was impossible to tell what time it was, but she suspected it was rather early.

"Breakfast time," called a voice. Allison looked through the slot and saw a tray being passed inside. She threw off the blanket and got out of bed, then walked over and took the tray.

"Surprise, surprise," she muttered to herself. The tray held actual dishes and flatware, where she had been expecting to find cheap plastic plates and sporks. Breakfast appeared to be coffee, scrambled eggs, and bacon, but there was a pair of biscuits and packets of butter and grape jelly. She set it all on the table and sat down, then glanced back at the slot in the door.

The woman who had passed the food to her had apparently moved on down the hall, but the slot was left open. She shrugged and began eating. The coffee was black and strong, but she didn't complain; at least it was coffee, even if it didn't have the sugar she was accustomed to.

The food was actually pretty good, and she had to admit there was plenty of it. She wolfed it down rather quickly and then buttered up the biscuits and slathered them with jelly before eating them, as well. When she was finished, she took the tray back to the slot and set it down so that it was balanced.

Fifteen minutes later, the tray disappeared and the slot was closed. Allison had gone back to the bed and turned on the television, and was scanning through the news programs. There was still nothing that seemed to relate to her situation, so she found a talk show and let herself zone out while it played.

It was a couple of hours later when she heard sounds in the hall, and glanced at the door just in time to see the slot open. There was a new young woman looking through at her, and she was wearing a smile.

"Hi, there," the girl said. "I'm Lucy, I got the snack tray today. Need anything?"

Allison cocked her head and looked at her for a moment, then smiled back. "I don't suppose you have any instant coffee and some sugar, do you?"

"Yep," the girl said. A moment later, she held out a plastic cup and a very small jar of instant coffee. Allison hurried to the door and accepted it, and found a spoon and several dozen packets of sugar inside the cup. "You have to use the hot water out of the sink, but it should be plenty hot enough. Do you need soap, shampoo, any of that kind of stuff?"

"Why, yes," Allison said, "now that you mention it. Incidentally, how often do they give us a change of clothing?"

"Oh, every day. That's usually shortly after dinner time, I think." Lucy glanced down the hall for a moment, then looked back at Allison. "I'm not supposed to tell you," she said softly, "but I heard that some people are coming to talk to you in just a few minutes. You might want to hurry up and get your coffee ready."

Allison smiled. "Thanks," she said. The slot closed and Allison dumped the contents of the cup onto the table, then went to the sink. It took only a few seconds for the hot water to become steaming, so she filled the cup almost to the brim and carried it back to the table. A spoonful of instant coffee and a half-dozen packets of sugar later, she took a sip and moaned with pleasure.

She carried the coffee back to the bed and continued watching television, but she didn't get to watch for long. It was about fifteen minutes later when she heard keys rattle and the door swung open.

"You got visitors," said a guard. She started to get up off the bed, but suddenly two men and a woman entered the room. Allison stared in surprise when she saw who her visitors were.

"Senator Duckworth? Senator Gibbs? Since when are either of you on the oversight committees?"

One of the two men, an older fellow who stood about six foot six, turned and nodded at the guard. The door was closed, and he turned back to Allison.

"Hello, Allison," he said. "Obviously, you recognize Gibbs and myself. This lady is Congresswoman Barbara Holloway, from California. And you're right, we've only recently been appointed to the committee. However, we are coming to see you for an entirely different reason, and I hope you're going to be cooperative."

Allison narrowed her eyes. "I'll listen," she said. "That's all the cooperation I'm gonna promise." She got up off the bed and walked to the table, taking one of three chairs and pointing at the other two. "Have a seat, Senator Holloway. One of these gentlemen can stand."

Holloway grinned and took the chair, but neither of the men bothered to sit in the third. "I heard you were quite a firecracker," Senator Holloway said. "Call me Barbara, please."

Allison nodded. "Okay, then I'm Allison. What is it you folks want?"

"Hopefully, the same thing you do," Holloway said. "A quick and satisfying end to this entire situation."

Allison looked at the two men, then back at Holloway. "At the moment, I don't even know what the situation is. Care to enlighten me?"

"First off," said Duckworth, "we want to let you know that you're not actually in any trouble, or at least not yet. The entire ruse about arresting you was to get you out of your office without letting anyone know what's really going on. Unfortunately, we can't turn you loose until we know exactly where you stand."

"Stand on what, you old buzzard? You know damn well I was appointed by the president to my position, and that the entire reason for the existence of my job at E & E is to make sure that no one can ever use it for personal reasons. If this is going to involve turning any of my assets against anyone within our government, you can turn around and walk right back out of here and we can just say we're done."

Gibbs, who hadn't spoken to this point, looked at Duckworth. "I told you she was sharp," he said. He turned and looked at Allison. "Allison, you need to hear everything before you make any decisions. There are some things going on that need to be dealt with, and they need to be dealt with soon. That's going to mean some eliminations, I'm afraid, and the people we are talking about are far too powerful to take down any other way."

Allison looked at Holloway. "Barbara, the men are sounding stupid. Why don't you explain this to me?"

"I'll be happy to," Holloway said. "Allison, there is a faction within certain parts of our government that is out to destroy everything America stands for. The idea is to bring us to a point of becoming a true socialist oligarchy, one that will literally eliminate all of the freedoms currently afforded by the Constitution and the Bill of Rights. This is a conspiracy that has been in existence for at least a couple of years, and some of us, including the three you see before you, have come to being concerned that it is just about to reach the point of achieving its goals."

Allison looked into her eyes for a moment, then looked at Gibbs and Duckworth. "I'm going to be completely honest," she said. "There is absolutely nothing about these two men that inspires trust or confidence in me. You, on the other hand, are an entirely new factor in the equation. I know who you are by reputation, because I follow what you people do, but if I recall correctly, you are something of a diehard liberal. Why would a socialist state trouble you at all?"

"I'm a diehard liberal, that's correct," Holloway said. "Do you have any idea what that actually means? It means that I hope to see our country become a mixture of all races and cultures, where everyone can actually consider themselves to be the equal of everyone else. It means I want to see poverty eliminated, so that no one in this country will need to go hungry, or go without medical care. It means that I want to see not fewer freedoms, but more. I want to see freedom from crime and avarice, I want to see freedom from envy, freedom from the fear of walking down the street. If wanting those things is bad, then I will happily plead guilty in any court that cares to bring me up on those charges."

Allison grinned at her. "Okay, you got some gumption of your own," she said. "Now, tell me about this socialist state that scares you so much.

Holloway glanced at Duckworth. "Marvin? This is where you come in."

Duckworth took a deep breath and looked at Allison. "Allison, about two years ago, I was approached by a reporter—one of those independent reporters, a freelancer from the Internet—who told me that he had evidence of a conspiracy that involved people from every level of our government. These people, he claimed, were working behind the scenes to eliminate our freedoms by coercing the people into giving them up in return for greater safety and security. I'll confess that at first, I thought he was a nutcase, one of those 'tinfoil hat' types. I dared him to show me any kind of proof, and he asked me to meet him privately the following day."

"Did he turn up dead before you got there?" Allison asked. "That's the way these stories usually go, isn't it?"

Duckworth chuckled. "No. Actually, we met right on schedule in a Maryland shopping center parking lot. I had driven my son's car, the one he used for going back and forth to school, so nobody knew who I was. I met the reporter, and we sat in my car while he showed me a lot of information he had compiled, information that was backed up by copies of emails he had intercepted, recordings of phone conversations, video of some of the conspirators discussing exactly how they were going to launch the next phase of their plan. From what I saw, he was telling me the truth, but I suspected there might be more to it than he even knew about."

"So, let me guess," Allison said. "You went to someone at the FBI? Somebody you trust, maybe?"

"That's exactly what I did," Duckworth said. "I went to Charlie McBride, who ran the field office out of Baltimore, and I showed him copies of everything I had seen. Would you care to guess what happened next?"

"I don't have to guess," Allison said. "SSA Charles McBride was murdered almost 2 years ago. The story was that he apparently surprised a burglar in his house late one night, and took a twenty-two caliber bullet through the head. I remember that, it was all over the news back then. You are thinking he was killed because he got too close to finding out the truth about this?"

"I don't have to think anything," Duckworth said. "Two of his agents came to me and told me that he had warned them that if something happened to him, they were to tell me that the plan was well advanced and that I should take whatever action necessary to stop it. I've been trying to do that ever since, but I keep running into brick walls. A year ago, I sat down with the directors of the NSA and DHS and laid this all out to them. They promised to look into it, and the next day I was told that they had concluded there was nothing to worry about, that it was all a conspiracy theory with no basis in fact."

Allison set silently, looking into his eyes for a moment. "So how did it go from there to dragging me out of my office in chains?"

"I've been quietly trying to build a case, sharing what I know with other representatives that I've come to trust. Gibbs and Holloway are two of them, but there's also Senators Ryan and Thomason and a few

others. Ryan, of course, is the chairman of the Senate's secret committee on intelligence oversight, and I went to him to ask for ideas. He's
the one who brought you up."

Allison snorted. "Now, why does that not surprise me? Ryan
and I have never gotten along, even back during my days with the
Agency."

"Well, you might be surprised at this," Gibbs put in. "Ryan didn't
suggest trying to get rid of you, he said the only hope we have of saving the country at this point is to get you on our side."

Allison's eyes widened. "Seriously? All the man has ever done is
try to block me from accomplishing anything. Why would he want
me to be part of this resistance movement?"

"According to him," Holloway said, "the only reason he has
fought your department is because he's afraid it will someday be used
against the political enemies of whoever might be sitting in the Oval
Office. It's not that he thinks you would allow that, but trying to put
some kind of restraints on the organization while you are still in the
top chair might be smarter than waiting until there's someone in the
White House that might try such a thing. If your successor has political ambitions, or likes to curry favor, E & E could become a serious
liability."

"That'll never happen while I'm in charge," Allison said.

"We know that, and so does Ryan," Holloway said. "The reason
he wants to get you involved in this is because, in his words, Allison
Peterson is the only one who could honestly have a chance at preventing the disaster that's coming. And the only way to prevent it is
to eliminate those people who are doing their best to bring it about.
And, incidentally, I was able to get him recruited into the organization. Like us, he's now working from the inside."

Allison looked at each of their faces for a moment. "You're telling
me that each of you is a member of this thing? Right now?"

"Yes, we are," Holloway said. "Each of us was recruited about six months ago, and we've been trying to gain information that would let us shut this thing down ever since. That's the very reason Ryan arranged to have us nominated to and appointed to the intelligence oversight committee. It gives us opportunities to get together and talk in a secure environment."

"So, you want to use me and my people exactly the way Ryan is afraid someone else might, in the future. Just what the hell is this disaster that's coming?"

Gibbs took the third chair and turned it around, straddling it and leaning on his arms atop its back. "Remember back when 9/11 happened, and everyone swore up and down it was an inside job? Well, we don't know whether it was or not, but it almost cost us a lot of the freedoms that Americans have come to depend on. This faction, which calls itself the Ascension Project, intends to generate three new mass terror events, and they'll probably make 9/11 seem like a Sunday picnic. We only have basic details on the first one, but it involves some sort of orchestrated disaster that will cost the lives of tens of thousands of children."

"Children?" Allison said, her eyes going even wider. "Keep going, tell it all."

"That's the problem, we don't know it all," Holloway said. "All we know is that there will be three events, and the first one is supposed to take out as many as twenty thousand children or more, ranging from toddlers to teenagers. That particular plan also refers to a lot of collateral damage, but only in the sense that it will help them to achieve a reduction of liberty. It is supposed to make it almost impossible to travel freely around the country. From what we understand, once it happens, there will be a move in Congress to require travel permits to even leave your home county. Anyone traveling without such a permit will be subject to arrest and incarceration without benefit of due process. The idea is that anyone who doesn't bother to let the government know where they're traveling to is probably traveling for an illegal purpose. Simply getting caught will be considered sufficient evidence for conviction and incarceration."

"Holy shit," Allison said. "What else is supposed to happen?"

"Like I said, we don't know," Gibbs said. "All we know is that there will be two more alleged attacks, and by the time they are finished, the American people will be willing to give up every freedom they got. Guns will be confiscated, and refusal to surrender them means automatic life in prison. Religions will be regulated, because terrorists often use the guise of religion to conduct their activities. Freedom of speech will be curtailed, because anyone speaking out against the government must be a terrorist. You see where it's going?"

"I see it," Allison said. "But, come on, there's been talk about this kind of stuff for the last thirty years or more. It hasn't happened, even though it's been predicted over and over and over."

"That's true, it hasn't happened yet," Holloway said. "On the other hand, it requires people in certain positions of power to pull off something like this. It would mean that the leadership of organizations like the NSA, DHS, possibly even some of the top people at FBI and CIA must be in on it. We know that they've already got some of the highest ranking military officers involved, because they've been caught on video. General O'Reilly, the guy who managed to make North Korea back down a couple years ago? He's in their camp, for certain, and he's made it clear to many of his subordinates that he expects their loyalty to be directed to him, rather than to America. He's built himself a fairly good sized private army, with enough clout to make a lot of the rest of the military follow his lead. When it comes time to round up the guns, he's probably going to be leading the charge."

"Who else is involved? Just spill it, don't try to sugarcoat anything." Allison's eyes had narrowed, and her face was showing anger.

"Try Lindemann, Martin, and Perkowski in the Senate, Anderson, Willamette, Borden, Majors, and Vincenzo in the House, Robinette, Morgenstern, Benton, Pickering, and Lewiston at the NSA, Mikesell, Scheiber, Romano, and possibly Rodriguez at DHS, and we are trying to lock down evidence against a number of others. The people I've listed have all been confirmed as being part of this organization, and they are all listed as holding specific positions in the oligarchy that is to come. Congress will be eliminated once they achieve their goals, and the president will answer only to something called the Ascension Council. Every agency and bureaucracy will be controlled by someone on that council, effectively putting every bit of the power of the country in their hands."

Allison was gritting her teeth, mentally chewing up the people listed so that she could spit them out.

"So we need to eliminate them? You want me to put my specialists out there taking them out?"

"Not all of them," Holloway said. "We know that you've got certain people who are extremely capable, and we need them. As it happens, we have actually found a friend within your organization, so we know who it is that we want, and we're doing our best to make sure they become available. The idea is to make it appear that some of your people went off the grid while you were indisposed in this situation, and that you have no idea what could've happened to them. Once that's done, the idea is for those people to be free to do what we need them to do."

Allison was staring into her eyes. "Tell me who it is you think you want," she said coldly. "And bear in mind, I still haven't promised any kind of cooperation in this."

Holloway looked at the two men, and turned back to Allison. "A few months back, you sent a team into Arkansas to take care of an organized crime outfit that was proving too tough to prosecute. What we've done is create a situation where the Ascension Project's members can believe that that particular team has deserted, run out on you and probably are trying to start a new life somewhere. We put you back in your office, where you pretend to become the good little girl who does what daddy government says, while that particular team stays off the radar and out of sight in order to bring the Ascension Project to a timely and bloody end."

"Cut to the chase," Allison said. "You claim you got somebody in my house? I want to know who it is, and I want to know who you think it is you want. You can either answer those two questions right now, or you can get the hell out of my cell."

"Allison, please," Holloway said. "I was just trying to give you a foundation for what I'm about to say. The person we've got on the inside of your organization is the only one you've got who was capable of understanding just how devious and despicable this plan really is. You know the old saying, it takes a thief to catch a thief? We needed someone who was just as devious as these people, and we found it in Doctor Nathan Parker. When we caught him during a recent visit to D.C. and showed him all of our evidence, he agreed to help us set up this whole thing. He's that convinced that the situation is dire."

"Doc Parker?" Allison said, incredulous. She burst out laughing. "Hell, if he's with you, then I probably am. Of course, I want to hear it out of his own mouth. I'm not taking your word for anything."

"Understandable, and we'll be glad to let him confirm it to you. As for who we want, I think you've already figured that out. There's only one team you've got who could possibly move through this kind of an organization and pick them off, and it's the one you sent to Arkansas. I'm talking about..."

"Yes, yes," Allison said. "You're talking about Camelot."

"Yes," Duckworth said. "Allison, we've seen enough intelligence reports about what he's accomplished to believe that he's the only one who might be able to pull this off. He'll be without the support of your organization, of course, because it all has to be done secretly, with no way to trace back directly to you, or to us. Parker tells us there is no one else who could possibly get him to do what needs to be done, that if the orders don't come from you, he'll ignore them. That's why we have to get you on our side, if we have any hope of saving America."

Allison stared at him for a moment, then leaned her elbows on the table and rubbed her hands over her eyes. "Who else have you compromised in my organization?"

"No one. I give you my word, Parker is the only one we've spoken with."

She leaned her face in her hands for several seconds, then leaned back and slapped the table.

"I'll think about this," she said. "For now, I want all three of you out of my cell. I need time to digest everything you said, so come back and see me in about six hours. Oh, and bring along some of this evidence you claim to have. I want to see it."

Holloway grinned. "I'm way ahead of you," she said. She reached into a pocket on her dress and withdrew a smartphone. She laid it on the table and pointed at it. "Everything we've got has been scanned and loaded into that phone. You can look through it all, but I'm told the phone won't work from inside this building. We'll go, and we'll give you your six hours."

She got to her feet and motioned toward the door, so Duckworth knocked on it. When it opened a moment later, she and the two men walked out of the room without another word.

Allison sat and looked at the phone, then picked it up. She powered it on and watched as it came to life, then shook her head. As Holloway had said, it had no signal.

Chapter ELEVEN

Parker was sitting in his office when the phone rang, and he snatched it up quickly.

"Parker," he said.

"Nathan, it's Marvin Duckworth. Are you secure?"

"Hell, yes, I gave you that damn phone, didn't I? What happened?"

"Well, she's pretty pissed off that we went to you first. Other than that, I think we're making headway. She's going to want you to confirm that you are part of this operation, but that's to be expected. What about the special team? Are they safe?"

"I've got them put away safely for the moment," Parker said. "Believe me when I tell you, though, they are not going to take these orders from anyone except her. To be perfectly honest, I'm not even certain they'll do it if she tells them to, unless she can convince them that this is real. Camelot is not the normal kind of man, he doesn't think like the rest of us. He's been known to completely change his mission objective on his own initiative, if he didn't believe it had to go down the way we plan."

"Hopefully, that will be his strength in this case. We are meeting with her again in six hours, and if everything goes according to plan, we will be taking her out of here. You may need to make arrangements in a hurry to get her to them."

"I can do that," Parker said. "I know approximately where they are, and I know who will be able to take her directly to them. You just make sure you got everything covered on your end, and I'll handle mine."

He hung up the phone without another word, and then leaned back in his chair. A lifelong skeptic, he had never believed that the day would ever come when he would willingly take actions against people who were supposed to be part of his government, but the oath that he took so many years before was to defend the Constitution of the United States against all enemies, foreign and domestic.

Most people didn't even think about what that line truly meant, but Parker had seen through it on the day he was enlisted into the United States Army. "All enemies, foreign and domestic," he had recited along with everyone else, but in his mind, he was thinking about what each word he spoke actually meant. By swearing to defend against all enemies, including those who would be considered domestic, he was taking an oath to take up arms against American citizens.

He'd never had to do that before, but the time had certainly come. While he might be too old to actually go after them himself, he wasn't a bit bashful about aiming the only weapon in his arsenal that might be capable of saving what America stood for, and that weapon was Noah Wolf.

DINNER HAD BEEN FANTASTIC. Noah actually considered asking Beatrice for her recipe for roast beef, but he decided against it. A true artiste had a tendency to guard his or her secrets, and Noah wasn't about to get on her bad side. A good cook can make something taste fantastic, but they can also make it inedible. He'd be eating her cooking for a while, so it might be a bad idea to get her riled.

After dinner, he and the others had gone for a stroll around the grounds. The air out in the countryside was incredibly clear, and he was surprised to realize that he could see stars appearing even before the sun had dropped all the way behind the horizon.

"Travis," Sarah said, following his order to make sure they maintained their view identities, "this place is incredible. Do you think there's any hope we might actually be able to stay?"

"I don't have any idea, at the moment," he said. "I thought about checking in again, but I'm afraid it might be too soon. We'll just have to wait and see what happens, but I'm certainly hoping that everything works out. If it doesn't, though, I'm hoping we can stay here for a long time."

"Yeah, me, too," Neil said. "Stacy actually likes it here, don't you, baby?"

"I sure do," Jenny said. "I don't think I've ever felt so peaceful inside. This place just makes you relax, doesn't it?"

"Oh, I know," Sarah said. "I think the only part about it I might not like is not being able to do our own cooking. I'm going to wait a few days, but I want to talk to Beatrice and see if I can sneak into the kitchen, now and then."

"I'm sure she'd let you," Noah said. "She might watch you like a hawk while you're in there, though."

"Hey, that would be okay. She might even give me some tips, and I could stand to learn a bit more about cooking."

"You know what I want?" Marco asked. "I want to get a rifle and go hunting. I've seen everything from rabbits to deer wandering around here."

"I saw a gun cabinet in the Great Hall," Noah said. "We ought to check out what weapons are available in it. I'm not sure I like not having a gun handy, just in case of trouble."

"I know what you mean," Jenny said. "Do you know how long it's been since I've gone anywhere unarmed? Makes me feel naked."

When the sun was fully down, and the sky was a beautiful latticework of stars, they finally headed back toward the house. There was no television on the main floor, but each of them had a large screen TV mounted on the wall in their rooms. At Sarah's invitation, they all decided to join her and Noah in their large room to see what programs might be available. There was a couch and a couple of chairs in the room, so there was plenty of room for everyone.

Noah took one of the big wingback chairs, and Sarah just settled into his lap. They found that they had satellite TV, and just about every channel was represented. After a few minutes of searching through the guide, they found a movie that sounded good and settled down to watch.

ALLISON READ THROUGH the files in the phone, and then took it with her to the bed and lay down while she went through it again. She had watched videos of politicians she had actually thought were reasonably faithful to their oaths of office, as they discussed massive loss of life without the slightest hint of remorse. She had read dozens of emails that hinted at the mysterious plan that would kill off tens of thousands of school-age children, and the rage that was boiling inside her was almost more than she could contain.

Of course, she realized that this evidence could be faked, and that thought occupied her mind to some degree. If that were the case, it was one of the most incredible forgery jobs she had ever seen, and she had seen a few.

The biggest benefit of the phone, however, was the fact that she could keep track of the time. When the slot popped open in her door, she shoved the phone under the blanket as she went to pick up her lunch tray and carry it to the table.

Lunch was a cheeseburger and fries, with some kind of ready-made cupcake for dessert. Instead of coffee, she had a can of cola, but that was okay with her. She popped it open, sat down at the table, and began to eat.

The things that she had read, however, had interfered with her appetite. She forced herself to finish the burger, but the fries were just a bit too greasy for her. She saved the cupcake for later and put the tray back in the slot, then climbed onto the bed and lay down as if she were going to sleep. The tray vanished about fifteen minutes later, and the slot was closed again.

She took the phone back out from under the blanket and began reading once more. She was still reading three and a half hours later, when the three politicians returned. They came in and waited for her to join them at the table.

"I'm ninety-five percent sold," Allison said. "You let me hear Doctor Parker say he's behind you on this, and that will probably be enough to make me want to help you. Until then, I don't know what else to say."

"That's good enough," Holloway said. "Are you ready to blow this joint?" Her face twisted in a grin.

Allison looked her in the eye. "To where? As far as I know, I'm still under arrest, remember?"

"We've already taken care of that," Holloway said. "Allison, we are taking some serious risks, here. Marvin Duckworth, Clarence Gibbs, and I are recently recruited members of the Ascension Project. We are also part of a—I guess you'd call it a resistance movement, within this thing. As far as the people involved know, we're completely in support of their efforts. Same goes for Ryan; as Marvin told you, he's also part of it all, but he's in with us. There are a few others, as well, including a couple other members of the intelligence committee."

Allison stared into her eyes as if trying to see through them. "You're playing double agents? You know they won't hesitate to kill you, right?"

"Not as long as they think we're valuable," Gibbs said. "The reason we're here is because they want to have you under their control. We were sent in to make sure you understand that you take your orders from them, now—through the intelligence committee, of course."

"That's never going to happen," Allison said, but Holloway raised a hand to cut her off.

"It has to," she said. "At least on the surface, you've got to appear to be cooperating. That's the only way you're going to be able to keep Camelot out there doing what has to be done. We've got to be able to report back that we have you firmly under our control, and we are going to claim that your capitulation came from threats we made against your people in Neverland."

"How the hell am I supposed to keep Camelot safe," Allison demanded, "if I'm kissing the asses of the people he needs to be taking out?"

"Who said anything about kissing any asses? All they want to do is take over making the decisions on who your organization eliminates, and you may have to do some of what they want if this thing takes any time to sit in the motion. Your Team Camelot is going to have to work on their own, while you're making it appear that you decided to be a team player."

"With bastards like this looking over my shoulder. How am I supposed to even keep in touch with Camelot under conditions like that?"

Holloway sighed. "The warrant for your arrest is going to be quashed, and you will be reinstated to your position. However, we need your help to get Camelot on board before you go back to your office. What we've got in mind is to take you out of here today, secretly, and meet up with Parker outside of Kirtland. We'll let you speak with him privately and make your decision. If you come in with us, then we'll move on to the next phase of our plan. If not, we will have to bring you right back here."

Allison's eyebrows came down. "Then, all of this really was just a way to get me alone so we can talk? Do you realize how Machiavellian that really sounds? I've seen movies about stories like this, and none of them were this convoluted, I swear."

Holloway shrugged. "We had to be certain that no one could possibly figure out what we were talking to you about. This was the only way that felt safe, to us. Remember something, we know without a shadow of a doubt that doing this could get us killed. None of us is ready to die, not unless there's no other way. At the same time, any of us would be willing to give up our lives if it means saving our country. I know you understand that, because you're just like me in that regard."

Allison sucked on her cheek for a second, then nodded. "You're right about that," she said. "Okay, then let's get this show on the road. What kind of hoops do we have to jump through to get me out of here?"

Duckworth knocked on the door and a guard opened it.

"We are ready to leave," he said. "All four of us."

"Yes, sir," the guard said. He held the door open wide and nodded to Allison. "Your escort is here," he said.

Allison glanced at Holloway, then got up and followed the three of them out of the room. She stopped in the doorway and looked back for a moment, then turned back to the Congresswoman.

"You know, Barbara," she said, "if you ever just need a break from the pressures of your office, getting arrested and thrown in here is a nice way to get one."

They walked back to the changing room where she had come in the night before, and she was given her own clothes back. After she had changed into them, the door opened again and she found Marshal Howard standing there.

"You're not going to arrest me again, are you?" Allison asked.

"Relax, Allison," Holloway said. "Howard is with us. We had to pull a few strings to make sure he was the one who arrested you, but it was worth it. We wanted to be sure you got here safely, and he just happens to be Duckworth's nephew."

Howard was grinning. "I wasn't allowed to tell you anything," he said. "But I wanted to. Sometime back, I was involved in a mop-up operation after one of your people took out some Russian mobsters. That's when I learned about your outfit, so when uncle Marvin called and said he needed somebody in my position, and told me what it was about and who I'd be dealing with, I was more than happy to volunteer."

Allison shook her head. "Fine, fine," he said. "Just remember what I said about if you ever want a better job."

"Oh, don't worry, you'll have my application within a couple of weeks."

They left the building and climbed into the back of a limousine that was waiting outside, and then it headed toward the airport.

"We've got a helicopter standing by," Gibbs said. "Parker is going to meet us at the airport at Xenia. You'll be able to talk with him for a bit, and then we'll discuss what to do next."

They made it to the airport in fairly short order, and climbed into the helicopter. The flight to Xenia took less than an hour, and Allison saw Doctor Parker standing on the tarmac as she stepped down to the ground. He had a car beside him, and the two of them climbed into it.

"I hope you're going to forgive me, someday," Parker said. "I swear I never would have gone along with this if I didn't think it was necessary."

"Hell, no, I'm not going to forgive you," Allison replied. "Why didn't you just come and tell me what was going on? As long as I've known you, I would've taken you seriously."

"Yes, but you might also have wanted to bring others into your confidence. That's what we couldn't risk. Allison, we don't know for sure that we have a clear idea of who all is involved, and some of the noise these people are making has actually implied that they have someone in every agency. If they got somebody in our outfit, then there was too big a chance they might figure out that we got you involved. I couldn't risk it, so this little dodge was the best idea we could come up with."

"Okay, fine, whatever. Just tell me, and don't pull any freaking punches, do you honestly believe all this is real?" She held up the cell phone Holloway had given her. "They let me read through all their files on this whole operation, and while it looks real, it's possible this is some kind of set up. If you honestly believe it's true, I want to know why."

"Because it would work," Parker said. "If the disaster strikes that kills off thousands and thousands of children, and the right people start making noises about how there's no way to protect those children in a world with so many freedoms, the people of America are going to start demanding that those freedoms be abrogated. Oh, sure, there will be plenty of diehards who insist this is some kind of plot to enslave us all, but the truth of the matter is that most people would go along with it. The vast majority of Americans think that life is pretty good; if the government thinks they'll be better off with an internal passport system, or without assault rifles, most of them are going to grumble for a few minutes and then they'll give in. If you don't believe me, just look back to when they started requiring guns to be registered. Every gun owner in the country complained, but he still went down and registered his guns."

She scowled at him. "Fine. I guess that's what I needed to hear. You're right, way too many people would go along with this idiocy. Now, tell me what you think about the idea of bringing Camelot in on this."

"There's nobody else who could do it," Parker said. "To be completely honest, we didn't know when the balloon was going to go up, and I think we're lucky that this all happened while he's got Cinderella out with him. Between the two of them and Noah's team, I think there's a good chance the head of this hydra can be cut off fast enough to keep them from growing all the way back."

"Have you got a plan worked out?" Allison asked.

"Me? I'm not the tactician. What we need to do is get you and Molly Hansen into a plane, send you out to where the team is hiding. All I know right now is that they're in England, and that they have been set up to the point they should be able to live under the radar for a long time. They'll need Molly, but planning a mission like this is going to have to be on Noah, for the most part."

"Does Molly know anything about this yet?"

"Nothing. I wasn't about to bring anyone else in on this until I knew you were on board. That way, if you decided to take me out and have me shot, nobody else was going to die with me."

"You old bastard. All right, let's do it. What's the next step?"

"We've got to get you to Noah. He's not going to accept orders like these from anybody but you, and I've made sure those people over there know it." He took a deep breath. "Allison, there's one more thing you need to know about."

She looked him in the eye. "Parker, if you're about to give me some bad news..."

"The worst. At this time, I don't dare let anyone inside our organization know the truth of what's happening. The reason for that is because there is one person involved whose name has been kept from you until now, because I know you well enough to know I'm the only person you would ever believe about something like this. Allison, I'm talking about the president, himself."

Her eyes shot open. "Jonathan Andrews? The President of the United States? Parker, you've got to be pulling my leg."

Parker picked up a tablet that was tucked down beside his seat and handed it to her. "This video was taken just under a week ago. It's already queued up," he said. "Just hit the play button."

Allison looked at the tablet in her hand and touched the power button, making it light up. There was a video all ready to go on the screen, and she touched the icon to make it play.

The video was grainy, and had obviously been taken by a camera designed to operate in low light and from a distance. It showed President Andrews standing in a parking lot with Senator Solomon Perkowski and Tom Lewiston from the NSA. Apparently, whoever got the video had used a shotgun microphone, because she could plainly hear them speaking.

"How soon are we talking about?" asked the president.

It was Perkowski who answered. "The first event will take place within the next sixty days," he said. "That will get us started, and then the second event will follow about three months later. The final event will come a week after that one. By that time, we'll have enough backing to install you as the Chairman I of the Ascension Council, and then we'll order a special election for a new president, to replace you."

"Can't happen soon enough to suit me," POTUS said. "I've had about all I can take of being hamstrung by your colleagues in Congress. We could've accomplished so much, if it weren't for all the partisan bull crap."

"It's not going to matter now," Lewiston said. "Once we are in power in the United States, the Russian arm will start working on setting up a council of their own. We'll form an alliance with them, and there won't be anyone left in the world who can stand against us. Within a year, our Council and theirs will replace the UN with our own Supreme Council, with you and Petrokov as co-chairs, and we can install governors in every other country."

Andrews shook his head. "I'm still amazed that we were able to recruit anyone in Russia," he said. "With both countries working together, though, we can finally put some common sense into government throughout the world. You know, I entered politics thinking that we had the best system in the world, that majority rule was the only way the world would ever know peace, but that was stupid. Letting the people have any say in how they are governed is only a recipe for disaster. It's no better than anarchy, because everyone thinks they know best."

"That's the whole point, Jon," Perkowski said. "The only hope the world has at this point, if we are going to avert the potential for a worldwide, global disaster like nuclear war, is to put rational minds in control of everything. Unfortunately, you can't do that if the people still have the right to protest against you. They've got to come to accept that only a true government can keep them safe and secure, and the only true form of government is an oligarchy of rational men and women."

Andrews nodded. "That's unfortunately the truth," he said. "Just let me know what needs to be done, and I'll do what I can from my end."

Perkowski laid a hand on his shoulder. "Jon, you already did the most important part. You brought us all together and came up with this plan."

"The only thing we need to be terribly concerned about right now," Lewiston said, "is gaining control over the agencies that are not already with us. I've been feeding some information to the permanent select committee on intelligence, and I've got Ryan's assurance that he's going to take action very soon. E & E has been without oversight for quite some time, and we need to get them under control. It's going to require a bit of a shakeup, but we think we can get its director to cooperate. Either that, or she can spend the rest of her life in Leavenworth."

"Do what you have to do," the president said. "If we can keep Allison, I think she could be very useful, but she was installed by the previous administration. I'm not sure I've ever gained any loyalty from her, so she's expendable, as far as I'm concerned."

The video ended, then, and Allison stared at the tablet for a moment before looking up at Parker.

"He knew this was coming? That they were going to take me down?"

Parker nodded. "Yes. I've been hammering him to try to put a stop to the whole thing, but that was just to keep him from finding out that we know he's involved. Allison, I know this is going to be hard to accept, but you're going to have to order Noah to assassinate the President of the United States."

Allison looked him in the eye. "I can handle it," she said.

Chapter TWELVE

M olly had just walked into her apartment when her phone rang, and she glanced at the display to see that it was Parker calling. She tried to answer quickly but missed the button and had to hit it a second time.

"Doctor Parker? It's Molly," she said.

"Hey, cutie," Parker said. "How would you feel about keeping an old man company for dinner?"

Molly jerked the phone away from her ear and looked at it for a second, then put it back. "Sounds good to me," she said. "Want me to meet you somewhere?"

"Yeah," Parker said. "How about the Sagebrush Saloon? I hear a lot of good things about that place."

The Sagebrush Saloon, Molly knew, was Noah's favorite restaurant, but she'd never heard of Parker ever going there.

"Cool," she said. "It'll take me about half an hour, is that okay?"

"Perfect," the old man said. "I'll see you there."

Parker had never invited her—or anyone else she knew—out to dinner before, so she suspected he was being deceptive and cautious. There must be something he wanted to talk about, with no one else aware that they were having a conversation, and it wasn't hard to figure out what it would relate to.

Allison's arrest had left Molly and almost everyone else devastated. Allison was the spine of the organization, and there were fears for its survival throughout the whole community. Molly hurried into her bathroom and checked her makeup, ran a brush through her hair, and then grabbed her purse and was back out the door. She rode the elevator down to the parking garage under the building and was almost to her car when she heard the squeal of tires and looked around.

A Ford SUV pulled up beside her, and the back door opened. Her heart began to race for a moment, not sure what was happening, but then she saw Allison grinning at her from inside the car.

"Get in," Allison said, and Molly obeyed without hesitation. She shut the door behind herself and turned to look at her boss.

"Oh, my gosh," she said. "You're out already? What's going on?"

"Nope," Allison said, "I'm still sitting in jail in Denver. You're imagining this, it isn't real. You're also going to imagine that you're about to get on an airplane and fly to England."

Molly's eyes went wide. "England? But I didn't pack or anything."

"Don't worry about it," Allison said. "We already arranged for luggage with a selection of clothing that will fit you to be loaded on the plane. Officially, you're calling in sick for the next few days. Doc Parker authorized you to stay home."

Molly glanced at Parker, who was driving. "Okay, is it too much to ask for somebody to tell me what's going on?"

"Not until we're in the air," Allison said. "I know this is kind of a shocker for you, but will you trust me when I say it's necessary? You and I have to go see Noah, and we need to make sure nobody knows."

Molly nodded slowly. "I trust you, you know I do. I'm just absolutely overjoyed to see you. This has all been such a shock, I'm not sure I'm not dreaming."

"It's not a dream, Molly," Allison said. "It's a freaking nightmare."

Parker went directly to the Kirtland airport, and then right onto the tarmac, where a Gulfstream G650 jet was waiting.

"The flight crew has no idea who you are," he said as he pulled up next to the stairs. He picked up a package from the console between the front seats and handed it to Allison. "Passports, cell phones, and ID kits for both of you," he said. "Allison, your name is Judy Walker; Molly, you're her daughter, Emily. The two of you are going to London on a shopping spree, because you're rich and can damn well afford to. The plane came from a leasing company, arranged through one of our dummy corporations that the GAO doesn't know about. When you get to London, call our station chief there. He'll make arrangements to get you to Noah. Call Holloway from a secure line when you're ready to come back, but they can only cover you being gone for four days. All the details are in your kits. Now, go. It's one a.m. in London, now, and the flight will last about nine and a half hours, so you will get there around ten. I don't know how long it will take you to get to Noah from there, but we don't have any time to waste."

Allison opened the package and looked at the contents, then handed one of the wallets to Molly.

"Leave your purse with Parker," Allison said, dropping the cell phone Holloway had given her on the seat. "Anything we need, we'll get when we get to London. Let's go."

With her eyes wide, Molly got out of the car and waited for Allison before starting up the stairs into the airplane. It was a luxury flight, and the two of them took seats that were facing each other as the flight attendant closed the hatch and made sure they had their seatbelts fastened. They made small talk with the flight attendant until she told them that it was time for takeoff, and the plane was in the air only ten minutes later.

Once they reached cruising altitude, the flight attendant brought them dinner and then disappeared toward the front of the aircraft. Molly and Allison, both of whom were hungry, dug in and ate the microwave meals, and then Allison began to explain to Molly what was happening.

An hour and a half later, Molly looked up at Allison and smiled. "I think I have the beginnings of a plan," she said.

"You damn well better," Allison said. "That's why you're coming with me. You and I are probably the only two people in the world

Noah trusts outside of his team, and we've got to impress on him just how important this is. Unfortunately, we've also got to explain that he's going to be completely on his own. We will not be able to provide support for this mission, so he's going to have to rely on his own wits, develop his own resources. I'm confident he can do it, but a part of me feels like we're throwing him to the wolves."

Molly smiled, but there was something wicked about it. "Yeah, well, who better to throw to the wolves than another wolf?"

NOAH AWOKE WHEN THE sun came through the window that morning, and managed to slip out of bed without waking Sarah. He went into the bathroom and took care of morning necessities, then got into the shower. He was running low on clean clothes, and most of what he had was designed for the desert; as he dressed, he decided it was time for them all to go shopping.

He sat in a chair and waited for Sarah to wake up, reading a book he had found on one of the many bookshelves in the Great Hall. It was a story about the struggles of an American cattle farmer who inherited a sheep farm in England, and the difficulties he had in adjusting to the life of an English country gentleman. Noah made careful note of some of the mistakes the character made, hoping to avoid making similar ones.

It was almost nine by the time he heard the sounds of some of the others moving around, so he decided it was time for Sarah to get up. He sat on the bed beside her and kissed her gently, and her face broke into a smile even before her eyes were fully open.

"Good morning," she said. "Mmm, that was a nice way to wake up."

"I think we need to go do some shopping in London, today. None of us really have the kind of clothes we're going to need for living here, and it might be nice to just act like tourists."

"Yeah, that would be great," she said. "What time is it?"

"It's almost nine," Noah said. "I heard Marco talking to Neil a moment ago, so I'm assuming they are all up. Why don't you grab a shower and meet us all down in the dining room for breakfast?"

"Okay, babe," Sarah said. "I'll be there in half an hour or so." She threw off the covers and climbed out of bed, while Noah slipped out the door into the hallway. He tapped on Neil's door. Neil opened the door, while Jenny and Marco were sitting on their sofa.

"Good," Neil said, "you're up. We were just thinking about going down to ask about breakfast."

"That's what I had in mind," Noah said. "Penny will be down in just a bit, she wanted to get a shower."

"Excellent," Jenny said. "These two guys have been trying to convince me they're starving to death, and I'll confess to being a little hungry, myself."

The four of them walked down the stairs, and Thomas suddenly appeared at the bottom.

"Good morning, sir," he said, addressing Noah. "Will you be having breakfast this morning?"

"Unless it's already too late," Noah said with a grin. "I have forgotten to ask what time breakfast would be ready."

"Sir, this is your home," Thomas said. "Breakfast will be served whenever you wish to have it. If you would like, there is both coffee and tea available. If you'll tell me which you prefer, I shall have it brought to the dining room."

They all chose coffee, and then went to the dining room. Thomas appeared moments later with a tray holding four cups and a large carafe, plus sugar and cream. He made a slight ceremony out of pouring the coffee and setting a cup before each of them.

"Beatrice asks if you have a preference for breakfast," he said. "She had a thought of preparing bubble and squeak with poached eggs."

"Bubble and squeak?" Jenny asked. "What is that?"

"Leftover vegetables from last night's roast, fried in shallow oil. In America, you would almost certainly call it hash. It is a staple of the British breakfast repertoire. Beatrice makes some of the best I have ever tasted, topping it with poached eggs."

Marco grinned. "You had me at poached eggs," he said. "Why don't we give it a try?"

The rest agreed, and Thomas disappeared into the kitchen again. Noah, Marco, Neil, and Jenny drank their coffee and chatted amongst themselves until Sarah came down. She had decided her hair was clean enough for another day, so the shower took less time than she had expected. Thomas appeared with another cup for her coffee, while Noah and Jenny explained to her about breakfast.

"Bubble and squeak?" she asked. "It's actually called bubble and squeak?"

"That's what the man said," Jenny said with a giggle. "He says it's pretty much like hash, back home."

Sarah shrugged. "When in Rome," she said. "So, we're going shopping today?"

"Shopping?" Jenny asked. "I'm up for some shopping."

"I think we all need clothes," Noah said. "I thought we'd take the Bentley into London and see what we can find. None of us really brought appropriate clothing for the weather here."

"Now, that's true," Jenny said. "I can definitely use a new wardrobe, and so can Penny. You guys, you probably don't care what you wear, but us girls have to think about it all the time."

"Okay, that's settled, then," Neil said. "I wanted to check out some of the electronic shops, anyway."

Beatrice and Lynn came in a moment later and began serving the breakfast. Each plate got a large pile of the bubble and squeak, which did resemble a sort of hash, and then two poached eggs were laid directly on top. As quickly as they had come, they vanished back into the kitchen and the five of them sat and stared at the plates in front of them.

"Well, I'm going to try it," Marco said. He picked up the salt and pepper shakers and applied both, then took up a fork and cut off a piece of egg so that he could scoop the mixture into his mouth. He chewed thoughtfully for a few seconds, and then his eyes smiled. He swallowed quickly and grinned, then said, "Hey, that's really good."

The rest of them dug in, and agreed that the new experience was a delightful one. Noah, Neil, and Marco even had seconds.

When breakfast was over, they all made a point of telling Beatrice how much they had enjoyed it, and then took the keys to the Bentley and headed for London.

THE PLANE TOUCHED DOWN at Heathrow airport at just before ten a.m., London time. Allison and Molly had slept through most of the flight, and were slightly groggy as they made their way down the stairs and into the terminal. Luckily, the customs line was empty at that moment, so they were able to walk straight up to the counter and present their passports.

"Do you have anything to declare?" The customs officer spoke with a German accent, but smiled politely at the two ladies.

"Nope, nothing," Allison said. "Not yet, anyway. Wait till we're headed for home, though. We're on a shopping safari."

The customs officer grinned at them, stamped their passports, and let them go. They took their bags and headed out through the front doors, then got into a taxi and asked the driver to take them to Westfield Mall.

Once they were moving, Alison took out the cell phone she got with her ID kit and scrolled through the contacts. She found the number for Leon Kendall, the station chief, and hit the button to dial.

"Leon Kendall," he answered.

"Hello, Leon," Allison said. "Seen any dragons lately?"

Kendall recognized her voice instantly. "Actually, I haven't," he said. "I understand they've become an endangered species."

Allison chuckled. "Rumors of my misfortune might be somewhat exaggerated. I happen to be in town, and need to get together with you. This is about as highly classified as you can imagine."

"Sure, no problem," Kendall said. "Where would you like to meet up?"

"We're headed toward Westfield Mall," Allison said, "and we're going to be ready for lunch when we get there. What's easy to find and easy on the stomach?"

"Westfield? Let's just meet up at Burger King. I haven't had a good American burger in months, anyway."

"Sounds good, we'll see you there." She ended the call and dropped the phone into her pocket.

The taxi got them there in fairly short order, and they carried their bags into the mall. There were lockers available, but they ended up having to rent three of them to make all the bags fit. Parker had instructed the costume department to give them both a complete tourist's wardrobe.

Once the bags were secure, they found a map and started toward the Burger King. It took them ten minutes to walk it, but there was no sign of Kendall when they arrived. There was a bench in the common way outside the restaurant, so they sat down to wait.

Fifteen minutes later, Kendall spotted them and came toward them, smiling.

"Ma'am," he said, "it is a relief to see you. What on Earth is going on back home?"

"More than I can go into, Leon," Allison said. "For now, you need to know that I am here in cover, and as far as anyone else knows, I'm still in custody back in the States. Leon, we need to get to Noah, AS-AP. Can you take us to him?"

Kendall's eyebrows went up. "Camelot? Ma'am, you know he's actually considered *persona non grata*, here, right? He's got to keep a very low profile, or the Brits will kick him out in a heartbeat."

"Don't worry, Leon, we're not going to activate him here. There's a situation I can't go into that I need to brief him about, but it won't involve any actions in the U.K."

Kendall nodded. "No problem, I just wanted to make sure you knew. To be honest, I was pretty surprised when I got the call from Jorge to set him up over here, and if it hadn't been for Catherine Potts, I might not have been able to do it. I think she twisted some arms up high, but then I got dragged in and questioned about some other things, so she took him out and got him set up for me."

Allison grinned. "I've heard a lot about her," she said. "See if you can arrange for us to meet while I'm here, would you?"

"Sure, no problem. Let's grab a bite to eat and I'll give Noah a call."

The three of them headed into the Burger King and placed their orders, then sat down to eat. As they did so, Kendall took out his phone and dialed the number that had been assigned to Noah's phone.

"Travis," Noah said when he answered.

"Hey, Travis," Kendall said. "It's Leon Kendall from the embassy. I was calling to make sure you're going to be around home today, I want to come out and see you."

"Hey, Leon," Noah said. "Actually, I'm on my way to London right now. We need to get a little shopping done, get some appropriate clothing for the local climate, stuff like that. Should I come by your office?"

"No, no. Where are you planning to do your shopping? I'm actually hanging out at Westfield Mall at the moment, and I got a couple people here who need to speak with you."

Noah muted the phone for a moment, then came back. "I'm sure we can find whatever we need at Westfield," he said. "I've got Gary checking now, and he says we'll be there in about fifteen minutes. Will that work?"

Kendall broke into a big smile. "That'll be perfect," he said. "We actually just sat down to eat at Burger King. We'll just wait here for you, okay?"

"Sounds like a plan, Leon," Noah said. "See you in just a bit."

Kendall got off the phone and smiled at Allison. "As it happens, he and his team are on the way here. They were planning on doing some shopping, and decided they can do it right here at Westfield. They should be here within the next quarter hour."

"That's a stroke of luck," Allison said. "I don't want to talk here, though. We'll go back to their place with them when they get finished with their shopping."

"Yay," Molly said.

NOAH PUT THE PHONE back into his pocket and turned to Sarah. "Something's going on," he said. "That was Leon Kendall, he's our station chief. He said he has a couple of people who need to talk to us."

"Okay," she replied. "Do you think this might be a problem?"

"This is why I hate being without a weapon," Jenny said. "Crap..."

"I didn't get the impression there was a problem," Noah said. "He was pretty cheerful. I think we're okay at the moment, but I'll confess I'm wondering what it's about."

"We'll know when we get there," Neil said. "Take the next right."

They followed the directions on Neil's GPS app, and arrived at the mall in slightly less than the fifteen minutes the app had estimated. They all climbed out of the car and walked inside, found the same map Allison had looked at earlier, and then followed the directions to Burger King.

They had actually gone inside and were looking around when Noah spotted familiar red hair and pointed toward Molly. "Look," he said, and Sarah turned to do so, and then she and Jenny both squealed and ran to throw their arms around Allison.

Chapter THIRTEEN

"**O**kay, okay, settle down," Allison said, her smile threatening to split her face. "I'm glad to see you kids, too, but there's a lot going on. Let's go do your shopping, and then we can go out to your place and get down to business."

Kendall smiled and got to his feet. "Looks like you're in capable hands," he said to Allison, "so I'm going to head back to the office. I'll speak to Catherine as soon as I get a chance, and see if she can get out to see you."

"That sounds fine, Leon," she said. "Thanks for everything."

Kendall shook hands with the men and walked away, while Molly and Allison got up to go with Noah and the rest. They spent a couple of hours with Sarah, Jenny, Allison, and Molly all going into several different ladies' clothing shops, while Noah, Neil, and Marco found everything they wanted at one store. When they were all done shopping, they met up near the entrance and collected Allison and Molly's bags, then carried them out to the Bentley.

Luckily, Molly was fairly small. With her squeezed into the back seat with Neil, Marco, and Jenny, and Allison riding shotgun beside Sarah and Noah, the Bentley was a bit of a tight fit. Allison waited until they were out of the parking lot and then began giving Noah a brief explanation of what was going on.

The ride lasted slightly over forty minutes, and everyone in the back seat was ready to climb out by the time they got to Feeney Manor. Noah parked the car in the circular driveway in front of the house, then he and Marco carried the bags for Allison and Molly while Neil and the girls brought in the shopping bags.

Thomas met them at the door and tried to take the bags.

"Here, sir," he said. "Had you given me notice, I would've had the lads here. Please, sir, allow me."

Noah smiled at him. "Thomas, we've got it," he said. "You don't want us to get fat and lazy, do you? These are our friends, Judy Walker and her daughter Emily. They actually surprised us, we weren't expecting them for a week or two, but I know there are enough rooms that would put them up, right?"

"Of course, sir," Thomas said, his feathers obviously ruffled. "Will the ladies be sharing a suite?"

"Sure, that's no problem," Allison said, and Molly nodded.

"Are you sure?" Noah asked. "Trust me, this place has plenty of bedrooms."

"Well," Allison said, "if it wouldn't be a problem. No offense to Emily, but I really do tend to like my privacy."

"None taken," Molly said with a giggle. "Besides, remember when I had to stay at your place a while back? You snore, loudly."

"Yeah? Let me tell you about that lasagna you made," Allison shot back, grinning.

"This way, if you please," Thomas said. He cast another glance at the bags, but then just led the way up the stairs.

Allison and Molly took the first two suites they came to, and decided to freshen up after their long flight. It wasn't long before the rattling of the pipes in the old house made it clear that both of them were taking showers, and they both appeared a half-hour later with wet hair. It was just getting close to three o'clock by then, and Allison suggested that all seven of them might find someplace private to talk.

"In that case," Noah said, "I think we should take a walk out into the fields. There are some picnic tables set up, so we can ask Beatrice for some snacks to carry along."

Allison nodded. "That sounds like a good idea. What we're going to talk about isn't something you want your staff overhearing."

The weather was nice, so they all trooped down the stairs together. Noah and Sarah went to the kitchen and spoke to Beatrice, who was delighted to put together a large picnic basket—she actually had four of them stashed in the pantry—with sandwiches quickly prepared with roast beef and Swiss cheese, bottles of ginger beer, and a towel-wrapped, chilled bottle of wine.

"Go on with yourselves, now," she said, "and have ye some fun. There will be mutton for dinner, but we shall hold it until seven thirty, since ye'll be having a mid-afternoon, all right?"

Sarah gave her a big smile. "Thank you so much, Beatrice," she said. "Seven thirty will be perfect."

Noah picked up the huge basket and carried it out to the great hall, where everyone was waiting. Marco took it from him then, and they traipsed out the front door and toward the woods to the west. They had seen a picnic area there the day before, and Noah thought it would be perfect for a private conversation.

It took them fifteen minutes to get there, but there was virtually no chance of being overheard. The grass on the grounds had been mowed recently, and it was still another half mile or so to the woods, leaving no place for anyone to hide and listen in. Marco set the big basket on the picnic table and started passing out bottles of ginger beer as they all sat down.

"Noah, I told you about the Ascension Project, the faction that is working to undermine the Constitution," Allison said, "but I'm afraid I haven't told you nearly enough. I've held back a few things until now, because—well, frankly, because they involve the hardest orders I've ever had to give."

"I could tell you were stalling," Noah said. "I figured you'd get around to it when you felt it was the right time."

"Unfortunately, that time is now. Noah, some of these people are folks that I've known for many years, some of them I even counted as my friends. Others, let's just say I've known them by reputation and find it somewhat difficult to believe they would be involved in such a thing. We don't know for sure what the three events are that they plan to use to coerce the American people into giving up their freedoms and rights, but we do know that the first event is supposed to involve the deaths of tens of thousands of children."

Sarah and Jenny gasped, and Neil and Marco simply stared at Allison.

"Children?" Sarah asked. "They plan to kill children?"

Allison nodded. "Again, that's the only part of their plan we've gotten. What we don't know is how or where or when, except that it's supposed to happen within the next six to seven weeks. I'm sorry to say that if they manage to pull it off, they are absolutely correct about we'll be willing to accept limitations on their freedoms if it means keeping children safe. It may be the most despicable thing I've ever heard, but it would be effective."

Noah was looking her in the eye, and she could tell that he was deep in thought. She waited half a minute, then cocked her head to the side.

"Noah? What's going on in that head of yours?"

"I was thinking about how I would go about it," Noah said. "If I were going to stage an event that would kill that many children, it would have to involve schools. You say 'tens of thousands...' Do we have any idea how many tens of thousands? Are we talking twenty thousand, fifty thousand, a hundred thousand?"

"I'm afraid we don't know that. When they refer to tens of thousands of children, no matter how many it ends up being, it's far too many."

"I agree," Noah said. "I'm thinking of schools in the major cities. They could be planting bombs, but since we'd be talking about at least a fair number of schools, there would be an awful lot of risk that one of the bombs would be discovered. I suspect we ought to consider truck bombs, or something from the air. Now, if we assume an average of a thousand kids per school, then the fact that they referred to 'tens of thousands' means we are talking about twenty or more schools. The only way I can imagine being able to hit so many of them all around the same time would be with some sort of vehicle, whether it's ground or air based."

Allison stared at him. "Good Lord, Noah," she said. "How the hell could we stop something like that?"

"The only way would be to establish a major security presence at every school, and that just isn't possible. Of course, even if it were, it would only tip them off that we were aware that something like that was coming. That would probably force them to abandon their initial plan altogether, and then we would have no clue about even one of the events." He closed his eyes for a moment, then opened them again. "How many people are involved in this plot?"

Allison grimaced and shrugged. "We honestly don't know," she said. "I have a few names, but that's all."

"Then I'll start with those," Noah said. "That's why you're here, isn't it? These people have to be eliminated, and they're going to be watching you and E & E constantly. You certainly can't send any of your current teams after them, so that leaves us."

"I told you he'd figure it out," Molly said.

"Shut up, Molly. Yes, Noah, that's why I'm here. The problem is that I've got to ask you to go after these people, but I can't give you any kind of support. You're going to have to handle it all on your own, from planning to weapons acquisition to strike. Now, in theory, I can still order you to take on the mission. In reality, since I won't be able to have any contact with you, you could take this opportunity for the five of you to simply disappear, and I wouldn't blame you if you do."

"But he won't," Marco said. "None of us will, even if we wish we could."

Allison looked at him, a sad little grin on her face. "Are you sure about that? That you all feel that way, I mean?"

"I do," Sarah said. "Don't get me wrong, I would love nothing more than to just run off with Noah and just have a life of our own, but that would mean abandoning you and all the people who would be suffering if this happens. I don't think I could live with myself if I felt like I was part of the reason that these people got away with what they were doing."

"I'll just say ditto to that," Jenny said. "Besides, we all know I'd go stir crazy trying to be normal. I'm in."

Everyone looked at Neil. "Oh, hell," he said. "Where Noah goes, I go."

Noah looked at Allison. "That makes it unanimous," he said. "How much information can you give me to start with?"

"We've got the names of three senators: Richard Martin, James Lindemann, and Solomon Perkowski. There are five in the House of Representatives that we know of: David Anderson, Anthony Borden, Charlotte Willamette, Bob Majors, and Lisa Vincenzo. At the NSA, there's Herschel Robinette, Ronald Pickering, Wilbur Benton, Harriet Morgenstern, and Tom Lewiston. At DHS, you got Edgar Mikesell, Simon Scheiber, Antonio Romano, and we're not certain, but possibly Armando Rodriguez." She waited for a moment as Noah committed the list to memory. "And there's one more," she said. "Noah, Jonathan Andrews is at the very tip of this thing. According to Solomon Perkowski, the whole damn thing may have been his idea."

Jenny's mouth fell open. "President Andrews? Allison, forgive me, but are you sure?"

"I'm afraid so," Allison said. "Doc Parker was given a video taken by someone working in deep cover inside the organization. It showed the president, Lewiston, and Perkowski having what they thought was a completely private conversation, and I've seen it. Their plan is to put Andrews in charge of what they call the Ascension Council. From what I've been told, that refers to the fifty people who will control all of the United States, but I don't think it had anything to do with how many states there are, or anything like that. The Ascension Council in the U.S. will partner up with a similar council that will be set up in Russia shortly after this one is in place. With the combined military forces of the United States and Russia under their control, it's a pretty safe bet that they can handle anybody else. They even have plans to replace the United Nations, and let Andrews and somebody named Petrokov serve as joint chairmen of some sort of Supreme Council that will replace the UN and rule the entire world."

Noah sat quietly for a moment and looked at her, then turned to Molly. "How do you see this playing out?"

Molly's face twisted in a grimace of her own. "An organization like this, when we don't have a full roster, is going to be very hard to put down. Unfortunately, you need to get more intelligence from the very people you also need to target. It's going to be a nightmare, trying to get them to tell you who else is involved when they know they're going to die. You can go at it from any of three different directions."

She pointed at her index finger. "First, you could take out the president. He has enough people who hate his guts that it would not be obvious that it was connected to this particular group. The problem is that any organization with any brains involved is going to have somebody ready to step in if the man they've chosen to lead is suddenly eliminated."

She touched her middle finger. "Second, you can abduct a few of the people whose names you know and try to get information out of them. I understand Jenny is particularly good at that, so you might want to let her give it a try. The only drawback is whether or not these people even know who else is involved. The fact that this organization has gone unknown for some time could indicate that they are using a cell system, or some other way of keeping identities under wraps."

She touched her ring finger. "Third, and the one I would least recommend, you can just start killing them off. We've got how many names? Nineteen, altogether? If half of them were to suddenly come up dead, there is a possibility the rest of them would scatter, drop the whole thing and disappear. That's not likely, but it could happen. I'd think it more likely that they would close up their ranks and even step up their agenda."

Once again, Noah sat quietly for almost half a minute, then turned and looked at Allison.

"I'll do it," he said. "Naturally, I'm going to need the whole team and Jenny. I'm also going to need money, and a lot of it. I don't want to tie any of this to the identities we're using now, so that means I can't use any of these credit cards. I'm going to have to find another source of financing. Any ideas?"

Allison chewed on her bottom lip for a moment, then shook her head. "I'm at a loss," she said. "We've got accounts all over the world, but getting you access to the kind of money you're talking about would be very difficult to do without leaving some kind of a trail. Hell, I don't know, rob a bank?"

"That's exactly what I've got in mind," Noah said. "Since we need to do this in such a way that it can't be traced back to you, we may have to resort to the kind of secretive and criminal tactics an actual terrorist organization would use. One of the things they do is rob banks."

Sarah's eyes were wide, and Neil was staring at Noah in shock.

"We're gonna rob a bank?" Neil asked. "You got a particular one in mind?"

"No, not yet," Noah said, "and only if there's no other way. We'll need to do a bit of research, but we can't take too long before we get started. We're also going to need other identities, passports, everything. We're going to need weapons, transportation, all the things that the agency normally provides, but we've got to do it on our own.

That's going to take millions of dollars, and the easiest way to get it might be to steal it."

Neil rolled his eyes. "Fine, fine," he said. "I'll start doing some research when we get back to the house. There's bound to be a bank around here somewhere we can rob."

"No, not here," Noah said. "We promised the Queen we wouldn't cause any problems in England, so we can't do anything here. It needs to be in the U.S., but that gives us the problem of how to get there. Once again, I don't want to compromise these identities. If this operation fails, we may need them just to survive."

"I might be able to help with IDs," Allison said. "Every station chief has a list of solid identities that can be used for any of our agents that might need one in a hurry. Leon Kendall, back in London, he might be able to put together some that can be burned. You could use them to get into the States again, but after that, you might be on your own. I couldn't guarantee they would get you back out."

"I'd rather find another way, something not connected to E & E or the U.S., but I'll use them if we don't have another choice. Neil, you start working on finding us a bank to hit. We do this the same way any other bank robbers would, a blitz attack that lets us get in and out in a hurry. We want the biggest possible yield with the lowest possible risk."

Neil nodded. "Okay, I'll see what I can figure out. What about weapons and such?"

Noah shrugged. "We steal them. Same for the getaway car, we steal it. The idea is to make it look like this is nothing but a run-of-the-mill crime, rather than a way to finance a series of high-profile assassinations." He turned to Allison. "The hardest one is going to be the president. It's nearly impossible to get close enough for a shot, and nowadays they clear an area so big that even the best sniper wouldn't have a chance. It's possible the only way to get him is going to involve a lot of collateral damage."

"Do you think I haven't thought about that?" Allison asked. "Noah, if there was any other way, I'd never ask you to do this. The simple fact of the matter is that you are the only possible team that could hope to pull this off. I just don't want to see you get yourselves killed in the process."

"I have no intention of dying," Noah said, "nor of letting anything happen to my team. We'll do this because it has to be done, but I'm not planning to lose anybody over it."

"I'm glad to hear that," Allison said. "Believe it or not, I'm rather fond of all of you, and that's on a personal level. Professionally, I need you all because you're the best. I don't want anything happening to you, either."

"All right," Noah said. "We know what we have to do. We'll let Neil do his thing for a while, and talk again tomorrow. For tonight, we're just a bunch of old friends having fun together. Who wants a sandwich?"

"Geez, I thought you'd never ask," Neil said.

Chapter FOURTEEN

L eon Kendall got back to his office at the embassy and finished his work day, completely forgetting the request Allison had made until it was after three o'clock. As soon as he remembered, he put in a call to Catherine Potts. Since she was E & E's liaison to British intelligence, he had a special number that allowed him to reach her without going through MI6. It forwarded through several different VoIP servers and then finally rang through to her cell phone.

"Catherine Potts," she said as she answered.

"Hey, sexy," Kendall said. "How's my favorite British girl?"

"Grumpy and tired," Catherine said. "There is something about you bloody Yanks that keeps me from getting any sleep at night, do you know that?"

Kendall chuckled. "That's because you lay there fantasizing about all the wonderful things I want to do to you."

"Oh, good Lord, what are you smoking? Seems to be a lot better than the stuff I get." She giggled like a teenage girl. "So, what is it you want this time, Leon?"

"Actually, I've got a bit of news. Are you secure on your end?"

There was a beep in the line. "All set," Catherine said. "What's the gossip?"

"The Dragon Lady is in town. It's pretty hush-hush, since she's still supposedly in custody, but I met with her at lunchtime. She was on her way out to see your friend from yesterday, but he happened to be coming into town and picked her up. She said she'd like to meet you while she's here."

There was silence on the line for several seconds.

"Catherine? Are you there?"

"I'm here," Catherine said. "I'm trying to figure out if you're pulling a prank. I just saw an intelligence report thirty minutes ago that said she was being held in some sort of secure facility in Denver. According to our sources, she's still there."

"That's what I'm trying to tell you," Kendall said. "She's doing something ultra-secret, actually gone into cover herself. I don't blame you for being skeptical, if I hadn't seen her, I wouldn't believe it either."

"And she's out at Feeney?"

"Yep. Your buddy and his friends picked her up at Westfield Mall. They were coming in to do some shopping and just happened to be at the right place at the right time. Saved me a drive out to Guildford, anyway."

"If she's here when every source we've got says she's locked up, there has to be something pretty big going on. Leon, thank you. I think it's time she and I got to know one another. Gotta go, luv, I'll call you later."

Catherine ended the call and stared at her cell phone for a few seconds. Her thumb hovered over a button for a moment, but then she simply clicked it back onto her belt. She got up from her desk and walked out of her office, then left the building and went to the car park. She climbed into her BMW and started it up, and started working her way towards Guildford.

Once she was out of the city, she opened the car up and let it run. She knew the road well enough that she didn't worry about getting pulled over, and the speedometer was bouncing on a hundred and forty km/h for most of the way. She made it to Guildford in under thirty minutes, then turned on to Tuppence Lane, the road that led to Feeney Manor.

She turned into the kilometer-long drive and followed it up to the house, parking behind the Bentley sedan she had seen the day before. She got out of the car and started toward the front steps, but then she heard a voice calling her name and turned to look for the source.

Noah and his team were walking toward the house from out in the fields, and she saw a couple of extra women with them. Since they were coming her way, she simply stood and waited for them. It was only a matter of a minute or so before they were close enough for her to get a good look at the newcomers, and she recognized Allison from the photos she had seen just an hour earlier.

She walked toward them, intercepting them about a hundred meters from the house.

"Bob's your bloody uncle," she said. "You really are here, aren't you? Oh, forgive me, I'm Catherine Potts." She held out her hand, and Allison grasped it firmly.

"It's a pleasure to meet you," Allison said with a smile. "I've seen your name in several reports, and I'm glad to have the opportunity at last to thank you in person for all that you do for us."

"Ha, there's no need to thank me," Catherine said. "I mean, you certainly pay me well enough, and it's my job. I just got a call from Leon, who told me you were here and wanted to meet up. Since my other job happens to think you're currently sitting in some kind of secret prison, I wanted to come and see for myself."

"I'm here on a very secret mission," Allison said, "and, while I realize it might put you in a delicate position, I'm hoping you will keep my presence between us. I can assure you that I will only be here for a short time, and there will be no official activities of any kind involved. I'm simply here to brief our mutual friend on a situation going on back home."

Catherine looked her in the eye. "Does that situation pose any threat to the U.K.?"

"I'm afraid that it will, if we are unsuccessful in stopping it. Unfortunately, I can't give you any of the details. This thing is so big that we do not dare let the people involved find out that we know about them. While I consider you utterly trustworthy, I can't always say the same about your other employers."

Catherine chewed the inside of her cheek for a moment. "And if you are successful?"

"If we succeed, then the threat will be eliminated. I will tell you this: if it becomes obvious that we are going to fail, I will see to it that you are informed of the situation. That's the best I can offer."

Catherine nodded. "Very well," she said. "I know your reputation well enough to know that whatever you tell me will be the truth. I can accept that, for now." She glanced over her shoulder toward the house, where Thomas was suddenly standing on the porch, and waved at him. She turned back to Allison. "The butler thinks I'm the estate agent that arranged the sale of the place," she said. "I gave him the name of Catherine Beasley, so calling me Catherine in his presence is perfectly fine. Shall we go inside and get to know one another?"

"I'd like that," Allison said with a grin. "By the way, I'm Judy Walker. The girl with the lovely red hair is my daughter, Emily. We are so pleased to make your acquaintance."

Catherine looked at Molly closely, then grinned. "Judy, Emily, so good to meet you."

Noah, who had been watching the entire exchange, pointed toward the house and smiled. "Come on, let's go inside. The way people are showing up today, we might end up with a party before the night's over."

"Party?" Allison asked. "Is there a bar in the joint?"

Thomas, who overheard the question, bowed slightly in her direction. "Why, yes, dear lady," he said. "There is a fully stocked bar in the Great Hall. If you would fancy a cocktail, I am rather skilled at mixing them."

"Oh, I like this guy," Allison said. "Can you make me a margarita?"

Thomas smiled. "It will be my pleasure," he said. He turned and walked toward the great hall, and they all followed. Marco carried the picnic basket back to the kitchen while the rest of them were getting drinks of their own and making themselves comfortable.

Noah was delighted with the beer that Thomas produced for him, while Sarah and Jenny decided to join Allison and Molly with margaritas. Neil and Marco, like Noah, had settled for beer, though Neil thought it was a bit too bitter and cloudy.

"I've got to admit," Allison said, "you got quite a place here, Travis. It's absolutely beautiful. If I ever got the chance to retire, I'd love to have something like this to call home."

"We like it," Noah said. "Of course, we're still getting used to it. We sort of bought it sight unseen, so it's been a bit of an adventure."

Allison grinned. "I'll bet," she said.

"I get a kick out of the armor," Molly said. "Any idea who used to live here? I mean, back when there were knights and jousting and all that stuff?"

"I don't know," Noah said. "Thomas?"

"The house was originally built between 1070 and 1072, when it was the home of Lord Tristan Percy, a loyal servant of William the Conqueror. At that time, there were no knights as we think of them; knights were merely lawyers who fought in battle, and not considered to be any part of the nobility. According to legend, Lord Tristan actually wore the armor you see beside the main door into the great Hall when he went into battle. There are three cuts in the armor, and it is believed that they were the ones which finally ended his life."

"He died in battle?" Catherine asked. She had been sitting quietly, just enjoying the company.

"Indeed. I'm afraid I don't know which battle it might have been, but there were many during the time in which he lived."

Thomas, it turned out, was a wealth of information about the history of the house. He told them about several of its previous owners, recited the story of how half of the house had been burned down in 1559, explained the differences in architecture between the remnants of the original house and the restored portions, and even showed them the entrance to a tunnel that was dug under the house during World War Two, when children from several European countries that were under siege by the Nazis were smuggled into England and hidden until they could be adopted by local citizens. Feeney Manor had taken in more than a dozen children from Austria and Czechoslovakia during that time, and some of them—now elderly—still lived around the region.

"This has been fascinating," Allison said after a couple of hours, "but I'm afraid I'm getting a bit hungry. I'm also afraid that I should not have been drinking on an empty stomach. Travis, would you mind helping me up out of this chair?"

Noah grinned and held out a hand. Allison grabbed it and let him pull her up from the chair, then held onto him for a moment while she got her balance. Sarah held up a hand of her own, and Noah took it to help her get up, as well. Marco ended up helping Catherine get to her feet, and she was suddenly full of giggles.

"I do believe," she said, "that I have gotten just a little bit drunk. Thomas, you naughty boy, did you double up on the tequila?"

"No, ma'am," Thomas said. "I made them the same way I always do."

"She's right," Sarah said, pointing at Catherine. "Don't ever let me drink Thomas' margaritas again, please? Ooh, you might have to carry me to the dining room."

Molly, who had already put away three margaritas, shook her head. She got up from her chair on her own and ended up helping Allison walk to the dining room. "You girls just don't know how to hold your liquor," she said. "Didn't you ever go to college? That's the main thing you learn in college, how to get drunk without falling down."

"My parents sent me to a Catholic college," Allison said. "No booze. Seriously, there was no booze."

"What's a college?" Sarah asked, and then she broke up in hysterical laughter.

"I did plenty of drinking at uni," Catherine said. "My problem is that I haven't done much since then, I'm afraid." She was leaning on Marco, clinging to his arm. "Goodness, you're a strong lad, aren't you?"

They made it to the dining room and managed to get seated, and Noah suggested that they all needed coffee. Surprisingly, there was a fresh pot already on and Thomas returned with a tray loaded with cups only a moment later. He poured coffee for each of them and let them get started on it as Beatrice and Lynn brought out their dinner.

Dinner turned out to be leg of lamb, rather than mutton, with peas, carrots, and the inevitable potatoes. They continued chatting as they ate, and hints of sobriety began to slowly appear among them. By the time they were finished eating, they were all speaking relatively coherently and Sarah had stopped erupting into giggles.

After dinner, they sat at the table for another hour. They had given up the idea of drinking any more alcohol, but Thomas produced bottles of cold Coca-Cola that made them all smile.

By that time, however, they were all beginning to feel tired, and especially Allison and Molly. At Noah's suggestion, they all decided to retire for the evening and made their way up the stairs. They all said their good nights in the hallway and disappeared into their respective rooms. Catherine took the one that was still unoccupied.

In their bedroom, Sarah looked up at Noah and gave him a sad smile. "Well, this was nice while it lasted," she said. "I should have known we wouldn't be able to hold onto it for long."

"I don't plan on giving it up," Noah said. "I had a brief word with Allison this evening, and she's agreed to let us keep this place. The way it's set up, it belongs to this Internet company that's actually one of the businesses she started when she built Neverland. It was never listed as being part of the organization, so it's been sitting on the back burner until it was needed. According to all the paperwork on it, we and our friends started it a few years ago and it just recently started making a lot of money. As far as the government knows, there's no connection. We'll be Travis and Penny Lightner from now on, whenever we choose to use those identities. Same for Neil, Jenny, and Marco, the new identities are solid. We can come back here anytime we want to, as long as we don't ever let it get connected to who we really are."

Sarah just looked at him for a moment, then the tears started running down her cheeks. "You know how wonderful it would be," she began, "to see children running around this place?"

"Maybe we'll get to see that, someday."

"Do you honestly think we're going to live through this? Noah, you're talking about assassinating the President of the United States. I don't know how in the world you expect to accomplish that and still manage to escape alive."

"I don't either, at the moment," Noah said. "But I will."

They got undressed and got into bed. A moment later, Sarah began giggling again.

DONALD JEFFERSON WAS sitting in his office, a few doors down the hall from Allison's, when his cell phone rang. He picked it up and glanced at the display, then answered it and put it to his ear.

"Jefferson," he said.

"How are things going over there?" The voice that came through the line was familiar, and Jefferson smiled. He and Senator Perkins had been friends for a long time.

"Bit of a nightmare, if you want to know the truth," he said. "How's it going up on the hill?"

"Let's just say I'm beginning to wish I had never gone into politics. Have you heard anything about Allison lately?"

"Nothing. We don't know where she's at, or what might be happening with her. All we know is that we've got FBI agents running loose all over the place, and doing their best to get us to make some kind of mistake they can use against us."

"Well, don't fall for it. I don't know exactly what's going on, Donald, but there are some screwy things going on back here in D.C. To be perfectly honest, I don't know who to trust. Some of my colleagues are acting like they're expecting to hit the jackpot any day, and others are scared to even ask the usual questions. Right now, all I know is that it's important to some people that your boss lady ends up under one of the oversight committees, and I know that's not going to go over well in Neverland."

"You can bet on that," Jefferson said. "She will resign before she let that happen. The whole reason the president agreed to give her autonomy was so that no one could ever use E & E for personal or political gain. As long as only she can make the determination of whether a sanction will be authorized, and then only based on all of the facts she can gather, then it's a viable tool. If it comes under any kind of political control, you're going to end up with the kind of fiascoes they have at the CIA, all the time."

"I know it," Perkins said. "If you get the chance to talk to her, you tell her to hang in there and don't give in. Some of us back here still believe in what she does, and we don't think much of the idea of anyone being able to push her buttons."

"Yeah, well," Jefferson said, "we feel the same way out here. Let me know if you find out anything, will you?"

"You know it," Perkins replied. "And you do the same. Talk to you later."

Jefferson cut the call and leaned back, then reached out and picked up his desk phone. He dialed Molly's number and waited, but got her voicemail message.

"Hey, Molly," he said, "it's Don Jefferson. Give me a call when you get a chance, please."

He hung up the phone and sat for a moment, then picked it up again. He dialed Parker, who answered on the second ring.

"Parker," the old man said.

"It's Don. Just wondered if you'd heard anything."

"Not a word," Parker said. "Any news on your end?"

"Bill Perkins called a little while ago. He said there's some strange stuff going on up on Capitol Hill. According to him, some of his colleagues are acting pretty strange, while others seem scared. You heard any ripples?"

Parker hesitated for a moment. "Only thing I've heard is that some of the stuffed shirts up there think they ought to be riding herd on top of us."

"Yeah, that's pretty much what Bill said. You don't think Allison will cave in, do you?"

"You know, normally I would say no," Parker said. "Under the circumstances, however, she might have no choice. It may be the only way to keep us all together until this thing gets completely settled."

"Damn," Jefferson said. "That would not be good. What about Camelot? What do you think is going to happen there?"

"Well, he can't come back while this crap is going on. He and his team have been given new identities and somewhere to stay off the radar for now, but it may become a permanent situation. I suppose there are worse ways to get out of this business."

Jefferson laughed, but it was filled with irony. "Yeah, you could say that. What worries me is Cinderella. Do you honestly think there's any chance she could retire?"

"No. Allison has managed to harness her need for the kill, but if she's taken out of this line of work, she's going to go full-blown serial killer on us. The best we can hope for is that Noah will be able to keep her from harming anyone who's innocent."

There was a sigh on the line. "Well, if she does, I'm sure he would deal with it. I just hate to see him put in that position. You know that she and Neil Blessing are something of an item, right?"

"Yes, I know. The kid is good for her, so that might help, but not enough. Between him and Noah, though, they should be able to keep her focused on targets that won't draw attention to them."

Jefferson shook his head. "Maybe she'll become a vigilante," he said. "Just keep me posted. By the way, have you heard from Molly today? She didn't come in, and all I get is her voicemail on the phone."

"Did I forget to tell you? She came to see me yesterday afternoon, started feeling sick while she was here. I told her to go home and take a couple days off. It's not like we can really plan any missions at the moment, right?"

"Yeah, you're right. Okay, I was just a little worried. Call me if you hear anything, and I'll do likewise."

"You got it," Parker said. "Maybe something good will happen."

Chapter FIFTEEN

A cross the Atlantic, Neil and Jenny were cuddled up in their bed. The past few days had taken their toll on the young couple, and they were trying to relax.

"So," Jenny asked, a playful tone in her voice, "how does it feel to be married?"

"It doesn't really feel any different," Neil said. "We've been together so long now, I don't even really think about it anymore."

"I kinda like it," Jenny replied, giggling. "Makes me feel a little bit more—oh, I don't know, maybe a little more like everything is right, with you being in charge."

Neil was quiet for a couple of seconds, then grunted. "Yeah, I guess it does feel a little bit more complete," he said. "Do you, um, do you think about wanting it to be, like, real?"

"I won't say I haven't thought about it," Jenny replied. "We've actually talked about it a bit, remember? What do you think?"

"I think," Neil said slowly, "that every time I think about asking you, I get nervous."

Jenny raised her head and looked into his eyes. "You little romantic," she said. "You really think about proposing to me?"

Neil nodded. "Every now and then," he said. "I get nervous, though, I think because I'm never sure what you might say."

"Well," Jenny said, "the only thing I can tell you is that, the next time you really think about it, you might want to give it a try." She leaned up and kissed him on the nose. "But for right now, I want you to shut up and kiss me."

"Excuse me? I believe that's my line."

DESPITE THE FACT THAT they had separate rooms, Molly was sitting in Allison's room with her. They were both still mildly feeling the effects of the margaritas, but sobriety was well on the way.

"What do you think?" Allison said. "About this whole idea of robbing banks to finance his operation?"

"Noah's right," Molly said, shrugging. "It's going to take an awful lot of money, and without the agency to bankroll him, it's probably the only real option. What's got you so worried about it?"

"Well, that should be obvious," Allison said. "I'm worried about him getting himself killed or caught. If he gets arrested, it's not going to be very long before somebody figures out who he is. That would be quite a disaster, from the standpoint of the mission and all of the personal lives involved."

"If Noah decides to rob a bank," Molly said, "you can bet on two things. Number one, he won't get caught, and number two, nobody will get hurt. He may be the most capable killer you've ever known, but he has a moral code that is all his own. He's not going to hurt anyone that he doesn't absolutely have to, and he certainly wouldn't hurt someone while he was already doing something he considered wrong. No, it isn't that way; if he plans a robbery, it'll be done in such a way that nobody is going to be hurt or killed."

"But so many things can go wrong," Allison said. "An off-duty cop inside the bank at the time, somebody managing to dial nine one one on a cell phone, any number of things could go wrong and end up with crosshairs over his face."

"Wait a minute," Molly said. "You're assuming he's going to walk into a bank with a gun to try to rob it. I don't think that will happen. He'll either find a way to get into it while no one is there, or he'll come up with a plan that lets him walk away with the money he wants with no one even being aware of it. I know him, and I know how he thinks. He won't take a chance on anyone being endangered over this."

Allison looked at her for a moment. "I hope you're right," she said. "I just wish there was more I could do. I'm asking him to go after people who will have their own armed security around them, and I can't even give him any actual support."

"What kind of support do you think he needs?" Molly asked.

"Hell, he needs Wally. If anybody can come up with ways to handle this type of mission, it would be Wally Lawson."

"Well, let's think about how we can get Wally involved. Do you think you can trust him to know what the mission really is?"

"Wally? Not a doubt in my mind. The problem isn't Wally, it's how we would get whatever Noah needed to him. From what both you and Parker have told me, the FBI and NSA are watching everything that goes in or out of Neverland. I doubt we could smuggle anything out without them being aware of it."

"Now, wait a minute. You're saying Wally could come up with the kind of things that could help Noah achieve his objectives, but you don't think he could devise some way to get those things to him? Sounds to me like you're selling Wally short."

Allison looked at her for a moment, and a grin began to spread slowly across her face. "Bitch," she said. "Don't you know it's not polite to correct me, even if you're right? Good Lord, why didn't I think of that? All we've got to do is tell Wally we need an untraceable way to get equipment and supplies and money to Noah."

Molly smiled. "See? There's a reason you keep me around." She yawned. "But for now, this girl is tired. I'm going to go to my room and get some sleep, and we can tackle this more thoroughly in the morning."

"That," Allison said, "sounds like an excellent idea. I am beat."

SOLOMON PERKOWSKI WAS sitting in his office, reading through a file on his computer when a particular icon appeared on the taskbar. It meant there was a message on the secure system, but the desktop in his office was too thoroughly wired into the system for any actual security. Rather than check the special email account that way, he cleared the icon and walked out of his office.

"Liz, I'm going out for a little while. I don't have any appointments scheduled this afternoon, do I?"

His secretary looked up at him with a smile. "No, sir," she said. "This afternoon is all clear. What should I say if anyone calls looking for you?"

"Just tell them I'm busy, and I'll call them back later, tomorrow at the latest." He nodded and walked into the hallway, then went to the elevator and down to the ground floor. His car was parked in the high-rise garage next door, so he went through the side doors and through the covered walkway that connected them.

As a senator, he had a special parking slot on the ground floor. He used the remote to open his car and got into it, then started it up and drove out of the garage before taking out his phone. Checking the special email only required tapping a single icon on one of the many secondary screens, and it was only a second later that he was able to glance at the message header.

There may be a problem, it said. It was from Tony Borden in the House.

That got his attention. Things had been going along smoothly, and they didn't need any problems at this point. He turned onto a side street and pulled the car into a parking spot next to a meter that still had time on it, then opened the message.

I just tried to schedule an appointment to go see the E & E director, and Barb Holloway seemed to be stalling me. She didn't even want to tell me where they're keeping her, and that worries me, Sol. Do we hon-

estly know where she stands? If she isn't really with us, there's no telling what kind of trouble she could be starting with that Peterson woman.

Perkowski leaned his head back and thought for a moment. He'd known Barbara Holloway for at least six years, ever since she first won her seat. They were both Democrats, and had often worked together on important legislation, but he knew little or nothing about her personal ideology. From the way she talked in their meetings, she was staunchly behind the project, but that could be nothing but a smokescreen.

On the other hand, she was a diehard ally and supporter of Marvin Duckworth, and if there was one person he could trust completely, that would be Marv. They had been through too much together to even imagine that Duckworth would be disloyal, all the way back to the WMD fiasco in Iraq. It was primarily their support that had made it possible for Bush to ram his crazy military operations through, and they'd had to stand firmly together ever since in order to avoid the fallout that would come if the truth ever got out.

He sent a quick message back to Tony, telling him not to panic and that he would check things out, and then he called Duckworth on the special number.

"Solomon?" Duckworth asked, his deep voice resonating through the phone. "How have you been?"

"I'm all right, Marvin," Perkowski said. "Are you clear, can we talk for a moment?"

"Yes, certainly. I'm all alone at the moment, and this line is completely secure. What can I do for you?"

"Marv, Tony Borden says he's trying to set up a meeting with Peterson, but that Barbara Holloway is keeping him from it. Would you have any idea why she might do that?"

"Well, of course," Duckworth said. "The committee sent us out to break her, remember? One of the ways we're working on her is isolation. Right now, she doesn't talk to anybody but Barb, and all Barb is telling her is that her world has come to an end. We don't dare let her talk to anyone else, or she might figure out that we aren't nearly as powerful as we're letting on. Want me to call Tony and explain it to him?"

Perkowski grinned. "I hate to ask," he said, "but would you mind? You know Borden, he's a drama queen of the highest order. He's part of one of the biggest conspiracies the world has ever known, but he sees a traitor in every corner. It might actually help if he hears the explanation directly from you."

"Sure, I'll be glad to," Duckworth said. "In fact, maybe Barbara and I should simply take him out to dinner tonight. She and I are meeting to go over her latest talk with the Dragon Lady, anyway, it might not hurt to let Tony listen in."

"No, that is an excellent idea. Why don't you do that, and I'll check in with you tomorrow. That okay?"

"That'll be fine. Talk to you tomorrow, Sol."

Duckworth cut off the call and leaned back in his chair. He'd have to give Barbara a call shortly, so that she had time to prepare what she'd want to say to Borden. At the moment, though, he just needed to take a moment to gather his own thoughts.

NOAH WOKE WITH THE sun the next morning as usual, and knocked on the other doors to make sure everyone else got up. He gave them all time for morning necessities and showers, then hurried them all down for breakfast. Beatrice already had bacon and sausage sizzling away, and it wasn't long before they were happily involved with putting away the best breakfast they'd had in some time.

Afterward, they announced that they were going for another stroll and wandered off once again into the fields. They chose another spot this time, just to avoid developing a habit, and sat down at another picnic table to talk.

"We had something of a brainstorm," Allison said. "It was actually Molly's idea, but it's a good one. I don't care for the idea of you robbing banks, so we decided to turn the problem of supplying you with money and resources over to the one person we know of who could possibly get it done. "

"Wally?" Noah asked. "I was thinking about him this morning, while we were getting ready to come downstairs. You're right, if anyone can figure out a way, it would be him."

"Which is why I'm going to cut my visit short," Allison said. "Molly and I are flying back today, commercially if necessary. I don't want to take a chance on causing any delays, but first we need to work out a method of communication. I need to be able to contact you, but without running the risk of any of the feds crawling all over Neverland figuring out what we're doing."

"We already have a way," Neil said. "Computer games. We can use the one we set up for the Arkansas mission. Molly still has an account, so she can message me that way, and I can relay to Noah."

Allison turned to Molly. "Would it work? And would it be secure enough?"

"I'm afraid not," Molly said. "The Arkansas mission is the one the Senate committee is screaming about, remember? That game was part of the mission, and was mentioned in the report. I would just about bet they have someone monitoring it. I don't think that would be worth the risk."

"What if I had an idea?" Marco asked suddenly. "I mean, I know I'm not the brains of this operation, but it occurred to me that we might have a resource that we've been overlooking."

"Well?" Allison asked him. "Don't just sit there, spit it out."

"Catherine," Marco said. "She's our liaison with British intelligence, right? And she gets coded messages directly from you all the time, right? Are you going to tell me that you couldn't hide a message inside a message?"

Molly and Neil looked at each other, then Neil turned to Marco. "Hey, you know what? You're not quite as dumb as you look. That can work, if Catherine will agree. Molly, I'm thinking of the Brubaker code."

"Gosh, yes," Molly said. "Brubaker is perfect for this."

Neil turned back to Allison. "The Brubaker code was developed more than two hundred years ago, and it involves using multiple books as references. For instance, you count the number of words until you find one that starts with the letter you want to use. Say it's the fifty-fifth word on a page, and the letter is an E. E, then would be translated as the number fifty-five, but then you also use the page number. If it was on page twenty-seven, then it becomes twenty-seven fifty-five. Now, for the next letter, you go to a different book, turn to a page and count words until you find the one that starts with the next letter. What you'll end up with is a series of number groups. The trick is to never go beyond page 99, so that you always know that the first two digits are the page number. Therefore, the first letter can be deciphered by going to the right page and counting the words in the first book, the second letter solved the same way in the second book, the third letter in the third book, etc. After the fourth book, you go back to the first one again and choose a different page. The only thing both the sender and the recipient need to know is the titles of the four books."

"I can write a program that will encode a message," Molly said. "Neil, if we use digital books, then the computer can encode and decode even a long message in a matter of seconds. The only risk would be if someone got hold of one of our computers, but I'm sure we could hide the program."

"Yeah, that wouldn't be hard. We can get started on that right away, download some old public domain books off the Internet."

"Then all I need to do," Catherine said, "is forward the message on, right? I can do that. I'm authorized to have secure communications with E & E, under the terms of our mutual cooperation agreement."

Allison nodded. "Okay, that solves that problem. Now, we'll let Wally figure out how to get you the things you need, and you can use the Neil-Molly code program to let us know what that might be, while we use it to tell you where to pick up whatever we send." She looked around the small group and smiled. "We make a hell of a team, don't we?"

"We do," Noah said. "Molly, get that program done as quickly as you can. We need to make this happen, and we need to make it happen soon."

Neil, Jenny, and Molly got up and headed back toward the house. That left Noah, Sarah, Allison, Marco, and Catherine sitting at the picnic table. Noah looked at Sarah, then turned back to Allison.

"I want to continue our conversation from last night," he said. "I want to keep this place as our private retreat. Not just me and Sarah, but for our entire team."

Allison nodded. "I'll need to take a look at some of the logistics," she said, "but I'd have to say you've earned it."

"What kind of logistics?" Catherine asked. "Kendall used one of the dummy corporations to buy it, and to set them up with long-term income. As far as he knew, this was going to be their permanent home."

"Yes, but I need to be sure that the corporation used isn't on any of the lists the CIA has access to. The last thing we ever need is for them to figure out what this place really is. Hell, I wouldn't mind vacationing here myself, now and then."

"You'd be welcome," Noah said. "But only under cover. I don't want to risk this place ever being connected to Neverland."

"I can definitely understand that. I'll keep this Judy Walker identity under wraps, just for trips out here to visit."

"Then you might as well let Molly keep hers, too," Sarah said. "She'll want to come sometimes, I'm sure."

Allison looked at Noah. "Have you decided how you want to tackle this situation yet?"

"Yes," Noah replied. "I thought about it during the night, and I think the best move is to get them shook up as fast as I can. It won't be long before they figure out I'm going after their group, but I don't want to give them a pattern they can analyze. For that reason, I've decided that the best move is to go straight to the top, first. My first target will be the President of the United States, and I'm hoping to make it happen within the next seven days."

Chapter SIXTEEN

"Seven days? We haven't even figured out how to supply you just yet," Allison said. "Don't you think you're being a little optimistic?"

"We don't have the time to waste," Noah said. "You said the first event is supposed to happen within the next seven weeks. That gives me less than two months to take out as many of their people as I can, and the best way to shake things up is gonna be by hitting them at the top. After that, I'll go after some of the lower ranks in order to gather intel on who else might be involved."

Allison looked at him for a moment. "I can't argue with you," she said. "This time, we've got to count on you knowing what to do in making the right decisions. I think that if you're looking for someone you might consider a lower ranking member of this conspiracy, I'd look at somebody like Simon Scheiber at DHS or Herschel Robinette at NSA. My gut says the actual politicians are more likely to be up in the higher levels."

"You're probably right," Noah said. "I don't know any of these people, so I'm open to any suggestions like that. Now, you mentioned having Wally work out how to send supplies and money. Have you got any ideas in mind?"

"There are a couple things," Allison said. "Wally has a massive budget, so funneling a few million out shouldn't be hard. What about setting up a dummy corp that supplies something he uses? Neil should be able to do that, and it would leave a viable paper trail if anyone looks at his expenditures."

"That might work. We'll talk to him about it when he and Molly get done with their coding project. Are you still wanting to leave today?"

She nodded. "I think I should. Our allies say I'm covered for four days, but the sooner I get back and agree to cooperate with them, the sooner I'm back in my office and getting all this put together."

"I know it probably bothers you to think of playing along with them," Noah said, "but there isn't really any other option. I don't think they'd leave Jefferson or Parker in place if they take you out; both of them seem very loyal to you, so they wouldn't trust them to follow orders. If you capitulate, on the other hand, they're probably going to be gloating so hard that they won't consider the possibility you're working against them."

"They won't even know that I know about this mess," Allison said bitterly. "That's how it has to be, for now, but I hope I get to look at least one of the bastards in the eye when it all crashes down around them. I'd love for some of them to know I was part of their downfall, when this is over."

"They will," Sarah said. "I know my husband, and he'll make sure of it."

"I will," Noah said. He turned to Catherine. "You're sitting there bouncing back and forth like you're watching a tennis match. You can ask Allison questions, but I can't guarantee you'll get or like the answers."

Catherine nodded and turned to Allison. "I've heard enough to know that there's a massive conspiracy of some sort," she said, "and of course, I heard Noah say who his target is, and it just about made me bolt. The problem is that I have come to know and trust him, and if he says your president needs to be eliminated, I'm going to assume he knows what he's talking about. Unfortunately, this leaves me with something of a dilemma; under anything resembling normal circumstances, I would feel it necessary to report what I've heard to my superiors, but I have the strongest feeling that doing so could jeopardize the entire situation. What I need to know, and I'm sure you'll understand, is how the situation is going to affect my country. Can you answer that?"

Allison looked into her eyes for a moment, then sighed deeply. "There is a conspiracy that involves people at the highest levels of our government," she said. "This conspiracy has as its goal the complete subjugation of the American people, by eliminating the basic constitutional guarantees of liberty that our country was built on. In order to accomplish this goal, we know that they are planning three major terrorist-style events, but the only one we have any details of is the first."

"And what might that be?" Catherine asked.

"We don't know how it's going to happen," Allison replied, "but they claim it will result in the deaths of, quote, tens of thousands of children, unquote. They plan to use that event to restrict some freedoms, including particularly the freedom to travel from one place to another without permission. The idea is to turn our republic into an oligarchy, with them sitting at the top and calling the shots. President Andrews has been credited with creating this entire plan, but it involves senators, congressmen, intelligence officials and operatives, and God alone knows who else."

"Children? Good heavens, children?"

Allison nodded gravely. "I was just as shocked as you are," she said. "Unfortunately, something like that would undoubtedly be successful in getting people to relinquish certain freedoms. Noah has speculated that it will involve truck bombs hitting schools, and that might be exactly what they have in mind. If mobile bombs are used to attack and kill our children, an awful lot of the people would be supportive of any plan to curtail the freedom of travel. I'm sure it would be presented as a way to make sure such a thing could never happen again, but the end result would be the same. You have to have some sort of passport or other permit to go from one town or county to another."

"But wait a minute," Catherine said. "The U.S. has a lot of allies, including us. At some point, it should become obvious that this is nothing more than some sort of coup, and surely your allies wouldn't stand still and let it happen."

"If it were only the United States, you might have a point," Allison said. "Unfortunately, I've seen intelligence that says there is a Russian faction working to achieve the same thing over there. It's already planned for the Russian ruling council to form an alliance with the one in the States, and then to use their combined military might to force other countries to capitulate and accept their rule." She grimaced. "They spoke of installing governors in every other country. I did not hear Great Britain mentioned specifically, but I have to assume you would be included."

"Oh, we'd never stand for it," Catherine said. "The PM would go bloody ballistic."

"Are you sure?" Noah asked. "If the American and Russian ruling councils were to succeed, are you certain your prime minister wouldn't accept an appointment as governor? If you look back into history, conquering nations have a tendency to absorb the political leaders of the conquered. They sell them on the idea that it's best for them to cooperate, so they can try to protect their people to at least some degree."

"Why, he'd never..." She closed her mouth and looked at him. "Of course, if it were presented in the proper terms, he might well consider it his obligation to accept such a posting. Merciful heavens, this cannot be allowed to succeed."

"And that's why a few patriotic Americans, who happened to be invited to join this thing, are playing double agent and asking me to put Noah on this. Catherine, there is very little chance that we can actually expose this conspiracy; the people involved are too powerful, too entrenched. My supporters believe, and I agree, that the only hope is to terminate them, but that means ignoring the rule of law and due process. I have the responsibility of deciding when such actions are justified, and I'm afraid I have to say that this is one of those times."

"But, if you're talking about high-ranking officials of your government, do you honestly believe that a single operative can eliminate all of them?"

"A couple of years ago, I would've said no," Allison replied. "But that was before I met Noah. I don't know how much you actually know about him, but he has certain advantages over other assassins, even other soldiers of any kind. Noah thinks purely in terms of logic, and he seems to be able to anticipate almost every eventuality he might encounter on a mission. He has no conscience, so he never hesitates when it's time to take a shot, and he is capable of the kind of super-heroic actions that your James Bond would have trouble emulating. If it were anybody other than him that I was sending on this mission, I would probably be trying to get out of the U.S. to someplace primitive, someplace these people won't even pay attention to for years and years."

"Allison, I don't know that I can sit on this. Simply as a loyal subject of the crown, I have an obligation to report this information to my superiors."

"And I have to ask you not to do that," Allison said. "Catherine, if these people are powerful enough to have already made agreements with their counterparts in Russia, do you honestly think they don't have connections in every other country? I told you that there are intelligence officials involved. We're talking about CIA, NSA, Homeland Security, probably all of them. Your people at MI6 all have their friends and contacts in our organizations. All it would take is for one of them to ask a few questions about this, and the conspirators will know that they've been found out. At that point, it may actually become impossible for Noah to do what has to be done."

Catherine stared at her. "Bloody hell," she said. "You're asking me to betray my country."

"No, I'm not," Allison said. "What I'm asking you to do is trust Noah to prevent this from ever happening. You said you'd gotten to know him and trust him, right? That's all I'm asking you to do, trust him."

Catherine's eyes bounced from Allison to Noah and back several times. "If I agree," she asked, "can I trust you to keep me informed about the progress? I want to be certain that I'm made aware of every detail, including both successes and failures."

"I'll agree to that," Allison said. "Noah can keep you advised."

"And you understand that, should I deem it necessary, I will go to my superiors?"

"You know how important this is," Allison said. "If you decide that telling your superiors becomes necessary, then it probably means you believe we're failing anyway, so I'll agree to that, as well."

Catherine sat there in silence for a few seconds, then turned and looked at Marco.

"I don't know you so well," she said. "I know that you replaced a man who gave his life trying to protect Noah and the others. Do you support him in this?"

"I absolutely do," Marco said. "In the time I've been with him, Noah is the only person I've ever known whose judgment I trust absolutely. If he says we are taking out the president, the only question I ask is where he wants me standing at the time."

Catherine nodded and turned to look at Sarah. "I'm sure he has your support," she said. "I'm fully aware that you married the man, so I would imagine you go along with what he wants."

"Of course," Sarah said. "But it's more than just the fact that I married him. There's also the fact that I've seen him walk into the jaws of death more than once just to keep me safe. I know that he'll do whatever it takes to keep these people from doing what they want to do, especially to all those children."

Catherine pressed her lips into a thin line, and slowly shook her head. "All right," she said after a moment. "I'll keep this to myself until such time as I feel it absolutely necessary to bring my superiors in on it." She looked at Noah. "One more thing. If you get any kind of information that specifically involves the U.K., I want to know about it as soon as possible. Agreed?"

Noah glanced at Allison, who nodded. "Agreed," he said.

"Very bloody well," Catherine said. "Then I need to get back to London. I'm going to play hell coming up with an excuse for my absence, even now." She turned to Allison. "While I wish it was under better circumstances, I am glad we finally got to meet. At least now I can put a face to the name of the person I'm cursing when I have to deal with issues like this."

Allison grinned. "I'll send you a picture, so you can have it made into a dart board," she said.

"That'll do," Catherine said, but she grinned back. "As I say, I've got to go. Noah, I'll be waiting for your reports, and I'll relay messages via email as soon as I get them. Tell your lad to get me an email addy to use, one that won't set off any alarms back at my office." She got to her feet and held out a hand to Allison. "Again, I'm glad we met. I wish you all the best in this effort, and I'll do anything I can to help, of course."

"Thank you, Catherine," Allison said, shaking with her. "Don't think for a moment that I don't know how much I'm asking of you."

"Of course you do," Catherine said. "It's your job, and this is mine." She turned to Noah, Sarah, and Marco and made her goodbyes, then walked back toward the house and her car.

Noah looked at Allison. "She's tough," he said, "but she's also loyal to the Queen. I wouldn't bet that she won't go to the palace tonight and tell Elizabeth."

"I trust Queen Elizabeth a lot further than I would anyone at MI6. That old woman has been through some of the worst times in history and survived. If anyone understands the necessity of secrecy and eliminations, it would be her."

"ALL DONE," MOLLY SAID. "The books we used, *Ivanhoe, Frankenstein, Wuthering Heights,* and *Robinson Crusoe,* are all loaded digitally into the program, so it can randomize which page it wants to key a letter from."

"I do know how it works, Molly," Neil said. "In fact, I think it was my idea, wasn't it?"

She stuck her tongue out at him. "Smart ass," she said. "Okay, well, it's done. I don't suppose you have a blank CD? An extra thumb drive?"

"Sure," Neil said. He reached into his computer case and produced a USB drive. "Here you go."

Molly stuck it into the USB port on Neil's laptop and copied the program onto it, then slipped it into her pocket. "Thanks," she said. "This should be extremely difficult for anyone to figure out. Without knowing the key books in the order of rotation, it would be just about impossible."

Jenny, who had been sitting on the couch beside Neil while Molly worked, got to her feet and pulled Molly into a hug. "I'm glad you got to come along," she said. "I was actually beginning to wonder if I would ever see any of you folks again. Now, if only you could tell my guys what's going on, but I know you can't. If you happen to run into them, just tell them you're sure I would want them to go on without me if anything happens."

"I will, if I get the chance. Come on, Allison is probably getting impatient. We need to get on the way back so this plan can go into action."

The three of them walked down the stairs and found Noah, Sarah, Allison, and Marco sitting in the Great Hall. Allison looked up as they approached.

"Everything set?" she asked.

"Yes," Molly said. She patted her pocket and smiled. "The program is on Neil's computer, and I have a copy on a thumb drive. We can simply type a message and run it through the program, and it comes out the other end fully encrypted."

Allison nodded. "That's what we need," she said. "Okay, let's get our stuff. Marco is going to drive us back to the airport, and I already called Barbara to arrange a plane. It'll pick us up in a couple of hours, so we got plenty of time."

She and Molly went back upstairs to get their things, and returned only a few minutes later. They hadn't really unpacked anything, so it was mostly a matter of closing up their bags. They had started to carry them down, but two of Thomas' sons spotted them and rushed to take them. They carried them out and put them into the car, and then vanished again.

"Well, it's that time," Allison said. She pulled Sarah into a hug, then did the same with Jenny, and Molly grabbed each of them as she let go. "Noah, I'm sorry to have dumped so much on you, but there's no one else I can trust enough to handle it. My thoughts and prayers are going with you throughout this entire mission."

"I appreciate it," Noah said. "I'm sure I'll do what has to be done, but I hope to be able to gain enough information to keep this from taking too long. The last thing we need is to let them manage to pull off even one of their so-called 'events.' Even without knowing what's behind it, the thought of our own elected officials doing something like this to the American people is just beyond comprehension. They've got to be stopped, no matter what I have to do."

"I could not agree more," Allison said. "Sarah, you take care of him."

Sarah smiled. "I try, but sometimes he makes it difficult."

"Oh, honey, that's just because he's a man." She turned and nodded to Marco, who led the way out the door and opened the passenger doors of the Bentley for them. Thomas' sons had already put their bags into the trunk of the car. Once they were inside and seatbelts were fastened, he walked around and got behind the wheel and started out of the long driveway.

"This is going to be a nightmare, isn't it?" Sarah asked. "And probably a long one."

Noah nodded solemnly. "I'm pretty sure you're absolutely right," he said.

Chapter SEVENTEEN

Forty-Eight Hours Later

Senator James Lindemann and Congressman Anthony Borden stepped out of the limousine and through the door that was being held open for them. This was the first time they had ever visited the so-called Lockdown House, the ultra-secure facility where extremely dangerous, high-level prisoners could be held at government order. They had been trying for almost 3 days to get this meeting set up, and they were in no mood for any further delays. They stopped past the guards that stood in the doorway, and waited impatiently to be escorted to their destination.

"We're here to see Allison Peterson," Lindemann said. "We've been stuck in traffic for the last two hours, so we're running a little late."

"That's not a problem," said the lead guard. "She's ready to see you. If you follow me this way, I'll take you right to her."

They walked through the long hallway, and the guard finally stopped just outside one door. He produced a key and unlocked it, and held it open for the two politicians to step through.

There she was, the famous Dragon Lady. Lindemann privately thought that she didn't look nearly as ferocious as her reputation seemed to suggest.

"Allison Peterson?" Lindemann asked.

Allison looked up from where she was sitting on the bed. She did her best to look broken and contrite as she nodded.

"Yes, that's me."

The two men stepped toward the table and chairs, and Lindemann motioned for her to follow. She got slowly off the bed and walked to the table, sinking into a chair without being invited to do so.

"I understand you know why we're here," Lindemann said. "Is that correct?"

"Yes," Allison said. "It's like I told Senator Duckworth, I'm more than happy to do whatever it takes to serve my country."

"You damn well should be," Borden said. "You sure as hell have been living high on the hog off the government for the last few years."

Try as she might, Allison couldn't keep the look of disgust out of her face. "I beg your pardon," she said. "If you're under the impression I'm getting rich at my job, you need to go back and take a good look at the accounting for my department. I've got technicians in our research division who make three times what I do."

"I'm not talking about money," Borden spat out. "I'm talking about power. You got half the people in Washington scared to death of you. They all seem to think you know something about them, something that could get them into trouble. It's almost like you've been blackmailing people, trying to make sure they know not to doublecross you."

"Who the hell is afraid of me? I'm a public servant, just like everybody else. I'm just not one that they talk about on PBS."

"None of that really matters at the moment," Lindemann said, glaring at Borden. "What we need to do is determine whether or not we believe we can trust you to continue running your division. You've been enjoying an awful lot of autonomy for quite some time now, and some of us don't believe that's necessarily a good thing."

I can't give in too easily, Allison thought. *They have to work for it, or they'll never believe it's real.*

"How many times do I have to explain this? The reason the president gave me autonomy was so that no one would ever be able to order me to approve a sanction. It was so that no one could ever use the inherent power of my department to favor themselves in any way.

That includes, just so you know, even people like me. While the decision on whether to approve a sanction is mine, I have to report each and every one after it's done for review. That's to make sure that even I can't personally benefit from an assassination."

Lindemann nodded, his face condescending. "We know, we know," he said. "Allison, the problem isn't that we actually think you got anything wrong. The problem is that you have the potential power to do so. Can you understand that?"

Allison let contrition settle into her face again. "I suppose so," she said, "though I still don't know where this came from. I mean, no one ever talked about this sort of thing before, right?"

"Perhaps not in front of you," Lindemann said. "However, I can tell you that the subject has been discussed many times on Capitol Hill. There's always been the concern that, should you ever decide to use the power you have with your position, it could be quite detrimental to everyone in Washington."

"So, what is it you want me to do? Whose ass do I have to kiss?"

"Oh, good grief," Borden said. "Do you honestly expect us to believe that you're stupid? There's a new paradigm, a new kind of power in Washington. Ever since President Andrews was elected, things have been shifting, becoming more dynamic. Are you trying to tell us you haven't noticed?"

"New paradigm?" Allison turned to Lindemann. "Just where did you find this monkey? Did you steal him from an organ grinder somewhere?"

"That's it," Borden said. "I've heard enough, I cannot go along with..."

"Tony, shut up," Lindemann said. "Allison, we're here to try to get you back to work as soon as possible, but we need to know that you understand that there will be a few limitations on you in the future. From now on, any sanction requests have to come through the committee, rather than directly to you. The committee will decide which ones to pass on, and then you will continue to do the job you've been doing. Is that really going to be such a problem?"

Allison looked at him for a moment, then squared her shoulders. "You want the flat, honest to God truth? I'll be delighted to have someone else take some of the pressure. Do you know what it does to you, when you spend every day having to play God and decide who lives and who dies? It eats at you, it tears away parts of your soul. I'll be more than happy to let you people make those decisions. I take it you're just going to leave me with the logistical problems of getting my teams out there to do the job?"

"I would say that's a fair assessment," Lindemann said. "You are certainly the most qualified to decide which of your people to send out on a mission. And speaking of your people, I understand that one of your teams has gone missing. Do you know anything about that?"

"Missing? Who?" Allison demanded.

"It's the team you call Camelot," Lindemann said. "We were able to determine that they were the ones who handled the Arkansas mission, and the committee was trying to find them to answer some questions. It appears that someone in your organization tipped them off, because they have disappeared completely."

Allison rolled her eyes. "Probably because they heard I was locked up," she said. "Camelot was the worst team I had about following orders. If they got the word that I was removed from my office, then I suspect they took the opportunity to vanish. It'll be a damn long time before we ever hear from them again, and they'll probably be rogue independents. Camelot is Noah Wolf, and if he hires out as an assassin, I pity whoever he's paid to kill."

"But wouldn't you have some idea of where he would go? And what about his team? According to some information in your files, he actually got married to his driver. You've got to have some idea of where he might go if he wanted to disappear."

Allison screwed up her face in a frown. "Well," she said, "maybe. I know that he had a thing for Russia. He's been there on three different occasions, and he's made the comment several times that he would have loved to live there."

"In Russia? That would be surprising. Why do you think he would choose to live there?"

Allison grinned at him. "One of the most effective assassins who ever lived? Can you imagine a better place for him to establish himself as a freelancer? The *bratva* would go absolutely nuts over him."

"Hmm," Lindemann said. "I guess that could be a good point. Does he actually speak Russian?"

"Oh, fluently. I didn't know that until his last mission, when he actually managed to get himself arrested in order to rescue another team. He pulled off a Houdini-quality escape that time, and it was only in the after action debriefing that I heard he was speaking fluent Russian. He could probably pass himself off as a native, if he wanted to."

Lindemann frowned. "This *bratva*, what do they do with somebody like him?"

Allison's eyebrows shot up. "With an assassin? What the hell do you think they would do with him? He'd make a fortune working for them."

Lindemann stared at her for moment. "Forgive me, but you don't seem all that concerned that he might have deserted you. Is there a reason for that?"

"Did you ever read his after action reports? Do you know how many times he went off orders, did things his own way? Now, sometimes it paid off, but other times he left us with a mess we had to clean up. That Arkansas mission you mentioned; he actually brought back a teenage boy that he thought would make a good assassin. Can you imagine what I went through, trying to justify all that with the paperwork?"

"This is bullshit," Borden said. "Let's just get down to the serious business. Are you going to accept the oversight of the committee, or not?"

Allison continued looking at Lindemann. "The monkey is making noise again," she said. "Apparently he didn't hear me when I said I'd be glad to let you guys make the hard decisions for a while."

"It'll be more than a while," Borden shouted. "We're talking about a permanent..."

Allison turned and looked him in the eye. "Do you think so? Do you honestly think that any of you really have what it takes to make those decisions, day in and day out? I give it six months before you're ready to hand it all back to me again. Hell, maybe less than that." She turned back to Lindemann. "I'm willing to play ball however you want me to. My biggest concern is taking care of my teams, and I can't do that from a jail cell. Not even one as luxurious and nice as this."

Lindemann looked at her for a moment, then nodded his head. "Okay, that's good enough for me. I'll be reporting back to the committee this afternoon, and we should be able to make arrangements to get you back to your office by tomorrow morning. And don't worry, you'll be dealing mostly with me or Barbara Holloway. We'll be the co-chairs of the new oversight committee for your division."

Allison let out a sigh. "That," she said, "I can live with. Let's get this show on the road."

"PARKER," SAID DOCTOR Nathan Parker as he answered his phone that afternoon.

"Nathan, it's Barbara," Holloway said. "We got it done. She'll be back tomorrow morning, bright and early. I'm actually going to fly out and bring her home this evening."

"Thank God for small favors," Parker said. "She said anything about her trip?"

"The only thing she told me was that it was a good one," Holloway said. "That was when she called for a ride home the other day. I haven't really had the chance to speak with her since then, so why don't you meet us for dinner somewhere tonight?"

Parker glanced at the clock on his office wall. "What time are you picking her up?"

"Should be about four thirty. Why?"

"Let's meet up in Fort Morgan at about five thirty. There is a hotel with a restaurant where I-76 crosses Highway 20. We should be safe enough there, and can actually talk."

"Alright. You're buying, I don't want it showing up on my expense accounts or credit cards."

"Damn, you're a cheap bitch, aren't you? Fine, I'll buy. See you then." He ended the call and went back to the paperwork he had been doing before the phone rang.

Because Kirtland was situated in what Parker thought of as "the middle of nowhere," he left his office at four and started to drive toward Fort Morgan. The trip should only take an hour, but he wanted to allow plenty of time to shake a tail, if necessary.

Twenty minutes later, he was glad he had taken that precaution. He had spotted the black SUV before he even got out of Kirtland, and had placed a call to one of the few people he thought he could trust.

"Wally? Nate Parker. I got a situation, old buddy." He explained about the tail and asked Wally if he could think of a way to get them off him. Wally had burst into hysterical laughter, and told him to drive slowly for a while.

He done just that, cruising the curvy two-lane blacktop that led up to the interstate at just over forty-five miles per hour. The big, black SUV stayed behind, about three car lengths back, but suddenly another car appeared in the rearview mirror. It was a big, black Dodge Charger, and it rode the bumper of the SUV for a couple of miles, then suddenly swung out to pass.

And then the most amazing thing happened. The SUV suddenly started slowing down, as if it were losing power. Parker watched in the rear view mirror as it moved to the side of the road and came to a stop on the shoulder. The Charger, on the other hand, sailed around Parker without even slowing down.

Parker watched for a couple of minutes, and then his phone rang. He glanced at the display and saw that it was Wally calling and put it to his ear.

"Whatever you did seems to have worked," he said without preamble.

"Oh, of course it did," Wally said in his inimitable, high-speed way. "Some of my kids came up with a new EMS gun, so we stuck it on the back of that supercar Noah likes so much and I sent it after you. I had Rodney drive it, he's the guy who designed it. He can handle it better than anybody else, and I wanted to get to you in a hurry. All he had to do was pass the car following you, and push a button. It shot an EMF pulse out the back that fried all the electronics in the car instantly. Those poor guys can't even call for a tow truck." He burst into laughter again.

"Good work, Wally," Parker said. "I'll talk to you later on, gotta go."

With the tail off him, Parker put his foot down on the accelerator and got back out to reasonable highway speeds. He made it to the interstate only a few minutes later and took a left onto the ramp, then set the cruise control at eighty and gave the car its head.

He arrived at the restaurant at a quarter after five, and went ahead inside to get a table. There was no sign of Holloway or Allison, but he asked the waitress for a table off by itself, explaining that he was expecting to meet some business associates who needed to discuss something very private. That wasn't much of a problem, since the place was almost devoid of customers. She led him to a table in the far corner, and promised to keep everybody else away.

Barbara Holloway, Allison, and the seemingly ever present Marshal Howard arrived about twenty minutes later. Parker waved as they entered the restaurant, and they came over to join him.

"Doc," Allison said, "if you ever get your ass arrested, I hope they put you in the same jail I was in. It was damn near like taking a vacation."

"They ever come to arrest me," Parker said, "they better bring a gun, because I'm not going to go quietly. I've given this country my whole damn life, and I'm not putting up with any of their political bull crap."

Holloway grinned at him. "It's not all political," she said. "Some of it's just plain insanity. Doctor Parker, this is U.S. Marshal Glenn Howard. Glenn, Doctor Nate Parker. If he ever gets you on his couch, you are probably on your way to the loony bin. He's the psychiatrist who works with Allison at Neverland."

"Good to meet you, sir," Howard said.

"Yeah? Why?" Parker asked.

"Because he's working for us, now," Allison said. "Or he will be, in a few days. It took some shenanigans, but I arranged for him to have the security detail in the headquarters building. He's one of the few people Barbara says we can trust, and he's Duckworth's nephew. He'll be our liaison with their little fifth column inside the conspiracy."

"Long as he understands it'll probably get him killed," Parker said. "Welcome aboard the hell-bound train. Now, be quiet so the grown-ups can talk."

Howard chuckled, but said nothing. Parker turned to Allison.

"So, how's the kids?"

Allison knew exactly who he was asking about. "They're doing well," she said. "I explained the situation, and they agree that it has to be taken care of quickly. I'm leaving the planning up to them, but we were able to work out a way to communicate. I'm going to leave it up to Wally to figure out how to get them money and equipment."

"Smart move," Parker said. "If anybody can do it, he can. We just need to be kind of careful not to let him get caught. Wally is the last person we could stand to lose."

"I agree. Listen, we also ran into a little bit of an issue. You know that we have a liaison in the British intelligence services, right? Well, she's a little concerned about not letting her office in on what's happening, but I think we got her to agree not to say anything unless it becomes absolutely necessary. She's also going to help with another little issue, which is our communications. Molly and Neil came up with a code program, something they're fairly certain none of the other agencies will be able to crack. We bury messages to our kids in the dispatches that go to our liaison, and she will forward them on. Both Molly and Neil have the program, and so they won't have any trouble encoding and decoding the messages."

"Sounds like her loyalties are a bit torn," Parker said. "Is she theirs, or ours?"

Allison shrugged. "I figure we'll know the answer to that soon enough."

Chapter EIGHTEEN

Donald Jefferson was sitting in front of Allison's desk at seven thirty the next morning when she came walking through the door. He jumped to his feet and stood there, staring at her, until she finally walked over and put her arms around him.

"I understand you held everything together while I was gone," she said. "Thank you, Donald."

Jefferson held her close for a couple of seconds longer than necessary, then let go and stepped back. "Just doing what I felt I had to do," he said. "How are you? Was it bad?"

"Bad? Goodness gracious, I should get locked up like that once a year. They took me to someplace in Denver, a place where they hold high-level prisoners, I guess. I was in a cell, but it looked more like a decent hotel room. Had a TV and everything, and they had people come around two or three times a day to see if you wanted a snack or a soft drink or a book to read. Other than being locked into a room, it was like a vacation."

Jefferson's eyes were wide. "Seriously? Well, I'm glad it wasn't something awful. Did you at least miss being here?"

"More than you can imagine," Allison said. "Now, do you know what's going on?"

He shook his head. "All they told me was that you'd be coming back this morning," he said. "I gather it means we have to live under some new rules?"

"Yes. There's a new Senate committee that will handle vetting the elimination requests, and every agency has to send them up there, first. Once they decide which ones we act on, they'll hand them off to me for assignment."

Jefferson glanced at the door, which was closed, then turned back to Allison and lowered his voice.

"And what about Noah and the others? Are they off the hook, now?"

"No. In fact, I was informed last night that they've gone completely off the reservation. Team Camelot is no longer with us."

This time, Jefferson's eyebrows tried to climb over the top of his scalp. "You've got to be kidding," he said. "Noah would never..."

"Donald, I'd rather let them retire and live their lives the way they want to than ever let these people get hold of them. We're talking about politicians; do you honestly think it would be good for them to know that we had a man with absolutely no conscience or moral compunctions? We wouldn't be able to keep him, anyway, because they would decide he needed to be assigned directly to their committee. Noah would be their personal hit man, and that's the last thing I want to see happen to him."

Jefferson stared into her eyes, and his face slowly relaxed. "Yeah, I guess I can see your point," he said. "It's just hard to think of this place without Noah and his team. Hey, what about Jenny? Will she be coming back?"

"You know how she feels about Neil," Allison said. "I suspect that if he can't come back, she won't. The only thing about that that worries me is her proclivity for murder. Noah might be able to retire, go without killing anybody, but she couldn't. She probably will end up hiring out to the highest bidder, and I just hope she doesn't get herself caught."

"If she does, I would imagine Neil will end up going with her." He shook his head. "They made a hell of a team, didn't they? We're going to miss them around here."

Good Lord, Allison thought, *this is Donald Jefferson I'm talking to. Don has never been anything but loyal to me, so why am I holding back the truth instead of trusting him?*

"Yes," she said simply. "We are. Now, what's the situation around here?"

"I've been keeping the FBI at bay for the most part," he said. "They've been trying to get into our files, but the lawyers have done a good job of keeping them out of anything that's classified special. I don't know whose bright idea it was to send them in here, anyway, because they don't have what it takes to really understand what we do. The NSA guys have been a bit less demanding, but I haven't been able to keep them from getting into the stuff they want. Luckily, they seem to have come to the conclusion that we've been doing our job exactly the way we were supposed to."

"Yeah, they would," Allison said, "especially since half our requests seem to come from them. They are not going to want too much exposure on their own activities, so they're not going to push that hard on ours."

"Right," Jefferson said. "Have you spoken to Doc Parker yet? He's been screaming at everybody from the president on down, trying to get you back here."

"So I heard. Yes, I actually talked to him last night on the phone. He knows I'm back, but he doesn't think we should let our guards down just yet. I told the committee I want all these other feds out of here ASAP, and they said they'll start pulling them out today. Hopefully that will make a difference, and we can actually get back to work. I know they've got a couple of assignments they want to send down today, but I don't know who the targets are yet."

"Okay. The only teams we've got at the moment are Aladdin, Robin Hood, Hercules, and Unicorn, but they are still in West Algeria. Most of the targets have been terminated, and President Abimbola is alive and well. Unicorn is fairly certain he's gotten all of the conspirators, so we could probably pull him out at any time."

"Good, do it. The committee has already taken away the requests we had, and the four that we are getting are out of that batch. I was planning to activate Team Pegasus in a couple of months, but we may need to go ahead and put the kid out there. Have we got a team assembled for him yet?"

"No," Jefferson said. "I had prepared you a list of candidates, but you never got a chance to look it over."

"Well, with Jenny gone, we've got an experienced team that's just sitting around on their thumbs. Let's put them over in Pegasus. Call them in this afternoon, and I'll explain the situation."

"Okay, that solves that problem. Only four assignments? You think this committee is going to slow us down?"

"Probably, for a little while, anyway. To be perfectly honest, Donald, I'm glad to let somebody else make the decisions for a while. I told Anthony Borden, he's apparently on the committee, that I don't give it six months before they want to hand it all back to me. I'll be glad to take the reduction in stress for as long as I can have it."

"I can understand that," Jefferson said. "I've never understood how you could cope with it, anyway. Not so much the decisions themselves, as the sheer volume they kept hitting us with. It always seemed to me you were constantly overworking yourself."

"I don't need a nursemaid, Donald," Allison said. "I assure you, I'm a lot tougher than I look. We'll just go back to doing our jobs, and if the jobs are a little easier to do for a while, be grateful and take what we can get. That's how I'm looking at it, and you should, too."

"I guess that makes sense," Jefferson said. "Okay, I'll call in the boys from Cinderella and tell them to get here after lunch. You know they're not going to like this, right?"

Allison looked up into his eyes. "Since when has that ever bothered me?"

RANDY, DAVE, AND JIM, who had been Jenny's support team for well over a year, didn't like it even a little bit. The thought of being with the new team leader, and especially an inexperienced twenty-year-old kid, set them all off. Allison let them rant and rave for half an hour, then shut them down.

"At what point did you decide this was some kind of a damned democracy?" she asked. "Despite the fact that we wage an entirely different kind of warfare, you are all soldiers, and soldiers take orders. Your orders, gentlemen, are to support Ralph Morgan and make sure he's able to complete the missions we assigned him. Do you understand me? I assure you, you will not like the alternative if you were thinking of disobeying my orders."

It was Jim Marino who spoke up. "Ma'am, we wouldn't consider disobeying," he said. "To be honest, we're just trying to wrap our heads around this. Until just now, we still thought Jenny was going to be coming back."

"Well, we live in a new reality. I suggest you get used to it. You will report to Mr. Jackson tomorrow morning to begin physical training with your new team leader."

"Yes, ma'am," they all said. They filed out without another word.

Allison leaned back and watched them go, mentally kicking herself for being so rough on the poor guys. This wasn't their fault, after all. She just wasn't going to be able to let them know that they might someday be back with Jenny again. There was too much of a risk that one of them might slip and let it out that Jenny might be returning.

The federal agents were almost all gone, with only a few from the NSA still wandering around in Kirtland. A couple of them had been up to see her, but they were staying out of her way for the most part. Donald Jefferson let slip the opinion that that might have been the smartest thing they could do.

Once those men were gone, Allison went down to Molly's office and invited her out to the Assassin's Club for a drink. Molly accepted with a big smile, and the two of them left the office an hour before quitting time.

On the way to the club, Allison called R&D. The receptionist answered and Allison simply asked her to tell Wally that he ought to come and join them. Since it wasn't uncommon for Wally to go to the club, she didn't think anyone would pay any particular attention to it.

Wally showed up only minutes after Allison and Molly got there, and it was obvious he was ready to get down to some serious drinking. Before that could get started, though, Allison drove him onto the dance floor. He protested all the way that dancing wasn't something he had ever mastered, but she told him to shut up and dance.

It was a slow song, so she pulled herself close to him and put her arms up around his neck. Wally, who wasn't the most comfortable man around women, put his hands on her waist and held them there as he tried to follow.

"I got you out here," she whispered, "so that we could talk privately. Keep your voice down and just listen, all right? I'm going to let you in on what's going on, but you cannot tell anyone. I don't care how much you think you can trust them, you don't tell anybody what I'm about to share with you."

"Um, okay..."

"I said just listen. There is a massive conspiracy going on at the highest levels of our government, and its goal is to strip the American people of their freedoms. There is a similar conspiracy going on in Russia, right now, and the plan is for the two groups who intend to take power in both countries to work together to bring the rest of the world under their control. This conspiracy involves senators, congressmen, people from every intelligence agency, and I don't know who all else. There's a small group of people who have infiltrated who are dedicated to stopping it, but there's not much they can do on their own. As a result, they managed to smuggle me out of the jail I would be helping and sneak me off for a private meeting with Camelot."

"Camelot?" Wally asked, also whispering. "There's a rumor that he's gone AWOL."

"Of course there is, I started it. Now, shut up and listen. Camelot has Cinderella with him, along with his own team. I've given him the names of the conspirators we've been able to identify, and he's going to start taking them out one by one. The problem is that he doesn't have access to equipment or money, and I need you to figure out how we're going to supply him. It has to be done in such a way that none of the other agencies can figure it out. Now, I have a means of communication with him, so when you figure it out, I can let him know. He's going to need money, more than anything else, but there will be needs for weapons, identities, etc. Think you can handle it?"

Wally giggled. "Oh, yeah," he said softly. "How much money are we talking about? I could funnel off a few million pretty easily, set it up in accounts that he can access without anyone ever being the wiser. I've got money stashed in accounts in six different countries, because sometimes the things I need just aren't available here. I'm not trying to brag, but I can guarantee you that the GAO doesn't know about some of those accounts. One of the beauties of a true black ops budget is that nobody really pays much attention to what you do with the money."

"Good. Let's get him about ten million set up as quickly as possible, and get me the information he needs to access it. Do you have anything in Europe or the U.K.?"

"Germany, yeah," Wally said. "He doesn't have to go anywhere to get it, though. I can set it up so he can draw money from anywhere in the whole world."

"He'll probably want to access most of it from somewhere here in the U.S., but it wouldn't hurt if we could find a way to get him a hundred thousand or so in England. That's where he's based out of, for now, but that's got to be the biggest secret of all. I don't want anyone finding out he's there, because we've got him set up with a safe house."

"Okay, okay," Wally said. "I can give you some instructions to send off to Neil, and he can take any debit cards and re-encode them to access this money. We can set it so he can withdraw up to seven thousand dollars a day, using different ATMs and cards. It wouldn't take long for him to have a pretty good stock in cash, that way."

"Good. Get those instructions together and get them to me as soon as possible. That sounds like the perfect answer to that part of the problem. Now, how are we going to get weapons to him?"

Wally giggled again, and Allison thought he sounded almost like a girl. "Are you kidding? We don't. What we do is send him a list of contacts I've got, people who can supply just about any weapon. They won't have any idea who he is, but they won't really care. These are the same people that most spies buy weapons from. As long as he's got money, that's all they care about."

Allison waggled her head. "Okay, I guess that takes care of that. The question is, what do we do if he needs some of your special equipment?"

"Give me a little bit of time to think about it," Wally whispered. "I can think of ways to send stuff out, I'm sure. Can we trust any of your other teams?"

Allison hesitated. "I'm not sure," she said. "I hate to say that, but right now the only three people I trust at all on this is you, Molly, and Parker. Nobody else knows what's going on, and I'm going to keep it that way for now. I haven't even told Donald."

Wally leaned his head back and looked into her eyes. "Allie, Don Jefferson would never betray you. You know that, don't you?"

"My head knows it, Wally," she said. "Unfortunately, my gut tells me not to trust anyone other than you three."

Wally let out a sigh and shook his head. "I'll get the instructions and contacts to you first thing in the morning," he said. "Just let me know of anything else you need me to do."

Allison thanked him, and then they went back to the table with Molly. Two hours later, Molly had to help Allison get Wally into the back seat of her car, so she could drive him home.

NEIL WAITED UNTIL BREAKFAST was finished before he caught Noah alone. "Got a message from Catherine this morning," he said softly. "I ran it through the program, and it's pretty interesting. Wally sent me instructions on how to modify debit cards so that they pull money out of a special account of his. I've still got a couple from Algeria, some that I forgot to get rid of. I'm going to use those, and then we can go to any big ATMs and withdraw a couple thousand at a time. He says we'll be able to pull about seven grand a day off each card."

Noah nodded. "I've got a couple of extra cards," he said, "and so does Sarah. The more you can set up, the more we can pull out, right?"

"Yeah, that's what he said. With four cards, we could pull out twenty-eight thousand a day. That would be an easy way to put a lot of cash together, and it might come in handy."

"Yeah, it might. Anything else?"

"Oh, yeah, lots more. I have a list of names and numbers scattered throughout the U.S., the U.K., and Europe, people who can produce weapons, ID kits that will pass inspection, that sort of stuff. We're going to need people like that if we are on our own."

"Yes, I agree. In fact, we need to get started on the IDs now. I want to be on the way to the States within the next three days."

"In that case, I need to get started on the cards. We'll need money to get the ID kits, and probably a lot of it. It'll take me a couple of hours to redo the cards, so give me yours as soon as you can."

Noah went up to his room and got them immediately, then passed them off to Neil. He was sitting in his room at his computer, and he took one of the debit cards and swiped it through a slot on the side of the computer immediately. He watched the screen for a moment, then turned and handed the card back to Noah.

"There is one," he said. "I just got everything set up, so we should be good to go within just a few minutes. The only question is, where are you going to find ATMs around here?"

"I don't want to use them around here," Noah said. "If we're going to pull that much money, I want to do it in London. These kind of transactions could possibly draw some attention, but is less likely in a bigger city."

Neil nodded and went back to work. A half-hour later, they had six separate debit cards that would draw money out of Wally's hidden super black ops account.

Noah passed the cards around, and the five of them got back into the Bentley and headed off to London once more. They spent almost two hours going from bank to bank, each of them going to walk-up ATMs individually and withdrawing the limit each time. By the time they were finished, they had amassed almost 30,000 pounds sterling, more than forty thousand U.S. dollars in value.

"Okay," Noah said as they headed back to Feeney Manor. "It's time to get this show on the road."

Chapter NINETEEN

They had gotten back to the house an hour earlier and found that it was lunch time, so they happily sat down to eat. Lunch was battered fish with chips—which Marco kept referring to as French fries—and was delicious. Afterward, they headed up the stairs to get started.

"We need identities," Noah said. They were gathered in Neil and Jenny's room so the whiz kid could use his computer. "Go through the list of contacts Wally sent and find us somebody who can create the documentation we're going to need. We'll need at least three sets each; one set to travel to the United States on, a set to use while we are there, and one set to get us back out. Passports, birth certificates, driver's licenses, everything."

"I'm checking," Neil said. "There's one British guy on the list, in Cambridge. Wally says he can turn out perfect documentation within a day, but we have to go to him."

"Then he's the one we want to use. He's probably going to be secretive and skeptical; does Wally say how to approach him?"

"Yeah, there's a kind of ritual. First step is an email that has to have certain codewords. After that, a phone call where you have to have answers to certain questions, then a face-to-face. That's when he decides whether to work with you or not."

"All right," Noah said. "Let's get it started."

Neil quickly typed up the message and sent an email off to Paul Tunney, the name Wally had given him. He was sure it would be a while before he got a response, but he had his current cell phone set to notify him when an email came in.

"Okay, next item," Noah said. "I want to hit the president away from D.C. Neil, I need his itinerary for the next 7 to 10 days. I want to know what cities he's going to travel to, what events he's going to attend, all of that."

"Okay," Neil said, "that shouldn't be too hard to find, but how do you plan to get close enough to him to make the shot? Secret Service clears everything within a mile, there's no way you'll get a weapon inside that perimeter."

"There's always a way," Noah said, "but we haven't even started to formulate a plan, yet. First we need to choose the location, so we can try to figure out what the possible options of attack might be. The choice of weapon isn't something we can even consider until we've got those things sorted out."

"But there is still the problem of all that security," Neil argued. "I don't care what the options are or what weapons you plan to use, I just don't see how you can expect to get past the Secret Service. I read somewhere that the president travels with more than a thousand people, and they are all involved in making sure he is safe. It's a pretty big number of people for one guy to try to get past."

"You're overthinking it," Jenny said. "Noah doesn't have to get past a thousand people, he only has to get past one: the one standing between him and his target."

"Correct," Noah said. "And as for weapons, the most effective weapon in this particular type of political assassination is usually one you have to improvise on the scene."

"Yes, but then I refer you to the work of Frank Olson, who made a point of explaining that improvised weapons are usually used during what's known as a 'lost' assassination, when the assassin is going to die with the target. I don't know about anybody else, but I'm not ready to give you up just yet."

"I second that," Sarah said.

"And you can both relax," Noah said. "I have no intention of sacrificing myself on this mission. My orders are not to take out just one man, but an entire organization. I don't intend to die on the first phase."

"Or the second, or the third," Sarah said. "Or any other phase. No dying, it's not allowed, you got that?"

Noah looked at her, and for a second it almost looked like he started to grin. "No dying," he said. "Orders received."

Neil was working away at the computer, and suddenly turned to Noah. "Okay, the president has two events scheduled in the next ten days. Three days from now, he's going to be meeting with children at an elementary school in Pittsburgh, Pennsylvania, and then five days later, he's going to be in Dallas to address an oil convention."

"Skip the one in Pennsylvania," Noah said. "The last thing we want to do is traumatize the school kids. Can you find out where he'll be staying in Dallas?"

"Ritz-Carlton," Neil said. "Secret Service has already blocked off three floors. That's standard procedure when the president has to stay in a hotel, and they've already got the staff scheduled that will be working the hotel while he's there. Apparently, some of them didn't pass the background check and will be taking a couple of days off. The hotel is calling in people from other hotels in the area who did pass."

"Is there any way you can get a list of who will be working while he's there? Particularly the people coming from other hotels."

"That's pretty highly classified," Neil said, "so it's going to require some hacking. Give me an hour or so to find my way into the Secret Service computers." He went back to tapping on the keyboard, and Noah turned to Jenny.

"I may need to use you," he said. "What I'm hoping is that we can pull a substitution, snatch one of those people and use their ID to get into the hotel. No matter what floor they keep him on, there will be certain areas he'll have to pass through. If one or both of us can get inside, we can set up some sort of ambush."

"What have you got in mind?" Jenny asked. "A bomb?"

"Possibly, but nothing conventional. They'll have detection systems set up to catch anything that uses explosives, everything from electronic sniffers to dogs. We'd never get a conventional bomb of any kind inside that hotel, so we might need to think outside the box."

"Then you have the problem of how to set it off," Neil said. "One thing they constantly scan for is anything electronic. They even take out all of the TV sets and telephones from the rooms they use, and install their own. No outside electronics are allowed, in order to prevent bugging and such. Some of their equipment can detect even the slightest electrical field, even as small as a hearing aid battery."

"I'm not even sure a bomb is something I want to use," Noah said. "One thing I would like to do is avoid collateral damage as much as we can."

Marco shook his head. "That's going to make this a lot harder," he said. "I understand where you're coming from, but I can't imagine that there's going to be any opportunity for a surgical strike."

"Then we need to create one. Let's think about other ways to take out a target that don't involve mass destruction, something that can be executed on a particular person. Any ideas?"

"It's got to be something that can get past detection," Jenny said. "A blowgun? Like some of the African tribes used to use, with poison darts?"

"That actually could be a possibility," Noah said. "We have to look into what kind of poison would be most effective, something that couldn't be quickly counteracted. It could also be propelled by compressed air, rather than just by breath."

"Hey, what about an air gun?" Marco asked. "Maybe something made of plastic or ceramic, so it won't set off a metal detector?"

"Another possibility. Instead of a trigger, it could use a simple valve. It would have to have an air tank built into it, one that can hold some pretty serious pressure."

"I'm thinking of poisons," Jenny said, "and a thought just occurred to me. Did I read somewhere that the president is deathly allergic to something?"

Neil glanced at her, then started tapping on the keyboard again. "Well, lookee there," he said. "It seems President Andrews is highly allergic to bee stings. He was stung once a few years ago and almost died. More than a couple of stings, and even atropine would not work."

Noah looked at Neil for a long moment. "Find out where I can get some bees," he said. "Preferably wild ones."

IT TOOK TWO DAYS TO get close enough to Paul Tunney to lock in a deal for identification, but once the man decided to take the job, he didn't waste any time. For three thousand dollars a set, he provided Noah with three complete identities for each of them less than twenty-four hours later. It required spending a few more hours hitting ATMs, but it was well worth it as far as Noah was concerned.

The following morning, they each used the first set of IDs to book tickets on an American Airlines flight from London to Dallas, and they told Thomas that they would be gone for a few days as they drove away. They drove the Bentley into London and parked it in a secure storage lot, then took three separate taxis to the airport. All three of them were on the same flight, but in different sections of the plane. In order to avoid drawing any attention, Noah sat alone, Sarah and Jenny appeared to be traveling together, and Marco and Neil sat beside each other toward the rear of the cabin.

For more than ten hours, they pretended not to know each other. It wasn't until after they had disembarked at Dallas and made it through baggage claim that they finally gathered together at the car rental counter. They drove out a little while later with a Nissan SUV, headed for a hotel that didn't have nearly the security requirements the Ritz-Carlton would have.

They arrived in the late afternoon, and despite the meals served on the plane, they were all hungry. The hotel they chose didn't have a restaurant of its own, but there were several within walking distance. They found a decent place to sit down and eat just a block away, and carefully acted like tourists as they had their dinner.

In order to keep an even lower profile, they had taken separate rooms. Noah and Sarah shared one, as did Neil and Jenny, leaving Marco all alone. When they got back to the hotel, Noah suggested they all get some sleep and be ready to start work the following morning, and the first thing to do was to send Marco and Sarah out to buy a vehicle.

"We need something big enough for all of us," Noah said. "I think the ideal vehicle at the moment would be something like a minivan."

"Sure," Marco said, "send me out to buy the perfect vehicle for a soccer mom."

"Hey," Sarah said, "I'll be with you, you can blame it on me."

They had been through so many different time zones in the last couple of weeks that all of them were exhausted. It wasn't that difficult for them to fall asleep, once they turned off the televisions, got their showers, crawled into bed, and relaxed.

The sun woke Noah at shortly after six, as it pushed enough light through the thick curtains to tickle his eyelids. He leaned over and kissed Sarah awake, then used the hotel phone to make sure the rest of them were up and out of bed. They went to the same restaurant for breakfast, and then Marco and Sarah went out car shopping. Neil,

Jenny, and Noah gathered in Noah and Sarah's room when they came back.

"Okay," Neil said, "I managed to get the layout of the Ritz, and it's really quite a building. The main entrance is on McKinney Avenue, but it's almost a certainty that the president will come in through the back. They're not going to take a chance on letting him walk right through the front doors, because controlling the environment would be too difficult. Granted, they try to set up a mile perimeter around his location, but even the Secret Service can't interfere with civil rights. Just because someone might not be fond of the president is no reason to run them out of their home or place of work, so they prefer not to let him be in the line of sight of anyone who might want to do him harm. That's why they generally bring him through the loading docks in the back of any building."

"It's not going to matter how he gets in," Noah said. "The only thing that matters to me is how I'm going to get in. Is there any way to find out what room he's going to be staying in?"

"Not the specific room number, no," Neil said. "I know that he'll be on the fourth floor, but they are very careful not to let anyone find out what room. As far as I can tell, there's absolutely no way to get that information short of being on his security staff."

"I don't think it's going to matter," Noah said. "Where did you get on the bees?"

"There is a supplier in Arlington, one of the suburbs of Dallas. Wilkerson's Honeybees in Arlington; they're located out between Dallas and Fort Worth, and they sell what they call a hive starter set. That's a queen and a couple of dozen of the female worker bees, which is what they say you need to start a hive. The worker bees are the ones that sting, especially if they think they are protecting the queen."

"That'll work," Noah said. "A couple of dozen bees ought to be plenty."

"Okay, then," Neil said. "Then you've got the issue of how you're going to get inside the Ritz, and I've actually found something that I think will solve that problem. You want to lean over here and take a look?"

Noah came close and leaned down to look at the monitor on Neil's computer, where the display showed a three-dimensional, wire frame layout of the entire building.

"There are only four actual entrances to the building," Neil said. "You got the front doors, the loading dock has three overhead doors and a walk-in door, and then there are two service entrances. Now, all of these are going to be under constant guard, naturally, but there's one other way in that I don't think anybody is going to pay any attention to." The display rotated on the screen and zoomed in on one particular section. "Do you see this square? That is an access way that was put in when the building was originally built, and it goes to an underground tunnel that was the original way utilities came in. Back in the late nineties, they completely redid the utility grid in this part of the city, and that tunnel is no longer used. That access hatch is situated behind a new high-efficiency furnace that was installed right around the same time, and you have to literally climb over the furnace to get to it. Since the hatch was welded shut, I don't think the Secret Service is going to consider it any kind of vulnerability."

"If it's welded shut," Jenny asked, "what good does it do Noah?"

"Quite a lot, actually," Neil said. "You see, the only thing they could have welded it to is the frame around it, which was put in from the tunnel side with bolts. Unbolt it, and the whole thing will lift right out. That leaves you with a thirty inch by thirty inch square hole that nobody can even see, but that isn't necessarily the best part of this little plot of mine."

Noah nodded. "Go on, I'm listening."

"Remember the new furnace? Right there on the back is the most vulnerable point of the ductwork. There's a panel that can come right off with nothing but a screwdriver, and the ductwork is big enough that they actually installed a ladder inside it. Go in through that hatch, and you're in a perfect position to get right into the ductwork. You can climb the ladder to get to the fourth floor, and then crawl through the ducting until you find the president's bedroom. He'll be sleeping alone, with his security detail in the anteroom to his suite."

Noah followed along on the display, as Neil manipulated it to let him see all of the details as they were described.

"What about the grill that lets air into the room? Would it be hard to remove?"

"Probably, at least without breaking it and making noise. On the other hand, it would be plenty big enough to let the bees get through. The only question is how to make them sting."

"That isn't all that hard," Noah said. "Bees usually sting because they think they're protecting the hive. If I can get a little bit of honey into the room, that will put them on alert. Any movement in the room will probably be enough to attract them and make them begin to sting."

Neil looked up at him. "I'm not sure I even want to know how you know that," he said.

"Something I learned when I was a kid," Noah said. "I found out the hard way, when I tried to steal honey out of a beehive."

"Okay," Jenny said, "but suppose you managed to get the bees in there. What happens if he gets stung, but lives through it? I mean, there's no way to know for sure that this is going to work, right?"

"No," Noah said. "At this point, all we've got is speculation. An allergy to bee stings, on the other hand, generally causes anaphylactic shock. If a single bee sting almost killed him before, dumping a few dozen riled-up bees into his room ought to get the job done."

They continued going over the plan for a couple of hours, until Marco and Sarah returned. They had picked up a late model Chrysler Town and Country, a seven-passenger minivan with a lot of room for baggage and cargo. It took a few minutes to bring the two of them up-to-date on the plan, and showed Marco the layout of the building.

"Okay, then," Marco asked, "what do we do first? What's the next step?"

"The first thing I want to do is get into that utility tunnel," Noah said. "Neil, have you found an entrance to it yet?"

"Funny you should ask that," Neil said. "I just happened to find one that is easy to get to, and far enough away that the Secret Service probably doesn't even know it exists. It's almost half a mile away from the hotel, and in the basement of an abandoned building. We shouldn't have any problem at all getting into it. From what I can tell, the door into the tunnel isn't even locked."

Noah nodded. "We'll find out tonight," he said. "Marco, you and me."

"You got it, boss," Marco said. "I guess it's likely to be dark down there. Maybe we should go buy some flashlights?"

Chapter TWENTY

The abandoned building Neil found had once been an auto parts store, and was currently sitting empty in a run-down neighborhood. Noah and Marco had no trouble finding it, and it was even easier to get inside. The building had been badly vandalized, with several windows broken and boarded over, but the boards had been ripped away. A side window offered easy entry, and they waited until they were well inside before turning on the flashlights they had brought with them.

It took them a moment to find the stairs leading to the basement, and then they spent another couple of minutes looking for the door that led into the service tunnel. That tunnel ran underneath the streets, so following it was not much different than following a map. It took them about ten minutes to walk through it all the way to where the Ritz-Carlton would be sitting above them, and then they had to hunt around for the sealed access way.

It was Marco who found it. "Over here, boss," he said. "I'm pretty sure this is it."

Noah took a look and nodded. Sure enough, just as Neil had suggested, the frame of the hatch was secured into the concrete wall of the tunnel with bolts. He took a couple of crescent wrenches from his pocket and they set to work.

The bolts had been there a long time, and were pretty rusty. It was a lot of work, but they finally got them out and then carefully pried the frame away from the concrete. They managed to do so without a lot of sound, and finally set it on the floor of the tunnel.

The basement was dimly lit, but Noah could see the panel that covered the ductwork maintenance entrance. He climbed inside the basement and then counted a dozen screws holding the panel in place.

He took a couple screwdrivers out of the same pocket and began removing the screws. He handed them carefully and quietly to Marco, and it was only a matter of five minutes before he was able to lift the panel away and lean it against the wall behind him. He stuck his head inside and looked upward, then climbed in and started up the ladder.

Someone in the maintenance department had obviously taken pains to mark each floor. When Noah reached the fourth floor ductwork, he carefully crawled into it. The soft clothing he was wearing made it quiet, but the duct was big enough that he could actually crawl on knees and elbows.

The ductwork went in two directions, and he followed it to the end both ways, just to be sure he was able to make it. It took him nearly 10 minutes to go each way, but a lot of that was because of being careful not to make noise. He didn't want to alert anyone to his presence, and that would be even more critical when the president was actually in the building.

Finally, confident that he could make his way through the ducting and find the right room, he went back to the vertical duct and climbed down the ladder. He and Marco put the panel back in place and secured it loosely with the screws, then climbed back into the tunnel and put the metal hatch back into the hole they had pulled out of. They put two of the bolts in to keep it secure, then made their way back to the old auto parts store.

"Can you imagine," Marco said, "having something like this underneath the city and nobody even knows it? I'm about half surprised that the local street gangs aren't using it. Find enough ways in and out, and you can just about move around the city with no one knowing how you do it."

"I'm sure some people know about it," Noah said. "Just about every building in this part of the city opens onto it in one way or another. What surprises me is that the Secret Service isn't stationing people down here to watch it. This is a serious vulnerability for a building where the president is going to be sleeping."

"Hey, don't jinx us. That would be the last thing we need." Marco shook his head. "Look, I still haven't gotten over the fact that we're going to kill the president. Noah, if anybody ever finds out it was you, you'll never be able to hide well enough."

"That's why they call this a secret mission," Noah said. "The only ones who are going to know are those who are with us on it. I'll be honest, I wish there was any other way to stop this thing, but I haven't figured out what it would be. Any conspiracy this big is one that won't be stopped by threats or even exposure, and it sounds crazy enough that it would be written off as a conspiracy theory, anyway. I've thought about it long and hard, and I don't see any other way to protect the country from the threat this thing represents."

Marco grimaced. "Yeah," he said. "I know. It just really sucks."

They got back to the parts store and carefully make sure they hadn't left any sign of their presence, then drove back to the hotel. There were still three days to go before the president would arrive, and Noah had planned each segment of the mission carefully. They would rest again that night, and then the following day, he would make a point of getting the honeybees.

When they got back to the hotel, they gathered up Neil and the women and went out to eat. They went to a different restaurant, this time, one that was in Arlington and not far from where the bees would be found. Noah wanted to drive by the place and get a look at it, and he was glad to see that it was nothing but an old building and a field full of wooden beehives.

They took their time over dinner, even allowing themselves to have a drink that evening. Since they would be going back to the hotel and sleeping, Noah said it was okay to relax a bit and let their hair down. The restaurant had a bar and even a small dance floor, so Noah actually dragged Sarah out of her chair for a couple of dances.

When they finally got back to the hotel, they all headed for their own rooms. Sarah was in a particularly good mood, and waited only a moment after the door was closed behind them before throwing her arms around Noah and letting him know that she wanted him.

IT WAS JUST AFTER TEN the next morning when Noah walked into the office of Wilkerson's Honeybees. A short, balding man looked up from where he sat behind the counter and smiled.

"Can I help you?"

"Hi, there," Noah said. "I'm here for my nephew. He's got a bee-hive, but something's happened and he said he needs a new queen. He told me to stop here while I was in the area because you sell queen bees?"

"I sure do," the man said. "I'm Don Wilkerson. Did you ever get to work with your nephew with the bees?"

"No, not really," Noah said. "I guess I just never found them all that interesting, but he does. He's my sister's kid, and his dad died in Afghanistan so I try to help out, now and then."

"Oh, I'm sorry to hear that," Wilkerson said. "Did he say what happened to his queen?"

Noah shrugged. "I'm afraid I don't know that much about it," he said. "Something about some damage to the hive from a storm, but he said he doesn't want to let the workers make an emergency queen, whatever that means."

Wilkerson nodded. "Well, an emergency queen is usually smaller and not as productive as one that was properly planned. That's the usual reason for a beekeeper to introduce a new queen, and that's why we sell them. Hang on, let me get you a queen set."

He disappeared into a back room and came back moments later with what looked like a large cigar box.

"This is your starter set, here," he said. "There's a queen in the box and about a hundred workers, they act like nurse bees. What they do is take care of the queen until you get them put into the hive, and then they help protect her until the hive catches on. It shouldn't take more than a day or so before the hide starts acting normal, again."

Noah looked at the box as if it made him nervous. "There's a hundred worker bees in there? Aren't they the ones that sting?"

"Well, yes," Wilkerson said, "but you don't need to worry. They can't get out of the box, and your nephew will know how to move them into the hive safely, I'm sure."

"Well, okay, then," Noah said. He paid for the bees and picked the box up carefully as he left.

"A hundred bees?" Sarah asked when he got back to the hotel. "I guess that ought to be plenty, but how are you going to get them into the room?"

"I'm just going to dribble a little honey through the vent into the room with a syringe, then open the box. From everything I've read, they should be able to smell the honey and go after it. Once they're in the room, all he's got to do is roll over to get their attention and that ought to put them into attack mode."

"I'm just thinking," she said, "but what happens if they come after you?"

"They should go after the honey. I'm going to hold very still until most of them are out of the box and going to the vent, and then I'll close the box and start moving back away as quickly as I can. They should be concentrating on the honey by then."

Sarah looked at him, and shook her head. "This scares me," he said. "Noah, if you get caught..."

"I'm not going to," he said. "Don't even let yourself think that way."

Wilkerson had explained to him that the bees had enough honey and moisture in the box to last a week, but that it should be kept in a cool, dry place until it was time to move them into the hive. He put the box into the closet in the room, and the waiting began.

The local news channel announced the arrival of the President of the United States a couple of days later, and Noah watched carefully. The motorcade made its way in the late afternoon from the airport to the Ritz-Carlton, exactly as scheduled. Everything was coming together, and Noah decided it was time to move that night. The ideal situation would be for the president to be found dead of bee stings the following morning, with no logical explanation other than a simple twist of fate.

Noah and Marco waited until after ten p.m., then went back to the old auto parts store. Someone had replaced the board over the broken window, but it was only a matter of a moment for Marco to pull it loose. They were back inside a moment later, and Marco pulled the board into place so that no one would notice.

The flashlights came on and they made their way to the stairs and down, then followed the same path to get back to the hotel. Noah put his ear to the access hatch and listened closely, but heard no sounds inside the basement of the hotel. After five minutes, they took out the two bolts they had secured the hatch with and carefully set it on the floor once again.

Just as he had done previously, Noah climbed through the hatch and removed the panel. Marco passed him the box of bees, and he started climbing the ladder.

At the fourth floor ductwork, he began crawling slowly along and looking carefully through each of the vents as he passed each room. Most of them had several people inside, and not all of them were asleep. He was very careful to make no noise as he passed, and was glad he had taken the precaution of putting some soft felt on the bottom of the box that he was pushing ahead of himself.

He found President Andrews inside the eighth vent he looked through. The president was in bed, but seemed to be tossing and turning. Noah waited several minutes, trying to decide whether the president was actually asleep or not, but there was no sign that he was awake.

He reached into a pocket and withdrew a syringe that was filled with raw honey, pushed its tip through the vent and depressed the plunger slowly. Honey began to drip out at the tip and onto the vent, then down the wall. He hadn't planned on using quite so much, but there was no help for it now.

He pushed the box close to the vent, then quickly opened the top and flipped the box up so that the open side was against the vent. The bees began to buzz gently, but the sound quickly lessened as the bees made their way through the vent grill.

Five minutes later, Noah set the box down and closed the lid. A few stray bees were still on the vent, but it seemed most of them hadn't even bothered to leave the box. There were enough inside the room, though, and Noah could see them flying around. Several were buzzing around over the president, where he lay sleeping.

"Well, guys," Noah whispered to himself, "it's all up to you, now."

Noah watched through the slots of the AC vent as the bees seemed to zero in on the president. He was still tossing around, and every time he moved the bees flying around him seemed to get more agitated. Several of them seemed to be hovering just over him, and when he turned over again he waved a hand right through the midst of them.

Noah couldn't tell if he actually hit one of them or not, but the rest of them suddenly became even more agitated. As he watched, several zoomed down to the president's face, and it was only seconds later that he let out a groan and tried to sit up. He raised his head and tried to get an arm under himself, but then fell back, his eyes and his mouth both open wide.

It was only a matter of a few seconds before he closed his eyes again, and the hand that was waiting in the air fell back down onto the bed. Several of the bees continued to attack, but Noah could see no sign that the president was even breathing or aware that he was being stung.

Noah began moving quietly backward, pulling the box after him as he made his way back to the ladder. When he got there, he started downward quickly. It took him only a couple of minutes to reach the basement again, and he passed the box out to Marco as he climbed out of the ductwork.

He put the cover panel back on and quickly secured the screws, then hurried through the access and helped Marco replace the hatch. This time, they put all four bolts back in, then turned and quietly hurried back to the parts store.

Apparently, the Secret Service had at some point begun checking on the president during the night. By the time they got back to the hotel, every TV station in the country was running the special announcement that President Jonathan Andrews was dead, after being stung by dozens of honeybees that had somehow gotten into his hotel room.

There was no indication that anyone suspected foul play, but it was too early to expect any such announcement. Noah sat with Sarah and the rest as they watched CNN covering the story, none of them saying a word until the commercial break.

"Do you think they'll figure it out?" Sarah asked.

"I don't think they'll ever know for sure," Noah said, "but there's bound to be suspicions. If they look into the ductwork, they're certainly going to find where I crawled through the dust. They will find traces of my DNA, but it isn't on file anywhere so they won't be sure it isn't from somebody doing maintenance years ago. I don't think there's any way they'll be able to say with certainty that the bees came through the AC duct, but even if they do, that only sends a message to the rest of the conspirators."

"Speaking of whom," Neil said, "I've been watching the names we have, and there's another one that's offering himself up as a target. Congressman Anthony Borden is going to be in Fort Worth day after tomorrow, because his brother is having surgery."

"Do you know where?" Noah asked.

Neil nodded. "I know where the surgery is happening, and I know where he's going to be staying. He's got a room reserved at the Holiday Inn that's just down the street from the hospital."

"Then he's next," Noah said. "A congressman is going to be easier to reach than the president. Find me a rifle..."

"Hey," Jenny said, "are you gonna hog all the fun for yourself? Congressman Borden is a well-known womanizer, let me have a crack at him. After all the stress the last week, I could really stand to let off a little pressure, know what I mean?"

Noah looked at her. "All right," he said. "This time, though, I want it to be very obvious that he's been targeted."

Jenny gave him her best evil smile. "Trust me, Noah," she said. "The whole world is going to know."

"Good enough for me," Noah said. He looked at Neil again. "The death of the president is going to probably create something of an uproar among the rest of them, and especially after Borden suddenly turns up dead. You may have to work to find me another target, but I want more of them as quickly as possible."

"I'll get them," Neil said.

It was past midnight, so they all decided to get some sleep. They were far enough away from the Ritz-Carlton to be outside the circle of investigation, even if foul play were to be suspected, so they headed for their individual rooms and went to bed.

PERKOWSKI WAS WAKENED by the insistent ringing of his cell phone, laying on the nightstand beside his bed. His wife shook his shoulder as he reached for it.

"Perkowski," he said sleepily.

"Solomon? Oh, dear God, have you heard?"

"Huh? Heard what? Who's this?"

"Solomon, it's Tom Lewiston. Solomon, the president is dead. It's all over the news right now, his Secret Service detail found him dead in his hotel room, they said it was from bee stings. Apparently there's thousands of bees inside his hotel room, and nobody knows where they came from."

Perkowski was suddenly wide awake. "Geez, are you serious? How the hell did bees get into a hotel room? Has anyone notified the vice president yet?"

"Yes, he knows. Solomon, this is going to cause us a lot of trouble, you know that, right? Vice President Cole isn't part of our little thing. Who's going to take Andrews' place?"

Perkowski shook his head, as if to clear it. According to the way the group had been set up, he was actually next in line. "I don't know," he said. "We'll have to call a meeting as soon as possible. This is something we'll have to talk out." He glanced over his shoulder at his wife, who had sat up and was staring at him, wondering what was going on. "Listen, Tom, give me a call tomorrow afternoon. I'm going to get up now and see if I can find out what's happening."

"Okay," Lewiston said. "Keep me posted, will you?"

"Just call me in the afternoon." He ended the call and set the phone down, then turned to look at his wife. "The president is dead," he said. "Something about bees."

Chapter TWENTY-ONE

The news spread like wildfire, and the entire world was shocked. As Noah had suspected, there were rumors of foul play but the official position was that there was no evidence to support those theories. The cause of death was quickly certified as anaphylactic shock caused by an allergic reaction to multiple bee stings, and the official position of the government was that the death was a tragic accident.

Every nation's leadership expressed condolences to America, and the people of the United States went into mourning. The flags were lowered to half-staff all over the country, and everywhere else in the world where the American flag could legally fly.

Jonathan Andrews had been a popular president. Despite the fact that the opposition party was convinced he had stolen the election through a number of unproven underhanded tricks, he had accomplished a lot of good in the fifteen months that he had been in office. Unemployment was down, jobs were up, and there was serious progress toward solving a lot of other national problems.

Vice President William Cole had been sworn in at nine o'clock that morning, with his predecessor dead less than twelve hours. Cole was not as universally liked as Andrews had been, but he was suddenly the man in the seat of power, and just as it had happened with Lyndon Johnson fifty-five years earlier, it became obvious in a hurry that he had every intention of making that power his own.

CNN devoted an entire news team to following the new President Cole through the rest of the day, and it was expected that they would stay on him for at least a couple of weeks. Every word out of his mouth would be history, every action he took would be momentous. They weren't about to let any of it slip by unnoticed.

IN KIRTLAND, COLORADO, Allison Peterson stared at her TV screen as she drank her fourth cup of coffee of the morning. She had been awakened by her own phone only minutes after the news had broken, and had been awake ever since. The sheer audacity of using honeybees had at first shocked her, and then made her laugh. If anyone could have pulled this off, she knew that it was Noah Wolf.

Her cell phone rang for the eighth time, and she glanced at it to see that it was Donald Jefferson calling. She had already spoken to him twice that morning, but she put the phone to her ear again.

"Yes, Donald?"

"Allison, word has just come down that the Secret Service is claiming they discovered evidence that the bees might have been planted into the hotel air conditioning ductwork. There is already rumbles of suspicion that this was an assassination, rather than a tragic accident."

"Yeah? Have they arrested any of the bees, yet?" Allison knew she was being snarky, but she didn't care.

"Very funny," Jefferson said. "What they want to know from us is whether we have any idea about any foreign assassin who might be able to do such a thing. Any thoughts on what I should tell them?"

"Tell them that there isn't a single foreign assassin anywhere who could even conceive of such a plan," Allison said. "Hell, I can barely imagine it myself. Honeybees? That's got to be one for the record books. Do they honestly believe they're ever going to convince anyone that this was a deliberate assassination?"

"I doubt it," Jefferson replied. "I think they're just looking for a scapegoat. Andrews was one of the most popular presidents out of the last seven, I think they just want to blame somebody."

"Oh, it's more than that," Allison said. "I'm sure the opposition is thrilled that he's gone, but they'll probably find themselves being blamed by all of the conspiracy nuts. They want someone else to point the finger at, but we can't help them. No, there aren't any Russian or Korean assassins lurking out there with beehives, I'm afraid. This is just Andrews' own bad luck." She cut off the call and dropped the phone on the couch beside her once again.

"Noah," she said softly to herself, "I hope and pray you never decide to get rid of me."

Her phone rang again, and she picked it up and looked at the display once more. It was Parker.

"Well?" Allison said as he entered. "What do you think?"

"It's like the old joke about a bus full of lawyers going over a cliff," Parker said. "What else can you say other than, 'it's a good start,' right?"

"I guess so. I'm not sure what the repercussions are going to be for us, but I'm sure they are going to be solved. Bill Cole isn't half the man Andrews was, but at least we can hope he's not out to destroy the whole country."

"Cole won't be a problem," Parker said. "He'll have too much on his plate to even bother with us, at least until the next election. It's going to be pretty hard for him to hold it all together at the moment, and he'll never make it if these people have their way. I'm pretty sure they'll get rid of him in a hurry."

"Well, maybe it's what he gets for going into politics. I've always wondered what could drive a seemingly rational human being to want to be involved in public office. It just doesn't seem to make any sense, not me. Why on earth would you want to have the whole world telling you what to do, just so you could pretend you had some kind of power?"

"Beats me. Closest I ever got to politics was running for class president in the seventh grade. I lost, by the way. To a girl, just so you know."

"That just proves that your class wasn't stupid," Allison said with a chuckle. "Considering how devious you are now, I can just imagine what you would have been like as a teenager."

"Well, anyway," Parker said. "I just wanted to touch base and see how you're doing."

"Me? I'm fine, but I'm not the one who has to do all this crap. We dumped that on the one person capable of handling it, and now we just have to hope and pray he can hold up to get it accomplished."

"He can. He's probably the only one in the world who can, which is why we dumped it all on him. Speaking of which, have you heard anything from him lately?"

"Nothing," Allison said. "He's in the wind, doing what he does."

PEOPLE WERE ALREADY beginning to make comparisons between Andrews and Kennedy, based mostly on the fact that both of them died in Dallas. Noah didn't understand why Neil and Marco seemed to think it was funny, but he didn't bother to ask, either.

Since no one was paying much attention to them, Noah decided they should stay where they were for the time being. Congressman Borden was due in later that day, the day after Andrews' death. Neil had been keeping a close eye on the situation and reported that Borden didn't seem inclined to miss his brother's surgery just because the president happened to drop dead.

Jenny had been getting herself ready, fixing up her hair and putting on her makeup and preparing to lure the congressman with her charms. She had gotten Marco to go out earlier that morning and pick her up a couple of knives, simple stilettos that she could easily conceal on herself. Marco would be her backup man on this operation, while Sarah would be her driver. Neil would be staying at the hotel, but Noah decided to put himself on as secondary backup.

"Okay, Borden landed at DFW half an hour ago, at just before three o'clock," Neil said. "Surgery is tomorrow, so he's probably going to go straight to the hotel."

"Right," Noah said. "Everybody ready?"

"I'm ready," Jenny said with a smile. "Hell, I'm impatient."

"Ready," Sarah said. Marco echoed her a second later.

"Then let's go. Jenny, you take shotgun in the front with Sarah. Marco and I will ride in the back seat, because we'll be getting out first. Sarah, I want you to drop us off in two different locations. I'll get out first a block from the hotel, then let Marco out before you turn into the parking lot."

"Got it," Sarah said. Despite the fact that she often wished for a normal life, there was something about being the driver for an assassination team that was exciting. She always felt a rush of adrenaline as a mission was about to begin, and this time was no different.

The ride from DFW to the Holiday Inn would take a little over an hour, while it would take slightly more than that for Noah and the team to get there. The idea was to let Borden get into his room and drop off his bags. He would undoubtedly come back down to the restaurant or lounge shortly thereafter, and Jenny intended to be close by when he did.

Sarah followed Noah's plan and dropped him off at the intersection a block before the entrance to the hotel, then stopped shortly before the entrance to let Marco out. Both of them would walk into the hotel separately, and keep an eye on Jenny while she took care of business.

Sarah dropped Jenny at the front door and drove away, circling around the block and coming back into the parking lot of the Cracker Barrel restaurant across the street. She'd be able to see the front entrance from where she parked, but she'd be waiting for one of the three to call her when it was time for pickup.

Inside, Jenny walked directly into the lounge and sat down at the bar, making sure she could be seen from the entrance. Borden was known for two particular things: he liked women, and he liked to drink. Between the two, she figured he'd find her pretty soon.

She was almost ready to go looking for him forty minutes later when the congressman came out of the elevator and walked directly into the lounge. She looked him in the eye and smiled, then turned away as if she didn't want to be noticed. The trick had worked for her many times, and this time was no exception.

Borden slid onto the bar stool beside her and pretended not to notice her for a moment. He ordered a Manhattan, then "just happened" to glance her way.

"Hi," he said. "Are you here all alone?"

Jenny gave him a sad little smile. "It seems to have turned out that way," she said. "I was supposed to be meeting somebody here, but I think I got stood up."

Borden tried to look sympathetic. "Oh, that's terrible," he said. "Who would do such a thing to a sweet little beauty like you? Listen, can I buy you a drink? No strings, I'm not trying to hit on you, I just feel bad that someone would stand you up."

Jenny let the smile brighten slightly. "Oh, thanks, but that's not necessary."

"Oh, come on," Borden said. "Look, to tell you the truth, I'm kind of just looking for someone to sit with for a little while. You know how it is, far from home on government business, don't really know anybody. It would just be nice to be able to look into your beautiful eyes for a few minutes. Would that really be so bad?"

Jenny looked down shyly, then shrugged as she turned her eyes back up to his. "I guess not," she said. "Okay, one drink. Vodka Collins."

Borden motioned for the bartender and ordered her a drink, then turned to face her a little more fully. He let his eyes roam over her completely, and made it obvious that he liked what he saw.

"Okay, something I like to do is guess what people's lines of work are. Looking at you, I'm going to guess that you are a fashion model. Am I right?"

Jenny giggled. "No," she said. "You're not even close. Try again."

Morton screwed up his face as if deep in concentration. "You're not a model? Boy, I would have sworn... Okay, if you're not a model, then I bet you are—I bet you're a doctor."

"Nope," Jenny said, giggling again. "Let me know when you give up, you will never believe it."

"I'm not ready to give up yet," he said. "One more guess. I think you might be a—are you a stewardess?"

"Beep," Jenny said. "Sorry, nope. I'll tell you, but I really don't think you're going to believe me."

"Okay, go ahead. What is it you do?"

Jenny giggled again, and this time she gave him her most coquettish look. "I," she said, "am a professional girlfriend."

Borden looked at her blankly for a moment, then shook his head. "You don't mean..."

"No! No, I'm not a hooker. A professional girlfriend is an actress, somebody who is occasionally hired to pretend to be the girlfriend of a celebrity or something. I put on a good act, like I'm really just crazy about whoever the guy is that I'm with, and it keeps them from having to deal with other women trying to get him into, shall we say, compromising positions?"

Borden stared at her. "Okay, I never would have guessed on that one. That is something entirely new to me. How do you do that? How do you pretend to be somebody's girlfriend?"

"Well, they have to fill out a lot of information for me," she said. "I memorize it, like some personal stuff so he can talk to me about things, so it looks natural if anybody's watching."

"And how did you get into this line of work?" Borden asked.

"Well, it all started because I wanted to be an actress. Unfortunately, you have to have some way to pay the bills while you're waiting for that big role to come along, and I was waiting tables when my agent got a call looking for someone to play a girlfriend for a certain movie star. My agent called me and asked if I wanted to give it a try, I did, and word kind of spread. I started getting calls from other celebrities, and—well, it pays pretty well. I'll probably keep doing it until I get a decent role on a TV show or something."

"That is amazing," Borden said. "I honestly have never heard of such a thing before. I mean, don't get me wrong, I can understand why just about any man would like being seen with you, but..."

Jenny looked at him, smiling. "But, what?"

"I was going to say," he said, "that I could understand why a man would want to be seen with you, but if it was me, I wouldn't want it to end after dinner."

Jenny winked. "It doesn't always," she said. "I mean, you know, if I really like the guy."

Borden smiled. "Well, now, I'm not trying to brag," he said, "but I might be a bit of a celebrity, myself. If I wanted to hire you as my professional girlfriend, what would it cost me?"

Jenny giggled again. "I get five hundred dollars an hour," she said. "And only for the hours that I'm seen in public with the client. If anything happens after that, it's always off the clock."

"Ah, I see," Borden said. "And was it a client you were supposed be meeting here tonight?"

"Well, no," Jenny said. "It was actually somebody who asked me out for real, but I guess he changed his mind."

"That is such a pity," Borden said. "I really can't imagine who would stand you up. I mean, after all, there are men who are willing to pay just for the pleasure of your company, right?"

"Well, yeah," Jenny said. "Of course, it's also nice to just be asked out on an actual date, once in a while."

"Oh, I'm sure. Tell me, what would you do if one of your celebrity clients were to ask you out on a date?"

"Oh, that's not allowed," Jenny said. "It's part of the business, I can't actually date someone who's hired me for this kind of work. Kinda frustrating, but that's how it is."

"Well, in that case," Borden said, "let's forget about me hiring you to be my professional girlfriend. I'd much rather, if you wouldn't mind, ask for an actual date."

Jenny looked down at the bar, smiling and trying to give the impression that she was blushing. "You would?"

"I would indeed," Borden said. "I'm very serious. Would you consider accepting if I did?"

Jenny tilted her head up so that she was looking at him sideways. "I'm Joni," she said. "Why don't we see how tonight turns out, okay?"

Borden broke into a huge smile. "Joni," he said, "I'm Tony. Tony Borden, United States Congressman from Texas."

Jenny let her eyes go wide. "Oh, seriously? Oh my goodness, I should've recognized you. I know who you are, you're awesome."

They sat at the bar and talked for quite a while, and Jenny made sure to keep an eye on Marco, who was sitting at a table toward the back of the lounge, and Noah, who was seated on one of the couches in the lobby of the hotel. Noah was holding a newspaper, but he kept glancing at the television that was on the wall in front of him. Anyone else would have gotten the impression that he was completely oblivious to his surroundings, but Jenny knew that he was watching her every second.

After an hour of sitting at the bar and talking, Borden suggested they go into the restaurant for dinner. Jenny agreed, and allowed him to take her hand as they walked from the lounge to the dining room. The hostess smiled and led them to the table, and Jenny watched as Noah followed her into the restaurant and took another table, joined by Marco a few minutes later.

Two hours later, Borden held Jenny's hand again as they left the restaurant and went to the elevator. Marco and Noah took positions in the lobby, just watching the elevators.

On the fifth floor, Jenny allowed Borden to lead her into his room, and then she let him pull her close for a kiss.

"Tony, this is awesome," she said. "If anyone had ever told me I would get to meet you, I would've said they were lying. Listen, you mind if I use your bathroom to freshen up just a little bit?"

"No, that's fine," Borden said. "Go right ahead. I'm going to get rid of this jacket and tie, if that's all right?"

Jenny smiled at him and winked. "That's fine," he said. "You'll be getting rid of more than that, shortly."

She stepped into the bathroom and closed the door, then begin taking off her dress. She stripped down to her underwear and hung the dress on the back of the door, then waited another minute before walking out in bra and panties.Forty-five minutes later, Noah and Marco saw her step out of the elevator. They waited until she had walked out the door and climbed into the passenger side of the SUV, and then both of them walked out and started strolling in opposite directions.

The news broke shortly before midnight, when Borden's brother called the hotel desk because he couldn't get an answer in the room. A maid was sent up to check on him, and entered the room when no one responded.

She stepped inside, and then suddenly began screaming. Several people came running down the hall to see what was wrong as she came rushing back out. She barely made it to the hallway before throwing up.

The police were called moments later, and one detective was quoted by a local news station as saying that they had never seen such a horrific crime scene. Congressman Anthony Borden had been sliced and stabbed so many times that he was almost completely unrecognizable.

As they watched the coverage on CNN and heard the quote, Jenny looked over to Noah. "What do you think? Will they get the message?"

"Coming right on the heels of Andrews' death," Noah said, "I suspect this group is starting to wonder just who or what is coming after them. That's exactly what I want them thinking." He looked at Jenny in the eye. "Very good job," he said.

"He was a talkative fellow, too," Jenny said. "Once he understood what I wanted, he was more than happy to give me names. Senator Dennison, Senator Lawrence, Congresswoman Bennett; oh, he also mentioned some names at CIA. Oberlin, Richardson, and Brent. All of them are handlers, he said, which is how they get a lot of their intel."

"Good." He turned to Neil. "Who's next?"

"Well, there is something exciting coming up in the next couple of days. Day after tomorrow, you're going to have five of the names we've got all gathered in one place. It's a meeting of the joint committee on immigration, and it includes Lisa Vincenzo and Bob Majors from Congress, along with Senators Perkowski, Lindemann, and Dennison. There are several others from both the House and the Senate on the committee, but none of them are on our list except Senator Duckworth, and he's on the DNK roster."

"DNK?" Noah asked.

"Yeah," Neil said. "The Do Not Kill roster."

Chapter TWENTY-TWO

Perkowski's phone had been ringing since before dawn, to the point that he had been almost unable to get anything else done since getting to his office an hour earlier. Lewiston and others had called, demanding his reassurance that the deaths of Andrews and Borden, coming so close together, were unrelated and purely coincidental.

Unfortunately, Solomon Perkowski wasn't sure he believed that. The police report, which he had managed to bully someone into faxing to him, described a scene that was so chaotic and horrifying that it was almost beyond belief. If the investigating detectives had actually recorded exactly what they saw, it seemed to Perkowski that Anthony Borden must have been the victim of a half dozen knife-wielding killers.

The problem was that the hotel was loaded with security cameras, and it was easy to track Borden's movements after he arrived there. He had first gone to his room and visited the bathroom, then went down the elevator and into the lounge. Three separate cameras were able to see him sitting at the bar with a young lady, a brunette, but none of them caught her face. Her hair was arranged so that it kept her face in shadow, preventing the cameras from even capturing her profile.

Sometime later, Borden escorted the young lady into the restaurant, but this did not improve the situation. A close look at her body language indicated that she had steered the hostess and Borden toward a particular table, where a single camera could only capture her from the back. Borden's face could be seen clearly, and he was obviously enchanted by his companion.

And then they left the restaurant and went to Borden's room. The detectives were excited, because they were sure that one of the many cameras in the hallways would get a clear image, but the girl seemed fully aware of each camera's location. She kept her face down and turned completely away from each and every one, all the way up to the point where she entered the room with the congressman.

Forty-five minutes later, she left alone. Once again keeping her face completely out of view of any camera, she went directly to the elevator, got in, and rode down to the ground floor, then exited the building without stopping. She got into the passenger seat of an SUV driven by what appeared to be another young woman, and disappeared into the night. Security cameras on the outside of the building were unable to get the license number of the SUV because it was obscured with mud.

Inside Borden's room, they had found Congressman Anthony Borden laid on his back on the bed. He was naked, and his wrists had been secured to the headboard with fur-lined handcuffs, and his ankles tied to the legs under the foot of the bed with nylon ropes. In his mouth was something called a ball gag, a rubber ball that was secured into his mouth by a strap that went around the back of the head to hold it in place.

Both he and the bed were covered in his own blood. Borden's chest had been flayed, sliced down the center and across from shoulder to shoulder, and the skin slowly peeled back to expose the muscles and viscera underneath. Someone—undoubtedly the young lady seen in the video—had taken the time to slowly slice away the tissues that held the skin in place, peeling it back a little at a time. The agony would have been unbearable to Borden, but the medical examiner speculated that he probably didn't last very long. Between shock and exsanguination, it was doubtful that he survived more than twenty minutes of such torture.

Afterward, for no reason anyone could determine, he had been sliced in various places all over his body. It was almost as if the cuts were random, with no particular purpose. And when that was done, the girl had gone and taken a shower before leaving the body right where it lay.

What kind of woman could do something like that, and then nonchalantly walk away as if she'd just had a good time? The thought sent a shiver down Perkowski's spine.

One of the detectives speculated further that it appeared as if Borden was being questioned. The torture, he believed, was meant to elicit information. This led him to the conclusion that Borden, United States Congressman, had been the victim of a Russian death squad.

Perkowski slammed the file shut. There may have been a death squad involved, but he was damn certain that it wasn't Russian. The only question in his mind was who, among all of the countries that spied on America, could have found out that Borden was part of the Ascension Project.

On second thought, there were two questions. Who could have figured that out, and how much information did he give up before he died? And as for the seemingly random cuts, Perkowski didn't believe they were random for a second. This was an attempt to send a message, a message that only a very few would ever understand, and he—Perkowski—was one of them.

His phone rang again.

"Perkowski," he said, answering.

"It's Ed Mikesell," said the caller. "Sol, have you heard anything more about Borden? I'm getting rumors that he was pretty much skinned alive."

"He was," Perkowski said. "I just read through the police report. The poor bastard was tortured, and there's no doubt in my mind that it was to get information out of him about us. Somebody knows what we're doing, and they're targeting us."

"Who could do that, Sol? Who could possibly find out and do something like this to Tony?"

"That," Perkowski said, "is what I intend to find out. What I can't understand is why whoever did this isn't trying to expose us. Why kill a congressman?"

"Especially right after we lost our founder. You know, some of our friends are saying Andrews' death wasn't as accidental as it seemed. Do you think someone actually managed to kill him?"

"Secret Service and DOJ are crawling all over it, but they haven't found anything to indicate actual foul play. The only weird part is trying to figure out how bees got into the air conditioning, but there have been stories of bees making hives in ductwork before. I gather they've gone through the entire building and haven't found anything that they can conclusively say indicates somebody got in who shouldn't have been there."

"I don't know," Mikesell said. "It just seems pretty strange that he drops dead, and then somebody plays slice and dice with Borden. Have they got any leads on who did that?"

"All we know is it was a girl, a young woman," Perkowski said. "She was a pro; she obviously knew where every security camera was, and never let a single one of them get a look at her face. The police say she was about five foot one, five foot two, weighs maybe a hundred pounds, and she apparently charmed him into letting her secure him to the bed. Tony always was one for the ladies, and I'm not surprised if he went for some of the kinky games out there."

"Good God," Mikesell said. "What a way to go, and I don't mean that in a good way. Sol, should we be worried? What if it's really about Ascension?"

"Well, I'm personally sure it was," Perkowski said. "I just can't figure why someone would do this; you'd think anyone who caught wind of Ascension would want to get in on it, not kill someone for being involved. Blackmail would have made more sense than murder, in this case."

Mikesell agreed, and then said he'd check in later. Perkowski was glad to get off the phone.

ALLISON WAS ALSO FIELDING calls that morning, and each time her phone rang, she wondered if it was going to be one of her new masters, demanding to know where Camelot was. She had to remind herself repeatedly that she was succumbing to the same thing that made a guilty man think everyone could see the guilt on his face, even though no one could possibly know what he'd done.

The only difference was that she knew she'd be suspected once it became obvious that someone was targeting the conspirators. They had gone to great lengths to make sure she was under control, and if they started to believe she wasn't, then she would probably find herself facing an executioner of her own.

Dying didn't scare Allison. It was dying before she had accomplished her mission that would give her nightmares. Unfortunately, the mission was out of her hands.

The phone rang again, and she picked it up instantly.

"Allison," she said.

"Allison, it's Barbara," said Senator Holloway. "Just want you to know, there are some rumblings going on about Borden. Just about everyone involved is starting to think there's a connection between him and Andrews."

"Oh, gee, I wonder whatever makes them think so?" Allison said, sarcastically. "Guilty conscience much?"

"That's funny," Holloway said. "I'd laugh, but I'm afraid someone might think I was laughing for the wrong reasons. Borden was butchered. All it's going to take is one or two more, and there won't be any doubt that it's got to do with the Ascension Project. Everyone involved is nervous, including those of us who are trying to prevent this thing from happening. Your boy does know that some of us are on your side, right?"

"Absolutely," Allison said. "I gave him the list of names you gave me, of our allies within the organization. None of you will be touched, I promise."

"I'm counting on it. It's bad enough to know that our compatriots in the conspiracy would be happy to see us dead; I hate to think we might be targeted by the good guys, too. Seriously, Allison, what about Andrews? Was that Camelot's work?"

"Now, you know how it works," Allison said. "I can neither confirm nor deny any such action, nor the existence of any such operative."

Holloway chuckled. "That's good enough for me," she said. "I'll be in touch."

The call ended and Allison hung up the phone.

"THE MEETING IS SCHEDULED to take place day after tomorrow at the Lincoln Club in D.C.," Neil said. "It'll be held on the rooftop patio, and the interesting thing about that is that the Club is housed in a three-story building that's surrounded by buildings that range from five to fifteen stories tall."

"Which means," Noah said, "that I can have an excellent line of fire. What about weapons? If it's happening in two days, that doesn't give me a lot of time to get a rifle and sight it in."

"According to Wally, that problem can be solved at the gun club in Silver Spring, Maryland. You go in and ask for Billy Daniels. When you're told he doesn't work there anymore, you ask whatever happened to his wife, Lynette. That's supposed to be a signal that Wally sent you and you can be trusted. They'll set you up with any weapon you need and you can take care of sighting it right there."

Noah looked at him for a moment. "Show me the city grid around the building," he said. "Let's see if we can figure out the approximate range I need to work with."

Neil called up a map and activated the Google Earth feature, then zeroed in on where the Lincoln Club was located. As he had said, there were several taller buildings scattered around it, and Noah pointed to one of them.

"What is that?"

"That is the headquarters of the Federal Employees Auto Insurance Group. Basically, it's a seven-story office building. The first two floors are occupied by the group itself, and everything above that is rented out. Security should be very light. Hang on a moment—yeah, they've got a single security guard sitting at a desk in the lobby. All three shifts are covered, but it shouldn't be that difficult to get past him."

"Especially if I have a little help," Noah said. "It'll work. From the roof of that building, maximum range should be less than three hundred yards. All right, we need to move. Marco, start loading everything into the van. As soon as we're all packed up, we'll check out and go drop off the rental car, and then we're on the way to D.C."

Everything was loaded into the minivan within half an hour, the Nissan was dropped at the rental agency thirty minutes after that, and they were on the road by ten a.m. The navigation app on Noah's phone said it would take almost twenty-four hours to make the trip to D.C., including stops for gas and food, so Noah decreed that they would take turns driving. He wanted to be in Washington as early as possible the following day, so that he had time to acquire a rifle and get it zeroed in.

They listened to the news on the radio as they drove, and the news stories slowly went from reporting the facts to expressing the opinions of the reporters. Some thought that Borden's death was related to his recent votes against certain regulations desired by the far left, including special protections for certain minorities. Borden was an outspoken critic of special protections for anyone, and there was a lot of speculation that someone had targeted him for that reason.

Others, however, were quick to try to connect his death with that of the president. While the official line still claimed that President Andrews had died as a result of natural misadventure, the conspiracy theorists were having a field day with it all. A number of them were already publishing what they claimed were documents hacked from various government sources, some of which seemed to indicate that the CIA may have had a hand in the president's death.

One of those documents had a strange reference to the fact that the president was allergic to bee stings, while the rest of it was devoted to a discussion of certain unpopular measures he had endorsed. Nothing in any of them actually made any statement regarding the subject of assassination, but the conspiracy theorists were happily explaining to various reporters that it was necessary to "read between the lines."

"Can we turn that off for a while?" Sarah asked. Noah was driving at the time, and he reached up without a word to turn off the radio. "Thank you."

"It's just the beginning," Noah said. "After the strike tomorrow, it's going to get even wilder."

"I don't mind the news as long as it makes some kind of sense," Sarah replied. "When they start talking about all these wild theories, though, it just starts to give me a headache. I mean, what's the point? They come up with all these conspiracy theories that nobody can prove, and most people won't even believe. Can you imagine what would happen if they knew the truth?"

"Yeah," Marco said from the seat behind her. "They'd be hunting us down. We'd all end up on death row, somewhere."

"Not if the whole truth came out," Neil said. "If the people knew what was really going on, we'd probably all get medals."

"I don't want a medal," Jenny said. "I just want to be able to go home and do my job."

They made a stop in Little Rock for lunch around two, running through the drive up at a fast food joint and getting back on the road. It was close to seven by the time they stopped again in Nashville, but this time they all needed a break. They went into a truck stop and sat down to eat, and both girls said they were grateful for a seat that wasn't moving, and the men agreed.

An hour later, they filled up the gas tank and were on the road again. Neil was behind the wheel at this point, and Noah and Sarah had moved to the rear seats so that Jenny could sit up front with him. Sarah quietly pointed out to Noah that the two of them were holding hands.

"Sometimes I wonder," Sarah said softly, "how Neil can handle knowing just how violent she really is. Of course, then I remember who I'm married to, but it isn't the same. She goes absolutely berserk on her targets, like what she did to Borden. You don't do that kind of thing. Do you?"

"Only if I think it's necessary," Noah said. "If there's a reason to send a particular message, or if I need someone else to be terrified of what might be coming. With Jenny, though, there's an emotional component that I don't have. I don't know if she actually hates the people she kills so much, or if it's just that she's one of those who enjoys the rush that comes from killing."

"Do you feel that kind of a rush?" Sarah asked.

Noah nodded. "To some degree," he said. "Violent death tends to stimulate the sex drive, for some reason. Even without emotions, I don't seem to be immune to that effect. After I've killed, I experience a great deal of sexual desire. From everything I've read, most people feel the same way after killing, sometimes after seeing someone die."

Sarah was quiet for a moment, then slowly nodded her head.

"I guess it's something built into us," he said. "I remember feeling it, after I killed Andropov. I couldn't wait to get you alone that night, remember?"

"Yes. I was expecting it."

Jenny took over driving around midnight, and Neil took the shotgun seat. Noah and Sarah were fast asleep in the back, and Marco had stretched himself across the two bucket seats in the middle. He was happily snoring away as they rolled through West Virginia.

Jenny was yawning by four, so Noah took over when they stopped for gas. Jenny and Neil climbed in the back and went to sleep, and Sarah moved up front, but she fell asleep again after a pretty short while.

They all began to wake up around seven, when the sun was up and bright. They stopped in Wellington, Virginia for breakfast, having eggs and bacon and sausage at a Waffle House beside the interstate. It took them less than half an hour, and then they were back on the road once more.

Noah let Marco take over, instructing him to go right through Washington and into Maryland. He wanted to get to the gun club early, and it would still take more than an hour to get there, though they had made good time. Even with the change in time zone that cost them an hour, they rolled into Silver Springs at just after nine, and found the gun club only half an hour later.

All five of them went inside, because Noah planned to buy more than just a single rifle. Each of them was to choose a handgun and take it to the range to get used to it. Neil, who normally carried a submachine gun when he had to have a weapon on a mission, said he wanted to find a compact thirty-two caliber automatic that he could hit the target with consistently.

Noah spotted the big, bearded man who seemed to be in charge and walked directly up to him while the others were staring at handguns in the display cases.

"Hey, there," he said. "I was wondering if Billy Daniels might be around today?"

The big man looked at him and gave him half a grin. "Man, you must have been gone for a while. Billy ain't been here in six years."

"Wow, really?" Noah asked. "I was really hoping to see him. Hey, you have any idea whatever happened to his wife, Lynette?"

The grin got wider. "She ran off with some guy named Wally," the guy said. "You know Wally?"

"Actually, I do. Good friend of mine, he's the one who told me to stop in here."

The grin turned into a smile and the fellow stuck out a hand. "I'm Stan Dorman," he said. "Any friend of Wally's is a friend of mine. What can I get for you?"

"I need a rifle, something that can handle a range of two to three hundred yards. Needs to be something takedown, something easily concealed."

Stan nodded his head. "Got just the thing," he said. "You ever seen the Paratus 16?"

"Yeah," Noah said. "You got one handy?"

Stan motioned him to follow and stepped through the door behind the counter. Noah had to move around it, then followed and found Stan waiting for him in an indoor firing range.

"The Paratus 16 is one of the best takedown sniper rifles in the world today," Stan said. He led the way through the range and into a separate section with a single lane, then stepped through yet another door and came out a moment later with what looked like a camera case for a medium-sized video camera. He set the bag on the shelf at the head of the lane and opened it up, then pointed inside. "Originally designed for SWAT teams and military, it's one of the most effective and accurate takedown rifles I've ever seen. This is one of the brand-new ones we just got in a couple days ago. It's chambered in .308 Winchester, there's a box in the case. Load it up and see what you think."

Noah stepped to the shelf and reached into the case, picking up the receiver and folding out the stock. He reached back inside and picked up the barrel, slid into place and screwed down the locking collar, then added the fore-guard and flipped the lever that clamped it solid. Last, he took out the Nightforce NXS scope and clamped it onto the top rail.

He laid the rifle down on the shelf and picked up the magazine, then opened the box of ammunition and quickly loaded twenty rounds. He snapped the magazine into place in the rifle and aimed through the scope at the man-shaped target hanging at the other end of the lane, then squeezed the trigger three times in rapid succession.

He lowered the rifle and looked at the target, and Stan touched a button on the wall. The target came rushing toward Noah, and he saw that all three rounds had penetrated just where the heart would have been.

"Again," Noah said. The target zipped back to the other end of the lane and Noah snatched up the rifle and fired six more times. When he set the rifle down, Stan brought the target back again. This time, there were six new holes. One through each eye, one in the center of the forehead and three overlapping ones where the nose would have been.

Noah turned and looked at Stan. "This is sweet," he said. "How much?"

"Sixty-five hundred," Stan said. "It's a special model, no serial numbers. If you lose it, it's not going to come back on any of us."

Noah nodded. "I'll take it. I need another box of ammunition, as well, and a spare magazine."

Stan went back into the other room and returned with a magazine and the box of bullets while Noah was taking the gun down and returning it to its case. Everything fit inside the case, and they carried it back to the front of the store.

The others were going in and out of the firing range, checking out the handguns they liked. Sarah had chosen her favorite Beretta nine millimeter, Marco had a very nice Kimber forty-five, and Neil was having a blast with the little thirty-two. Jenny chose a Colt 380 Mustang.

By the time they were finished, the total came to just over eleven thousand dollars. Noah counted out the cash without a word, and they got back into the minivan and drove away.

Chapter TWENTY-THREE

Allison was getting nervous. It had been two full days since Borden was killed, and the members of the Ascension Project were crawling all over her.

Of course, officially, she was unaware of the conspiracy. The senators and congressmen who were calling her constantly were part of the new committee set up to oversee E & E operations, and they were demanding answers about Noah and Team Camelot.

Unfortunately, Allison had no answers to give them. All of her reports agreed that Noah Wolf and his team had vanished, had taken advantage of the opportunity when she was arrested to disappear and start new lives of their own.

Solomon Perkowski wasn't convinced, though. He had gotten hold of some of Noah's previous after action reports and let it be known that he suspected Noah as Borden's assassin. Allison argued that Noah would never have torn the man up the way he was found, and only thanked her lucky stars that they had not realized Jenny Lance was also missing. Allison had enlisted Molly's help to scrub any reference to Team Cinderella from their records, and so far it seemed to be working.

She finally broke down and called Senator Holloway. "Barbara, it's Allison," she said. "Can we talk?"

There was a beep on the line, and then Holloway said, "Okay, I'm secure. What's going on?"

"What's going on is Perkowski," Allison said. "I don't know how, but he's figured out that Noah is involved, which means he's suspecting me. If he starts talking to the rest of them about his suspicions, this whole thing could blow up in our faces. Remember, you're the one who vouched for me and got me back in my office."

"Damn," Holloway said. "Perkowski is trying to position himself to take over the project, now that Andrews is gone. The trouble is, I'm afraid he's going to make it. Just about everybody else is afraid of him, because he knows where too many bodies are buried. And yes, I do mean that in the literal sense. Some of these people have skeletons in their closet that are still rattling, and a lot of them went to Perkowski to help cover up the messes. He ended up with an awful lot of power, simply because he knows enough to put some of them away forever."

Allison leaned back in her chair, the phone clamped to her ear. "Then we need him gone. I can get a message to Noah and ask him to put Perkowski high on his list. That's the only way I can see to nip this in the bud before it becomes a bigger problem."

"Okay, and it'll help throw the project into another uproar. By the way, there is some sort of meeting tonight among a few of the members. I don't know for sure what it's about, but it could have something to do with stepping up the timetable. Unfortunately, I'm not high enough in the ranks to be included in such discussions, so I'm hoping that Duckworth will be able to learn something. Gibbs is trying, as well, but he's about the most junior member of the whole thing, right now. I'll let you know if I learn anything."

The phone went dead and Allison replaced the handset. She waited only a moment, then pushed the button to ring Molly and asked her to come to her office.

"We need to send a message to Noah," she said. "Senator Perkowski is starting to become a problem. He keeps asking for more information about Noah, and he's asked me point blank several times if Noah was the one who took out Borden."

"Then Perkowski needs to go soon? Okay, I'll send it off. Hopefully, Neil will get it quickly and they can shut this guy down."

"Go, make it happen."

Molly left her office and Allison leaned back in her chair. She wondered how soon Perkowski could be eliminated, because she suspected he was getting close to having the same thoughts about her.

THE MEETING AT THE Lincoln Club was scheduled for six p.m., but Noah wanted to be in place before it ever got started. At five p.m., Jenny and Neil walked through the front doors of the insurance group building and smiled at the security guard sitting behind the desk.

"Hi," she said brightly. "I'm Yolanda Rivers, a reporter for D.C. Interrogator, the TV show on the History Channel. I'm doing a story on the security guards' union, and I'm going around to local buildings and speaking to their security guards. Can you give me a few minutes of your time to answer some questions?"

The security guard, a chubby, balding man in his forties, smiled back. "Why, sure, little darlin'," he said. "What can I do for you?"

Jenny turned up the wattage on her smile. "Oh, that's awesome," she said. "I've been having a rough time getting any interviews. Well, at least getting any interviews with someone who would look good on camera. You don't mind if my cameraman sets up, do you?"

The guard shrugged and kept smiling. "Fine by me," he said. "I'm gonna be on TV?"

"Yep. This episode will air in about three weeks, so you want to tell all your friends to watch it." She winked at him. "You never know, some TV producer might spot you and decide to make you a star."

Neil had pulled out a large video camera and tripod, and was setting up so that it would be aimed at the security guard. He got it all assembled and turned on, then looked up at the overhead lights.

"Hey, Yolanda," he said. "This lighting is terrible."

Jenny looked around for a moment and then pointed at a couch that was in another part of the lobby, facing away from the doors. "Hey, could you come sit over there? These florescent lights right over your desk, they really mess with our video quality. Would you mind?"

The guard glanced at the video monitors on his desk, then slowly got up out of his chair. "Yeah, that's okay," he said. "I just can't be away from the desk for too long."

Jenny nodded. "I understand, this won't take long at all," she said. "And besides, you'll only be right there, so you'll hear if anybody comes in or something, right?"

The guard nodded again, this time taking the opportunity to look Jenny over thoroughly. "Yeah, it should be all right. Where do you want me, right there?"

They walked over to the couch with him and Jenny got him situated, facing away from the desk and the front door. She kept up a running chatter the whole time, and then Neil took out a lapel microphone and joined her as he clipped it onto the guard's shirt.

"Could you say something, please, so I can get a sound check?" Neil asked.

The guard chuckled. "What would you like me to say? Want me to say how pretty Ms. Rivers is?"

Neil grinned at him. "She is, isn't she? You gotta be careful with her, though, flattery goes right to her head."

"Well, then, I should add that she's got the most beautiful eyes I've ever seen," the guard said. "You really are absolutely beautiful, you know that?"

Jenny pretended to blush, smiling at him the whole time. "Oh, come on, don't do that," she said. "I get all embarrassed, but thank you anyway. And may I say that you really look good in that uniform?"

The guard seemed to sit up a little straighter all of a sudden. "Yeah? Do you think so?"

Jenny leaned down close and whispered in his ear. "I don't admit this very often," she said, "but men in uniform make me hot." She pulled back quickly, giggling.

Behind the security guard, the front door opened slowly and quietly, and Noah stepped through it. The soft-soled sneakers he was wearing made no sound as he walked quickly across the marble floor toward the entrance to the stairs. He stopped beside the door and looked toward Jenny and Neil, then quickly opened the door when he saw Jenny lean close to whisper again.

"Mmm," Jenny said in the security guard's ear, "I also have a thing for older men. You're not married, are you?"

The guard's smile started to slip, but then he brightened up. "I am," he said, "but we're talking about getting divorced. Would that matter?"

Jenny giggled again. "Not a bit," she said. "Maybe after the interview, we can talk about getting together after you get off work tonight."

"Yolanda," Neil said, "you know you're not supposed to date your interview subjects. You keep it up, the producers are going to get mad."

Jenny winked at the guard. "So don't tell them," she said.

Noah made his way quickly up the stairs, carrying the case with the Paratus tucked inside. He got up to the roof door, then had to stop and pick the lock. Luckily, there were no alarms on the door, and he was able to step out onto the roof a moment later.

The wind was blowing, but it wasn't terribly hard. He made his way to the edge of the roof and looked over the parapet down toward the top of the Lincoln Club, and saw that the patio was already set up for the festivities. He set down the case and took out the rifle, quickly assembling it. When it was all put together, he slapped a magazine into it and leaned it against the parapet, then settled in to wait.

He didn't have to wait that long. People begin appearing on the roof of the building next door about forty minutes later, and he looked through the scope to help him identify his targets. He saw Bob Majors, the Congressman, speaking with the man he identified as Tom Lewiston. Lewiston wasn't on the list that was supposed to be attending that evening, but he was definitely on Noah's target list. He decided to watch closely and see if any other conspiracy members happened to show up.

At six o'clock, the party started in earnest. There were several tables set up, and Noah took notice that Majors and Lewiston had taken one early, and all of the others Noah was watching for slowly came and joined them. Lisa Vincenzo was first, followed a moment later by James Lindemann. Robert Dennison appeared a few minutes after that, and finally Solomon Perkowski arrived at about ten after six.

That was everyone, Noah thought. Lewiston would be a bonus. He scanned the patio once more, just making sure he wasn't missing any other potential targets, then brought the scope back toward the table and moved it quickly from one target to the other, setting their positions in his mind.

And then he fired. The first shot took Majors through his forehead, the second did the same for Lewiston. Lisa Vincenzo reacted before anyone else, turning her head and staring at Lewiston, so the next bullet went through her right ear. Lindemann tried to get to his feet and fell over backwards, so Noah passed him and moved to Denison, putting a bullet through his left eye. Lindemann was scrambling, trying to crawl away, but he came out from behind the table and the next shot caught him in the back of the skull, obliterating his face on its way out. Noah snapped the scope back to Perkowski, but he was up and running. Noah followed him with the scope for a couple of seconds, then moved it slightly ahead and squeezed the trigger.

Perkowski's next step put his head directly in line for the shot, and the bullet entered his right temple at a slight rearward angle. The whole left side of his head exploded into a gooey red mist, and then everyone on the patio was screaming and running.

Noah took down the rifle quickly and put it back into its case, then picked it up and headed toward the stairway door. He went down the stairs three at a time until he got to the ground floor, then peeked out to see the security guard standing just inside the front doors, staring at the police cars going by.

Noah nonchalantly walked out and approached the front desk. The security guard, still standing at the front doors, didn't notice him until he spoke.

"Hey? Can you sign me out?"

The guard turned and stared at him, his eyes wide. "Who are you?"

"I'm Jackson, from Robinson Computers," Noah said. "I've been up at that lawyer's office, fixing his computer system. What's going on, why are all the cop cars out front?"

"I don't know," the guard said. "They just started showing up a few seconds ago. Were you signed in?"

Noah raised his eyebrows. "I thought I was," he said. "David Jackson, don't you have me down there? The guard that was on duty this afternoon asked me for my name, so I figured he put me down."

The security guard scowled. "That was Chandler," he said. "He's a dweeb. Doesn't look like he bothered, so you're all good."

"Okay, sorry about that," Noah said. He started toward the door and then looked back. "Thanks, man." He stepped out onto the sidewalk and turned right, walking slowly until he got to the corner. There, he turned to the right again and climbed into the open side door of the minivan.

Sarah started it up and put it into gear, and they pulled away from the curb as Noah shut the door. They drove straight for several blocks, then turned left on to H Street NW. Sarah followed it for three more blocks, took another left onto Third Street, and followed it until she was able to merge onto 395 South.

Just over twenty minutes later, they pulled in at the Night's Rest Motel, where they had rented rooms when they'd arrived in D.C. They listened to the radio all the way back to the motel, waiting for news of the assassinations to break, but there had been nothing on any station throughout the ride.

"Let's get inside and check TV," Noah said. They all followed him into the room he shared with Sarah, and waited as Noah turned on CNN.

The banner for a special bulletin was just beginning to cross the screen, and one of the regular newscasters suddenly appeared.

"Washington, D.C. police are currently on scene at the Lincoln Club on North Capitol Street, where reports say a number of shots were fired into a gathering of elected officials on the rooftop patio. Guests at the club are saying that a sniper fired into a crowd, killing at least six people. Initial reports say that there are senators and congressmen among the dead. Our Nathaniel Rogers is on the scene. Nathaniel?"

The scene cut to a camera on the street, facing a clean-cut young man holding a microphone, with the Lincoln Club behind him.

"Chris, I'm here at the Lincoln Club, where a number of people say that a sniper opened fire onto the rooftop patio, killing six people. I've just spoken with an official of the National Security Agency who was just coming onto the patio when the shots began, and I've been informed that Congressman Bob Majors, Congresswoman Lisa Vincenzo, Senator James Lindemann, Senator Solomon Perkowski, and Senator Robert Dennison have all been killed, along with Deputy Director Tom Lewiston of the NSA. Police responded about twenty-five minutes ago to a nine one one call, and they say that they came upon a scene of chaos when they arrived. People were running out of the building and screaming, and it took them a minute to find out what had happened and get up onto the patio. Paramedics have responded, but it's my understanding that none of the victims have survived. I'm waiting for Captain Janet Lieberman of the Washington police, she's going to come and give me a statement here in a moment. I'll keep you updated as soon as I know more."

The camera cut back to Chris Libby, the anchorman.

"Thank you, Nathaniel," he said. "That was Nathaniel Rogers at the Lincoln Club. If you're just joining us, there has been a sniper attack at the Lincoln Club that seems to have taken the lives of several of our representatives. Congressman Bob Majors, Congresswoman Lisa Vincenzo, Senator James Lindemann, Senator Solomon Perkowski, and Senator Robert Dennison are reported among the dead. Also killed, according to reports, are Deputy Director Tom Lewiston from the National Security Agency. We are currently waiting for a statement from the Washington police, and will bring you that statement as soon as it becomes available."

"Six at once," Marco said. "Nice shooting, boss."

"Lewiston was a freebie," Noah said. "His name wasn't in the list that Neil found, but this was supposed to be a meeting of the immigration committee. Considering that my targets were all sitting in a single table, I think it was really a meeting of the conspirators. I sat and watched for a few extra minutes, just to see if anyone else sat down at the table with them."

"And nobody did?" Sarah asked. "Babe, you may have just taken out their top people. I wonder if there's any way to find out."

Neil picked up his computer, which he had left in the room earlier, and opened it up. "Let me see what I can find out," he said. He called up a browser and typed, then noticed a flashing icon. "Wait a minute," he said. "We got an incoming message."

He opened the email from Catherine Potts to find a message containing strings of numbers. He quickly copied it all and then opened the code breaker program and pasted it in. He tapped the button to tell it to run, and a moment later the message was displayed on the screen in simple English.

Urgent. Urgent. Perkowski becoming a threat. Eliminate soonest possible. Urgent. Urgent.

"Well, will you look at that?" Neil said. "The Dragon Lady wants Perkowski out of the way, ASAP. We actually beat her to it, boss."

Noah nodded. "I don't think you need to bother replying," he said. "I suspect she knows already."

"Probably," Sarah said. "But we can worry about that tomorrow, and I'm hungry tonight. We haven't had dinner yet, remember?"

Noah nodded. "You're right," he said. "I don't want to go back out tonight, the police are probably looking for anyone that fits my description after the security guard told them all about me. Marco, would you go out and grab us a bucket of fried chicken?"

"Sure thing, boss." Marco got up and headed toward the door, and Jenny got up and walked out with him. She came back a couple of minutes later with soft drinks from the vending machine and passed them around.

"Don't know about anybody else," she said, "but I was getting pretty damn thirsty."

"Thank you," Noah said as he took the bottle of root beer. He looked around at the rest of them. "I think we need to relax the rest of the night, and get back on this in the morning. Marco should be back before long with dinner, let's see if we can find a movie to watch."

ALLISON WAS JUST ABOUT to leave her office for the day when the phone rang on her desk, and she picked it up. "Allison," she said.

"Allison, it's Barbara. Have you heard the news?"

At that moment, Molly Hansen came rushing through the door. When she saw Allison on the phone, she stopped and motioned for Allison to put her hand over the mouthpiece.

"Hold on a second, Barb," he said. She covered the mouthpiece and nodded at Molly.

"Perkowski and five others just got assassinated in D.C.," Molly said. "Vincenzo, Majors, Lindemann, Dennison, and Lewiston are the other names I heard. Turn on CNN, it's all over it."

Allison picked up a remote and pointed it at a mid-size TV on her wall, powered it on, and switched it to CNN. She watched the replay of the comments by Nathaniel Rogers, and then the scene cut to Rogers with the police spokeswoman. Captain Lieberman confirmed the names of the dead, and then stated that the police were looking for a single shooter, a tall, blond man who was seen by a security guard leaving a nearby building.

Allison smiled and put the phone back to her ear. "Well, well," she said. "Seems like our boy took care of the problem for us. What about those others? What was a group like that doing all together in one spot?"

"Well, they were all on the joint immigration committee," Holloway said, "but that's really nothing but a cover. Perkowski, Lindemann, and Lewiston were closest to Andrews, while Vincenzo, Majors, and Dennison were all important to the plan in some way or another. Again, I just don't have the standing in the group to get much more than that. Duckworth is supposed to be in touch with me tomorrow, and I'm hoping he will have found something out."

"So am I," Allison said. "We've already gone through most of the list that I had; can you get us more targets?"

"We'll try," Holloway said. "I'll be back in touch soon."

The phone went dead.

Chapter TWENTY-FOUR

"**I**'ve got one Senator left on our current list," Neil said, "and two congresspeople. Senator Richard Martin, Congressman David Anderson, and Congresswoman Charlotte Willamette. Other than that, what we've got are some names at NSA and DHS, and a couple from CIA."

"I think we've shaken up the politicians enough for now," Noah said. "Let's have a go at the others."

"Okay," Neil said. "In that case, there's Herschel Robinette, Ronald Pickering, Wilbur Benton, and Harriet Morgenstern at the NSA. At DHS, you got Edgar Mikesell, Simon Scheiber, Antonio Romano, and Armando Rodriguez, but Allison said they weren't actually certain about him. I'm doing a search on all of these names, and, oh, look at that, Wilbur Benton and Edgar Mikesell are going to be briefing the new president tomorrow morning at eleven-thirty. They're scheduled to meet at the NSA headquarters at Fort Meade at nine, and a White House limousine is picking them up at ten."

Noah looked at him for a moment. "Fort Meade would be tough," he said. "Just getting onto the base with any kind of weapon would be hard enough. On the other hand, they'll undoubtedly be on the Baltimore-Washington Parkway. Can you find me a vantage point along it, somewhere I could get a good shot at the limo?"

Neil scoffed. "Does a duck swim?"

"Sarah, Jenny, I'll want the two of you to go to Fort Meade in the morning and try to watch for them to leave. You should be able to get on the base as tourists, just leave your weapons behind. NSA HQ is a tall glass building, actually a couple of them. What I want you to do is watch and see if the limo is marked as a presidential car, or get a description of it if it isn't. I don't want to be shooting into the wrong limousine."

"We can handle it," Sarah said.

SENATOR MARVIN DUCKWORTH walked into Senator Richard Martin's office and closed the door behind himself. Martin had called him first thing that morning, demanding to get together and talk. Duckworth had suggested that they meet in Martin's office, rather than his own, claiming that his secretary was driving him crazy and spying on him all the time.

"Richard," Duckworth said as he entered. "What's got you so shook up?"

"What's got me shook up? Good god, man, don't you listen to the news? Perkowski, Lindemann, all of them, they're dead. Borden is dead, and the president. Are you going to tell me this doesn't seem a little fishy to you?"

Duckworth nodded. "Of course it does," he said. "Somebody is trying to take us out, that's pretty obvious. The only question is who is behind it. Any ideas?"

Martin shook his head as he paced around. "I don't have any idea," he said. "Andrews was supposed to be the head man in this thing, and then he dropped dead from bee stings, of all things. Right after that, Borden gets himself filleted down in Texas, and now every other high muckety-muck in this thing gets blown away by a mad sniper. Hell, Marvin, it's really starting to look to me like we might be next. I don't know about you, but I didn't sign up for this kind of thing."

Duckworth looked him in the eye. "Then what did you sign up for? Richard, aren't we trying to turn this country into what it should be? We stand to hold positions of power that will reach throughout the world, did you think there wouldn't be some risks involved? That's pretty childish thinking, Richard. I would expect more from you."

"Don't give me your high and mighty bullshit," Martin said. "You're no better than me, Marvin, you want your slice of this pie just as bad as I do. And what the hell is wrong with that, anyway? If somebody is going to be on top, what's wrong with wanting to be the person in that position?"

Duckworth shrugged. "I never said there was anything wrong with it," he said. "I simply said that you have to accept the risks that come along with the possible rewards. That's the name of the game in politics, you know that. We all play this game, we make deals behind the scenes that benefit our constituents, but in order to get those benefits we end up having to give something else to one of our colleagues. If we can keep it all balanced, everybody is happy, but let something get out of balance and everybody points their fingers at us. Suddenly we're the bad guys, right? It's the same with this; as long as we make it happen smoothly, we'll be heroes. Let anything go wrong and we are also the ones that are going to catch the blame."

"Geez, you sound like my dad," Martin said, sinking into the chair behind his desk. "He was in politics, you know. He started out as a small town mayor and ended up serving fourteen terms in the Senate. He said the same kind of thing you just did, that the only difference between being a hero and being a villain in politics is how many of your friends you can keep from stabbing you in the back. Well, we seem to have somebody out there doing a lot worse than stabbing us in the back, he's shooting us through the head. I don't know about you, but while I don't mind taking a risk, I'm not going to put my life out there. I'm not going to die for this thing, you can bet on that."

Duckworth sat down in a wing chair and looked at Martin.

"What do you think about the Ascension Project, Richard? What do you honestly think about it? The whole thing was conceived as a way to bring about some serious changes that might help us avoid letting our country slip completely back into the dark ages, right? Isn't that the reasoning that Andrews gave for coming up with this entire plan?"

"Yeah, yeah, I heard the sales pitch. What I'm trying—"

"Shut up and listen," Duckworth said. "While I believe that our dearly departed former president had his good points, if you really sit down and take a look at what the Ascension Project is out to do, it's not going to make the world a seriously better place for anybody except those of us who end up on top. Oh, the little people will benefit to some degree, but it's really us who will be the winners. That seems to be what the entire plan was all about from the beginning, except that poor old Andrews thought he was going to be the top guy. Maybe he's making a deal with the devil in hell right now, because I can't imagine him giving up the chance to rule somewhere. So now, Andrews is gone, and who were we going to put in his place? I know Perkowski wanted the job, but I'm sure Lewiston would have jumped at it, as well. Well, guess what, both of them are dead now. Who's going to run this thing for us with them gone?"

"Hell, Marvin, I don't know. I don't even know what you're talking about, who the hell cares who is going to be in charge of it now? Getting promoted is probably the best way to get a target painted on your head, have you thought about that?"

"Of course I thought about it," Duckworth said. "The question is whether or not you have thought about it, Richard, because I'm planning to call an emergency meeting of the remaining members and nominate you for the top position. I thought it over pretty hard, and out of all the remaining members, you are the only one that I can see who might be able to bring this thing all the way through to its conclusion."

Martin's eyes were wide, and his eyebrows looked like they were trying to fly away. "Me? Why on Earth would you think I would want to be on top? Are you not listening to anything I've had to say? What I want to do is crawl my way down into the sewers and stay there until they catch whoever this sniper is and put him away. I don't want to die, Marvin, can you understand that?"

"I'll tell you what I can understand," Duckworth said. "Somebody has to take over. Now, I thought you might be the right guy for the job, but if you don't want it, then we need to find out who does." He scowled and looked like he was deep in thought. "Well, dammit, the problem is that I just don't know that many of the remaining members. I'll tell you what, we need to put together a meeting and we need to do it soon. I'm going to contact everyone I know, and I want you to do the same. We can all meet out at my place, you know where it is?"

Martin nodded, but he didn't seem happy. "I know where it is, out past Bethesda." He seemed to think about the proposal for a moment. "When do you want this meeting? I can call everybody I know in the organization, and they can pass it on to the ones we don't know."

"I think tomorrow night," Duckworth said. "I wish it could be tonight, but I'm sure some of them are going to have to make arrangements in order to attend. Let's try to put this together fast, but we need everybody possible to be there. Somebody has to step up and take command, and I don't know who's left that's really qualified, other than you."

"What about you?" Martin said suddenly. "Look at you, you're the one who's trying to save this thing right now. You're the one who's talking about taking risks and not being afraid, why don't you take it over and run it?"

Duckworth smiled at him. "Oh, I would," he said. "The only problem with that is that the rest of the members don't know me well enough. I've only been in the outfit for a few months, they don't even bother to trust me with knowing about the events. If they're not going to trust me to know what I'm part of, I sincerely doubt they're going to trust me to make the decisions for them. Wouldn't you agree?"

"No, I wouldn't. I just happen to know that quite a few of the members think very highly of you, Marvin, so I might just nominate you, myself. I could get a second on the motion, and if I present it the right way, I can probably get it to carry. How about it, are you willing? If I can sell them on putting you in charge, are you willing to wear that target on your back?"

Duckworth shook his head. "Richard, Richard," he said. "I told you, I would be more than willing to do whatever it takes to bring the project to fruition. We've got our entire reputations staked on this, we don't dare fail to complete it, now. Can you imagine what would happen if the Russians pull off their end of it, and we can't complete our own? We'd be the laughing stock of the world, and America cannot afford that. You want to nominate me? Fine, go right ahead. If the members are desperate enough to actually put me in charge, I will do everything I can to help this come to the best possible conclusion."

"That's good, then," Martin said. "And it would settle the issue about letting you know all the details of the plan. The events are already scheduled, there's no stopping them, now, but we need to have somebody in the head spot who can step up during the aftermath. The people respect you, maybe more than they respected Andrews. You'd be perfect for the job."

Duckworth left Martin's office a few minutes later, completely amazed at how the meeting had turned out. The last thing he had ever expected was that Martin might want to turn the tables on him. The reason he was talking about trying to put Martin in control was because he knew the man was an idiot, a fool who would help to bring the project to ruin without even really knowing what he was doing. The chance to put a nitwit at the helm of a ship that should never sail in the first place sounded like a good idea, but if Martin's crazy plan to move Duckworth into control could, by some miracle, succeed, then Duckworth would have access to all of the names in the conspiracy, all of the information on the planned terror events, and an awful lot of information about the Russian contingent.

He headed back toward his own office, and finally let himself think about his former colleagues who died the night before. A part of him hated to think about them at all, because he was fully aware that he was part of the reason they were dead. True, he didn't believe there was any other way to stop the worst possible thing that could happen, but it still felt terrible to him to know that he had participated in arranging the deaths of his peers. Some of them weren't really all that bad, but had fallen under the sway of Andrews' charisma.

He glanced at his watch, the same one he had worn since he first came to Washington thirty years earlier, and saw that it was approaching lunchtime. He was supposed to be meeting with Barbara Holloway for lunch, and decided that he might as well tell her about that crazy meeting with Martin.

BARBARA HOLLOWAY WALKED into the Good Stuff Eatery at ten minutes to twelve, ordered her burger, fries, and toasted marshmallow milkshake, and carried them on the tray to the second floor, where it was possible to find a table that afforded some basic privacy. She wasn't terribly surprised to find Marvin Duckworth already waiting there, and smiled as she sat down across from him in the booth.

"You got here first, today," she said. "That's unusual, you must have something important you want to share."

"You could say that," Duckworth replied. "I had an interesting meeting with Richard Martin this morning. He's panicking over what happened at the Lincoln Club last night."

"Good. I hope they're all panicking. What makes this meeting so interesting?"

"Dick was ranting and raving about how the leadership of the Project is all getting killed off," Duckworth said. "I played the good little comrade, of course, told him that we were naturally going to be facing some risks in taking on such a vast undertaking, but he's downright terrified. Watching him trying to fight back tears, I got this wild idea of suggesting that we call together a meeting of all the surviving members we can reach and nominate Dick to take over as project head."

"Dick Martin? The man is a tit, Marvin."

Duckworth chuckled and grinned. "And you can think of a better way to destroy the project? Don't worry, he isn't going for it. In fact, he's insisting that he could sell the remaining members on putting me in charge."

A French fry stopped halfway to Holloway's mouth. "Are you serious? He actually thinks he could do it?"

"Says he does," Duckworth replied. "I personally have my doubts, but if everyone is as shook up over the assassinations as he is, he might actually pull it off. I told him we need to set up a meeting for tomorrow night, out at my farm, so we can talk about it. I'm thinking about seven o'clock. Can you make it?"

The fry got put back on the plate and Holloway stared at him. "Marvin," she said, "are you actually considering trying to take it over?"

"Of course not," Duckworth said. "What I am thinking, however, is that Martin claims the events are already set up and can't be stopped. Well, we know that Allison has a way to contact her people, and I think we should invite them to this meeting. Barbara, we need all the information we can get, and they are just the ones who can get it. Some of these people know about the events, and just how far along they really are in planning and preparations; if Martin is right, we need to know that, right now. They would also know about the Russian connection. I'm not sure how we would handle it, but we have to stop them, too, or we could all end up under Kremlin rule."

Holloway was quiet for several seconds, then slowly nodded her head. "I can be there," she said. "I'll spread the word among the members I know. Should we say anything about you being nominated to take over?"

"Oh, no, let's let Dick get the egg on his face for that one. He may talk about it, but if anybody asks, you just say that we need somebody who knows more about it in charge. I don't want anybody thinking I'm actively trying to campaign for the spot."

"Okay. You want me to contact Allison?"

"I think that would be safest," Duckworth replied. "We've got the rumor going around that you and she are friends, so that would look least suspicious."

Holloway took out her phone. "Hang on, I want to do this now." She dialed the number and put the phone to her ear.

"Allison," she heard a moment later.

"It's Barbara, sorry to bother you again," Holloway said. "Can you talk?"

There was a beep, and then Allison came back on the line. "I'm secure," she said. "Go ahead."

"There's been a major new development," Holloway said. "Marvin spoke with one of the other members this morning, and it led to setting up a meeting of all the surviving members tomorrow night. The meeting will be held at his place outside Bethesda, his old family farm. We were thinking that we might want to send an invitation to your friends, because there's a lot we need to know and these people know it. Marvin was told that the 'events' are already set up and ready to go, so we need to find out what we can about how to stop them, but these people will also have information about the people in Russia who are involved in the Ascension Project. They have to be stopped, as well."

"Good God, Barbara," Allison said. "Give me the address, and I'll get a message out to them immediately."

A moment later, Holloway ended the call and put the phone back into her purse. "Okay, she'll do her best to get word to them. Now, the question is what do we do with the rest of the members after the interrogations are over?"

Duckworth grimaced. "That's going to be a tough call," he said. "Do you think there's any possibility we'll be able to trust them afterward? Because, if not..."

"Exactly," Holloway said. "If not, then they need to be eliminated anyway."

Duckworth shook his head. "It amazes me that you can accept that so calmly," he said. "Even though I know what they were trying to do, even though I agreed it had to be done, I still feel dirty over being part of the assassinations that have taken place already. You just seem to take it in stride."

"Marvin, assassination is nothing but a political tool. Politics is the business we're in, and sometimes we have to use whatever tool is available."

Duckworth looked at her for a moment, then shook his head once again. "I hope and pray I never end up on your bad side," he said.

Chapter TWENTY-FIVE

Neil was at the computer, scanning the countryside along the Baltimore-Washington Parkway. He had hacked into one of the spy satellites and was seeing the roadway in real time. Noah was leaning over his shoulder as the two of them worked together in Neil's room. The rest of the team was watching TV in Noah's.

"There," he said, pointing at a stand of trees. "What about that spot? Is it likely to still be like that now?"

"This is live," Neil said. "This is satellite G-444, one of the NGA's supposedly secret ones. It used to be over Central America, but the last president wanted a better look at the neighborhood around the White House, so he ordered it moved."

"Good," Noah said. "That looks like a good place for me to set up, and..."

A chime sounded, and Neil pointed at an icon in the task tray. "Message from Molly," he said. "Give me a minute to decode it." He clicked on the icon and collected the message that had been relayed through Catherine Potts, a new series of number groups, and copied it. A moment later, he pasted it into the program Molly had written and let it crunch them.

"Here's the message," he said, leaning aside so Noah could read it on the screen.

All remaining members of the Ascension Project should be gathered at 99875 Potter's Mill Road, Bethesda, Maryland at 8 PM tomorrow evening. Allies within the organization request your presence for interrogation and disposition. Urgent we learn about planned terror events already set to happen and Russian compatriots. Highest possible priori-

ty. Allies include Holloway, Duckworth and Gibbs, possible others to be revealed on site.

"Holy crap," Neil said. "Boss, what do you think? Could it be a trap?"

"It says allies request our presence," Noah said. "That means someone Allison trusts is making the request, so I think it's legitimate." He looked at the message again. "She refers to the 'planned terror events.' Is it possible they've already been set in motion?"

Neil shrugged. "Molly said they might speed up their timetable. If they've already got the plan to kill a bunch of kids started, we need to find out how to stop it, and fast." He looked at Noah. "You're gonna need to turn Jenny loose on them, boss."

Noah looked at him for a moment and nodded. "Send back, 'Happy to attend the party,' and we'll go tell the others we've got a party to attend. We're all going in on this one."

"All of us?" Neil asked, as he encoded and sent the message. "Boss, you know how much I hate it when when you kill someone right in front of me."

"Can't be helped," Noah said. "We have no idea how many people are in the group of surviving members. It could take all of us to maintain control of the situation." He pointed at the message on the screen. "Wait just a minute. Can you get us a look at that location?"

"Yeah, give me a minute." Neil went back to the satellite view and made some adjustments. The view slid sideways and then began to zoom in. "Looks like some kind of estate," Neil said. "Big house, there are several barns or outbuildings. That looks like a fence line around it, so it's probably several hundred acres." He gave an approving nod. "To be honest, boss, it looks like the ideal place to interrogate a bunch of prisoners. There's not going to be anybody close by to hear the screaming."

"That's what I wanted to know. Let's go." They left Neil's room and went to Noah's.

"Okay, gang," Noah said. "We've just received a message. I'm not sure of the details, but somebody has arranged for all of the remaining conspirators to be gathered up in one place tomorrow evening. We're going to crash the party. Marco, you, Sarah, and Neil will need to keep everyone under control while Jenny and I handle interrogations. It appears that these people will know the details about the so-called 'terror events' they've been planning, and we need to make sure they're not going to happen. In addition, some of these folks will have information about the Russian end of this thing, which also has to be stopped."

"If they know anything," Jenny said, "we'll get it out of them. Where is this going to happen?"

"It's a secluded estate outside Bethesda. I'm guessing it probably belongs to one of them. We'll have at least three allies in the place, the people who've been working with Allison to get us information. We don't let anything happen to them, but we don't want to out them in front of the others. As far as I know, we're not going to leave any of the conspirators alive, but there may be a reason to do so and I don't want any retaliations against the people who have been helping us."

"Of course," Sarah said. "What about Benton and Mikesell? Are you going to go ahead and take them out in the morning?"

Noah shook his head. "No, scratch that plan. Another assassination this quickly could make them panic, cancel this meeting. This is a stroke of good luck, as far as I'm concerned. We can end the American part of the Ascension Project tomorrow, and hopefully get enough intel to be able to put a stop to it in Russia, as well."

"COME IN," ALLISON SAID after a knock on her door. She glanced up to see Molly Hansen slip in, closing the door behind herself.

"Message came back," Molly said. "Noah says they will be 'happy to attend the party' tomorrow night."

Allison nodded. "Excellent. Maybe we can get this thing shut down for good. What do you think?"

"If Noah and Jenny can get information about the events they were going to stage, we can probably make sure they don't ever happen. It all depends on just how widespread their plans were, geographically. When you talk about 'tens of thousands of children,' you're not talking about one single attack, but many. The other thing we've got to consider is the Russian angle; these people may not know enough to let us shut it down completely, but we should get at least some names. I'm sure the CIA has contacts in Russia that would accept the intelligence and take whatever action they deem necessary."

Allison nodded. "I agree." She sat quietly for a moment, just looking into Molly's eyes. "I'm seriously considering going out there and attending this little get-together myself. To be perfectly honest, I think I would enjoy the looks on some of their faces if I walked in."

"You don't think it might cause a problem, if you suddenly disappear from your office?"

"Do I look like I give a damn? Molly, these people were behind the attempt to shut us down. The only thing that saved us was the fact that Holloway, Duckworth, and Gibbs were able to get themselves on the committee that was supposed to force me into compliance. If anyone else had been sent with them, we might still be in the dark. Yeah, I'd love to see the looks on their faces when they find out I was behind the whole operation to eliminate them."

Molly shrugged. "I can't say that I blame you," she said. "On the other hand, what kind of excuse can you use? You still haven't let Mr. Jefferson know what's going on, have you?"

"No, not yet," Allison said. "It's not that I think he's dirty, I actually trust him completely. Unfortunately, the situation was so critical that I made the decision not to involve anyone I didn't absolutely have to, to minimize the possibility of a leak." She smiled softly. "In fact, I think it may be time to rectify that situation. Would you ask him to come in, please?"

Molly returned the smile and walked out. She returned less than two minutes later with Donald Jefferson right behind her.

"Molly said you wanted to talk to me?" Jefferson asked.

"Sit down, Donald," Allison said. "I'm afraid I've been keeping a big secret from you, but it's time to let you in on it."

CLARENCE GIBBS DROVE his car into the parking garage and spotted Duckworth instantly. He pulled up in front of the man, who climbed in the passenger seat and shut the door.

"Marvin, what the hell is going on?" Gibbs asked. "I've had half a dozen calls today telling me that we're meeting at your place tomorrow night, something about choosing a new project leader." He put the car in gear and drove out of the garage, cruising along the streets as they talked.

"It's a setup, Clarence," Duckworth said. "Dick Martin called me up yesterday in a panic, and we ended up talking for a while about who should take over leadership. I actually suggested that it should be him, but he's trying to dump it on me. It gave me the idea that we needed to get all of the remaining members together to talk about it, but that's just a ruse." He took a deep breath. "Arrangements have been made for Camelot to show up there."

"Camelot? Good Lord, Marvin, he'll kill us all!"

"No, he's fully aware that we've been working as double agents. You, me, Holloway, Ryan, Thomason, and Whitehall, we'll all be perfectly safe. The idea is to let Camelot and his people find out everything they possibly can about the events and the Russians. Dick Martin claims that the events are already set up and scheduled, that they can't be stopped, but we have to find a way to stop them. If it takes letting Camelot and his people torturing the rest of them to get that information, then so be it. They bought the ticket on this train, they can take the ride."

"I don't know, Marvin," Gibbs said. "If any of them get wind of this, they're going to be looking straight at you, and then at me and Holloway."

Duckworth turned and looked hard at Gibbs. "If any of them get wind of it," he said, "it would mean you told them. I haven't let anyone else know the real reason for this meeting, Clarence. As long as you keep your mouth shut, they won't find out anything. Understand me?"

Gibbs nodded. "I understand completely," he said. "What you're actually saying is that if they find out, you'll send Camelot after me. Right?"

"I'm saying that I've carefully limited the knowledge of what's going to happen," Duckworth said. "A leak would probably get us all killed, so there cannot be one. Are we good?"

Gibbs cursed softly, and nodded. "We're good," he said.

"Then take me back to my car. I've got other issues to deal with besides this."

"I WON'T SAY A PART of me isn't hurt," Jefferson said. "I have a hard time believing that you didn't trust me with this, but at the same time, I understand the need to keep it close to your vest. I'm just worried about you going out there. Allison, if anything goes wrong, you could be walking into a trap that you wouldn't survive."

"I'll be fine," Allison said. "Noah and his team will be there, along with Jenny, and I won't go unarmed, myself. I'll confess a part of me just wants to be there when they realize they've been had, but I also want to hear what they've got to say about these events. According to Duckworth, they may already be set up to the point that they'll happen if we don't find a way to stop them. I'm not going to sit by and let that eventuality come to pass."

Jefferson looked into her eyes for a moment, then nodded his head. "Okay. Have you talked to Parker about this yet?"

"No, and I'm not going to. I've made up my mind, Donald, and I'm not going to change it now. What I need you to do is figure out how to get me there without alerting anyone. Can you do that?"

"I've already got it worked out," Jefferson said. "I have a personal JetBlue account, so I can arrange a jet to pick you up at the airport here without anyone being the wiser. I use them now and then when my wife and daughter want to go on their shopping sprees, so they've been seen here plenty of times. I'll drive you out myself, and take you straight to the plane like I always do for them; no one will think anything of it, and you'll be in D.C. within hours."

Allison smiled. "That's perfect. How soon can it be here?"

Jefferson took out his phone and tapped a number in his contacts. "This is Donald Jefferson, account number 55547874. I need a light jet at Kirtland, Colorado airport, going to Dulles International. Can you give me a time frame for departure?" He listened for a moment, then smiled. "That'll be fine," he said. "Thank you."

He put the phone into his pocket and grinned at Allison. "Plane will be here in two hours," he said. "It's almost five, now. Would you ladies care to join me at Charlie's for dinner? Maggie and Elaine are actually in Denver for tonight, doing some of that shopping they love so much."

Allison grinned. "Best offer I've had all day," she said. "Molly?"

"Hey, I never pass up a free meal," Molly replied with a grin. "Let me grab my bag and I'm ready to go! Hey—do you want me to send a message to Noah that you're coming?"

"Yes, just a quick one," Allison said. "Tell him I have my personal cell phone with me."

"Okay, be right back."

Allison watched her hurry back to her own office, and then went to a closet and retrieved the travel bag she always kept handy. She set it on her desk and reached into a desk drawer for her Kimber Ultra Covert forty-five and its clip-on holster. She shoved them into her bag and closed it again.

"Is taking a gun going to cause any problem?" she asked.

"Not a bit. Relax, this is a private flight. You won't have to go through security. Incidentally, I'm also arranging a rental car for when you get there. It'll be in your name at the Enterprise counter."

Allison turned to face him and smiled. "You always take care of me, don't you, Donald? I probably don't show my appreciation nearly enough, but I really am grateful for you."

Jefferson grinned. "Aw, shucks, ma'am," he said. "'Tweren't nothin'!"

Molly returned then and they all headed down the elevator and to Jefferson's car. A few minutes later, they walked into Charlie's and found a booth. Molly and Allison took one side, while Jefferson sat on the other, and they were looking at menus when a voice caught their attention.

"Well, well," it said, "the people you run into when you least expect it."

They all looked up, and Allison broke into a smile. "I was wondering when I was going to see you again," she said. "Donald Jefferson, Molly Hansen, this is Glenn Howard. He's a former U.S. marshal that I recruited. Are you getting all settled in, Glenn?"

"I am," Howard said. "Personnel says I start next week as day security in your office building. From what they tell me, it will be just me and one other security officer."

Allison smiled, but there was a hint of a grimace in it. "Must be kind of a step down from your last job," she said. "Maybe I can find you something more suitable."

"Oh, no, I'm happy where I'm at," Howard replied. "I found a house here in town today, and my kids will be joining me this weekend. Do you know how great it is that I'll be able to be at home every night, now?"

"Well, yes, that's a benefit," Allison said. "You mention your kids, but how does your wife feel about it?"

"Oh, it's just me and my kids," Howard said. "I'm afraid my wife passed away a couple of years ago."

"Oh, I'm sorry," Allison said. "I wasn't aware."

"It's okay," Howard said. "I'm afraid she had cancer, and it was pretty rough. By the time she passed away, it was something she was looking forward to." He glanced around behind himself and started to turn away, but Allison suggested he join them.

"Oh, thanks, but I can..."

"Glenn," Jefferson said, "let me tell you the first rule of survival at Neverland. Always, and I mean always, do what the boss lady suggests."

Howard broke into a smile and slid into the booth beside Jefferson. "Far be it from me to break a rule of survival," he said. He found himself sitting across from Molly, who seemed to be fascinated with his face. "Have I got something on my nose?"

"No," Molly said. "I'm just trying to figure out who it is you remind me of. Look like somebody, but I can't quite put my finger on it."

Howard chuckled. "Well, I've been told I look like Harrison Ford, back during his Star Wars days."

Molly leaned a little closer and stared, then shook her head. "Nope. That's not who I'm thinking of. Don't worry, I'll figure it out."

"Well, when you do, please let me know. You got me worried now."

Molly's eyebrows shot up. "Worried? Why?"

"Because you might be thinking I look like somebody ugly."

"Oh, no, not at all," Molly said. And then she blushed.

"Donald, are you buying?" Allison asked quickly.

"Might as well," Jefferson said. "I'm going for the T-bone."

"Well, my appetite isn't as big as yours," Allison said, "but the filet mignon looks good. Molly?"

"Cheeseburger," Molly said. "I just want a cheeseburger."

Howard was obviously trying to hide a grin. "Hey, you know what? A cheeseburger sounds like it would really hit the spot."

The four of them placed their orders and chatted while they ate, killing some time over coffee when they were finished. At five thirty, Jefferson looked up at Allison.

"It's about time to go," he said, then turned to Howard. "Glenn, it was good to meet you. I'm sure I'll be seeing you around."

Molly had to slide out of the booth before Allison could get up, and she surreptitiously motioned for Allison and Jefferson to leave. "You guys go on," she said. "I think I'm just gonna walk home."

Allison looked at her, a hint of a grin on her face. "You sure? You don't exactly live right around the corner, you know."

"Oh, it's not that far..."

Howard smiled. "I'd be more than happy to give you a lift," he said. "If that's okay, I mean?"

Molly broke into a wide smile of her own. "Sure, yeah, that'd be nice."

The two of them walked out the door and Jefferson looked at Allison. "Does he have any idea who she is?"

"Not that I know of," Allison said. "Why?"

"Well," Jefferson said, "I'm sure he's a pretty smart guy, but her IQ isn't far from the number of the national debt. Do you honestly think a guy like him is going to be able to cope with a girl who is that much smarter than he is?"

Allison glanced toward where Molly and Howard were walking away, then turned back to Jefferson. "She's extremely smart, right?"

"And then some."

"Then I'll bet she's smart enough to keep it under wraps until she gets him hooked."

Jefferson rolled his eyes, then paid the check and walked out with Allison. They got into his car and he pointed it toward the airport. They talked a little bit on the ride, mostly about what was going to happen the following night, and a little over forty minutes later, Allison stepped into the Cessna jet that was waiting for her.

Donald Jefferson stood beside his car and watched until the plane was in the air, then got back into his car and went home.

Chapter TWENTY-SIX

It was almost 11:30 by the time the plane landed at Dulles. Allison walked off and made her way to the Enterprise rental counter, picked up the car that was reserved—a very nice Mustang convertible—and then went to find a hotel room for the night. She chose a moderately priced hotel and was in her room and asleep before one o'clock.

She was awakened at eight by her phone ringing. She picked it up and looked at the display, but didn't recognize the number. She cautiously put it to her ear and said, "Hello?"

"Camelot," came Noah's voice.

Allison smiled. "Good to hear from you," she said. "How are you holding up? All of you."

"We're doing okay. It's been a wild few days."

"I'm certain of that," Allison said. "I gather you got the message?"

"Yes. I just wonder if this is really a good idea."

"If I didn't think so, I wouldn't be here. We've got to get some information out of these people, and I want to be there to hear it. If you're worried about what you'll have to do to get it, don't. I'm not the squeamish type."

"All right," Noah said. "Do you want to go with us, or on your own?"

"I figure I'll let you go in and secure the situation, then show up once you've got it under control. You can text me when you're ready for me, okay?"

"No problem. The meeting is scheduled for seven, so I plan to let them have a few minutes for any stragglers to show up before I make my entrance."

"That's what I figured. I'll be close by, somewhere out of sight. When you give me the high sign, I'll come on in."

"All right, but be careful. I'm sure some of these people are going to be armed, so I want to take them by surprise. I don't want to give them the chance to draw or use any weapons."

"Smart thinking," Allison said. "And don't worry about me, I'm also armed, and I'm not a bit bashful about using it. I'll see you tonight."

She ended the call and dropped the phone onto her nightstand, then lay back down on the bed and drifted off to sleep again.

DUCKWORTH WAS IN HIS office at ten o'clock when his secretary told him that Senator Perkins was on the line for him. He sighed and picked up the handset.

"Hello, Bill," he said. "What can I do for you?"

"You can tell me," Perkins said, "why I'm being told to come to your place tonight."

Duckworth's eyebrows went up a half inch. "You? Really?"

Perkins chuckled. "Didn't know, did you? There's a reason for that, but it may be a moot point, now. Dick Martin is saying that you need to be the new top guy for the Project. From what I'm hearing, he's actually getting some support for you. I thought I'd call and see how you actually feel about the idea before I make any commitments either way."

Duckworth felt a chill go up his spine. Bill Perkins had been a friend for a long time, and was one of the most respected men in the Senate. If he was part of the Ascension Project, then it meant that he was probably going to die that very night.

Of course, Duckworth had known that there were others from the House and Senate involved, people whose names had been kept from him. It just hadn't occurred to him that any of them might be people he thought of as friends. Hell, Bill Perkins was almost family; he'd been at the hospital with him when Duckworth's daughter gave birth to his grandson.

All of that went through his mind in a split second.

"I don't really know what to think, Bill," he said. "I actually suggested maybe Dick would be the one to step into the President's shoes, but he turned it around on me. I didn't think he was serious, though, and that's why I suggested a meeting and volunteered to host it."

"Well, you need to think about it. Dave Anderson and Wilbur Benton are backing him up on it, saying they think you'd be the best man for the job. Of course, you know what that means, right? It means they want to make sure they don't get stuck with it, but there's a pretty strong chance they're going to sway the vote your way. If you want your name pulled out of consideration, you need to say so soon."

Duckworth narrowed his eyes. "Why wouldn't one of them want to be at the top? Are they really scared of the assassin?"

"I'm sure that's part of it," Perkins said. "More than that, though, I'm thinking that they don't want to be the guy who has to make the big announcements. When the events happen, there are going to be a lot of very unhappy people in the country, and whoever is top of the chain in the Project is going to be the one who has to explain that the only way we're going to save our country is by tightening security to the max. If that's you, you're gonna be pretty unpopular for a while, until people get used to the new way of doing things. See what I mean?"

Duckworth frowned. "Yeah, I guess I do. Still, I guess Andrews was going to have to deal with it, too, right? It's all part of making the Project work."

"Well, Andrews had Perkowski," Perkins said. "He was gonna be the guy in the hot seat, writing the bill to subjugate the Bill of Rights and putting it before Congress. All Andrews had to do was be ready to step into his role when the Ascension Council was formed. Now, with him gone, it's all gonna fall on whoever steps into those shoes, and right now, they're trying to make that guy be you. If it turns out that way, you and I will end up spending a lot of time together. I'll have to introduce you to the Russians, things like that."

"So, wait a minute," Duckworth said, trying to sound like he didn't quite understand. "Are you saying that the top guy now is not going to be the head of the Council? I thought that was the whole point of being the project leader, to get that spot."

Perkins laughed. "You sly old dog," he said. "Yes, if you get the top spot now, you keep it for life, council and all. You had me going for a minute there, old buddy. I was starting to think you didn't really want all that power, but you're just like the rest of us, aren't you?"

Duckworth forced himself to chuckle. "Hey, just wanted to keep my humble image, right? Of course I want the job, if I can get it."

"That's what I wanted to know," Perkins said. "that's not a problem. I'll go ahead and throw my weight behind you, too, and I think we can make it happen."

"I appreciate it, Bill," Duckworth said. "I'll see you tonight, then?"

"I wouldn't miss it to save my life," Perkins said. "Talk to you then."

The line went dead and Duckworth slowly replaced the handset. He sat there and stared at it for a moment, then put his hands over his face. Images of the many times Bill Perkins had been there for him over the years went through his mind as his tears began to flow.

EDGAR MIKESELL WAS on his way to brief the new president with Wilbur Benton when the stress got the better of him. He leaned over toward Benton and whispered, "What do you know about this meeting tonight? All I heard is we're going to talk about who's going to take over for Andrews, now that Perkowski is gone."

Benton glanced toward the chauffeurs compartment, but the divider window was tightly closed. "I heard the same thing," he said softly. "Word is that some of the members want to tap Duckworth for the job. They think his reputation in the Senate will help him handle everything when it all starts to go down, and that he's got the kind of temperament we need at the top of the Council."

Mikesell nodded. "Duckworth is a good man," he said. "I've had to go to him for favors in the past, and he's always come through. Personally, I think the guy is just about fearless, which he'd have to be if he accepts that position. Good God, it would be like putting a target over your face."

"Sure seems that way," Benton said. "What I can't figure out is who could possibly have gotten our names. I can't believe we have a traitor in our midst, but it almost seems like the only possibility."

"I don't find it all that hard to believe. All it takes is one of us to let a few names slip, or talk too much about what we're trying to do, and then, of course, you got Borden. Poor guy was obviously tortured, so there's no telling how many of us he gave up."

"Yeah. Poor bastard."

"What a way to go," Mikesell said. "I heard he was damn near skinned alive."

AT THREE O'CLOCK IN the afternoon, Noah and the team climbed into the minivan and Sarah drove them out toward Duckworth's farm. Noah wanted to get some familiarity with the place before the excitement began, so they went to reconnoiter.

The drive took about forty-five minutes, but they found the place with no problem. Once they had it located, they begin cruising around the area and planning a strategy for the attack.

"We need to park this thing somewhere and get closer to the house," Noah said. "The whole estate seems to be surrounded by woods, there ought to be somewhere we can leave the car out of sight."

They found a spot just a short distance from Duckworth's property. Someone had apparently started to cut a driveway into the woods, but it was grown over with weeds and small brush. Noah told Sarah to drive into it, and they found that it curved so that the van was invisible from the road.

With the trees for cover, they exited the vehicle and moved quietly through the woods and into Duckworth's land. The trees showed signs of cultivation, and it was easy to move through them even though they were fairly dense. Noah carried the Paratus rifle, fully assembled, while everyone else had their handguns out and ready.

It took them nearly fifteen minutes to get through the woods so they could get a good look at the house. It was a large, somewhat rambling old farmhouse, one that had probably been originally built sometime in the early or mid eighteen hundreds. It looked to be in excellent condition, though, and Noah suspected it had been renovated many times in its history.

There were no signs of life around the place at all, so they jogged across the intervening lawn until they got close to the house. They split up then, with Neil and Sarah staying close to the house while Noah, Marco, and Jenny checked out the outbuildings.

The place was completely deserted, so Noah had Marco slip the lock on the back door so they could get inside. They all hurried in and closed the door behind them, and then began carefully searching through the house. It took only a few minutes for Marco to find the circuit breaker box, and he quickly deactivated the security lights that were mounted outside. Once that was done, they all familiarized themselves with the layout of the house.

It was Noah who first found the library, a massive room lined with bookshelves and with four large sofas and almost a dozen chairs.

"If I were holding a meeting like this," he said to the others, "this is where I would put everybody. A couple of dozen people could sit in here, and I'm sure they could bring in more chairs from the dining room if they needed to."

"I think you're right," Marco said. "It would make sense, anyway."

"All right, we'll use that as our working hypothesis. Now we need to figure out the best way to surprise them."

"Hide in the closets?" Neil asked. "I mean, they probably wouldn't be expecting that, right?"

"That's not actually that bad an idea," Noah said. "Sarah, I want you and Neil to go upstairs. Find a hiding place big enough for both of you and get into it. Keep your guns out and handy, and listen for me to call you."

Sarah looked at him for a moment and bit her bottom lip, but then nodded. "Come on, Neil," she said. "Let's go find somewhere to get comfortable for a while."

"Yeah, and let the grown-ups deal with all this crap," Neil said, rolling his eyes as he followed her.

Noah looked at Jenny. "There's a hall closet that seems to be full of winter coats. Get yourself in behind them and wait for the fun to start."

"You got it," she said. She disappeared into the closet and pulled it shut behind her. They could hear rustling for a couple of seconds, but then it stopped.

"Marco," Noah said, "there's a closet off the dining room, looks like it was used for storing serving dishes, utensils, that sort of thing.

It's got some boxes in it, but I think there's room for you to get down behind them."

"On my way," Marco said. It took him a moment to rearrange a couple of things, but then Noah shut the door for him as he sat on the floor behind boxes of neatly packed dishes.

Noah went to the parlor at the front of the house and sat down in a chair, looking out toward the driveway. He made himself comfortable and waited. According to everything Neil had been able to learn, Senator Marvin Duckworth lived here alone, ever since his wife passed away four years earlier. If he brought anyone home with him, Noah wanted to know it.

It had been close to five by the time everyone was hidden away, and Noah expected Duckworth to come in sometime after six. He was surprised when he heard gravel crunching at just after five thirty, and looked up to see Duckworth's Cadillac Escalade just pulling up in the circular driveway.

He sat still and watched, but Duckworth stepped out of the vehicle alone. He walked unconcernedly up the big front steps and onto the porch, holding a key in his hand as he approached the front door. Noah waited until he had closed the door behind him before getting up out of his chair and stepping into the foyer.

"Senator Duckworth," he said, and the old man almost fell over.

"Good heavens," Duckworth said. "Who the hell are you?"

"Camelot," Noah said. "I was told you invited me to attend your meeting tonight."

Duckworth was leaning with one hand against the wall, the other hand pressed against his chest. "Oh, my God, you almost scared me to death. Forgive me, but I just wasn't really expecting to find you standing inside my house. Are you alone?"

"My team is here, hidden away. I just wanted to talk with you for a few minutes before this begins."

Duckworth glared at him for a few seconds, then nodded. "Fine," he said. "Let's go in there and sit down." He indicated the parlor Noah had just come from.

Once they were seated in chairs facing each other, Duckworth reached up and loosened his tie. "All right," he said. "What's on your mind?"

"Some questions," Noah said. "First, do you know how many people will be coming?"

"Not exactly, no. I'm anticipating between sixteen and twenty-five, but that's only a guess."

"And you will be holding your meeting in your library?"

Duckworth nodded. "That's where I conduct a lot of business," he said. "Especially if it involves any group of people."

"Good. Of the people that you know are coming, how many of them are definitely on your side, against letting the Ascension Project reach its goal?"

"The only ones I'm certain of are Senator Holloway, Senator Thomason, Senator Ryan, Congressman Gibbs, and Congresswoman Whitehall. There may actually be a few others, but I'm not aware of them."

Noah nodded. "I'll know Holloway, Ryan, and Gibbs when I see them," he said. "Thomason and Whitehall are not names I've heard before. Could you manage to keep the two of them right next to you? Considering the risks that all of you have taken to bring this organization down, I don't want to take a chance on accidentally harming any of you."

"Yeah, I can do that. Thomason won't be hard to spot, he's about six foot four and almost eighty years old. Brenda Whitehall is also very tall, like six foot one, I think. Blonde hair that she keeps very short, you should be able to spot her, as well."

"All right, got it. Now, with the others, do you know of any of them who would have extensive information about the events they've been planning?"

"Well, there are two specific ones that I know were involved in setting them up. Edgar Mikesell is one of them, and the other is Herschel Robinette. I suspect Wilbur Benton and Charlotte Willamette, as well, but I'm not absolutely certain."

"And what about the Russian situation? Who would know most about that?"

"It's funny," Duckworth said, "but I didn't have any idea about that until today. Senator William Perkins; there are probably others as well, but I know that he knows who's involved on their side, at least the top levels. This meeting, believe it or not, is so that the remaining members can decide who's going to be put in charge of completing the project, and a particular idiot named Dick Martin has nominated me for the job. Perkins told me today that, if I get it, he'll be the one to introduce me to our Russian counterparts."

Noah cocked his head slightly to the right and looked closely at Duckworth. "You must've done a good job as a double agent," he said. "Most of the time, they try to keep a low profile and avoid any sort of recognition."

"Yeah, well, this certainly wasn't an honor I went looking for. Now, can I ask you something?"

"Yes. Go ahead."

"Are you going to kill them all?"

"I expect to, yes. My orders were to eliminate all genuine conspirators involved in the Ascension Project, by which I mean those who were actually adhering to its ideals."

Duckworth made a sour face and shook his head. "I understand the necessity," he said. "I just hate the thought of all that blood in my house. This place has been in my family for five generations, and this will be an extremely dark day in its history."

"I'm curious," Noah said. "Considering how you feel about that, why did you choose this location for the meeting?"

Duckworth shrugged. "First, I figured it would be better here than someplace where innocent bystanders might get in the way. Second, inviting them into my home would be less likely to arouse suspicion. Don't get me wrong, I completely agreed with going to Allison and asking her to bring you into this, but I feel the guilt of every death it has caused. Even a traitor's death weighs heavy on my soul, when I know that it came from the decision I made."

Noah looked at him for another moment, then nodded slowly. "Of course," he said. "Many of these people have been your friends and coworkers for years. I think it's only natural that you feel remorse over the action you were forced to take, but you need to remind yourself that they are the ones who set out to betray our country. No matter how altruistic their motives might be, stripping the American people of their constitutional rights is treason of the highest order. By accepting the responsibility of putting a stop to their plans, you are demonstrating yourself to be a genuine patriot. You are as much a hero, sir, as the soldier who stands between us and our enemies, but you'll have to come to accept that for yourself."

Duckworth shook his head. "As I said, I understood the necessity, but I really don't feel like much of a hero, Mr. Camelot."

Chapter TWENTY-SEVEN

Duckworth looked at his watch. "They'll be arriving shortly," he said. "That's an impressive rifle you've got, but I think you might want to have it out of sight before these people start coming through the door. One look at that, and they're going to know who you are. And frankly, most of them are downright terrified of you already."

"That's good," Noah said. "The more afraid they are, the more inclined they will be to talk. Could you suggest a place for me to hide until they're all here?"

Duckworth's eyebrows went up. "Hide? Is there any possibility that any of these folks know what you look like?"

"I highly doubt it. My appearance is a very closely guarded secret."

"Damn, I wonder why. Oh, never mind, that's just an old man being sarcastic. Still, if you put that rifle away somewhere, I don't think you need to hide at all. As you say, it's very doubtful any of these people have any clue who you are or what you look like. All I've got to do is say you're my nephew, visiting for a few days. Any of these folks who know me are fully aware that I have several nephews who occasionally come to visit me."

Noah nodded. "All right," he said. "I want to keep the rifle close to me, so where is a good place to put it so that I can reach it in a hurry from the library?"

"Oh, that's easy," Duckworth said. "Follow me."

Noah followed Duckworth into the library and pointed to a pair of hooks on one wall. "I sometimes keep a rifle of my own right there," the old man said. "Just hang it up there, and no one will even pay attention to it."

Noah nodded, and lifted the rifle up and set it on the hooks. The Paratus was a nice-looking weapon, and looked right at home hanging on the wall.

"That's perfect," Noah said. "Now, the rest of my team is hidden in the house. They'll come out when everything starts. They'll hear me fire the first few shots, and they'll come in a hurry. Each of them is armed, and will be ready to fire. How many of your guests do you expect will be armed?"

Duckworth pulled away his own jacket so Noah could see the snubnosed revolver he kept clipped to his belt. "Probably all of them," he said. "There are enough whack jobs out there who hate all politicians that most of us have decided to be responsible for our own self-defense. Some of them might even try to draw their weapons, but most probably won't. If you come at them quickly, they'll probably be too scared to even remember they have a weapon."

"That's certainly possible, but if you can think of any who would be likely to draw and fire, it would help."

Duckworth seemed to be thinking about it. "Wilbur Benton. Robert Chambers. Ed Mikesell, he definitely will try. I'm sorry, I just don't know most of them that well, and there will be some people that I might not even know at all."

"Benton and Mikesell I can recognize. What does Chambers look like?"

Duckworth grinned. "If I had to describe Robert Chambers, I'd have to say he looks like that actor from that TV show, can't think of the name of it. The one about FBI profilers? He looks like the Italian guy."

Noah nodded. "That'll work. Now, is there anything you need to do before your guests start to arrive?"

"I guess I could set up the big coffee urn," Duckworth said. "That would probably be something I would do if this was a legitimate meeting."

"I'll help you, Uncle Marvin," Noah said.

He followed Duckworth into the kitchen, where he found a six-ty-cup coffee urn and used a pan to fill it with water, then put its filter basket in place and poured in coffee grounds. It was sitting on a wheeled cart, and they pushed it back to the library before plugging it in and turning it on.

It wasn't long before the aroma of coffee was filling the room.

THE FIRST CAR TO PULL in arrived a few minutes before seven. Clarence Gibbs got out from behind the wheel, with Barbara Hol-loway stepping out from the passenger side. Duckworth went to the door to let them in.

A moment later, he brought them into the library. Noah was standing near one wall, not far from the rifle.

"Clarence Gibbs, Barbara Holloway, I'd like you to meet my nephew..." He suddenly looked blank. "Oh, the hell with it," he said. "Clarence, Barbara, meet Camelot."

Gibbs looked like he was about to bolt and run, but Holloway held out a hand. "I can wish we were meeting under other circum-stances," she said, "but I am delighted to make your acquaintance."

Noah took her hand and shook it gently. "Considering the fact that you put yourself in jeopardy to help protect our country, I feel the same way." He turned to Gibbs and extended a hand, and the man took it nervously. "Congressman, I consider you a hero, sir."

It took a moment, but Gibbs finally started to relax. "I wasn't ex-actly expecting you to be here already," he said. "On the other hand,

I'll confess that I'm glad you know which one is me." He tried to grin, but it didn't quite work out.

Another car could be heard on the gravel, and a glance out the window showed two more approaching.

Duckworth took a deep breath. "It looks like things are about to begin."

"James Wilcox," Noah said. "I'm your nephew, James Wilcox."

Duckworth nodded, and for the next twenty minutes he greeted newcomers and introduced them to his nephew. Noah made himself useful by playing host, offering coffee to each person as they arrived. He was particularly gracious to Herschel Robinette, and to Edgar Mikesell when he arrived a few minutes later.

At ten minutes after seven, Senator Perkins arrived. He looked around the library at the twenty-two people who had preceded him, and nodded.

"Looks like everybody is here," he said. "I suppose we should get on with the business at hand. If nobody has an objection, I shall serve as chairman for this meeting. Is that all right with everyone?"

"I second that motion," Holloway said, chuckling. "Better you than me, anyway."

There were a few lighthearted laughs, but no one seemed to object. Perkins took a position where everyone could see him and stood tall, his hands clasped behind his back.

"Well, I think most of you know that the reason for this gathering is to decide who will serve as our new leader for the project. Senator Martin has proposed that we offer that distinction to Senator Duckworth, who I personally think would be an excellent choice. However, in fairness, the chair will entertain other nominations. Do I hear other nominations?"

"What about you, Bill?" Senator Ryan asked. "I thought you wanted the job."

"I would certainly serve if that were the will of the members," Perkins said, "but I'm not sure that's where my greatest value to the project would lie. I've been busy with other aspects, and I'm sure some of you know what they are. It might actually cause us some difficulty if I had to pass those off to someone else at this point. And I note, for the record, that no one jumped up to second that nomination."

There were a few more polite chuckles.

"How about Ed Mikesell, then?" Wilbur Benton asked. "I think he'd do a great job."

"Hey, no," said Mikesell. "I'm not the leadership type. Besides, I'm a lot more important where I'm at. The Council is going to need somebody in intelligence, and I'm already well entrenched."

"Well, that's two nominations and no seconds. Senator Martin, would you like to nominate Senator Duckworth formally?"

"I so move," Martin said.

"I'll second that one," Holloway said quickly. Duckworth looked at her, and saw the mischievous gleam in her eye.

"I have a nomination and a second," Perkins said. "One more time, are there any other nominations?"

Every eye was on Perkins as Noah reached up and quickly took down the rifle. "I have one," he called out, and as everyone turned to look at him, he raised the rifle and fired four times in rapid succession.

Congressman David Anderson, Simon Scheiber, Ronald Pickering, and Congresswoman Harriet Morgenstern all died instantly where they were sitting, a single bullet penetrating directly between the eyes of each of them.

"I nominate me," Noah said. "Anybody care to argue?"

Another shot rang out as Jenny and Marco came rushing into the room. Senator Robert Chambers had leapt to his feet and drawn a pistol, and it was Jenny's shot that took him through the throat. He dropped his weapon instantly, reached for his throat, then gurgled and fell onto his face.

"Anybody else want to be a hero?" Jenny asked. "Come on, give me a chance to blow your head off." The smile on her face seemed to terrify all of them, and those few who had been reaching for weapons suddenly made sure their hands were quite visible.

"One at a time," Noah said, "I want each of you to take out any weapon you might be carrying and toss it onto the floor over here by me." He aimed the rifle at Mikesell. "You first. Move very slowly."

One by one, each of them did as they were instructed. Once they were all disarmed, Noah took out his phone and punched a speed dial icon he had set up.

"Go ahead," Allison said as she answered.

"All clear," Noah said. "Come on in."

"I'll be there in two minutes." The line went dead and Noah put the phone back into his pocket.

"Ladies and gentlemen," Noah said, "please allow me to introduce myself. I'm afraid I'm not really Senator Duckworth's nephew. Those of you who know of me at all would only recognize me by one name. I am Camelot."

There were a couple of muted gasps, and a few more quiet curses.

"Not long ago, I was informed about the Ascension Project. Now, the people who told me about it didn't have a lot of details, but they did know enough to be certain it wasn't something America could allow to happen. For that reason, I was ordered to bring it to an end as quickly as possible. Those orders compelled me to eliminate every person, regardless of who it might be, who was an active participant in the project. For those of you who wonder, honeybees don't normally live in a high-pressure air conditioning system. It was actually necessary, and quite difficult I might add, to carry a number of them into the air conditioning ductwork and entice them into the room occupied by President Andrews. A little bit of honey dripped through the vent was all it took to make them believe they were somewhere near their hive, so when the president began moving about, they took it as a threat and they attacked. That eliminated my first target."

"Tony Borden was mine," Jenny said with a smile. "And by the way, if every politician is as big a scumbag as Congressman Borden was, I personally think you should all be taken out and shot. All he saw when he looked at me was a girl he wanted to drag into the sack. Well, he kinda got his wish. Of course, it didn't exactly go down the way he wanted. Me, though? Oh, I had a blast. My, how that man could scream. He screamed your name, and your name, and your name..." She pointed at different people as she talked.

"Then you're going to kill us all?" Mikesell asked. "You found out about this meeting and decided to take us all at once?"

"Yeah, something like that," Noah said. "But first, you're going to tell me and my friends all about the events you've got planned."

Neil and Sarah entered the room at that point, and Neil took out a cell phone and panned it around the room, capturing all of their faces. Several of those present tried to look away or block the camera with a hand, but he walked around until he had gotten them all.

A moment later, the front door opened. Sarah was still standing in the doorway and spun toward it, but she recognized Allison before she could even aim her gun. Allison smiled at her and walked into the library, and almost everyone present began to groan or grumble.

"Well, hello, boys and girls," Allison said. "I see you met my friend, here. How's it going, Camelot?"

"I was just explaining to them that I want information," Noah said. He looked around the room for a moment, then pointed at Mikesell with his rifle. "Mr. Mikesell," he said. "Tell me about the events."

"Up yours," Mikesell said. "You're going to kill us all anyway. At least I'll die with the satisfaction of knowing that the country you love so much is going to suffer."

"Eddie, Eddie," Allison said. "What on earth has made you so cynical? You honestly want the country to suffer? The people?"

Mikesell sneered at her. "The people? Do you mean the people who continue to allow their children to be sacrificed on the altar of liberty? We have mass shootings every other week, school shootings even more often, and then we have the fact that there are at least fifty ISIS training camps within our borders, running radicalization campaigns and recruiting from among our own youth, something the government knows but prevents the intelligence community from doing anything about. This country needs to be shaken up. If the Ascension Project does nothing else, maybe it will wake them up to the fact that their freedoms are what allows these things to happen."

"Those freedoms are the very foundation of our country," Allison said. "They are guaranteed and sanctified by the Constitution of the United States, the same Constitution that you swore to uphold and defend. I don't know how you managed to delude yourself into believing that you're doing something good with this effort, but what you've really done is commit treason. You even planned to benefit from it, and you have the nerve to complain about the very freedoms that have allowed you and your compatriots to accomplish what you've already done?" She turned to Noah. "Find out what he knows. We want everything."

Noah looked at Jenny and nodded, and Jenny handed over her pistol to Sarah, who took it and kept it, along with her own, aimed toward one of the sofas, where four people were sitting.

Jenny reached around her back and pulled out the stilettos she had used on Borden, then walked toward Mikesell.

"Eddie, Eddie," she said, mimicking Allison's tone. "How much would you like to bet that I can make you scream even louder than Tony Borden did?"

Mikesell shrugged. "Do your worst," he said. "I'm not going to tell you anything."

Jenny's hand flashed, and Mikesell screamed, along with several of the others, as his right ear fell into his lap. He picked it up without thinking, staring at it, then turned to glare at Jenny as he put his hand against the side of his head.

"That was a love tap," Jenny said. "If I do it again, I'll get serious about it. Now, tell the nice man what he wants to know."

Perkins started to take a step toward her, but Marco, who had been standing close to him and watching, suddenly reached out and grabbed him by the shoulder. He pushed downward and kicked the back of Perkins' right knee, forcing the man to kneel on the floor, and then put his gun against the back of Perkins' head. Half the people in the room turned their faces away.

Mikesell was trembling, but he had his jaws clamped shut. Several of the others in the room were whimpering, and there were a lot of tears. Jenny glanced around at the rest of them, then reached out and took hold of the hair on top of Mikesell's head. She tilted his head back and heard several wails of anguish, as everyone else in the room thought she was going to cut his throat.

She held one of the knives in front of his face. "There are a number of extremely sensitive parts of the human body," she said. "One of them is the ears, but we already dealt with that one, didn't we? Would you like to know what the others are?"

Once again, Mikesell kept his mouth shut, despite trembling from the pain he was suffering. Jenny suddenly yanked his head forward and downward, and then dragged just the tip of her stiletto across the back of his neck.

The man screamed and tried to jump out of his chair, but Jenny yanked him back. The cut wasn't deep, but blood was flowing steadily from it, running down his back and all over the chair. Mikesell was almost having a seizure, he was shaking so hard, and he was obviously having a hard time controlling his hands. They were gripping the arms of the chair at one moment, and clenching into fists the next.

"Now, you were asked a question," Jenny said. "I would suggest you answer it while there is still the possibility you might survive."

Mikesell opened his eyes and glared at her, but still refused to speak.

"Okay, we'll move on to lesson number three," Jenny said. Her left hand continued to hold onto his hair, and the knife in her right flashed forward. The tip pierced Mikesell's bottom lip at its edge, and she dragged it across quickly, flaying it open.

That was the end of his self-control, as he tried to lunge and grab her by the throat. Jenny's stiletto sliced quickly across both hands, making him yank them back as he continued to scream in agony.

"Lips are very sensitive," Jenny said, "but so are the hands. I guess you were impatient to get to lesson four."

"Oh, for God's sake," shouted Congresswoman Charlotte Willamette. "Stop this, it's uncivilized! You can't torture people!"

Allison turned and pointed her gun directly at the woman. "Are you serious? You're part of a group that wants to basically enslave most of the human race, for the benefit of a few who will become rich and powerful, including yourself, and you dare to speak to us about morals? I'll tell you what, we'll stop what we're doing to Mikesell, and you can start talking about the events. Now."

"Hell, I'll tell you," Willamette said. "I'm sure as hell not willing to die to keep it a secret, not when it's obvious you're going to shut us down, anyway."

"Jenny," Allison said, "take a break for a minute. All right, Congresswoman, start talking."

Willamette glared at her for a moment, then let out a sigh. "Event number one is scheduled for a certain date, a few weeks from now. It's been in the planning stages for about two years, now, and it's all set and ready to go. We have people, through our intelligence agencies, in every terrorist organization. We've used them to recruit fanatics to drive over three hundred large cars, each of which is equipped with a package of high-yield, incendiary explosives..."

"Charlotte, shut up!" Mikesell screamed, but Jenny put her knife to his upper lip and he closed his mouth again.

"We might as well tell them, Ed," Willamette said. "It's over, can't you see that?" She looked back at Allison. "These people are true fanatics, the kind who believe America is a great evil. When it's time, each of them will get into their cars and drive from their current locations to a certain school in a neighboring state and crash into it at high speed. The explosive packs that are built into the car are powerful enough to level a large building. Because each bomber traveled across state lines, a bill would be introduced in Congress to require limitations on travel. Americans would be required to have permits for any traveling they wanted to do, and those permits would require vehicles to be searched, so it could never happen again."

Allison stared at her for a moment, and her finger almost squeezed the trigger. She caught herself just before it would be too late, and nodded. "Go on. The next event?"

"One month after the school explosions, a hundred mass shootings will take place in different places around the country, all at the same time. Once again, the shooters are fanatics we have recruited. Each of them would be targeting a crowded event, so imagine a hundred Las Vegas shootings, happening all at once. Each of them would be wearing a suicide bomb. If it appeared they were going to be captured, they would detonate."

"With further devastating loss of life, of course," Allison said. "What's the benefit to the project?"

"With so many gun-related deaths happening all at once, Congress would respond to the people who would be screaming for gun control, and outlaw the sale or possession of any weapon that can fire more than three rounds. Hunters would be required to keep their rifles and shotguns in centralized locations, and to sign them out when they want to go hunting. Civilians would not be allowed handguns at all."

"And the third event?"

"That's the one that would cinch the whole project. Two weeks after the mass shootings, twelve small nuclear devices would go off. They are already planted, some of them in specific cities and some in small towns that no one would ever expect to be targeted, and they would do a lot of damage and cause a lot of death and injury. It would result in a complete suspension of the fourth amendment, allowing any person or place to be searched at any time, for any reason, so that such a thing could never happen again without warning."

"Dear God," Allison said. "You people are crazy. You'd end up with a revolution on your hands."

"Oh, I doubt it. In total, the death toll from all three events would exceed two hundred and fifty thousand people, about a third of them children less than fifteen years of age. The people would be told that it was all the work of terrorist groups, and that there was no way to protect everybody and still have all the freedoms we've been enjoying. By this point, except for some diehards, pretty much everybody would be willing to give up most of their freedoms if it means their families are going to be safe."

Allison stared at her for a moment. "How do we stop them?"

"I don't know that you could stop the events from happening," Willamette said, "not without my help. If you were to close down all of America's schools, the actors would simply wait until they reopened. I doubt there's any way you could cancel all of the different crowd-drawing events that would be targeted by the shooters, and even if you put every resource you possibly can on finding where those nuclear devices are, there's no way you would find most of them. Without specific information, you're pretty much SOL."

"And do you have information on which schools would be bombed, where the shootings would happen, where the nukes are?" Allison asked.

"As a matter of fact, I do," Willamette said. "And I'll give it to you, once I'm assured that I will be able to survive and live out my life without reprisal."

Chapter TWENTY-EIGHT

Allison stared at her for a moment, then slowly shook her head. "You absolutely amaze me," she said. "All of you. You have callously planned the deaths of a quarter million people with no other genuine motive than your own comfort, wealth, and power. Congresswoman, there is absolutely no possibility that you will continue to live your life as you've known it. You have proven yourself a traitor to your country, possibly even to the human race, and you deserve absolutely no compassion or comfort." She looked around the room. "Who else knows the details of these events? Is there anyone here who has that information and understands that the best you can hope for is life in a federal prison?"

Half a dozen hands waved in the air, and Allison looked back at Willamette. "It appears that you've been outbid," she said. She reached behind her back and drew her pistol, calmly aimed at the Congresswoman's face, and squeezed the trigger.

The loud report caused half the people in the room to scream and cover their ears, and several actually vomited as the congresswoman's head exploded. Her body bounced against the back of the chair and then slithered out onto the floor, her head turned so that the gaping wound where her eyes and nose had been was visible to most of them.

Allison looked at Mikesell. "Are you interested in survival?"

Edgar Mikesell, Director of Intelligence at the Department of Homeland Security, raised one bleeding hand and extended his middle finger. Allison aimed her gun at his head, but then lowered it.

"Finish him," she said to Jenny.

The girl flashed her a big smile, then turned and drew her knife across Mikesell's throat. Blood sprayed out for a few seconds, and his head sagged down onto his chest as he died.

"Now, listen up," Allison said. "I have absolutely no reason to be merciful to any of you. However, in the interest of preserving life in this country, I will make one offer." She paused, then motioned for Neil to come close to her and whispered in his ear. He listened, then nodded his head, and Allison looked around again. "One by one, you will each tell this young man everything you know about the horrific events that you helped to plan. He will make a video recording of your confessions, which absolutely will be used to guarantee that you will spend the rest of your lives in a federal corrections facility. Now, in the interest of justice, I must first state that you do have the right to remain silent. However, under Classified Presidential Action Directive Number 92, in matters of National Security that involve charges of treason, the Director of Elimination and Eradication may, upon a request from any American agency involved in preserving said National Security—*or on her own volition*—order the immediate elimination of any suspect who refuses to cooperate. Do all of you understand what I'm saying?"

Most of those present nodded or stated that they did understand, and Allison nodded her acknowledgment.

"Neil," she said, "take one at a time into another room. Record everything they say, be sure to have them identify themselves and state their confession to being part of the Ascension Project on the video. Sarah, you go with him to keep them covered."

Hands shot up again, and Neil pointed at Herschel Robinette. "You first," he said. Sarah had handed Jenny's gun back to her, and now aimed her own at Robinette as they walked out of the room.

"Now," Allison said, "while they're having a little chat, there's something else I want to find out about. We know that you people have been working with a group in Russia that is trying to accomplish the same thing over there. I want names, and I want them now. Who's going to give them to me?"

Several of the people looked at each other, confused, but no hands went up. Noah raised his rifle again and pointed it at Perkins. "I understand Senator Perkins has been handling a lot of the contact with the Russians," he said.

Allison turned to Perkins. "Bill? I'll give you the same deal I offered before. You talk, you live, but in federal custody."

Perkins gave her a sour look. "Do you think a federal prison, with underpaid and undertrained staff, could keep the *Bratva* from getting to me if they wanted to? That's who we deal with over there. They'd kill me if I give up any information."

"I'm going to kill you if you don't," Noah said. "Which way do you expect will let you live longer?"

"I'll make you a counteroffer," Perkins said. "I want witness protection, but under your division. I don't care if you turn me into your house boy, I don't care if you put an ankle monitor on me, I don't care about anything other than not being where they can get to me."

Allison looked at him for a few seconds, then cocked her head slightly. "Do you honestly think the information you've got is that valuable to us?"

"I guarantee it," Perkins said. "And it's doubly valuable for its rarity. I'm the only one still alive who knows our contacts over there. Lindemann, Perkowski, and I handled that, no one else."

"Then you've got a deal. Marco, whatever happens, don't let any harm come to him."

"Yes, ma'am," Marco said.

A woman raised her hand, like a school kid waiting to ask a question. Allison pointed at her and nodded. "Go ahead," she said.

"I—I just wanted to ask," the woman began, "what happens if we don't know anything? What if we don't know any information to give you? Some of us—we were just kind of dragged into this thing.

I mean, I'm only part of this because..." She licked her lips nervously. "I only got invited in because I've been sleeping with my boss, and he doesn't want it to end." She glanced at Senator Lawrence, her face red with shame.

Allison smiled at her, the kind of smile a shark wears just before dinner. "Trust me, dear," she said. "You probably know more than you think you do. As long as you give me a full and complete confession of your involvement, the deal for prison instead of a bullet stands. There might even be the possibility of some kind of leniency, in certain cases." She looked around. "Just bear in mind that the more information you give us, the more comfortable that prison stay, or the possibility of mercy, is likely to be."

She looked around and pointed at another man who had been sitting quietly near Duckworth. "Senator Ryan," she said.

"Yes, ma'am?" Ryan said cautiously.

"You are the Chairman of the secret Senate committee on intelligence oversight, am I correct?"

"Yes, ma'am, you are correct."

"I further believe that you have been using your position within the Ascension Project to assist in providing intelligence and evidence to help shut it down. Am I also correct on this?"

"You are," Ryan said. Several of the others were staring at him, some hatefully and some in disbelief.

"As the chairman of that committee, you are empowered to call a meeting of the committee at any time, so long as you have a quorum of the members. How many members are on your committee?"

Ryan grinned. "Thirteen," he replied. "And I'm sure you're aware that seven of us are here at this moment."

Allison nodded. "Yourself, Duckworth, Gibbs, Holloway, Whitehall, Thomason, and Bennett. Are you confident that all of them can be trusted?"

"Absolutely," Ryan said.

"And with a quorum present, you can vote on and issue indictments for treason."

"Once again, you are absolutely correct. Shall I convene a meeting at this moment?"

Allison smiled. "I do believe it's time," she said.

"THE HEAD GUY IS ANTONIN Petrokov," Perkins said. "He's a major boss in the *Bratva*, but has also had his finger on the pulse of the politics in Russia for years. President Feodor has been a puppet of his since the election, but for the last year he's been trying to outgrow his britches. With Petrokov in command of the Russian Council, his puppet strings will be even more firmly attached."

"That's one name," Allison said. "Give me the rest."

"Yuri Romanov, he's the new defense minister over there. He and Petrokov are old friends. He'll be number two in the Russian Council. Number three will be Alex Gorky. Those three are running the whole thing over there, but there's also a guy named Sergei Rubinsky and a woman named Anastasia Kaminov. I'm not sure what their positions are, but they're both deeply involved in murder and money laundering."

"Five names? That's all you've got?" Allison shook her head. "Bill, it's going to take more than that to get witness protection. You made it sound like you can give up the entire operation over there, but this is..."

"It's all there is," Perkins said. "The Russians, they play it all close to the vest. Petrokov is the head guy, he's the one who calls all the shots. Out of the others, only Romanov and the woman, Anastasia, have any real power. Gorky and Rubinsky are tough guys, but they don't have the brains for any kind of management potential. That's one thing about the *Bratva*, they punish intelligence. The only way to rise in the ranks is to be smart enough not to let anyone notice how smart you are."

"So there's no one who could step into Petrokov's shoes? Take over the operation to keep going, if we eliminate him?"

"Romanov could, or Anastasia. Nobody else. If I were you, I would still take out Gorky and Rubinsky, just to make sure everyone else knows what will happen if they try, but as long as Petrokov, Romanov, and Anastasia are dead, what's left of the Moscow *Bratva* will be content to go back to running drugs and girls."

Allison was seated at a table, with Perkins sitting across from her. Marco was right beside him with his gun still trained on Perkins' head.

Allison leaned back into her chair and just looked at Perkins for moment. "Assuming that you've given us accurate information that is genuinely enough to shut down the Russian faction, just what is it you really expect in return?"

Perkins smiled and raised his eyebrows. "Best case scenario? Keep my involvement under wraps and send me back to my office in D.C. You'll have your own private pet senator, ready to keep you in the loop on everything going on up on Capitol Hill. But that isn't what you asked me, is it? You asked me what I really expect. Well, I suppose the right answer to that would be that I only expect to stay alive. Like I told you, if you want to lock me up in your basement and use me for your personal whipping boy, then so be it. The only thing I would ask is that I could have occasional visits with my family. Any possibility you go along with that?"

"Hold that thought," Allison said. "Marco, don't let him move." She got up and left the room, walking down the hall to where Duckworth had taken Ryan and the committee for their private meeting.

She tapped on the door and waited for Ryan to tell her to come in, then stepped inside.

"Perkins just made a suggestion that may have merit," she said. "Senator Ryan, it occurs to me that there might be some value in having Perkins remain in the Senate. Of course, he's promised to be my personal eyes and ears on the Hill, but I'm wondering if you might have any thoughts on this matter."

Ryan grinned. "Are you planning to do to him what you did to Monica Lord? That little chip she carries around that keeps you aware of everything she does or says?"

Allison gave him a smirk. "Hell, Ryan, you know me too well. Of course I would; you honestly think I'd trust a politician?"

"He could be useful," Ryan said. "My only concern would be that it would give you an awful lot of power. What say you to that?"

"I think you know me well enough to know," Allison said, "that power is among the last of the things I want. I confess, however, that it wouldn't break my heart to have someone on Capitol Hill watching my back and doing what he can to protect my interests. The last thing I ever want is another trip to the hoosegow, no matter how luxurious it might be. Any chance you'd let him onto your committee, just to make sure you don't send the goons after me again?"

Ryan burst out laughing. "Oh! Oh, Allison, if you ever decide to leave public service, you really should go for a career in stand-up comedy. That was the funniest thing I've ever heard. Of course not, we already know the man is a traitor. That may be what makes him perfectly suited to your purposes, but I'm not about to let him get hold of top-secret, compartmentalized information."

"Yeah, I thought you'd react that way. Frankly, if you had said yes, I would've started to worry about your honesty and integrity. How are you all coming along in here?"

"We agreed to order indictments against all of the conspirators," he said. "As soon as you're done here, we'll arrange for all of them to be arrested and taken into custody. If you want Perkins, I have no objection, but take him out of here when you leave with your people. I'd rather leave his name out of it completely than let anyone think he was working with us."

"Some of the others are bound to give up his name under interrogation. You'll help me handle that when the time comes?"

Ryan nodded. "We'd give him immunity, based on the fact that he cooperated voluntarily. We'll even imply that he had kept documents of information and was just waiting for the chance to turn them over to the right authorities. That should clear his name with the public, and he can pretend to be some kind of hero."

"The only problem, then, is his Russian mob connections. Any suggestions on how I keep him safe from the *Bratva*?"

"That's easy," Duckworth said. "We issue a statement that one of the others gave up the Russian names, one of the ones that didn't survive. They take the heat for that, so all he needs to do is keep on being their friend. If you put a monitor chip on him, he becomes a source of intelligence about what the *Bratva* is doing."

Allison shot him a look of pleasant surprise. "Why, Marvin, that's actually a brilliant, albeit devious, idea. Make it happen. I will let him know he's the luckiest bastard that ever lived. How soon do you want us to leave? Don't you want to have FBI here to take care of your prisoners before we slip off into the night?"

"That probably is a good idea," Holloway said. "The only question is how we explain the dead bodies."

"We don't have to explain them," Ryan said. "This committee has the power to request eliminations from E & E, and did so. Publicly, Delta Force will probably get credit for these kills, as part of a secret operation to put an end to the Ascension Project and capture its membership."

"Good," Allison said. "Other than a few conspiracy theory websites, we've managed to keep any information about our organization away from the public. I want to keep it that way."

"So do I," Ryan said. "I'm calling the FBI right now. If you leave us some handguns, we can keep our prisoners under control until they arrive. You need to get your people out of here."

"Done."

THREE DAYS LATER

"You'll be happy to know," Allison said, "that the White House is going to announce the arrests of the Ascension Project membership this afternoon. You did good work, kids."

Noah, Sarah, Jenny, Neil, and Marco were sitting around the conference table with her and Jefferson. She had given them a couple of days off, and called them in that morning for debriefing.

"And E & E is back to normal?" Noah asked. "No more oversight?"

"All back to normal. President Cole is coming out here tomorrow for our first meeting, but I spoke with him on the phone and he's as firmly behind the concept of what we do as the president who created us in the first place. Now that we got Ryan on our side, things should go smoothly for at least a while."

"Well, I've got a question," Jenny said. "First thing I did when you let us know the other night was call Randy. What's this about them being transferred to Team Pegasus? I've been waiting two whole days to ask about that."

"Yes, I transferred them over to Pegasus," Allison said. "Ralph needs an experienced team, and your guys are tough enough to help him grow into the asset I know he can be."

"Yeah, fine, but what about me? You gonna make me start over with a brand-new team?"

Allison's eyes went wide. "Jenny, I thought you would have figured out by now," she said. "The events of the last few days have taught me a valuable lesson. I sent you out originally with Camelot to help out with the West Algeria situation, but you were a major contributor to the success of Operation Ascension. I'm not going to give you another team; you're staying right where you are."

It was a tossup whether Jenny's eyes were wider than Neil's, but both of them seemed absolutely delighted with this turn of events. They stared at Allison for a moment, then grabbed each other for a passionate kiss.

"Okay, that tears it," Marco said. "Boss lady, you see what I gotta put up with? I got to go out and work with two happy couples. I'm going to need more time off to spend with my girlfriend, if this keeps up."

"What are you talking about? You guys generally get a month or two between missions, and you're rarely out for more than a week or two at a time, even then. If you can't spend enough time with your girlfriend when you're off duty, that sounds like a personal problem."

"I've got a question," Noah said.

"Sure, go ahead," Allison replied. "What is it?"

"We are keeping the house in England," Noah said. "But I'm also keeping the house here. I'd like to take the team back to England for a month, just to relax and take it easy. Any chance Renée could get time off to come with us?"

Allison glanced at Marco, then grinned as she turned back to Noah. "I actually think that might be an excellent idea. Say hello to Catherine Potts for me, would you?"

SPECIAL OFFER

B uilding a relationship with my readers is the ultimate goal with writing. At least, it should be. Without you guys, us writers would just be making up stories for ourselves...which would be weird. That's why I like to connect with my readers in a way many big name authors don't.

I occasionally send newsletters with details on new releases, special offers and other bits of news relating to Sam Prichard, Noah Wolf, and the other varies series and stand alone novels that I write.

And if you sign up to the mailing list today, I'll send you this free content:

- A free copy of the first Sam Prichard novella, FALLBACK (plus the audiobook version)

- A free copy of the first Noah Wolf novella, THE WAY OF THE WOLF (plus the audiobook version)

- Exclusive content and pricing to my mailing list – you can't get this anywhere else. Every book launch I set a discounted price for my mailing list for a couple days. This is exclusive to my list *only*, and something that isn't publicized anywhere else.

You can get the novella's, the audiobook's, and the exclusive discounted pricing **for free,** by at: www.davidarcherbooks.com/vip

NOTE FROM THE AUTHOR

If you enjoyed this adventure, would you please consider taking a moment and leaving your thoughts for others who might also enjoy this book?

It takes only a handful of seconds to leave a review, but can literally make or break a self published career. Please don't feel any obligation to do so, but if you had fun, or perhaps enjoyed yourself at all, then I'd sincerely appreciate it!

Thanks so much,
David Archer